NOTHING TO SEE

PIP ADAM

VICTORIA UNIVERSITY OF WELLINGTON PRESS

VICTORIA UNIVERSITY OF
WELLINGTON
TE HERENGA WAKA

Victoria University of Wellington Press
PO Box 600, Wellington
New Zealand
vup.wgtn.ac.nz

ISBN 9781776563159

A catalogue record is available at the National Library of New Zealand

Published with the assistance of a grant from

Printed by BlueStar, Wellington

for Sheila, Brent and Bo

When I'm broken, I am whole.
And when I'm whole, I'm broken.

—Björk, 'Quicksand'

1994

1

'Huh?' Greta was lying on Peggy's stomach.

'Everything seems so dark,' said Peggy. They were both reading. They'd gone to their room with the intention of reading. 'We're just going to read,' they'd said to their flatmate Dell. But for the last half hour or so they'd been staring out at their room over the top of their books. They were just learning how to spend time.

'Like everything,' Peggy said.

Greta was sleepy. They'd been up too late. The cold and heavy of the Sunday evening was settling down.

'When I think back to what we did this week or last week or the week before. It's all so dark.'

'We've been up a lot at night,' Greta said. She put her book on her chest.

'Yeah.' Peggy turned round so she could see out the high window above their bed. Greta's head moved with the change in Peggy's position. 'You're right.'

They sat like that for a moment. Peggy wound round to look up and out the window, watching the grey sky. Greta staring at the ceiling, book on her chest, and head, precarious now, on Peggy's stomach.

'We should get some food,' Greta said.

'Yeah,' said Peggy. 'Do we have any money?'

Greta scratched her head. Her hands were swamped in a long jumper and she scratched her head through the sleeves. Her dark, short hair stood up. She wiped her nose with the sleeve of the jumper. 'Not much.'

'Enough for tom yum?' Peggy's voice lightened a little.

'Yeah?' Greta said. 'How much is tom yum, again?'

'Eight bucks,' Peggy said. She was getting up now. Greta fell off her lap. 'Eleven, if you have noodles. The noodles are three dollars. If we have the noodles we only need one bowl of soup.'

'What's the date?' Greta said.

Peggy shrugged. 'Like, the sixth?'

'We should be golden.'

'Can we get spring rolls?' Peggy asked. They'd both put on heaps of weight since they'd stopped drinking. A few weeks ago, Peggy worked out that if they took more Antabuse than they were supposed to it gave them diarrhoea. The counsellors at rehab were dark on dieting or vomiting but Peggy was pretty sure they'd get away with it now they were out. Except, Greta pointed out, if they both kept taking more than they were supposed to, they'd probably need more Antabuse sooner than they were supposed to.

'What date does rent come out on?'

'Like, the fourteenth?' Peggy was pulling on their Converse All Stars. She pulled a floral dress over a long-sleeved top and leggings. The dress had been bigger. She was looking around for their fisherman's rib jumper. Then she stopped. 'But . . .' She rubbed her eyes and the black eyeliner left over from the day before smeared more. 'We can't fly too close to the wind, 'cause it's not like if we spend the rent it'll magically come again from somewhere else.'

'How much do we have in cash?'

Peggy started going through the pockets of the jackets and trousers on the floor.

They'd gone to a budget advisor. He hadn't said much and had mainly looked at the pieces of paper their case manager had sent. He'd cut their credit card up in front of them – while they were still sitting there. They'd looked in the rubbish bin at the fragments of plastic while he moved on to other things. He rang the gym that had sent their debt to a debt collector, and worked out 'terms'.

They were on a sickness benefit, but every now and then they'd sleep with men for money. The counsellor at rehab said if they sat in the barber's chair long enough they'd get a haircut, which as far as they could tell was true (the others from rehab were falling like flies), but sometimes the rent was due and it wasn't like anyone would give either of them a job. A job that still left time to go to meetings and counselling and doctor's appointments. 'That's what the sickness benefit is for,' the counsellor said as he signed the forms for them before they left rehab. 'So you can concentrate on staying sober.'

They wanted to stay sober more than anything. They sat up late into the night talking about how much they wanted to stay clean. How much they wanted to start a new life. What they'd do to stay away from a drink. 'If I was like ... if I thought I was going to drink, I'd fucking ... I'd go to the police station and say "Arrest me" and if they wouldn't, I'd break a window.' 'Yeah,' they'd both say. 'Yeah.' They went to a meeting every day – most days they went to two meetings. They were making friends. They got invited to go tenpin bowling. They got sick together and they'd get well together.

'Three dollars,' Peggy said. She was resting the combination of coins in her hand – they had small hands.

'Well,' said Greta, who was still lying on the bed. 'That's the noodles already. Like, in your hand.'

'There's so much fucking money,' Peggy said. They'd pissed a lot of money against the wall. Things were tight now, but they had a roof and some clothes and they had enough for noodles without even checking their EFTPOS card.

'Fucking love being sober,' Greta said.

'Fucking *love* being sober,' Peggy said.

'I'm going to check the wallet,' said Greta, and she grabbed their canvas army surplus bag and pulled everything out until she found the wallet. There was a five-dollar note. Greta looked up at Peggy with a smile so broad her face might come apart at the seams. 'We're fucking loaded! We've got like' – she counted it – 'eight bucks!'

'We must have three in the bank?' Peggy said.

Greta looked at her.

'For the noodles.'

'For the noodles,' Greta agreed.

It stopped them for a minute. How lucky they were, and they just stood and looked at the wall and basked in the luck.

'Shouldn't we be happy with just the soup?' Greta asked. 'Like, finding that eight bucks – that's pretty awesome.'

Peggy thought about it. 'I think god would want us to have noodles.'

Greta wondered.

'God didn't save us from drowning for us not to have noodles on the shore,' Peggy said. 'God wants us to have a noodle life.'

Greta laughed. Peggy did, too. It was okay to joke about god a bit. It wasn't that kind of god. It was like a small 'g' god. Their counsellor at rehab had made them look at the hills surrounding the rehab buildings. 'Are the hills bigger than you?' 'Yes.' They were never surer of anything before in their life. They couldn't stop drinking and the hills were big.

Their flatmate Dell was in the lounge. She was reading too – staring at the wall, book in lap. They didn't have a television and the days without drink were long.

'Are you guys going to a meeting?' she said. They'd all moved in together after rehab. It had seemed safe but it really wasn't. Their other flatmate, Heidi, had started drinking again – or maybe she hadn't. She was never home, or maybe she snuck in and out without them realising. None of them liked to be left alone.

'We're going for tom yum,' Peggy said. 'We went to a meeting this morning.'

'And at lunchtime,' Greta said.

'Oh.' Dell looked at her watch. 'I think I don't have time for dinner. Carol's picking me up.'

'For the one over that way?' Peggy asked, pointing in the direction she thought the meeting was.

Dell nodded. It was a pretty great meeting, but Peggy and Greta had already been to two meetings and they were hungry and they'd found the money. Just before they left rehab, they'd been told to go to meetings, they all had. Peggy and Greta wanted to be sober more than anything, so they did what they were told. The meetings were weird. Peggy and Greta had no idea what was going on. They had been about to give up going to meetings when a woman called Diane came over to where they were waiting for their bus home. Diane had been coming to meetings for a long time. Diane hadn't had a drink for a long time. She gave them her phone number, written on a small piece of paper in blue ballpoint. 'We don't know what to do,' Peggy said as Diane was walking away, and

Diane stopped and came back. 'What do we do?' Diane said she didn't know what Peggy and Greta needed to do, but she could tell them what she did. Diane said that to begin with she went to daytime meetings on Sundays. Sundays were hard and Peggy and Greta often wanted a drink. Diane said maybe they could go to daytime meetings, and on Sunday nights they could get ready for Monday. Routine was good.

'Will you get something to eat?' Greta asked now. 'You have to eat dinner.'

'Oh yeah,' said Dell. 'There are some baked beans and I can make some toast.' Now Peggy and Greta felt like they should stay and have baked beans on toast too. Should they save the eight dollars for buses and savings? What were they supposed to do? If they went out for tom yum would they drink again? If they stayed for baked beans would they drink again? Diane had told them not to overthink things. Carol was Dell and Heidi's Diane. She seemed a lot more loving than Diane. Diane never picked them up for meetings. She told them to pick up ashtrays at the end of the meetings, to talk to newcomers, forget themselves. Carol told Dell and Heidi to treat themselves like their best friend.

Peggy and Greta wanted to stay sober. Wanted to stay sober more than they wanted their old life back. Their old life had been rape and beatings, and drinking had stopped helping, stopped working – completely. The people they knew from rehab who had started drinking again told them that some people could drink, and that was true, and Peggy and Greta and Dell tried not to have an opinion about whether Heidi was one of those people, but they all knew to their core, just right now, that none of them could drink safely again. Every now and then a thought would sneak in, but when they talked about it they could see what their mind was up to. So, they decided not to have a drink just for now. Just now they wouldn't have a drink, and now, and now, and now, and then it was another day and today it was ten months and three weeks and two days.

'Well, we're going to have tom yum,' Greta said. Peggy nodded.

'Cool,' Dell said. 'Have a good time.' Dell was way chiller than Peggy and Greta. It was like she knew more, or understood more, or was older. It was one of the things they stayed up late talking about. Maybe it was Carol. Maybe the whole 'treat yourself like your own best friend' thing made Dell feel like she had everything she needed. That there was no need to be sad, or angry, or anxious. Maybe it was easier to accept baked beans on toast for dinner when you were looking after yourself well.

Greta and Peggy fought everything. Everyone said, 'Let go.' Anything Peggy and Greta let go of had teeth marks in it. They laughed about that as they walked down the street. The heavy dusk was falling in. It felt like they were walking underwater. It was all so heavy.

'It's so dark,' Peggy said.

Greta nodded. She was kicking a stone in an obsessed way like their life depended on it. The road they lived on was busy. Where were people going? It was five o'clock on a Sunday.

'Dark,' Peggy said.

'Yeah,' Greta said.

When they were tiny, like, really small, there had been a very hot summer and all the mothers took all the babies to the paddling pool in the Botanical Gardens. The story went that everyone was sunburnt before they reached the end of their street. The pushchairs were all made of metal, they didn't even have cushions in them. They weren't adjustable except the back of the seat could be dropped to lying down. Being a baby wasn't meant to be a cakewalk. Neither was being a mother. Peggy and Greta weren't particularly wanted. When mothers like theirs were angry this is what they would tell daughters like Peggy and Greta. 'I never wanted to have a baby. But I did my best.' And they did, except when they didn't. Mothers like Peggy and Greta's were not happy about Peggy and Greta getting sober. Neither were fathers like Peggy and Greta's, or brothers like theirs, or any of the girls at the parlour or the married men they'd been sleeping with before they got sober. Greta and Peggy felt very alone. 'If it wasn't for you,' they'd say to each other as the sun came up. As they got on their knees and begged for one more day sober, as they picked up ashtrays at the meetings in the old stone building by the grassy square. 'If it wasn't for you,' with their eyes, with their heart, to god – to say thanks. 'You've taken almost everything,' they'd say in their braver moments to something that was powerful and terrifying, that they couldn't understand, something like the big hills, 'but thank you for giving me her.'

When they got to the wide avenue at the end of their street, Greta slowed. She looked down the tree-lined footpath. 'We could go to the Krishnas?' she said. 'It's heaps cheaper.'

Peggy thought about it. 'All that fucking chanting, though.'

'It's not that bad,' Greta said. 'It's good for us. Probably.'

'I really want tom yum. We're sort of all prepped for tom yum.'

'Yeah,' Greta said. 'But we should go to the Krishnas next week.'

'If we're alive.' Peggy pushed the button on the traffic light so they could cross. 'If you and I – or one of us – is still alive next Sunday we'll go to the Krishnas and eat prasadam and chant like motherfuckers.'

'But not get married,' Greta said. A woman they knew had gone into the Hare Krishnas and been married to a man, and then she'd left the Hare Krishnas. Every woman who married this man left. They left and the Hare Krishnas found him another wife. No one had seen her since she got married. Peggy and Greta had no idea if she'd left the Krishnas, they just heard from someone. There was a lot of that – gossip, intrigue. Things were boring without drinking.

'Agreed,' said Greta. 'No marriage, just prasadam.' She looked behind herself because she'd lost the stone she was kicking. They were both like that. Acutely obsessed and wildly distractible. Peggy looked around, took a step and picked up a small, round stone. She dropped it at Greta's feet and Greta smiled. She patted Peggy on the arm to say thanks. If it wasn't for you.

They couldn't walk straight through the grid system to tom yum. There were a couple of houses that still held a bit of a pull. It was best to avoid them, especially on a depressing Sunday night. One day it wouldn't tempt them. One day they'd joke and say, 'There's not enough alcohol in the whole wide world to satisfy the deep hole in us, so why start?' But there were men in the houses, and where there were men there was the illusion that Peggy and Greta could get what they needed. A habitual idea that the men could give them enough alcohol and drugs to satisfy the deep hole. They'd been raped in both the houses. Lots and lots of times. Once on a terrible night towards the end – smashed in the face and smashed apart by all the men in the house. To an amateur that would seem like enough to put them off. But when they first got back from rehab a week before Dell and Heidi they'd found themselves outside the house, thirsty, starving, telling each other how it wasn't that bad. Not really. On balance.

Compared to not having a drink or a taste ever again. The sun set while they stood there. The lights had come on in the house, they could see the men walking around in the windows. The guy who'd pissed on Peggy and Greta while they lay bleeding and naked in the lounge came out onto the deck because he thought he'd seen them from inside. 'Peggy,' he'd shouted. 'Greta, is that you?' and they'd stood and looked at him without answering. Looked at how much bigger he was than both of them. Realised, again, like they always did, that they didn't stand a chance against how much bigger he was and how he had all the others on his side. Still, they thought, maybe. Maybe it'll be different tonight. Maybe they could get in and get what they needed and then leave. Maybe just steal money – or ask for money. Ask for money for all the times they'd fucked him for free, for drugs. Like debt collectors. And then he walked to the front gate and shouted at them again. And they'd said, quietly, in something only slightly louder than a mumble, 'No.' No, it wasn't them. It was someone else. And they'd walked away realising it wasn't a lie. They were someone else.

They weren't sure they could do it again, so they avoided the house and walked a strange elliptical route to the short mall where the Thai place was.

'Hello,' the woman at the counter said. 'One tom yum soup?' They both nodded. 'With two noodles?' she asked.

'One noodles,' Greta said, and the woman nodded and Peggy and Greta sat down.

The hot soup always made their stomach play up. Peggy thought it was the mushrooms but Greta said she was dreaming. 'It's really spicy,' Greta said. 'Our stomach sucks.' They'd spent a lot of time vomiting. Vomiting because they were piss-crook, vomiting because they drank too much, vomiting because they were too fat. How could they expect their stomachs to work properly, now? Especially when they poured spoonfuls of fiery hot soup into them.

They sat at a table near the door and Peggy played with the chopsticks.

'Did Dell say Heidi had been home?' Greta asked.

Peggy shook her head.

'I wish she'd come home,' Greta said.

'Me too,' Peggy said. The guy Heidi was with was dangerous and awful. His name was Ian. He lived way out in a place that was like the country. In a house on a big swathe of land. Ian was in the meetings but he always shared about how much he hated them. How men didn't like him. How he thought everyone else in the meetings was fake. The first time they met him, Peggy and Greta raised their eyebrows at each other. They knew men like Ian. Staying away from men like Ian was a big part of how their new life was going to be different. Peggy had seen him come up to Greta after the meeting. She was across the room picking up ashtrays. She shouted, 'Greta, we've got that thing.' And Greta said, 'Oh yeah,' and apologised to him and went to help Peggy. He'd cornered both of them at a meeting a few days later and told them he knew what they were up to with the whole 'We have that thing' routine. Peggy looked at the ground the whole time he got in her face, telling her if one of them wanted to talk to him, they could talk to him, telling them they didn't own each other, despite what it looked like. Diane had a word with him and he had never spoken to either of them again. Diane was hardcore. They both said it to each other. Like, she wasn't perfect, no one was perfect, but she was pretty fucking awesome – for someone who didn't drink.

The other men in the meetings tried to talk to Ian but he

said they were ganging up on him and jealous. Men like Ian thought everyone was against them and that if there was a real victim in the situation it was them. Peggy and Greta could see it in Ian's body and hear it when he talked – above everything, this was what made him the most dangerous.

At another meeting, Ian started talking to Heidi. Peggy and Greta yelled, 'Heidi, we've got that thing.' But it didn't work – Heidi waved at them and smiled. Then Heidi didn't come home for four days and the three of them, Dell, Greta and Peggy, sat round the table and tried to talk each other into calling the police. 'He could have killed her,' Dell said. And while they wanted to say 'Don't be ridiculous', Peggy and Greta knew men like Ian. Women were killed like that all the time. Women they knew were killed like that. Stabbed, strangled, left in rivers. Sometimes Greta and Peggy thought they were overreacting, that they'd seen too many movies. They used to live in a big city further north, before there were two of them. One morning, they woke up and looked around the room. There was a gun by the door and a safe, and men had come the day before to ask where the money for the drugs was. They were lying next to the man who had offered them as payment, and it hit them hard and immediately that this was not a movie. It was their life. They crept out of bed, too scared to get their boots. Too scared to look for their cardigan, and they snuck out and walked the two kilometres back to their flat. There were too many guns in the city, they decided that morning, and they moved south and then before they knew it – maybe four weeks later – they were in a room with a gun and a safe and another terrible man. If they were going to make a change, it had to be more than geographical.

Heidi turned up with Ian on the fifth day. She said they all needed to stay out of her life. That her life was her life.

Especially Dell, Dell could stay the fuck out. Heidi and Dell hadn't met many men like Ian. Greta and Peggy saw it on that day. They had rich parents who sent them to private and expensive counsellors and self-improvement courses before they went to rehab. It was possible Heidi and Dell had only met nice men. It was possible that Heidi thought Ian was a nice man under a big barrel of sadness and that if she could wash away that sadness she'd be left with just the nice man. Then Heidi started coming home with bruises on her arms and then just to get clean clothes and then with a black eye and with the sharp tang of vomit on her. Peggy and Greta and Dell watched her go back and forth from the laundry to her room to the kitchen, pleading with her. Then she said if they really wanted to help, maybe they could loan her, like, twenty bucks, and then everyone started shouting and Dell punched Heidi and Heidi threatened to call the police. Dell and Heidi were already on parole for drink-driving, so Peggy and Greta gave her the twenty-eight dollars from the jar by the oven they'd saved for the electricity bill, and then Heidi left and Dell, Peggy and Greta sat in silence and worried about how they would pay the electricity bill and whether Heidi had moved out. But she hadn't. She still had a key and they were sure she was sneaking in when none of them were there.

'You'd think we would have seen her.' Peggy looked intently at the chopsticks and the fork she was balancing them on. 'Like, in town.' The chopsticks fell off the fork and almost rolled onto the floor before she could catch them. 'It's small here.'

Greta nodded. 'Maybe she just stays at his house now. With Ian.'

Peggy nodded. 'Maybe.'

They saw Ian all the time. He was at most of the meetings

they were at. Ian hadn't drunk. Ian was still sober. They fucking hated Ian. But they needed to realise Ian was a sick person – they all were. How could you hate a sick man? Otherwise, Ian had the power to really fuck them. To ruin everything. No amount of hating Ian was worth dying or being raped for. That's what they thought, as long as they went to lots of meetings and stuck together. If either of them was by themselves they hated Ian so much they dreamed about taking a large, strong swing with a softball bat at his face. They played it over and over and over and although there was some relief in it, it really just tied them to him. It just gave him power. That's what Diane said. They doubted Diane knew what the fuck she was talking about, but they had nothing else. So they kept telling each other that if they hated Ian they'd drink and if they drank they'd die – or worse. But sometimes, when they were in the shower or walking home when it was cold, they rehearsed it again in their heads. One strong, even, beautiful swing breaking almost everything in his face.

'We're all just walking each other home,' Greta said, and they laughed, disgusted at the bullshit of it all, and the soup arrived.

2

By Wednesday they still hadn't heard from Heidi. They were in the kitchen after a meeting and it was about nine o'clock, a couple of weeks since the big fight and the electricity money. Dell said Max had told her that Heidi had been at the rehab aftercare class. Greta and Peggy shook their heads. She hadn't. Everyone else had been. Some people had brought notebooks and pens. The counsellor gave a talk about relapse prevention. It was boring. Michael, who wore better clothes than anyone else and owned a clothes shop and went on holidays to Asia a lot, looked bored. Then he noticed something in the leg of his trousers, a lump. He worked it down the leg of the trousers – it was a pair of underwear. Peggy and Greta watched the whole thing. Bored. The counsellor was talking for too long about drinking, so they started watching Michael. Michael was handsome and married. Peggy and Greta wondered about fucking Michael. Just to pass time. He seemed a lot cleaner than them. They looked down at their hands and they were sort of caked in dirt. They had no idea where it came from. They rubbed the skin and it sort of flaked off – the dirt or their skin, they weren't sure which. They asked Dell once how often people normally showered. Dell shrugged her shoulders. 'Once a week?' she said. 'That's what we thought,' Peggy said. Then Greta called out from the other room, 'What about clothes? How often do you wash clothes?' 'Trousers?' Peggy asked. 'And sheets,' Greta shouted. Even Dell didn't know that, and she and Heidi worked in a clothes shop.

'I reckon you can wear trousers quite a few times if you hang them up in between,' Peggy said.

'Like ten?' Dell asked.

'At least,' Peggy said.

'Sheets depends on whether you've had sex in them or not.' Greta was being brave but really she had no idea. It had just occurred to her that it might be gross to sleep in a bed that had been fucked in.

'What about clothes?' Dell said.

Greta was in the room now, and she and Peggy looked at Dell, because that's what they'd just been talking about.

'Like if you have sex in them?' Dell said.

'Oh,' said Peggy. Peggy and Greta had sex for money and sex with each other – which was really just masturbating so maybe didn't count. Sometimes they had sex with each other to help themselves fall asleep, sometimes they did it because they were bored, sometimes they were sad and just needed a little bit of cheering up. Sex with anyone else couldn't do those things and at the moment that was all they wanted.

'Good point,' Greta said, in a voice silenced to a whisper by what a good point it was. A few days ago, Greta and Peggy had had sex in the skirt Greta was wearing now. One of them pushed the skirt up and up – it was tight and took some effort, this was how they knew they really wanted to have sex, because the tight skirt gave plenty of opportunity for either of them to change their mind. Kissing and hitching the skirt up – it took coordination. It felt heated. It was like that sometimes and sometimes it was just a lazy fuck. Hardly any effort at all. Like taking part in a familiar task, diligently but with no great passion. They always knew exactly what they were doing, and when. Although it was hard to tell when it started, when it was finished, and when it was over.

'Straight away?' Peggy asked.

Dell nodded. 'I think clothes should be washed straight away if you have sex in them.'

'You shouldn't wear them again,' Greta said, like it was obvious. The skirt had ridden up a little bit – she pulled it down again.

'But trousers you haven't had sex in,' Peggy said, 'I reckon you can wear them a few times.'

Michael had worn the trousers he had on at least once before today. Unless the underwear somehow got in there from the washing machine. Peggy and Greta weren't sure.

Greta had incinerated their striped thermals the week before. She'd hung them on a chair and put the chair too close to the heater to dry. They hadn't washed the thermals much, possibly ever, and they only had one pair so they needed to dry them quickly. They didn't have a dryer. No one did. Dryers were expensive and none of them had much money. Not now the credit cards had been cut up. Dell and Heidi were paid one wage between the two of them into their one bank account. They called it job-sharing. It was a rush now – for Dell – to get to the bank on pay-day lunch breaks to take as much of the money out as she could before Heidi did. Usually she was too late because Heidi had stopped turning up for work, so she had all the time in the world to wander into the bank and withdraw the money. Their boss didn't mind who turned up – both of them, one of them – it made very little difference because they were rostered on as if they were one person. Dell was going to ask about getting paid in cash, but it sounded dodgy and she needed to approach it carefully.

Probably their boss thought they were both still coming to work. Possibly Dell hadn't done a lot to correct her. It was another thing Peggy and Greta talked about in the dark, in whispers, when they couldn't sleep and they were trying to work out how honest was honest enough not to die drunk and naked in a river.

As Michael pulled the underwear out of his trousers he looked around and Peggy and Greta had to look away quickly. They looked at the counsellor and nodded their heads like they'd been listening the whole time. She was talking about being careful not to compare themselves to people who could leave half a glass of wine on a table at dinner. Everyone laughed. It was funny. It being funny was part of why Peggy and Greta needed to stop drinking. That and the sleeping on the streets and just about dying. There was lots to laugh about. When they laughed it meant they knew. When a room full of people trying to stay sober laughed while you were talking, it meant they understood. They'd done it. They knew.

The counsellor kept talking. Peggy looked at their wristwatch, which Greta was wearing. Greta shifted her arm so Peggy could read the watch better. The talk was nearly over. Greta had made them both sandwiches for after the talk. They got hungry a lot. They'd left home at about quarter past nine. They could eat the sandwiches as they walked to the meeting that went from twelve till two every day. They went to the lunchtime meeting every day. The aftercare talk was a bit of a bonus. The days were long. You were only meant to go to part of the lunchtime meeting. It was designed so that people who had lunch from twelve till one and people who had lunch from one till two could go, but people like Peggy and Greta went for the whole two hours. It was great. It meant that after the meeting there were only five hours before they'd be picked up for the next meeting, which started at seven-thirty.

Meetings, they both agreed, were great because no one ever offered you alcohol at a meeting. There were never ads for alcohol at meetings. In meetings they felt safe. Everywhere else, not so much. Some people said things like, 'I don't have a drinking problem anymore. I have a thinking problem.' Peggy and Greta didn't laugh at that. They very much had a drinking problem. The week before last, they'd been walking into town to go to an appointment at the dole office when they saw a half-empty bottle of beer in the doorway of an empty shop. It stopped them in their tracks. They looked behind themselves and further in front of them. No one was there. No one would know. That was what they found the hardest. They had organised their lives so that it was very unlikely they would be anywhere they could buy alcohol, but what about this? Did it count if you drank half a beer off the side of the road? Was it just cleaning up? They told a woman after the lunchtime meeting and she told both of them that if they were tempted they still had an alcoholic mind. And they did. The woman said they needed to work harder – they weren't working hard enough, sobriety was for people who wanted it. It upset them. They rang Diane when they got home and called the woman a 'fucking bitch' and said they wanted to punch her in the face and was it true? What she said? Was the temptation because they weren't working hard enough? Was it impossible for them to stay sober?

'There's a name for an opinion like hers,' Diane said.

'What?' they both said.

'Bullshit,' said Diane, and laughed. She got them to read a story in a book about someone who didn't get over the urge to drink for two years. 'Just 'cause it's not easy doesn't mean you can't stay sober,' Diane said. 'Don't drink, and go to meetings and keep doing the work you're doing. And keep talking to me.' She said goodnight and told them to go to sleep.

'Heidi wasn't at the aftercare talk,' Greta told Dell while they were trying to do the dishes.

'Oh,' said Dell. None of them could get the oven dish clean. They tried the brush, then a Steelo pad, then Greta got some Jif from the laundry and they were trying that.

'Will that poison us?' Peggy asked.

Dell and Greta didn't think so. 'People clean the oven with it,' Greta said. 'Surely if it was going to kill us it would have killed everyone by now. The fumes.'

Peggy shrugged. And they tried again.

Before the meeting, they'd made cheese on toast for dinner. Someone had brought them round some cheese – it was a housewarming present, they said, but they'd been in the house for a while now. They looked at the cheese for a long time after the person left. They all knew cheese on toast was a thing. Dell and Heidi had had it when they were kids. Heidi wasn't there to ask, though, and Dell knew what it looked like but not how it was made. Peggy and Greta couldn't remember ever having cheese on toast on account of them being fat kids and being on a diet since they were five. They backward engineered it from what Dell could remember and it was pretty good. The first slice was the worst. They tried it one slice at a time – so as not to waste too much. They experimented with toasting the bread first. Then they added some Vegemite from a food parcel Social Welfare had given Peggy and Greta on the half-drunk street beer day. They saw the Vegemite as a reward from god for not drinking the beer. 'Which was probably actually piss,' Peggy said.

'Which was probably actually just a beer bottle half-full of piss,' Greta agreed.

They'd all left straight after the cheese-on-toast dinner. Greta and Peggy thought maybe they'd left the oven on. They hadn't been able to concentrate on the meeting. Not really. They just kept thinking about what would happen to their bond if they burned the flat down. They were pretty sure they'd go to jail. Then someone said something that caught their attention and they were in the house taking off their coats before they remembered how scared and sure they'd been that they would be arriving home to a pile of ash.

Dell was putting all her effort into scraping off a piece of baked-on cheese.

'Are you supposed to use baking paper?' Greta asked.

'I don't remember anything about baking paper,' Dell said.

'It seems really unlikely it's meant to make this much mess,' Peggy said.

'I think this oven tray is old,' Dell said. She stopped scrubbing and let the tray fall into the sink.

'Shall we soak it?' Greta said. Almost ecstatically.

Peggy nodded, with an impressed face. 'Yes,' she said. 'Let's soak it overnight.' It seemed right. Maybe that was the problem. They'd left the tray on the bench when maybe they should have left it in the sink full of water and dishwashing liquid.

Dell dried her hands and they all pushed on the tray in the sink one last time for luck and went and sat in the lounge. Peggy stayed in the kitchen and made them cups of coffee. Someone had said it wasn't a good idea to drink coffee after five but it was instant, so they figured it was okay. Dell said if she didn't have a cup of coffee before she went to bed she couldn't sleep. Someone had told Peggy and Greta a good way to test if someone would benefit from Ritalin was to see if Coca-Cola calmed them down.

'Everyone would benefit from Ritalin,' Greta joked.

And they all sat for a minute looking out the window at the dark night thinking how great Ritalin was. Then they remembered the dreadful things they'd done for Ritalin. Then they remembered how fucking terrible it had been detoxing from Ritalin. Then they all sighed, almost all at once and thought how fucking lucky they were to be sober today.

Dell's day at work had been okay. The clothes shop was in the mall. Dell and Heidi had worked there for nearly five years. The clothes shop had stood beside them – through everything – but their boss wasn't quite ready to let them back near the money. They'd stolen a lot of money and their boss called the police and there was a restorative justice hearing and their boss agreed that if they went to rehab they wouldn't press any further charges and Heidi and Dell could keep their job. There were conditions. They still weren't allowed near the money, but their boss said if they proved themselves they'd be allowed the key to the cash register sooner or later.

'Like, in a few months.' Dell blew on her coffee so the steam rose up into her face. Peggy and Greta looked at her like it was unbelievable. That any of them could get a job and keep a job and maybe one day be allowed near the money. They hadn't known Dell or Heidi when they were all drinking. They'd met in rehab. Peggy and Greta had heard what Dell and Heidi were like when they were drinking, and they couldn't imagine there was a job that would stand by people who'd acted like that.

Peggy and Greta had wanted a job so badly. They'd never had a straight job. Their case manager had been trying to help them with a CV ever since they got out of rehab, but it hadn't gone well. There were massive spaces. 'What do you do about that?' Greta asked. The case manager had shrugged. There was a job board in the dole office with lots of small cards pinned to it. Each card had the details of a job on it. If a jobseeker saw a job they liked the look of, they unpinned the card and took it to the counter. When Peggy and Greta had nothing to do and it was too soon to go to a meeting, they'd look at the job board. They weren't jobseekers though, they were on a sickness benefit – there were no jobs for Peggy and Greta. They just liked looking at the cards, because they didn't know that some of the jobs even existed. Most of what they knew about jobs was from Richard Scarry and things they saw on TV. They knew about working in a shop, and they knew about being a doctor or a lawyer, but they really didn't know much about many other jobs. They'd never really thought of sleeping with men for cash or stealing as a job. That was the only experience they really had and there were never jobs like that on the job board.

One day, a couple of months ago, they'd been looking at the job cards and their case manager called them over. Their case manager had talked to her boss and her boss thought it might be a good idea for Greta and Peggy to do some volunteer work. They nodded.

'The Salvation Army runs shops,' the case manager said.

They nodded, because they knew the Salvation Army shops.

'Could we volunteer in a Salvation Army shop?' Greta said.

'Probably not to start off with.' Their case manager copied down an address on the back of a card that looked a bit like one of the job cards. 'But you could sort the clothes.'

Greta and Peggy thought that would be fine.

'If I call them and tell them you're coming, you'll have to go.' Their case manager was not fucking about. 'If I call them, I'm putting it on your file that you'll go. That it's a condition of your benefit.'

They both nodded. Really, she couldn't do that. Really, they were on the sickness benefit. But really, they weren't supposed to be asking about jobs and making CVs and looking at the job board if they were on the sickness benefit, so they nodded and said they would definitely go tomorrow.

At the warehouse they talked to the supervisor and it went well, and now – on Mondays and Thursdays and Fridays – Peggy and Greta went to the warehouse and sorted through donations.

They were allowed first pick of the clothes. Their supervisor said the Salvation Army had needed to work out a way to do that, otherwise the volunteers just stole things. If Peggy and Greta saw something they liked, they could set it aside and take it to the supervisor at the end of the shift. The supervisor would tell them how much it would cost, and if they had the money, they could have it.

It was dangerous. Peggy and Greta both agreed. Dangerous financially. They both loved clothes and they both felt like shit. They'd had to leave fast, that last night. It was a now-or-never situation and no one thought it was a good idea to go back and get any of their things. So now they needed clothes. Someone, maybe even someone from the Salvation Army, had sent them both tracksuits when they were up the line in rehab. It was kind, and to begin with they really were fine with anything that kept them warm. In a flash of wanting to change and commit to being sober, they'd taken out all their piercings. 'I regret it now,' Greta had said, only a couple of days later, as she and Peggy sat on the steps of the large hospital block at the rehab, looking up at the hills. Their hair was growing out. No one in rehab was allowed scissors. Their short hair grew long and flopped to one side, the shaved bits underneath were growing back and everything was fluffy with the big bottles of shampoo in the communal showers. The tracksuits were fine but Peggy and Greta didn't know who they were in them. Which was fine. Peggy and Greta didn't know who they were in anything – not sober.

They'd stand in line for breakfast, holding up the queue, looking at the bain-maries. 'Do we like marmalade?' Peggy would ask. Greta would shrug. They didn't know if they'd ever had marmalade. 'I think it's nice with peanut butter,' someone behind them said. 'If you can get one of the crusts from the toast and put, like, peanut butter and marmalade on it. I reckon that would be nice.' They tried it, and she was right. You had to take other people's advice. That's what they learned. Their thinking was a bit broken in regard to a lot of things. It was like trying to fix a broken machine with the same broken machine. That's what the counsellors told them at rehab.

But when they'd got back to town and paid the bond for the flat and before the credit card had been cut up, they'd bought some clothes out of the big bins in the secondhand store on one of the roads that led out to the port. You could fill a bag for five dollars. The bag was splitting a bit at the sides, but the person taking their money looked at their tracksuits and let it pass. They wouldn't get their faces re-pierced. It was too expensive and their body was kind of in revolt. It was as if the alcohol and drugs had been keeping a whole bunch of infections at bay. Both of them got thrush and eczema and nits. They would walk to the after-hours in the dark, late at night, having come to their wits' end with the scratching after spending all day telling each other they could handle it. Chemists were dangerous but there was a small photo of them behind the counter that said they were drug-seekers. So that was helpful.

Two weeks after they started at the warehouse, they went to the computers at the dole office and typed '1994 – present: Warehouse Contractor' into their CV and clicked Save. It was a really happy day. They walked next door to the café and got a huge cup of coffee each, and then another one, then another. Peggy was pretty sure they were going to drink until they got an effect. They loved coffee so much.

They sat in the lounge now with their cups of coffee looking at the place in the room where a TV would have gone.

'Should we try calling his place?' Greta said, finally.

Dell looked at her. Then at the ground.

'It would at least be good to know if we needed to get another flatmate,' Peggy said. It was the wrong thing to say, but it was said now. 'Sorry,' she said. 'Sorry.'

'How does it play out, though?' Dell blew on her coffee. 'We call. He maybe answers. We ask if we can talk to her. He says no, we worry. He says yes, we talk to her. She tells us how great things are going. And' – she fished around in the coffee for something with her pinky finger – 'we worry.'

'I think she's been here,' Greta said.

Dell and Peggy looked at her.

'Some of your stockings were in the laundry – like, for ages – and when we got home today they were gone.'

No one else had moved them. Peggy and Greta had thought about it. They liked the stockings. They were thick denier and black. They looked warm. They'd just got a floral dress from work; the stockings would be great with it. The only leggings they had were the stripy thermals which were footless and melted, now. They only had seven socks. None matched. They'd held the stockings as they hung in the laundry. Run them through their hands, thinking how good they'd look with the dress and Converses. But they hadn't taken them.

At any moment like that, Greta and Peggy would hold their hands out, like scales. They'd look at one hand: 'Stockings.' Then the other hand: 'Dying drunk in a ditch – alone.' They'd make a weighing-up action. Sometimes dying drunk would still look good, so they'd add something to it. 'After being raped,' Greta would say, and if that still didn't work, Peggy would say, 'Anally.' 'By a roomful of men.' Eventually, not stealing the stockings would win – or not stealing the electricity money, or the lunch in the fridge at work, or the shampoo that Dell and Heidi left in the shower. They usually had to put something that had really happened to them in the mix. They talked about how they both worried that one day even that wouldn't work.

Dell looked at Peggy.

'We didn't take them,' Peggy said. Dell believed them – and, realistically, she wouldn't have cared that much. Carol had told Dell and Heidi that honesty was fluid. That it shouldn't be rigid.

They all looked at each other a moment longer, then Dell put her cup down next to where she was sitting, and they all stood up.

Dell and Heidi's room was off the lounge and not very big. The four of them had flipped a coin for the bedroom that was off the dining room and kitchen, and Peggy and Greta had won. No one had said it but everyone was pretty sure the damp dark room was not a win, but that was how they sorted out that Heidi and Dell could have the room off the lounge which had a window and slightly less mould than the other one.

Coffees in hand, the three stood, looking through the open door like it was something in a gallery. It looked as if someone had just walked out. Or maybe it looked like Heidi could be sitting somewhere they couldn't see her. There were clothes on the floor, shoes scattered. It was a mess, but the bed was made – they all made their beds. Making your bed was what sober people did after they got up so that they didn't go back to bed and hide there for days and days. Dell looked behind the door. The winter jacket she and Heidi had bought from work with their first paycheck after rehab wasn't there – maybe it had never been there. Maybe Heidi was wearing it when she first left.

The three of them realised almost telepathically and in unison how stupid the idea was. No one had any idea what she'd taken with her on the first day. Not really. Dell and Heidi had lots of clothes and Dell didn't wear them all very often. They all found ways to share. Peggy and Greta had way less clothes than Dell and Heidi, but even they found a way to clothe themselves with their meagre wardrobe.

'Is anything missing?' Peggy asked, hopefully.

Dell shrugged.

'Have you missed anything since she's been gone?'

'Not overly,' Dell said. Dell and Heidi had a lot of clothes.

'Make-up!' Greta said.

It was a good idea, because although Heidi and Dell also had lots of make-up, Dell would have done her face that morning for work and maybe she could figure out if Heidi had taken anything during the day.

Dell went to the bedroom and looked at the set of drawers covered in socks, underwear and mail. She picked up the lipsticks and compacts that were there. 'I take most of it to work.' She put everything back down.

They were all in the room now. Greta started picking up clothes, folding them and placing them on the mattress Dell and Heidi had on the floor. Dell flicked through the papers beside the mattress. Peggy sort of moved the shoes at the end of the mattress with her feet. There was a poster of Björk on the wall. Heidi and Dell had tried, but they'd never really moved in, and then Ian had come along. Some people they talked to about it said they needed to detach with love. That Heidi was a grown-up. They all were. Sometimes, Peggy and Greta wondered if it was all about the intrigue, if they didn't really care about Heidi or Dell and just wanted to know what was going on.

Life was pretty boring without drink and drugs. Life with drink and drugs was pretty boring, too. Sometimes, in the days of working out how to get a drink then drinking then needing more drink, they'd say to each other, 'I wish something bad would happen,' because sometimes drinking felt like a rat-wheel. Getting more drink, the day spread out ahead of them like the plains on the way to the treatment centre up north. One day, they'd been trying to work out how to get to the warehouse in the rain and how to stop the rain coming in the hole in the bathroom window and Peggy had said, 'So many problems to deal with.'

'With drink, all your problems just become one problem,' Greta said.

'Getting more drink,' Peggy said.

'Getting more drink.'

A woman who had been sober for five years said, 'Alcoholics love drama.' It had made them angry. It was after a meeting, and Greta had been telling a group of people about Heidi and the situation at home and the others had been listening, nodding and saying, 'That's tough,' and then the woman had said that. She followed it up by saying, 'Drama. Drama. Drama.' Like a song, and then, 'Am I right?' and a few people agreed. Nodded their heads and laughed. 'She could be dead,' Peggy said. The woman shrugged. 'Not your business.' Then she left to get another cup of coffee.

They couldn't tell if anything was different in the room. They'd made it look different now, though. The clothes were on the bed and folded – badly – and the papers were on top of each other in a pile. It felt sort of like a cunning trap. If Heidi came home again and saw they'd moved things she'd want to know why. She might leave a note, *Don't touch my stuff* or something like that, and then they'd at least know she was alive and able to write.

It was a bit of a useless cunning plan, but it felt like something.

'I think I'll go to bed,' Dell said, running her hand through her hair. All their hair looked so bad.

'Yeah,' Greta and Peggy said. 'Yeah.' And they left the room, closing the door behind them.

3

Greta and Peggy saw the poster up in the record store. They spent a bit of time in there in between meetings. Flicking through the albums, reading liner notes, listening to everyone talking. They'd left all their records at the flat the night they left, so sometimes they tried to find all the records they used to own. Every now and then they found the actual records they used to own – their name in ballpoint. Sold by the other people in the flat. Which was fair enough, really. Maybe it would cover some of the rent they still owed. Probably not. They could never afford to buy the records back. They never had that kind of money, but it was funny sometimes and sometimes it was sad and sometimes it was infuriating – the way things had turned out. It all depended on the day. Like a rollercoaster, someone had said at coffee after a meeting the other day. People said it a lot. Peggy and Greta had never been on a rollercoaster but they nodded. 'Yes,' they said. 'It was exactly like a rollercoaster.'

The guy in the record store was putting the poster up. He was sort of leaning over Greta and Peggy to do it. They all laughed. He was a nice guy. They saw him sometimes – at the supermarket, in the street. They always said hi, even though neither of them ever bought anything from the record store. Except, once, a sweatshirt. Years ago, when they'd missed a

Henry Rollins concert because it was in the city they didn't live in anymore and there was no way to get there, they'd gone to the store and bought a Henry Rollins sweatshirt. They paid using a lot of small coins and notes – ones, twos, fives – but the guy didn't mention it. They'd stolen the money from a donation jar at the needle exchange, a little bit at a time. The sweatshirt was falling apart now. It had only been a year but they'd bleached their hair in it one night and now it had holes.

The poster said Bailter Space were playing. Peggy and Greta looked at it. They were playing at a bar, but surely if the two of them went and if the two of them went not to drink but to listen to Bailter Space – surely that would be okay. They rang Diane when they got home. Before they called, they talked about it for just about every available second, how they would ask. What was the best way of asking? Diane wasn't the boss of them – she didn't run their life, she made sure they understood that, said there was no way she could run anyone's life, not even her own. But if they talked to her about it and she thought it was a bad idea, or if they didn't talk to her about it at all, they'd never be able to get that out of their heads.

It was like the sex for money they were doing on the side. They talked to Diane about it because if they didn't it would feel like an elephant in the room when they spoke to her – a massive hole in the conversation that they were stepping around. It wasn't that Diane had opinions – it wasn't that. She just knew things. Maybe it wasn't even that. Maybe it was just that she'd done things, she knew what worked and what didn't. Diane had definitely slept with some people for money so they felt like Diane wouldn't sell them a bill of goods. But, also, they were still in that phase of wanting what they wanted and trying to work out the best way to get it and maybe thinking they had more power than they did to make people

42

do things and say things – things they wanted them to do or say. Like, if they just asked Diane in the right way, they'd get the right answer.

This, now, was a whole new way of living. Where the 'right' answer wasn't as easy to work out. Plenty of things that had looked good had gone bad. Someone at treatment told them a story about a man who got a horse and everyone said, 'Isn't it great you got a horse,' and he said, 'We'll see,' and then his son fell off the horse and was paralysed and everyone said, 'Isn't that terrible,' and he said, 'We'll see,' and then a foreign army came through and took all the able-bodied men and everyone said, 'Wasn't that good.' In truth, neither of them could remember the story – other things happened to the man – but they got the gist. Things that looked good weren't always good. Things that looked bad weren't always bad. They needed to give up judging whether they were lucky or not. No one knew. Some people they met said only good things happened. Like, even if it looked bad there would be a reason. They knew that was bullshit. Terrible things had happened to them and if anyone tried to tell them it was for a good reason, they would punch them in the face. Neither of them was sure about god. They didn't really even like saying the word.

'If we tell her it would be a good night out,' Greta suggested.

'Like a test?' Peggy said. Diane wouldn't like that.

Greta shook her head. 'She won't like that.'

'We could say we're going with some other people?' Peggy said.

That seemed like a good idea. A sober outing, like bowling a few weeks ago. But it was at a bar. There would be alcohol and drugs.

By the time they got home they had an elaborate story that included quite a few lies. But they needn't have bothered.

Not really. Diane told them to go if they wanted and had the money, but to go to a meeting beforehand, and if one of them needed to go home they both should go home, to make sure they had a way home – not to rely on anyone else. Greta hung up the phone and they both looked at each other and said, 'Awesome.'

Bailter Space were playing on a big stage in a big hall. There was wood on the floor and a bar at the back. Greta and Peggy got a stamp on their wrist and didn't buy drinks. They didn't really want drinks. It was amazing how un-thirsty they were when it came to drinks. The support band was good. Then Bailter Space came on and they played some good songs and then Peggy and Greta got in a fight with someone. It was a girl called Tyra, and they couldn't quite remember what they'd done but Tyra remembered both of them and emptied her glass over Peggy's head. It was just water but it was frightening. Neither of them had a moment to think or stop. One of them just punched Tyra in the face. They were much better fighters sober, which was dangerous. They realised how dangerous it was as soon as they landed the first punch and Tyra sort of tripped over herself. They looked at each other. Tyra was bleeding and some people were calling the bouncers over. As the bouncers rushed towards Tyra on the floor Peggy and Greta wove quickly through the crowd and towards the exit, heads down, and they left and ran down the street and Peggy asked, did Greta think Tyra knew their names or where they lived, and Greta didn't say anything, just ran and took a look behind them, and Peggy said, 'Shit.'

They'd really let themselves down. Maybe this would be it? Maybe they'd go to jail. They had several bits and pieces on their record – people had given them a million chances.

'Fuck,' Peggy said, and they started to cry, but not for Tyra, they were crying for themselves, for how shit it all was that they'd got this far – fought to get this far and now they'd fucked it up with one punch. What would they do? Diane would make them call the police. Turn themselves in. They'd lose the volunteer job at the least. 'Fuck.' 'What were we thinking?' Greta said. It was a rhetorical question.

They were both in trouble, even though only one of them had done the punching. The bouncer who knew them from around had shouted, 'Greta!' He'd seen one of them punch the woman but no one could be sure, especially not in a dark room. 'Peggy!' he'd said, just to cover his bases. He'd kept shouting both their names as he chased them through the crowded room before he watched, helplessly, as they left. So, really, they were both in trouble.

4

Everything came in on them when they woke up the next morning. It was like sleep had let them escape and then everything was waiting, after, to smash into them. It reminded them of why they liked to drink. It was so easy just to make everything blank, just to keep moving.

Dell was in the kitchen when they came in. She had a small notebook open on the bench and was stirring a cup of tea with one hand and holding the notebook open with the other.

'Heidi called,' Dell said.

'Oh.' Greta reached up high beside Dell to get a cup.

'She doesn't want us messing with her stuff.'

Greta and Peggy looked at each other.

'Did it work?' Greta said.

'Maybe she just guessed,' Dell said.

Peggy and Greta shrugged. It was hard to tell, because it was a pretty easy guess. With them being them and Heidi being her. Wherever she was, Heidi would know that eventually they'd be fucking with her stuff. There was a joke going around. What's the difference between an alcoholic and a drug addict? An alcoholic will steal your wallet and a drug addict will steal your wallet and then help you look for it. None of them could be trusted. They all knew that. They were living in a weird code where they knew none of them could be trusted and that if any of them didn't rip the others off on any given day it was exceptional. But they were getting better. Dell and Heidi liked to steal things. Every day Dell would have to go to where Carol worked in the mall and show her what she'd stolen, and Carol would make her take it back. It was a new, better way of living, but it was going to take some bedding-in.

'How was the gig?' Dell asked.

'Don't ask,' Peggy said.

'Trouble?' Dell took a tentative sip of tea – it was too hot.

Peggy nodded. Greta was eating raw cereal, straight from the box.

'Was there violence?' Dell asked.

'You know us,' Peggy said.

Dell nodded. 'Fuck.'

'Fuck,' they said and looked out the kitchen window onto the neighbour's wall.

The whole day it worried at them. In their tenuous state everything felt like it might be the end or the beginning of some new level of dreadful life they didn't think they could stoop to. They tried to shake it. They went to the lunchtime meeting, but hated it. The feeling that they'd fucked up in such a big way they were doomed to drink again separated them from everyone in the room. They felt like they were just visiting. Like it was all just about over. The people who spoke, spoke for too long, the room was hot, and there was too much talk about god. Maybe it was a cult. Maybe they were too young. The old men who had been coming for a long time were misogynist and homophobic. Greta and Peggy could tell by the way they sat and looked at everyone. Everything about it was old-fashioned, the whole thing was hopeless. They were hopeless. They kept living the moment over and over again and being furious that they hadn't stopped and not punched her. They listened to the radio but, as Greta said, it was one punch and she was pretty sure Tyra had got up. It wouldn't be on the radio or on the TV.

'Isn't there someone we can call?' Peggy asked again.

Greta shrugged. They had friends in common but then what? Please don't fuck up our life? Please don't make us go to jail? We don't want to go to jail because we're trying to make a go of being sober? Sorry about your face? No. It just wouldn't do. It was hopeless. The meeting ended. They said the prayer – the fucking prayer. Why was there so much fucking god? They'd packed a lunch, a slice of white bread with some butter and grated carrot. One of the important things they'd learned in hospital was that a body needs three meals a day. They walked to a patch of grass by the river. Tourists were being punted up it. They knew a guy who worked as a punter. They used to think it was funny but now everything just looked dark. The tourists, the punters. Maybe they could move. The sandwiches tasted dreadful. They didn't call Diane until eight.

'Well,' Diane said. 'These things happen and then, if we don't drink, we get a choice about what we do next.'

They talked to her for about an hour, Peggy holding the phone so they could get both their ears to the receiver. They cried. They were happy to be back. Together, with Diane, they decided they needed to contact Tyra, and tell her where they were, in case she wanted to press charges. They needed to say they were sorry, out of line. And then they needed to shut up and hear what she had to say and then they had to wait until she decided what she wanted to do. They had to try better and ask to be given the strength to do better. Ask the god they didn't believe in – the one they had no idea what shape it took – to try to take away their anger, their quickness to anger, their rage, and help show them a better way to deal with disappointment and fear. They all agreed it was the best way to find some happiness. That it was the best way to deal with a situation that no one could change, now. Before the receiver was back in its cradle Peggy and Greta started to doubt it. They would do it, but they cried again because this was where they had come to. 'Eunuchs,' Greta said, and they cried some more. They'd been someone to be frightened of and now this – apologies. Putting themselves in clear sight of their enemies. Where was their life? They looked around the small, damp flat. Where was the life they got to choose? How had it come to this? They'd had no life before and now they had this. Life was long. They both knew it, and then they found the address book and rang someone who knew the phone number for someone else who knew the number for Tyra who they had punched and they called her and she swore at them and told them they were fucking psychotic and hung up. So, before they went to bed they found all their bank stuff and information stuff and put it in an envelope in their bag, in case they were taken away quickly by the police. Then they slept so well, tucked up, not knowing where they stood, but knowing what they had done and who they were.

5

The next morning they were all in the kitchen. Dell was trying to get ready for work. She was holding it down at work. No one had noticed Heidi wasn't coming in anymore. Their boss told her a couple of days ago how proud she was of both of them for making a go of it. Dell said she'd pass it on to Heidi.

'You can't keep lying like that,' Peggy said.

Dell knew but, they all agreed, desperate times called for desperate measures. What Heidi did fell on Dell. Their boss needed to think they were both doing great. Dell and Heidi always used to look beautiful when they went to work. Dell still did. She had a full set of make-up on by the time Peggy and Greta were up, and her clothes were often new and always fashionable. She was sipping coffee – it was too hot to drink. They all gulped everything, waiting for a hot drink to be cool enough that they could swallow the whole cup in one. While it was hot they'd worry at it the way Dell was now. One day Peggy swallowed an instant coffee in one gulp and one of the guys said, 'You can take Peggy out of the pub but you can't take the pub out of Peggy.' He was handsome. And right in the head. Peggy and Greta both liked him. They were having sex with each other and the only other people they were having sex with they were having sex with for money so it wasn't proper sex, but, they agreed, if he asked, they'd have proper sex with him. He wouldn't look at them, though. Not this guy. He was well enough to see what it was to prey on vulnerable people. He didn't want to be that person, so he didn't look at them like that. Not at all. But he was handsome.

Peggy suddenly said, 'Did you say yesterday that Heidi called?'

Dell looked up but didn't take the coffee cup away from her lips. She said, into the cup, 'Yeah.'

'What did she say again?' Peggy and Greta must not have been listening at all yesterday. Greta tried to sound like they had been listening but just not completely, so that Dell would tell them what Heidi had said again.

'She said we needed to stay away from her stuff.' Dell was blowing on her coffee. It made her cheeks shine.

'So, she was here?' Greta looked around like she expected Heidi to be there. Their memory was shot. Neither of them could remember the conversation until Dell said, 'I don't know. Remember, we weren't sure. We thought she might have guessed.' Then they remembered the whole conversation – the trying to work out if it was a game. It was hard to tell. It always felt like a game with Heidi.

'We were only trying to make sure she was safe,' Peggy said. She was thinking about toast, and whether it was better to have toast or cereal for breakfast. About which was most likely to keep them sober. Neither of them believed in god, so everything felt like a complex superstition or ritual. They were trying to placate something they didn't understand. That was what they thought this was about. That if they just did the right things, then some complex form of karma, some cosmic equation, would right itself in their direction. If they had cereal, Tyra wouldn't call the police and they'd be able to carry on as they were. And, perhaps in their better part, if they ate the right thing for breakfast then Heidi would be safe. 'Is she drinking?' Greta asked. It was probably the worst thing you could say about someone and none of them had said it until now. They were all thinking it, wondering it. Sometimes when they thought it, they were wondering what it meant to them – if it made more room in the cosmic equation for them to stay sober or whether it was catching. If Heidi drank, would they all drink? Like a cold. But now Greta was asking it. It was because she hadn't been paying attention. She wasn't thinking. She was thinking about breakfast, too – cereal or toast. But then it would be bread for breakfast and lunch, which was fine with her, but was that addictive? Could they get addicted to bread?

Dell shook her head. 'I haven't seen her.' They both knew what it meant. Dell hadn't seen her at meetings – neither had Peggy or Greta. That didn't necessarily mean anything, because every time they were at a meeting there were three other meetings on. But also, it meant she hadn't *seen* her – looked her in the eye.

To begin with, it felt like everyone was drinking. Falling off the wagon, busting, slipping. They went to so many meetings and for a while it seemed like there was always someone who had a look in their eye and a story to tell. They knew what drinking looked like. Or they thought they did. Really, they had no idea. Lots of things looked like drinking – breaking up, losing a kid, getting a bad diagnosis – but really they had no idea. Some people said they could tell, but then one day they'd look in the mirror and see it – the loss of light – but they hadn't been drinking and they'd realise there was no way of telling except to yourself. Except in your own skin. Except when you lay down in bed and the world fell away and you were by yourself and you thought, 'I have to lie down by myself,' and at the same time, 'In the end, when I take my last breath it will be me and whatever semblance of a spirit I have.'

There was an energy around any discussion of Heidi, a push and a pull, a tension between caring – or maybe even just wanting to appear to care – and being intrigued and wanting the problem to get worse. For the situation to become even more intense. Partly it was about wanting to be in the middle of something. When people asked them 'How's Heidi?' Peggy and Greta loved it. Their faces would make a certain type of shape – one that looked like they were so worried, like they didn't really want to say, but they so wanted to say. They would talk in hushed voices about the terrible things that were happening to Heidi. Dress it all up as concern, as wanting to help, but inside they loved to gossip. It put them on a high horse. By confessing Heidi's sins they were trying to show they didn't have any. That they were above the pull of some human kind of wanting. That they could stand on their own feet. That they were committed to staying sober above everything else, but perhaps without realising it they were actually showing that they too would love a door that led to a drink – some way of taking an understandable drink, a justified drink, a drink they could get away with. When people asked, they would tell them exactly how they thought Heidi was and sometimes the people who'd asked would love it. Sometimes they were as interested in this higher ground as Peggy and Greta were. But most of the time their eyes would start to wander, they would say something about Heidi's life being Heidi's, or that maybe it was okay for Peggy and Greta to just say 'I haven't seen her' or 'Not sure'.

The three of them were like a tableau in the kitchen now. Peggy saw that Greta was having cereal and decided to have cereal. Dell was drinking her coffee and looking into the space in front of her. Sipping. Head slightly lowered, a stare in her eyes that hid her mind, busy at needing to be at work soon and how it was tiring and how she would have liked a day off and how she was a little jealous of Greta and Peggy and how sometimes she wished they'd get a job so she wasn't the only one working. Peggy and Greta weren't sure Dell even liked coffee. They wondered if she was just holding on until things got better. Until Heidi came home. Holding the coffee to give her time to think these things over and wonder where Heidi was, when she would be back, if she really had been home and really was angry at her. Dell must have been jealous of Peggy and Greta because they still had each other and she must miss Heidi so very much.

6

A lot of the days in the week following the concert were spent looking at the phone. Dell said one day everyone would have a phone in their hand all the time – but not for a while yet. One day, Dell said, they'd be hard pressed to find a moment away from their phones. There'd be meetings in their phones, and friends, and they could talk to anyone anywhere and send pictures. Dell was concerned about the future in a way that the future did not seem concerned about her. It was like she thought she could win it. There would be video phones inside the phones that everyone would have in their hands all the time. There was a magazine article she'd read. Not yet, though. For now, Peggy and Greta had to watch the phone that sat on a pile of phonebooks in the lounge, plugged into the wall. Watching and waiting to see if Tyra would call or the police would knock on the door. But they couldn't do that all day. Part of the day they had to go to the warehouse and sort clothes and part of the day they had to go to meetings and some of the day they had to clean the house and themselves, and eat and make cups of tea. So, part of the day the fear was very acute because all their energy was going into watching the phone and then it would subside into a backburning fear that lay on top of them and behind them, like when they were swimming and the thing could come from anywhere.

The days were getting cooler. It was darker now when Peggy and Greta walked to the warehouse. One day the supervisor came up and asked if they'd like to train to do the shop. They were very keen to do the shop. The shop looked like fun and felt like a step up. Like, maybe if they did the shop, there might be some kind of way they could get a job that paid – in a real shop. Not that the shop wasn't real. The responsibility was huge. There was money and customers and the things to be sold in the shop, and when you worked in the shop you were responsible for all of it. Not one person but everyone who worked there was responsible together.

They met the manager at the shop so they could see the open-up. The keys were a big responsibility, so big that most of the time only the paid manager looked after them. People volunteering in the shop met the manager at eight-thirty so they could be ready to open at nine. The manager unlocked the door and the people volunteering that day came in and then it was locked again. There were usually piles of clothes outside the door, but you ignored them to start off with.

Inside, the manager would turn on the lights, because they knew where all the lights were. While the manager turned the lights on and went to the till, Peggy and Greta would go around the store and tidy up. Sometimes this was a bigger task than it should be. The people who locked up were meant to check the store for rubbish or any clothes on the floor or in strange places. They were meant to put the dresses back with dresses. The trousers with the trousers, and all the oversized clothes went in one part of the store – to save people time. Sometimes they would look at an item and not be totally sure where it went, but they were allowed to make an educated guess and it wasn't a blaming culture. Sometimes the end of the day was busy – customers looking around right up until the last minute and wanting to buy something at three minutes to five, just before the till closed, and maybe the people who locked up had other things to get to: meetings, after-school pick-up, dates – so sometimes that first clean-up would take until ten in the morning, an hour after the shop opened. There was no way the manager could wait until the clean-up was completed to open the door. That would be crazy. There wasn't much else to do other than clean-up. It made up the bulk of the work and it could be done while there were customers in the shop. In between cleaning up there was the labelling and eventually Peggy and Greta would be taught how to use the till.

Peggy and Greta were told all this by Dorrit, the paid manager, on the first day they worked at the shop, and they understood it to be true. They'd thought a lot about working at the shop during the week they had to wait before they started. They imagined themselves working there: first as the person who didn't know what to do, then as a person who perhaps ran the shop, and then as a person who ran several shops, who maybe had a job at another shop like Heidi and Dell did. But, as Dorrit showed them around and explained the job, their ideas about how they would progress disappeared and, instead, they were pretty sure they would steal the money, or wreck the shop, or one day get drunk and break in so they had somewhere to sleep. Before this happened, they were sure they would say something rude to someone or consistently put the oversized clothes in the wrong place or some undersized clothes in with the oversized clothes. There seemed very little possibility they would be there for anything like the time it took to get a paid job.

Eventually, Dorrit had told them everything they needed to know to work in the shop. When she asked if they had any questions, Peggy asked when lunch was.

It was usually between twelve and one but they liked people to stagger when they went so that there were always two people in the shop. They'd be counted as two in the shop but one when it came to lunch and on the roster, because they probably wanted to have lunch together and work together. Peggy and Greta nodded because they did. If they had to have a particular time for lunch, Dorrit said, maybe they had an appointment – they should let someone know first thing. There were some cafés around but it was always best to bring lunch. Peggy and Greta said they always did that. It was one of the things they'd learnt at rehab. Making lunch was cheaper, but the really important thing was that if they made it and put it in their bag when they left home they would always be close to something to eat. Alcohol had a lot of sugar in it and hunger could make you want to drink – it was important to have food close. They had both lost weight in the first months, and now they were putting it on again. They were probably fatter than they had been in their lives but it was a different type of fat – they'd been puffy when they arrived at rehab, and bloated. Theo, one of the guys at rehab, had pointed out that they had a beer pot. It probably wasn't cute. He hadn't said it to be mean. He'd said it in a sort of revelatory tone – like he was realising again that alcoholism had physical effects, like any other disease. His father was in meetings but they hadn't seen Theo since they all got out of rehab. He was handsome and kind.

One Sunday afternoon at rehab, Peggy and Greta lay under a tree in the dappled sun and talked about how Theo was the kind of guy maybe they could go out with. Like, someone who was clean and trying to make a better life. Like maybe they could have a house, Greta had said. They'd dozed off a bit and both had the same dream. A single image – they were standing at a sink washing dishes, and above the sink was a window and above the window a concrete path at eye level and above the concrete path a deck and a large pōhutukawa tree. In the dream, they were struck with an overwhelming sense of contentment. Not joy or ecstasy, just the quiet weight of being where they said they'd be, doing what they said they'd be doing, when they said they'd be there. When they woke up they were in each other's arms, smiling, the feeling lodged in them from the dream. When they told their counsellor, he said the image, the feeling, was something worth holding on to, so they did.

They liked working in the shop. Each day was different and there were different people coming in all the time and new things to learn and they were good at what they did. It felt good to be working in the shop. Lunchtime was nice. There was a small park a couple of blocks away. They'd go and sit on the grass and eat the sandwiches they made at home on the kitchen bench in the mornings. Usually it was butter and grated carrots. Every now and then at the end of a meeting, someone would say, 'Does anyone want to take the rest of the biscuits?' and occasionally Peggy and Greta would say, 'Okay.' So sometimes they would have biscuits as well as the sandwiches.

Greta held up a Shrewsbury and said, 'Where even do these come from?' and they both laughed, because neither of them really knew. Some people in the meetings baked – like almost obsessively. Their friend Michelle had made a chocolate cake for them a couple of weeks ago when they were at her house – like in front of them.

Michelle went to meetings mainly out of town, by the dock, and had a kid. Her drinking had been different from

59

theirs. She'd learnt to bake because she had a kid, and baking was cheaper so she had more money for alcohol. Baking was also a great excuse for drinking. She laughed at that. A lot of the women they met drank at home and were able to do a lot of drinking because they were alone a lot – doing the dishes, the laundry, looking after the kids while the kids slept. When they were at Michelle's watching her bake the chocolate cake, they asked her the whole 'How many times can you wear something before you have to wash it' question and she listed off all the clothing items and their respective when-to-wash times. Underwear you only wore once, but a bra you could get maybe four or five wears out of, depending on what you were doing in it. If you had sex in anything it needed to be washed straight away, so Dell was right. Cardigans and sweatshirts could sometimes go seven wears. It was a good idea to maybe do a weekly wash of sheets and towels. 'Really?' Peggy said, and breathed out. 'Wow,' said Greta.

They wrote it all in a small notebook they carried around. The notebook was for writing things down in. They kept a list of everything they spent money on. That was about their money stuff, not their drinking stuff. They were money drunks as well. They needed to put everything they spent in the notebook so they could tell how much money they had left and where all the money went. They didn't have much money. They needed to get used to that. There was the sleeping with men for money but both of them and Diane agreed that probably couldn't go on for ever. It was hard and messed with their heads and they often felt like the only way to keep doing it was to get drunk and often the guys were drunk or liked them to play drunk. When they were well and truly done with it they would have even less money.

Or maybe something would change in them and the work

would get easier and they would find a way to do it without getting drunk and start to pay taxes and it would be like Dell's job in the shop. It was illegal, but they could set themselves up as contractors and say they were in the entertainment business and pay taxes. People did that.

It would all become clear. That's what Diane said, not because she was any kind of expert, just because that was what had happened for her. Peggy and Greta had thought maybe they were the only ones sleeping with people for money but when they talked to Diane and the other women they realised most women were doing it in some form or another. Or had done it in some form or another.

Talking to women was good. Before they got sober, Peggy was the only woman Greta talked to and vice versa. They didn't trust women. Women were competition and scary and reflected back a little too starkly what they were and who they could be. But being sober was different. Women were great.

All sorts of people came into the shop. Sometimes their old friends would come in and that could be a bit disconcerting. They would ask what Peggy and Greta were up to and they'd both shrug and look around, maybe at their hands holding a T-shirt or a scarf or something.

'You know,' they'd say.

'Yeah, 'cause I haven't seen you around.' Sometimes the old friend was sizing them up. Did Peggy and Greta get paid for working in the shop? Could Peggy and Greta loan them some money?

'Yeah. You know,' they'd say. Knowing that there was no way their old friend could know. Knowing what they would have thought if the shoe was on the other foot. Knowing they would know nothing.

'You finishing soon?'

A look at their watch or a look towards the counter, where the clock was. 'Nah.'

Sometimes they wished they were finishing soon. Some days when the work was boring, or things were frightening them. Maybe there was a bill they weren't sure they could pay – those times they would want so badly to go with the old friend. Surely they could have a drink today and come back tomorrow? Surely, just to take the pressure off? The pressure.

'We're working all day.'

It was a habit. So much of it was about habits. Habits had got them in trouble and habits would get them out.

'We're working late. Then we've got a thing.' But we want to, every part of them would scream, hoping maybe the friend could read it, would insist, would save them from the hell of being so much in the real world and the here and now. Pick them up. Tell them they were being stupid, that things would be fine, that it was just a drink.

But then the old friend would shrug too, and say, 'Well, you know where I am.'

And they did. They knew where it all was. Knew how long it would take to get there and how they would get there and what bus to take and what to say when they got there.

When they talked to other sober people about it, the people said how when things like this happened they were always happy they hadn't said yes. But Peggy and Greta hadn't felt that yet. Every now and then they would feel grateful – and they said it a lot in meetings, because it was part of what you said. 'I'm really grateful to be sober.' But they were pretty sure they weren't. It was more of a stick situation – no carrot, just a massive stick. Those last few months of drinking had been terrifying, traumatising. They still had nightmares. Woke up gasping. There was some kind of deep terror of going back to that. Sometimes the terror of what had happened was so big it seemed insurmountable. Sometimes they thought a drink was the only way to get rid of it but drinking had stopped working. Completely. They didn't know much, but they knew there was no comfort left in alcohol. So they would say, 'Yeah, see you later. Have a nice day.' And watch their old friend walk out of the shop and into the sunshine.

They never went too near the edge. Never thought too hard. After the old friend left, Dorrit would come and tell them they could go for lunch and they'd look out the door again and think maybe they wouldn't come back from lunch but that would mean the next people wouldn't get their lunch.

The sandwiches generally ended up squashed at the bottom of their bag. They'd discovered hummus. That you could buy hummus at the dairy and make it last a week. They put the sandwich in a plastic bag they'd taken from the staffroom, but everything in their bag still smelled of garlic. They'd take the sandwiches to the car park at the back of the shop. They couldn't be bothered walking to the park anymore. If there was sun they'd sit in the sun. Not talking to each other. Angry. Sad. Wondering what the fuck they were bothering for. Looking at their sandwiches – the soft carrots, the wet bread – and somehow remembering food before sobriety as delicious, or perhaps remembering how they hadn't needed food before they stopped drinking – like they were superhuman. They were staying sober despite themselves, they decided. They had no idea what was keeping them from following their friends. From the outside, when they looked at themselves, at each other, it looked like fear, but there was something more annoying than the fear. They had no idea what it was. Laziness? Were they tired?

'After lunch,' Greta would say. Peggy nodded. After lunch, they'd throw it all in. From somewhere high and with force, they would throw it all in and have a drink and try to forget about all of this. Then the sun came out and some old lady would walk past and say, 'Nice day.' And they said, 'Yeah. This sun!' And they could do it for another few minutes. And then they had an okay bite of the sandwich and maybe they had just been hungry and maybe something better was waiting for them. Then lunch was over and they went back inside and got busy and labelled fifteen T-shirts and had a chat with someone and helped someone else to the dressing rooms and said, 'That looks nice,' and the person would smile a bit and something felt a bit more awake in them and, before they knew it, it was five and there was a meeting starting at five-thirty and there they were, another day. Another day at work without walking out.

They hurried a bit to lock up. Often, when they were halfway to the five-thirty meeting, one of them would say, 'Did we check the changing rooms?' and they'd both fall silent. One day they told Diane, and Diane recommended making a checklist. Just for themselves, in their notebook. And it worked, but not always. The things they did every day didn't often settle in their memory. They read somewhere that you needed to tell yourself what you were doing. 'I am locking the front door.' 'I am brushing my teeth.' Otherwise it didn't stick. Their short-term memories were a bit fucked. Alcohol did that. People would ask, 'Where were you?' and they'd shrug. It was hard to remember things. But they knew where the meetings were. And if they forgot, they had a folded A4 sheet of paper with all the meetings on it and it was always in their pocket or their bag.

Today it was sunny. There was a bit of heat in it. It would

be full spring soon. Peggy and Greta had fifteen minutes to get to the hall. It wasn't far away. Mainly, the people who went to the five-thirty meeting were workers. They had gone a lot before they started at the shop because it meant they could get to three meetings in a day, but they particularly liked to go now they were workers too. There were quite a few cars. The central city wasn't that busy, but people drove through it to get places. They didn't say much on the walk. They thought a lot. Too much probably. Today they were worrying whether Tyra would call them, or if she'd called the police.

'Surely we would have heard?' Peggy said, finally, pushing the pedestrian crossing button over and over. A woman stood next to them, looking at them both.

'You'd think so.' Greta was looking out to the hills. Peggy was looking down and pushing the button over and over. Someone had told her it made the cross sign go faster and they were always in a hurry. Which wasn't true – they thought they were in a hurry but they were just impatient. Wanted everything to happen faster and then when it did felt sad it had passed so fast. They'd feel that way about life, soon, how they had wished away the first weeks and months of their sobriety when in reality magical things were happening to both of them and they were walking past them every day.

'But could she be talking to the police and it's just taking a while?' Greta said.

'She's a bit of a fuck-up,' Peggy said, and Greta nodded. They could only say that because they were fuck-ups too.

A few months before Peggy and Greta got sober, their friend Shay had stopped drinking. They'd hated him for it. He was a wowzer, they said. 'My dad says there's nothing worse than a reformed anything,' Peggy said to Greta, leaning on her in a drunken way, too close, breathing all over her face.

Greta's eyes were closed. She was standing and holding a cigarette close to her mouth but not smoking it. 'Mine too,' she said, smiling, and shook her head, and they both laughed like they wouldn't stop. It wasn't until they went to their first meetings that they realised Shay had been going to meetings. He was drinking again now. They'd seen him just after they got out of rehab. He was on the street, out of it, just in town for the weekend. He was living at a camping ground miles from anywhere. Did they have any money? Peggy? Greta? Surely, they had some money? Then, 'The light in your eyes.' And a sadness took him over, then anger. 'Fuck you,' he yelled, and spat in their direction. 'Fuck you.' They hadn't helped at all when he'd tried to stop drinking. They'd called him a loser and talked about him behind his back. They told people where he was if anyone was looking for him. They drank and smoked in front of him and bought him drinks and got angry when he wouldn't drink.

'He's not wrong,' Greta had said as he walked away, shouting and flinging his arms at them.

Peggy shook her head. 'Fuck us,' she had said. And Greta nodded. They had mentioned it in passing to Diane. Not out of any concern for Shay, but to lift themselves, to look good, like they had this and he never would, and Diane shook her head and made a clicking noise. 'You,' she said. 'Come on.' And, of course, she was right. They were eligible for it all. There was nothing special about them.

Neither of them understood it. People explained to them over and over that it was a disease. Neither of them completely believed that, but then, one by one, people they knew drank and people they knew died and people they knew with everything to lose lost everything and they started to suspect maybe they really were drinking despite themselves.

That maybe there was something physically different between them and people who could drink half a glass of wine. It seemed like a cop-out. They had done terrible things. Drunk like pigs. To say they were sick was such a fucking cop-out.

'Fuck us,' they'd say occasionally, in memory of Shay – who died three days after they saw him. He was hitchhiking home and got drunk and fell asleep in a shed and vomited and choked. They heard about it three weeks after the funeral. No one had known where to get hold of them. People were pretty disgusted with Peggy and Greta. Get clean, forget everyone. 'Not very spiritual,' one of their friends pointed out to them. They were right. Things felt selfish so often. Not returning calls. Staying away. Crossing the street. It all felt so fucking tentative. Everything tempted them. Talked to them. Everything seemed too hard. They needed to pretend they were new people. Needed to do new things. But, they said to each other all the time, they should have tried to help Shay. They had done nothing to deserve what they had except act like arseholes for a very long time. They didn't deserve it any more than Shay. In some ways, Shay maybe deserved it more because he was gentle and kind and had tried so fucking hard to stay friends with them. 'Fuck us,' they would say. 'Fuck us.'

7

By the end of May they'd both stopped sleeping with men for money. Well, stopped sleeping with the men they used to for money. There was a place, and the men there were all new. They couldn't guarantee they'd stopped altogether. But it was falling further and further down their 'good ideas for money' list. Anything they used to do that they tried now sent them into a mass of physical cravings. It would sideswipe them. Sometimes a song would play from a passing car. Sometimes they'd smell something. Sometimes someone would shout in a particular way. The clothes at work were tricky. They all smelled but, also, they were often from mass-produced lines. So, it would look exactly like Jimmy's T-shirt, or when they put their hands in the pockets of a jacket they were sure they'd find Laura's wallet which they'd stolen one night, took everything out of then returned.

'What's the difference between an alcoholic and an addict?' Greta would ask.

Peggy would shrug. They liked saying the punchlines. Remembering the punchline from a joke was huge and it was nice to get the chance.

'An alcoholic will steal your wallet and an addict will steal your wallet then help you look for it.' They would both laugh. Every time. Remembering the punchline was one thing but remembering how it felt was another thing altogether. They had talked about it one night. Someone else had told the joke. They'd heard it from another room. They were at Diane's house. A dinner, maybe it was someone's birthday. Not the day they were born on, but the anniversary of the day they got sober, or the last day they drank, or the first meeting they came to. Those birthdays were big. Cakes, candles and a potluck dinner like this. Greta and Peggy brought chips. One bag. Dell brought some bread from a bakery at the mall but hadn't brought any butter, but Diane had some. Diane's house was really nice. She'd been sober for over ten years, which seemed ridiculous. The house was so cool.

'If we had a house,' Peggy said, 'it would be exactly like Diane's.' It was an old villa with a really nice kitchen and the bedroom was painted forest green – dark, like you were sleeping out in the bush.

'Like witches, like,' Greta said. The lounge didn't have a TV. There wasn't a TV in the whole house. Hardly any of them had TVs. 'The drug of the nation', someone had said, but Peggy and Greta were pretty sure it was because they were always at meetings when anything decent was on TV.

The lounge was decorated with amazing things. Diane knew artists and there was art on the walls, original pieces of art. Peggy and Greta had started going to the art gallery and getting books out of the library about art. Out of everything, they probably wanted to be artists. Diane said the people she knew who were artists had gone to university. Peggy and Greta didn't have University Entrance. Diane said they could ring the local high school and ask about what they would have to do to get University Entrance. The person they talked to said they needed to get School Certificate first. There were night classes. They'd got the high school to send them booklets about it, but it seemed unlikely. Then Erin and Kitty told them about Workbridge. Erin and Kitty had gone to Workbridge and now they were doing a course. It was work-based training. They were working at the electronics factory, learning how to solder.

'Can anyone ring them?' Peggy and Greta asked.

'Anyone who's on the sickness benefit,' Kitty and Erin said. If the work-based training worked out, Kitty and Erin would have a job. It felt a bit like a shortcut. Shorter than the whole School Certificate thing.

'We're on the sickness benefit,' Peggy and Greta said.

When they got back from treatment the counsellor had given them the form to take to Social Welfare to say they needed to concentrate on staying sober. The person looked at their file and the arrests and the trouble, and agreed. They'd never been on a benefit before. They'd always worked – usually illegally but it was so much easier than dealing with Social Welfare. They'd been lucky. Even though they were very drunk, most of the work they did could be done drunk. 'Lying on your back,' they laughed. They looked up the number for Workbridge in the phonebook and now they had an appointment in five weeks. Erin and Kitty said that one of the other women was doing a graphic design course. Which was sort of like art, they all agreed. They were going to ask the Workbridge people about that. That's what they'd been telling everyone. The art on Diane's wall was what made them want to be artists. They wanted a house like this. They wanted to know artists. This made them feel good. From Diane's sink, you could look out on a lawn. Or back at yourself if it was night time.

They'd had cake. They'd sung happy birthday. People were laughing. Peggy and Greta wondered if it was a show. They'd hung out with straight-edge punks for a while. Drinking in toilets and closets and pretending they hadn't been. 'Can anyone else smell booze?' 'Nope.' The music was great but the straight-edge punks were the worst. The direct action – one night they'd superglued the McDonald's doors shut, and the good-looking guy they hung around the straight-edge punks to be around was arrested for throwing a brick through a butcher's window. There was a rumour that a drummer from one of the bands worked in a freezing works but that was probably bullshit. What made the straight-edge punks the worst was they were constantly trying to prove they didn't need drugs to have fun. Instead, they did all sorts of exhausting fun activities.

One night, one of the straight-edge punks called out to Peggy and Greta from under their bedroom window. 'Don't answer,' Peggy said. But he wouldn't stop calling, so they leaned out and he said they were all going somewhere awesome – come on. First, they drove around the streets for hours pulling real estate signs off their posts. Then they drove up a dormant volcano and slid down the crater on the signs. Peggy and Greta had been drinking heavily in their bedroom before the straight-edge punks had called them away for the fun activity so they were sobering up awake, which sucked. The whole thing was exhausting and they were miles from any more drink. They started to shake a bit. That was in the early days. In the late days, like in the months before they went to rehab, they shook like nothing on earth. They joked about how they had around ninety minutes of sobriety each day – between about nine and ten-thirty each morning and man, someone else would have to roll their cigarette and someone else would have to light their cigarette and not even the nicotine would help and they were only twenty-four! They kept saying this.

They still hallucinated now. They'd hear people calling their names when no one was calling their names. There were small, brown, furry things on four legs with no heads – about the size of a large hedgehog – that would strike out from under cars and behind doors. When they saw something, they checked to see if anyone else saw it first. They perfected the sideways glance. 'Did anyone else see that?' They were twenty-four. They hadn't done that many drugs. Alcohol was the only detox you could die from, the doctor had told them as they shook and fevered and scratched. Or maybe the doctor didn't say that at all. Those first days were fucking terrible.

Someone at Diane's potluck told the 'What's the difference between an alcoholic and an addict' joke, and everyone laughed. Peggy and Greta were sure some of the people were forcing the laugh out. Some of the women threw their heads back, raising their necks to the ceiling. Peggy and Greta were still in the kitchen, leaning in a doorway, a bottle of Coke each in hand, no straw, no glass. It all looked fake. No one could be that happy without drink. No one. They'd all been telling stories about their drinking. This was their drink, Peggy said as they walked home powerfully and angrily from that last dinner party at Diane's. Talking about their drinking was getting them drunk. What kind of sobriety was that? They weren't happy, it was all a ruse. They were whistling in the dark.

Someone else told a joke and despite themselves Peggy and Greta laughed – it was frightening, this weird noise coming out of them. Laughing with people rather than at them. It shocked them. They were about to raise their eyebrows at each other, about to look at each other in a way that said, 'Fuck these bitches.' But instead they were caught off guard by the laugh which came out of them.

Whenever they heard the 'What's the difference between an alcoholic and an addict' joke, they never laughed. They'd stolen Laura's wallet. She'd gone to the toilet in a crowded bar and asked them to watch her jacket. They stole it and Peggy went through it while Greta kept an eye out for Laura coming back. Laura had just been paid – in cash. There was two hundred dollars, sorted, separated by folded pieces of paper that said *Rent, Food, Power*. They weren't sure what to do with the pieces of paper, so they took those too and put the wallet back in Laura's jacket pocket. A few days later, Laura rang. Not for 'Where the fuck is my money?' Just for 'How's it going? Are you going out tonight?' But she mentioned the money. 'Man,' she said. 'I spent all my money the other night. What a fucking loser.' And then, 'Maybe some of it must have fallen out when I was paying for something.' Peggy and Greta said they weren't sure and 'I guess these things happen' and 'We'll buy you a drink tonight.' And it was settled. They burnt the pieces of paper in the kitchen sink while they drank some of the vodka they'd bought with Laura's cash.

'Tell that one,' Peggy said. And they laughed their wry, fuck-you laugh and tried to forget about the other laugh. They were half in, at best. No one in their right mind wanted to fully commit to this. Not when you had to close your eyes and think about Shay and Laura and Tyra. Not then. Peggy and Greta had done nothing to deserve a laugh like that. They'd walked home from the potluck angry. It was dark. They wished they hadn't gone. When they got home, the phone rang. They picked it up and for a second there was someone on the other end and then they hung up.

Dell came into the room. Peggy still had the phone in her hand and they were both looking at it.

'No one there?' Dell asked. She was drying her hair.

Peggy and Greta shook their heads.

'Weird,' Dell said. 'Has that been happening a bit?'

Peggy and Greta thought about it, and maybe it had.

'Do you think it's Tyra?'

They hadn't thought about Tyra for a month or so, thought they didn't need to worry about Tyra.

'Weird,' Dell said.

Peggy and Greta hung the phone up.

'Maybe you should keep a list of every time it happens?' Dell said. 'In case.'

They looked at her and she was making sense. 'In our notebook,' Greta said.

Dell pulled something out of her pocket. 'You could use this one,' she said. The notebook was empty and new.

'We could.' Peggy took it.

'Keep it by the phone and just jot it down every time one of those phone calls comes through,' Dell said.

'I guess it makes sense,' Greta said.

'You don't need to tell Heidi,' Dell said.

'We don't see Heidi,' Peggy said.

'Yeah,' Dell said. She was wrapping her wet hair up in the towel. She was wearing day clothes, so she must have washed her hair over the sink. 'But, like. If you see her. You wouldn't need to tell her.'

8

They'd been hearing about the picnic for weeks in meetings but none of them expected to go – hadn't given it a second thought. No one actually went to those things, did they? Dell was clearing out her bag and pulled out the flier. Someone had made photocopies of it. Peggy and Greta couldn't imagine how someone would have the wherewithal to photocopy something. It had a picture of a tree and under it was a picnic table. The type with chairs attached to it. There were some dates on the flier. Dell was looking at it. And soon, because there wasn't anything else going on, Peggy and Greta got up and came and had a look. It was on that weekend. There was a number if you needed a lift. It looked like there'd be volleyball. Dell was holding the flier and Peggy and Greta stood either side of her and held the two top corners up so they could read it.

'Are you working?' Greta raised it first. They were all thinking about the possibility of going, but Greta was the first and backed into it slowly.

Dell shook her head.

'Who'll be there?' Peggy asked.

Dell shook her head. It was a mystery. God only knew who would turn up.

'Why are they having a picnic in winter?' Peggy asked.

'It's spring,' Dell said.

'Is it?' Peggy said.

'Is it for couples?' Greta asked.

Dell and Peggy didn't think so.

'Is it to get into a couple?' Greta asked.

Dell and Peggy laughed. Meetings were full of damaged goods. Anyone who appealed to them wouldn't touch them with a barge pole. Peggy and Greta were making money out of sex and had been raped horribly so would be happy if a man never came within ten feet of them again. Dell and Heidi usually slept with women, which made what Heidi was doing with Ian even more confusing. There were women in the meetings, but Dell was having nice casual sex and wasn't looking for anything. They'd all seen what had happened to Heidi. A lot of people were sleeping with each other in the meetings. People would arrive together. There was a bit of intrigue, because it wasn't totally a good idea. When two alcoholics got together, shit got intense. That was how someone had described it to Peggy and Greta. It worked sometimes but rarely. Usually one of them would drink. There was some weird psychic antagonising agent when two alcoholics slept together. Suspicion, passion, rage, obsession. It was usually a bad combination.

None of them had been to anything social to do with the meetings. Ever. There was plenty going on. Except bowling. Peggy and Greta had gone bowling, but not really. A group of young people went bowling. Peggy and Greta had agreed they never wanted to go bowling, but they went and it was okay. They talked to a few people and it was okay. The bowling was okay. Someone paid for them to go and then someone bought them a Coke and they sat around and then, before you knew it, there was another day. Another day closer to death, they'd say to each other and laugh. But it was a good way to waste time.

Saturdays sucked. There was no work and walking around was depressing because the streets were weirdly lonely and the parks were packed with families with kids. The weekends dragged and there were only two meetings in town and another one too far away for them to get to.

'Maybe we should go?' Dell said. She missed Heidi and wouldn't go by herself.

Peggy and Greta put their lips together and raised their eyebrows high like they were kind of surprised about it and nodded.

Greta climbed her hand down the flier. 'It says you have to bring a plate.' It was a curse of being sober. Everywhere you went you had to bring a plate. Alcoholics loved food. Greta and Peggy brought chips. Dell brought bread. They were vegetarian, so it usually meant they ate chips sandwiched between slices of bread at the potluck meals.

'We could make a quiche,' Greta said, like she was the bravest person on the planet.

'Really?' Dell said, then, 'How the fuck do you make a quiche?' Dell had eaten them before, they all had, but they thought they were made in some special quiche factory and only sold to bakeries.

'We saw it in the Alison Holst book,' Peggy said. She went and got it from the kitchen.

The cover was hideous. Some sort of stoneware or aluminium bowl held a terrifying collection of raw things – star anise sat on top of cashews, which nestled against kale sprouting out of an ear of wheat. There were raw mushrooms, and slices of pale cheese, raw pasta, spring onions – someone had taken a lot of time arranging the food. It made them all sick. The mix of sweet (grapes, carrots) with raw and just-picked-from-the-ground. But by far the most awful thing was the single, whole, raw Brussels sprout next to quarter of a boiled egg. 'All the fart-smelling things,' Dell had said the night they'd been given the book. It was a long Wednesday night. None of them could sleep and they'd sat in the lounge not saying anything, but the book had been on the coffee table because they'd just been given it and then Greta said, 'Fuck. That cover' – and they dived in. Fuck. The cover. Dell made gagging noises that started off sounding like a joke but then they all felt the wheat catch in their throats and smelt the cheese and farts, and started saying 'Stop. Stop' and 'Why would you put that on the front of a cookbook?'

Now Peggy put the book on the bench and Greta looked up the index.

'Oh,' Greta said.

'What?' the other two said.

'Something's up with the crust.'

'Do quiches have crusts?' Dell said.

'It's called "self-crusting",' Greta said.

'Oh,' Dell said.

'All the better,' Peggy said.

'Surely,' Dell said.

'Here it is.' Greta found the page. 'Self-crusting Potato and Vegetable Quiche.'

They fell silent and read.

'What's a flan tin?'

'I bet there's one at work,' Greta said. There were always tins and things. People brought cooking stuff in all the time.

'We could ask?' The person with the keys must know which tin would work for a self-crusting quiche.

'How will we keep it hot?'

'I think we can cook it and then take it to the picnic cold.'

'Or wrap it in tin foil.'

'Tin foil.'

'We should try and make one before Saturday to make sure it works.'

Someone looked at their watch. There was a supermarket up the end of the long road they lived on. They'd started getting their bread and hummus and carrots there because Diane explained it was cheaper than the dairy. It was the sort of place you went for cigarettes, but all of them had given up smoking at treatment, because if you're going to have several horrible detoxes you might as well have them all at once. The supermarket was small, but they thought it might have the things in the recipe. They could easily walk there in fifteen minutes.

'How much will it be?' They were already putting their jackets and shoes on – it was already decided. But they didn't have much money.

'I think we should take the cookbook,' Greta said. 'So we don't buy more of anything than we need.'

Everyone agreed. It was genius. They all turned out their pockets and wallets. Between them they had about eight dollars and there was seven in the jar for flat expenses, like toilet paper. They convinced themselves it would be enough, but they had no idea.

'If we get there and it's not enough we'll just get what we can – the things that'll keep – and then get more tomorrow.' No one wanted to ask how they would have more money tomorrow, because the quiche was the most exciting thing that had happened in ages. Peggy and Greta were thinking if it wasn't enough they could probably find someone to sleep with for money tomorrow after work to get the money for the rest of the quiche ingredients.

The night was big. Big sky. Everything was built low around where they lived and the sky was always so big. There were no hills to box them in until the huge hills way in the distance, which seemed to make the sky even bigger. Peggy and Greta always walked with their hands in their pockets. Dell swung her arms a bit more, but they all walked with their heads down. It was dark. Someone honked as they sped past. None of them looked up. The walk was flat and Dell was carrying a backpack to put all the stuff in and the book. They needed 1 large onion – chopped, 2 garlic cloves, 1 Tbsp butter, 3 eggs, ¾ tsp salt, 1 cup milk, ½ cup self-raising flour, 2 cooked potatoes, 1 cup of drained cooked asparagus or spinach, or mushrooms or broccoli, and 1 cup of grated Tasty cheese. They had none of it. Dell was stealing tea and coffee from her work, and milk powder and sugar in sachets from the café at the mall. Sometimes she didn't have time for a cup of coffee at work so it seemed fine to take it home – the cup of coffee she didn't have at work.

'We've got the butter,' Greta said suddenly. Into the silence of them walking and the dark of the night and the big, big sky. The others nodded.

'It's only a tablespoon of butter.'

The store was bright compared with outside. Did they need a trolley, or maybe a basket? Everything was cheaper than they thought it would be and in the end they had enough money for a new flan dish 'with a solid (not push-out) base' and they still had most of their money.

'Cooking is cheap,' Dell said.

They paid and walked home. The walk and their success at the supermarket made them feel more awake rather than sleepier. On the way home they talked and talked. Greta held the flan tin above her head. Every now and then they'd get a bit of a run on.

'We'll never need to buy salt again,' Peggy said, holding up the huge container they'd bought. 'We'll be splitting it up between us at our fiftieth birthdays when we finally have enough money to move into our own places.' They laughed and then fell silent. The future wasn't any of their business, and where was Heidi and why wasn't she here, with Dell?

At home they started getting everything together. They only had breakfast bowls so they made the mixture in three parts. Dell was good at converting everything into thirds. They often had thirty per cent off sales at her work. They turned on the oven. They hadn't used the oven except for making toasted cheese, but it smelt okay. The people before them must have cleaned it pretty well. They didn't have a cheese grater so Greta used a butter knife to cut up the cheese very small and then not so small as she lost interest in the task. Finally, it was time to put the mixture into the flan dish. It looked good. Then they put it in the oven and turned the light on and took turns looking at it through the oven door. It bubbled and shifted, and a few times they thought they'd fucked it up. They talked excitedly about what else they could make. They took turns looking through the cookbook. There were recipes for bread – could they make bread? It seemed impossible. They'd buy a grater. Maybe they could catch a taxi to the big supermarket across town and buy other stuff. Maybe they could meal-plan? Peggy had seen a magazine article about it.

The time was up. Dell wodged a couple of tea towels into her hands so she wouldn't burn herself and she lifted the quiche out and it looked amazing.

'Is it cooked in the centre?'

It was cooked in the centre.

They looked at it for a moment. It was late.

'It'd be nice for breakfast.'

But they decided to eat it now. While it was warm. At least some of it, and then they would all take it for lunch tomorrow and see what it was like cold, and if it was okay then they'd make it on Friday night and wrap it in something and catch a bus and go to the picnic at the beach park. They wouldn't ask anyone to take them. That seemed like something they wouldn't do. Maybe they'd change their minds. You always needed a back door.

It was delicious. All the better for the walk there and the cheapness and the walk home in the fresh air and the making of it themselves. In the end they ate half of it straight out of the flan dish. Maybe they needed to grease the flan dish a bit next time, but they could always take the dish and the quiche to the beach. They put it in the fridge once all of them had had enough.

Dell stood in front of the fridge. She wished Heidi was there. There was plenty of time for more laughs, but Heidi wasn't there.

'Maybe she'll come home soon,' Greta said, and she and Peggy put their arms round Dell's shoulder.

'Maybe,' Dell said. 'No one's seen her for months.'

'Someone's seen her,' they said. Then, 'There was that phone call.' And everyone nodded a bit.

'It's late,' Dell said, shutting the fridge door.

They started getting ready for bed. They all ended up in the hallway at the same time, standing at the doors of their rooms. It was late and they were tired and everything seemed off-kilter without Heidi. 'Night,' they said to each other, and Peggy and Greta went to bed and tried not to think about Dell by herself in the half-filled room.

*

The quiche might have tasted even better the next day, and it was decided. On Friday night they repeated the trip to the supermarket, but this time they didn't need some of the stuff because there was still enough left over from the first quiche. They worked together in a similar way, except now they had a bowl that Greta and Peggy had bought from the shop. They hadn't been able to find a cheese grater but when Greta opened the cupboard to get a cup to measure with, there was a cheese grater on the shelf next to it.

'Where did this come from?' Greta said.

Everyone shrugged.

With the proper bowl they were able to mix everything in one lot. The mystery grater made the cheese a much better shape and nothing fell over the sides of the bigger bowl. They were worried about these changes. Was there some special magic spell to the way they did it last time? But when it came out it looked really good – maybe better, and they resisted it and put it in the fridge and went to sleep. Greta and Peggy had bus timetables from the library and they had worked out a bus and which bus stop they needed to be at before ten-thirty the next morning. There were hardly any buses on Saturdays, but, realistically, if they missed the bus, they decided, they could take the quiche to the park in town and eat it under a tree by themselves.

None of them had togs or shorts or sundresses. They dressed in their boots and polyester frocks. It was going to be an unseasonably hot spring day, the type that comes out of the blue. None of them had sun hats. Someone might have sunblock. Was it really possible to get sunburnt on a day like today? Dell looked outside. Even though it was hot, it was a bit overcast. Would the picnic even be on? Again, it didn't really matter if no one was there, they were happy by themselves. Possibly happier. They each packed a backpack. Peggy and Greta packed another cardigan, a wallet and their keys. As they walked down the street they could feel their make-up moving. It was so thick and so matte. Whenever they had photos taken they looked like ghosts. Someone told them it was because of the reflectors in the foundation they used. Dell's fringe kept falling in her face and she was carrying the quiche so she had to blow her hair up and out of her eyes. They made it to the bus stop in good time, and the bus came on time, and they got on and Peggy and Greta sat on one seat and Dell and the quiche sat on another seat.

They weren't quite sure which stop to get off at, but Dell had the flier and it said the road the picnic would be on. They got off the bus and there was a picnic area on the grass next to the beach. There were picnic tables under a large pine. Several people from the meetings were already there.

'It's you!' three of the bowling people said at once.

'Yup,' they said together. As soon as they saw the others they wondered if maybe it had been a mistake.

'We made a quiche.'

'Nice.'

Peggy and Greta and Dell stood back while the others put up the volleyball net and unpacked things and put out rugs and started the park's barbecue that someone had rung and asked the council to unlock. They stood back and drank Cokes someone gave them. They scowled. It was a bit of a mistake. It was all a bit lame. Peggy and Greta kept looking around to make sure no one they knew could see them. It looked a bit like they were at a Christian thing. The other people from the meetings were very loud. They laughed loud and sang – someone had brought a guitar and someone had a boom box that played music loudly. They were all so concerned with looking like they were having a good time. Dell and Peggy and Greta should have taken their quiche to the park in town, but now they were stuck. It was on the table with the other food and, while they could leave the quiche, it was still in the flan dish and if they wanted to make more self-crusting quiches they would need the flan dish. Peggy and Greta did the arithmetic, quietly. They could buy another one but they really wanted a bigger spoon and a cake tin. Michelle had given them a recipe for the chocolate cake that had no eggs, just vinegar and baking soda, and they wanted to make that. Dell looked all wrong. Poor Dell. Like a one-armed coat-hanger. Where was Heidi? Why didn't she come home?

'Hi.' Someone was beside them all of a sudden, panting and indicating towards the volleyball game, like that was why he was puffed.

'Hi,' Greta and Peggy said.

'Nice day,' he said. Maybe he was Mark? Diane had joked about how most of the men were Catholic, so most were named after one of the apostles, so if you just went through those you'd probably hit on it. Simon. Andrew. James. Was he James? He was the secretary at one of the lunchtime meetings.

'Yeah,' they said. 'Not too hot.'

He laughed. They weren't sure why. Soon a woman came up and stood beside him. 'Hi,' she said.

'Hi,' Peggy and Dell and Greta said, then it was silent for a moment, and they all looked out at the volleyball game. It was going okay. Some people were taking it a little too seriously. There might be a fight. It was weird seeing everyone trying so hard. Greta and Peggy knew one of the guys serving. He had been in a band, a good band, and then he'd taken all the band's money – they'd been given a grant to make a music video and he'd emptied the bank account before they could make it and had pretty much injected it all into his arm. He was cool. And here he was, shirt off, tattoos out, serving the ball over-arm. It was all they had left. When they talked to him, he was all in. So committed it was terrifying.

Peggy and Greta were pretty sure the meetings and all this was a cult. When they raised this most people said, 'Oh yeah, that's what some people think.' But when they talked to the band guy about the meetings it felt like it was a cult. He was about six months clean and sober and did everything like his life depended on it, because it did. All of their lives depended on it. Peggy and Greta were under no illusion – if they drank again they'd die or go crazy. It was just some days the choice between dying and going crazy or playing volleyball at a daytime picnic wasn't an easy one to make. When they told people in the meetings this, they'd say, 'Yeah,' and nod their heads. When they told people outside the meetings this – counsellors, the Christians at work – they said, 'What?' and Peggy and Greta would change the subject.

The silence went on and on but it was actually okay. Someone did a good shot, and Peggy and Greta found themselves clinking their heavy rings on their Coke cans like they were clapping.

'Do you want to play?'

Peggy and Greta did not want to play. But Dell shrugged and followed the others up to the line of people waiting to play. When it was Dell's turn she tucked her frock into her underwear and hit the ball back once, twice and just kept moving around until she was serving. Peggy and Greta didn't know Dell could play volleyball or smile. Then they saw them. Heidi and Ian. They must have parked quite close. Dell hadn't seen Heidi yet. Ian had his arm over Heidi's shoulder – like he owned her. That's what it looked like. He had sunglasses on and a leather jacket and dark jeans with motorcycle boots. He had long hair which Peggy and Greta were pretty sure he spent a lot of time on – to make it look like he didn't spend any time on his hair. And still Dell didn't see them. Heidi and Ian couldn't have come on his motorbike because they were carrying too much. They walked closer and closer. Peggy and Greta shifted their stare from Ian and Heidi to Dell and back, wondering who would break first. As Heidi got closer, they saw that she had changed her hair and was wearing some kind of fake tan. She'd pierced her lip and as she took off her glasses they saw she was wearing coloured contacts and had had some of her teeth taken out. She was wearing a dental bridge that changed the shape of her face slightly. She'd contoured, and it looked like she'd taken half of one of her ears off and then, as the light hit her, they saw she had a scar, a new scar, across the bridge of her nose and down to her jaw. It hadn't worked at all. She still looked exactly like Dell. Just like Peggy looked exactly like Greta, and Kitty looked exactly like Erin, and so on out into the handful of women who had divided into two in an instant, one night eighteen months ago. And as Heidi got closer to Dell, they could see her starting to notice it. Starting to realise it hadn't worked, that they still looked exactly the same. Not like a mirror, not like a twin, but with every cell divided and the same, and even with all Heidi's effort and pain they were indistinguishable – it was like she'd done nothing. Whatever was intrinsically Dell and Heidi had not been extinguished in Heidi. As they watched Heidi walk past Dell, all of the women who had a woman who looked exactly like them looked at her and then at all the women who didn't, and they remembered how odd it was and that it hadn't always been this way. Then they looked back at Heidi, hating her for making the shame obvious again.

Most of the time no one noticed them. They could blend in. At first, people were interested, but not much. There were only a few of them and most of them were not women people took much notice of – drunks, sluts, crazy.

There'd been one of them and then, in an amount of time which was too small to measure, that one had divided into two.

One night, eighteen months ago, about two-thirty in the morning, something happened. Maybe to the world, maybe just to them. A handful of women, among four avenues, who'd been very drunk and blacked out and probably split inside themselves – conflicted, broken – split into two identical women. These few, drunk women found themselves one in one moment and two in the next – shoulder to shoulder, or face to face, as if the seams hadn't quite finished. Maybe they'd been in the bathroom or the kitchen or walking somewhere. One second, they were drinking by themselves and the next they felt the warmth of someone next to them and they weren't drinking alone anymore. It only happened to the drunkest and the most ruined. It was a shock – but an embarrassing shock, like coming to halfway when shouting at someone, or suddenly realising you weren't wearing any pants. So, they quietly took up slightly more room. In the wardrobes, in the single beds, they all just wandered around with each other, arrived at their jobs together, took buses together and bought cigarettes together. Everyone who saw them knew what it meant and wished they hadn't seen them. No one talked about it. If you acted like nothing had changed, everything was the same. If you pushed it down, they read like one person, like they always had, except for the odd feeling you got when you were around them, like something was a bit off, maybe by a couple of centimetres. It was worse when they tried tricks like the one Heidi was pulling now, because it threw everything sideways a bit. You had to readjust your eyes.

There was very little interest to begin with, and by now what interest there had been had almost completely worn itself out. It was a handful of women who had made bad decisions and couldn't be trusted. Women who would do anything for drugs or a drink. But everyone knew it was rude to stare, no matter how strange they looked, so they stopped staring and when they stopped staring eventually they stopped seeing them.

Peggy looked at Greta. Greta looked at Peggy. Something that ran through them suddenly ran cold. They looked around the park, and Kitty was looking at Erin, and Vi was looking at Lettie, and Jem was looking at Mimi and they were all looking in the same way. And even though none of them would talk about it, Peggy and Greta knew they were all thinking about that night. And as Kitty and Erin and Vi went to tell Dell that Heidi was back, Peggy and Greta had a moment to stand and be cold in the hot, hot sun.

9

It happened all the time. Margaret had come to in all sorts of places doing all sorts of things with all sorts of people.

But that night, she'd been drinking alone in the lounge and then she was in two places. Divided. Sitting to the left and the right of herself – forearms, thighs touching.

'Right,' she said, filling up a glass with straight gin and handing it to herself, and, 'Right,' she said back to herself and took a drink, and suddenly everything was crystal clear and they were almost as sober as they would be in the next twenty-four-hour period.

It happened all the time – waking up talking and moving, coming to mid-action like someone was moving her around like a piece in a board game.

'So good to see you,' Greta had said, and she hugged Peggy tightly around the waist.

'So good,' Peggy said, and she drained the glass and the crystal clear feeling was gone.

The next morning, the bed seemed too small for both of them. Face to face, they didn't recognise each other at first but then they rubbed their eyes with fisted hands and each of them came into focus. They were both hungover, so they rubbed their faces some more and dragged flat hands through their short hair. They needed to go to the toilet. When they walked through the kitchen their flatmate Orla was home, eating cereal at the table. She was looking at each spoonful of cereal as it made its way to her mouth, not looking up at all. Peggy and Greta groaned hello. Orla raised her spoon and groaned back. She'd worked all night and she was tired.

Peggy sat on the toilet and Greta turned on the cold tap, wet her hands and placed them flat-palmed to her face. They could both see the old coffee mug everyone put their toothbrushes in. They both counted them, then Greta took the toothbrushes and put them in a line. She was leaning against the sink and the tap was still running. Peggy reached over as she peed and moved the toothbrushes around, trying to get them to match the people in the house. Orla's toothbrush was green and Jimmy's was red. Phil had one with all-white bristles, all the same length – like it was made for children. Roxana's toothbrush was see-through green. Peggy held it up to the light before she put it next to the others. Everyone had their own toothbrush except for Peggy and Greta. They had just one blue toothbrush between the two of them. It was a solid blue that bent just before the bristles, which were punched into the handle in a rectangle. Shame ran through them. Everyone could count. But Greta looked at Peggy in the mirror and shrugged. Lots of people probably shared toothbrushes. They could probably get another toothbrush today. It was totally time to replace the old toothbrush. Maybe there were actually two toothbrushes and one of them had just taken the other one somewhere. Maybe there had always been two of them. Maybe people just needed to mind their own fucking business. There were plenty of perfectly reasonable explanations and then there was the hovering doubt about what had happened last night and what yesterday had been like and whether they would be able to get another drink soon. It felt like there had been a monumental shift in the night, and at the same time nothing had changed – like every morning. Maybe people wouldn't even notice there were two of them now. Maybe it wasn't their fault. Maybe this also happened to people who were fucking saints. Neither of them would own up to not knowing exactly what had happened, so the question would never be asked. It was grotesque, they could hardly look at each other. They knew that no one who saw it from the outside would want to talk about it. It was pushed under something.

Peggy wiped herself and pulled her pants back up. Greta sat on the toilet and Peggy turned on the cold tap, wet her hands and placed them flat-palmed to her face.

When they got back to the bedroom, Greta sat on the side of the bed and lit a cigarette. 'I need a drink,' she said.

Peggy looked out the window onto the street. 'We don't have any money.'

Greta nodded, picking tobacco off her tongue with her thumb and index finger. 'There's some mouthwash in the bathroom,' she said.

Greta got up and they both went to the bathroom again, opened the cupboard under the sink and drank Jimmy's mouthwash. It took the edge off but now they needed another drink. They needed to find some money for another drink and some more money to buy Jimmy a new bottle of mouthwash and themselves another toothbrush, but also fuck that, people needed to mind their own business.

'That was a temporary solution,' Greta said, holding the bottle up.

'I might throw up,' Peggy said.

'Don't waste the mouthwash,' Greta said, and she was right. Peggy vomited a bit in her mouth and swallowed hard.

'Is it Saturday?' Greta asked.

Peggy shrugged. They both called out to Orla, who said it was Sunday and she better not be drinking Jimmy's mouthwash again and then they were all in the bathroom and it turned out the reason the bottle had been full was that Orla had just replaced it for Jimmy from the last time Peggy and Greta drank it.

Orla was kind to them. She looked from one to the other, seeing them for the first time that morning, and she looked disgusted. She said, 'What the fuck have you done now?' Then she tried to wrestle the mouthwash bottle off them. Orla wrestled Peggy and Greta into the bath and they all sprawled around in there for a while, which didn't solve the problem of getting another drink, until Peggy said, 'The café!' and everyone agreed and went to their bedrooms to dress so that they would look like a walking group just popping into the café for lunch and a quiet wine.

'None of this solves the problem of money,' Greta said as they all stood in tidy shorts and sandshoes in the hallway. Then Orla pulled a credit card out of her windbreaker pocket, and they all said, 'Oooh.'

'Where'd you get that?' Peggy asked.

Orla touched the side of her nose with her index finger. She'd stolen it off one of her clients last night.

'No one will ask whose it is for a bit,' Orla said, 'and by then we'll be gone.'

Peggy and Greta doubted it. Once they got there they'd be there for ever, or as long as the café would let them sit there drinking. If Orla went to the toilet or wasn't looking they'd steal the credit card. There were two of them now.

10

Everyone else at the picnic had stopped watching, but Peggy and Greta wanted to see what Heidi would say to Dell. But Heidi just said 'Hey' without stopping, and walked towards the picnic table.

Dell was holding the volleyball. She was going to serve again. She said 'Hey' back, and waved slightly. She watched Heidi for a little bit, then turned back to the game and, smiling, she served the ball.

Ian grabbed two cans of Coke and handed one to Heidi. They came and stood next to Peggy and Greta. Peggy said hi, and Ian and Heidi looked at her and said hi too. Heidi's face was a mess but she was still the same old Heidi. As soon as they'd said hi to each other, they all turned to look out at the game where people on Dell's side of the court were cheering and high-fiving each other. Greta moved slightly and said hi to Ian and Heidi, and they said hi back and then looked away. Greta stood beside Peggy who was still drinking the can of Coke. It was warm from her hand and the bubbles had gone out of it.

'We made a quiche,' Peggy said.

Heidi pursed her lips together and nodded once.

'It's more of a frittata than a quiche,' Peggy said.

'Is it?' Greta asked.

'I think so,' Peggy said. They'd looked it up in another cookbook at the library. Quiches without crusts tended to be frittatas, not quiches. Quiches had a short pastry base. Greta had been reading over her shoulder but now she was trying to make conversation over the silence that Ian and Heidi were wiping all over everything.

'Fancy that,' she said. 'A frittata.'

They didn't need to talk. They'd had that explained a lot. It was okay to be quiet. No one could force Heidi or Ian to explain themselves. But it was uncomfortable. It wasn't so much the silence or even Ian and Heidi, it was being at the picnic in the first place. Dell was playing the game – literally – but Peggy and Greta had stayed on the periphery. Watching. It probably looked weird but it felt worse. They didn't fit in because they wouldn't take the actions to fit in. The few people who had come to talk to them had only stayed a short while. They were trying hard, Greta and Peggy suspected. Everyone was trying hard. Heidi was using one of the serviettes on the picnic table to take off her lipstick and wipe some of the contour off. She'd surrendered to the fact that it had all been a waste of time.

At the café that first day, with Orla and the stolen credit card, an ice-cream truck drove past playing 'Greensleeves'.

'When I was tiny,' Greta said.

'There was a really hot day,' Peggy finished. They'd been sunburnt before they got to the end of their street. They remembered it – being so close on that hot, hot day, on top of each other, inseparable it seemed. One baby, one mother, one pushchair, one tiny little towelling jumpsuit. One head nodding instead of two. When they said to people, 'I remember that,' they were just making the best estimation. Maybe it had been a cold day and it was windburn. Maybe one of them hadn't stolen the money from Laura's wallet or run away from the other city and the guns? But they had. They both had – as one.

Peggy and Greta looked from Heidi to Dell, who was wiping sweat off her face with the back of her hand. Maybe if they drank, another one of them would turn up. Or another two? They were pretty sure that was how division worked. It felt like it could happen. Then the bed would be really overcrowded. Soon it would smooth over again and they wouldn't see it as sharply, but for now it was odd and sad and hard to take.

'Have you been well, Heidi?' Greta asked. Someone had told them questions worked in conversations.

'In what sense?' Heidi asked.

'Any sense,' Peggy replied. Now it sounded like they were trying to work out if she was sober, which was no one's business but Heidi's. It had all pretty much backfired and they were only two questions into the conversation.

'I'm fine.' Heidi linked her arm through Ian's, which was bent at the elbow from his hand being in his pocket.

'Cool,' said Peggy.

'Are you well?' Heidi said, not looking at them but waving her can between the two of them.

Greta and Peggy looked at each other and nodded. Then, realising Heidi wasn't looking at them, they replied at the same time, in unison, 'Oh, yeah. Yeah. Good, thanks.'

Ian laughed.

'Your weird's showing,' Heidi said.

'We've started at the Salvation Army shop,' Peggy said, by herself this time, like a normal person.

'Nice,' Heidi said.

'And we've got an appointment at Workbridge in about a month,' Greta said.

'What are you talking to them for?' Heidi asked. She was watching the volleyball game, but none of the four of them wanted to be there. Having this conversation.

'Have you got your car?' Greta asked.

Ian turned now because none of them had spoken to him in so long.

'Yeah,' he said.

'You didn't bring your bike?' Peggy asked.

'No,' he said.

'We could go, I suppose?' Greta said. 'With the quiche.'

'I suppose,' Heidi said. She looked at Ian, who shrugged his shoulders.

'Shall we bring Dell?' Ian asked.

Heidi drained her can and looked inside it, like maybe there was another drop left. It was an alcoholic move. 'Yeah,' she said. 'There's room, eh?'

And Ian said, 'Totally.'

Peggy made eye contact with Dell and with her head waved her over. Dell left the game seamlessly. She knew straight away what they were up to.

'Are we going?' Dell said. She was still hot from the volleyball. Slightly wet with sweat.

Dell picked up the quiche off the table and they walked to Ian's car without saying goodbye to anyone. Nobody cared and if they did they didn't make it obvious. There was a temptation to make the exit as attention-grabbing as Heidi's entrance had been, but no one had the energy for it. Not now that Heidi was home, or at least back where they could see her.

'We could eat this at home,' Peggy suggested. She was squashed in between the other two in the back seat with the quiche on her lap.

'Yeah,' Dell said. 'Why not.'

While Greta, Peggy and Dell took the quiche inside, Heidi talked to Ian at the gate. There was some shouting – from him. They could hear it from inside. Peggy looked through the lounge curtains. The neighbours didn't like it when there was too much noise. Ian punched Heidi in the face and she doubled over. The other two came over and looked out the window as well.

'Should we help?' Greta asked.

'Nah,' Dell said. 'She'll be fine.'

As Heidi stood up, Ian slapped her across the side of her head and spat in her face. Then, just like that, he stepped back and said, 'You fucking freak,' and got back in his car and drove off. Heidi waved at them as she walked down the driveway and they waved back.

They sat in the lounge. Dell had put some music on, and they ate the quiche with their hands.

'You know what would go good with this?' Heidi said.

The others had their mouths and hands full so they just nodded to say, 'Go on, tell us.' Heidi said, 'Sweet chilli sauce.' And everyone agreed, with big smiles and nods. She was so right.

'Can you just, like, buy that?' Greta asked.

'Totally,' Dell said. 'I saw it at the supermarket the other day. In glass bottles near the tomato sauce.'

'Oh.' Greta was licking each of her fingers. 'I thought you could only get it from takeaways.'

'And potatoes,' Peggy said. 'Like mashed. Or roasted or something.'

Everyone nodded.

'Even a salad,' Dell said. 'It'd be like a whole thing.'

'French bread,' Heidi said. No one was really concentrating

on it now – they were all just eating, really, and watching everyone else eat. Watching themselves eat. Feeling doubly full. Feeling all but done even though they were eating some more. Picking the quiche up when the other one did. Stuffing it in their mouths. Thinking about the next time they would make it. Not sad at all that they'd left the picnic. Glad they were together again. Glad Ian was gone.

'Is Ian gone?' Dell asked. Really only Dell could ask. She had leaned to face Heidi and was stroking her face where the new scars were, where the teeth had been removed and replaced.

Heidi freed herself from Dell's hand and said, 'For now.' Then she made an excuse to stand up. She held her body in a way that made an excuse for her standing up and made to leave the room but first she turned back to Dell and stroked her face back – Heidi's old face. Then she left the room and they heard water running in the kitchen.

In about half an hour it would be time for them to be picked up for a meeting. Someone was picking them all up, in a van. Heidi was doing the dishes. Maybe she wasn't waiting long enough for the water to heat up. None of them could see her. Maybe she wasn't even using dishwashing liquid. Maybe she was spitting some new infection into all their plates and cups and cutlery. None of them could see. Someone from the picnic would probably be at the meeting and they might ask where they'd gone. It was hard to tell. None of them had ever been to a social event before. Except the bowling that Peggy and Greta had been to – but they'd stayed until the end. No one knew. But they could all point at Heidi now and say, 'Ian's gone,' adding, quietly so the other person might not quite hear, 'for now.' So, everyone would forgive them for leaving the picnic early. No one would think it was impolite or drinking behaviour. It was fine.

They peeled off to their bedrooms. Peggy and Greta both went to grab the jeans that were on the floor.

'Were you wearing these last?' Greta asked. They were both looking at them, still on the floor like a dead safari park animal.

'I thought so,' Peggy said.

'Me too,' Greta said.

'You thought I was wearing them?' Peggy asked.

'No.' Greta touched them with her foot, almost like she was turning them over. 'I also thought I was wearing them last.'

'Hm.' Peggy looked at their wardrobe. 'I could wear the black ones.'

'Would you?' Greta seemed grateful and relieved.

Peggy thought about it. 'Yeah. Yeah.' She walked towards the wardrobe. 'I can totally wear the black ones.'

Everyone got ready. They walked around the common areas looking for bits of clothing and jewellery they'd taken off in the lounge or the kitchen or the bathroom.

'Is that them?' Peggy said a couple of minutes later, when it sounded like the van had arrived.

'Can you tell them I'll be there in a sec?' Greta was putting liquid eyeliner on.

'Me too,' Heidi yelled from Heidi and Dell's room.

'And me.' It was Dell, of course.

Peggy walked out to the van.

'Greta!' the woman driving the van said.

'Hi, Kadie,' said Peggy.

'How are you?'

'Pretty good,' said Peggy, and climbed in the back. 'The others are just coming.'

'Oh,' said Kadie. 'Cool. No rush. Did you go to the picnic?'

'For a bit,' Peggy said. 'We made a quiche.'

'Cool,' Kadie said.

'It was more of a frittata,' Peggy said. The others were leaving the house now. Locking it up.

'Baking, Greta,' Kadie said. 'Wow.'

'Yeah. Cool, eh?' said Peggy.

The others climbed in.

'Heidi,' Kadie said. 'Great to see you.'

Heidi said hi.

'Dell.'

'Hi.'

'Peggy. Hi,' Kadie said.

'Greta,' Greta said.

'Sorry?' Kadie was probably looking at Peggy now for some kind of explanation, but Peggy was looking out the window so she couldn't see her.

'I'm Greta,' said Greta. 'That's Peggy.'

'Oh,' Kadie said. 'Cool.'

The meeting was in a community hall above a library. As they walked up the stairs there were people ready to greet them. Erin was greeting, and Kitty was in the kitchen getting the tea and coffee ready. Erin was shaking everyone's hand. You had to walk through the kitchen to get to your seat. Greta and Peggy always sat three rows back and four seats in. They'd been told by Diane to try to always sit in the same seat. That way, if they weren't there, someone would notice and wonder why and call them. People were saying hello to Heidi. Everyone was happy to see her, although most people probably hadn't noticed she'd been gone. Dell hadn't missed a meeting, and although she had looked sad and lonely because they were usually always together, people filled in the gap that was there. Anything unusual about them needed to be brushed over. Seeing one of them by themselves had become something unusual. That's what seemed to be happening. Peggy and Greta talked about it a lot. No one wanted to know they were there. It was too hard. They knew what it meant if there were two of you. They knew what sort of woman you were. What sort of things you'd done. It had only happened to the drunkest women. Only the most blacked-out. When they looked at women like Peggy and Greta or Heidi and Dell, a discomfort went over them. A mix of horror and shame – knowing it could have been them, but disgusted all the same. So, no one mentioned it and slowly it was just going away. They talked themselves into it without talking about it. Each person was helping out with a new reality. If nobody saw it, there was soon nothing to see. Except for the women who were in two places at once. The ones who saw themselves.

'Why'd you do that?' Greta asked.

Peggy looked at her with high eyebrows, like she wasn't quite sure what Greta was talking about.

'In the van?'

Peggy didn't say anything.

'You have to tell them,' Greta said. 'It's fucking rude if you don't. Jesus. We're not animals.' The names meant nothing to Greta and Peggy – they didn't feel discrete – but they helped them blend in. People liked that they had different names. Some people thought they could tell them apart. They couldn't. Not even Heidi, not even now she'd fucked up her face. The names were interchangeable, but it helped if they each stuck to one, if they corrected people when they got it wrong. It drew less attention to it. Peggy had drawn attention to it. 'You've got to tell them,' Greta said again, under her breath.

Peggy opened her mouth to try and explain but then Kitty

came and sat next to her and said hi and started talking about how hard the coffee job was. Kitty and Erin had gone straight to the meeting from the picnic but they were getting a ride home in the van with Kadie.

The meeting was a speaker meeting, so one person spoke for a while, then they had a break. Kitty sighed to show how hard the coffee job really was when everyone came back for the second half, where sobriety chips were handed out and the chair started picking people to share. People shared, then they closed the meeting and it took ages for Kitty to clean up and for everyone to leave. Peggy and Greta helped with the dishes, so they got to hear Kitty exasperated about everything she had to do. Of course, she didn't do much. Peggy and Greta did most of everything and Kitty complained about how much there was to do. That's how it went.

Finally, Kadie was ready to drop everyone off.

'Where did you four go?' Kitty asked when they were in the van. Like she'd only just remembered they'd left the picnic. Peggy shrugged and Greta replied, 'Home.'

'Oh,' said Kitty. She didn't really care, but it was nice to ask after people, and maybe something interesting had happened. She hadn't really noticed anything because she'd been looking at a man who was playing volleyball.

When they got home, everyone was exhausted. Sometimes they would have a cuppa together after the meeting but really, what with the sunshine and the excitement and the late meeting, they were all ready for bed.

'Goodnight,' Peggy and Greta said to Heidi and Dell.

'Goodnight,' said Heidi and Dell to Peggy and Greta.

When they turned the lights out, Peggy and Greta talked about having Heidi back. It was a vacuous conversation. That's what they both thought as they sank into sleep. Sometimes they didn't talk about what was really important, sometimes they just talked about the surface. Where had Heidi been for so long and why had she done that to her face? Who had done that to her face? Was it Ian? Surely you couldn't do that to yourself without passing out? That's what they really wanted to say to each other, but instead they talked about how good it was to have Heidi home and they could maybe go shopping in the next couple of days and make the quiche again. The fucking quiche. They were so close to sleep. The quiche was beginning to define them. Greta rolled over and was breathing heavy and warm and sleepy into Peggy's face. They were so close to sleep, drifting in and out. Everyone thought they wanted to drink but sometimes they wondered if what they really wanted was just to be alone again. Maybe they didn't want to work in the shop anymore, and then they were asleep. Gone. In a dark unconsciousness where time travelled weirdly or not at all. Where they dreamed they were a butterfly – not realising they were asleep until they woke up the next morning. Beside each other, listening to Heidi and Dell moving around in their morning ways, unsure whether they were people who had dreamed they were a butterfly or a butterfly dreaming they were them.

11

In the New Year it was busy in the shop. Lately, it was always busy. They asked, but Dorrit said there wasn't really a busy time of year and just sometimes it was busier than others. Peggy and Greta talked about it, though, when they were pricing things out the back. When the students were first around, it got busy. That's what they'd noticed about the last few weeks. The students arrived in January to go to university. Some of them, most of them, had a big course-related-costs cheque in their bank. They had cash, most of them. And they came into the shop. Peggy and Greta watched them, sometimes. It seemed like they were changing their image for university. Lots came in wearing clothes from Glassons and Shanton and Farmers, and some even had moleskins and fob chains, but they weren't buying those sorts of clothes. Peggy and Greta were having to be faster with the dresses they wanted. Some of the students had new Docs on. Peggy and Greta's Docs were old and the tongue had shifted round to the side so they were pretty uncomfortable. They'd seen some Blundstones in a shop in town which were much cheaper than Docs, and they were thinking of getting a pair. One of them wore the Docs every day and Peggy asked Greta if she thought maybe they were ruining something in their feet. The Docs needed resoling but it was almost as expensive as buying a new pair.

It was nowhere near as expensive as buying a new pair, but it was expensive. Sometimes the students would leave their Docs outside the dressing rooms while they tried on trousers. It made Peggy and Greta's mouth water. They were so close. Often, the Docs were their size or at least they were slightly bigger and could have worked with an insole. The job in the shop paid nothing. They were still volunteering. They knew stealing was a sure-fire way to slip back into drinking, but often it was just the effort that put them off. The effort, and having to face one of the students. The students were horrible to Greta and Peggy most of the time, although some of the guys were friendly in a creepy way. The boys were all living clean lives and it made them creepier to Peggy and Greta. The guys had no machismo, so they were sort of unsure, and that made them storm through boundaries and do it all nervously, like it was Peggy and Greta's fault. They were rude when they said no. Peggy and Greta suspected they weren't said no to very often and probably not by shop girls.

There were nice students. Some of them were poor like Peggy and Greta, just looking for a waterproof coat or a new pair of shoes. They'd repaired their Vans over and over with shoe-goo but that was all coming to an end so now they needed a new pair – a pair that was new to them. Peggy and Greta would help them out. Take them to their personal stash of canvas shoes. It wasn't really kosher but they would hide some shoes away from where the shoes normally were. Put them on display way back at the end of the store where really they weren't on display at all. No one could see them, but when a nice person came in and was looking for canvas shoes they might say, 'Oh, wait here,' and head back to the end of the shop and grab the Converse All Star low-tops or the PRO-Keds and bring them to the customer and say, 'Do these work?' and the person might say, 'Wow. Yeah,' and smile and it would make Peggy and Greta smile. They suspected they were a long way off, like if they were really spiritual giants they would bring the shoes for the rich students as well, or just put them with the other shoes, but they felt like they were getting there. Slightly. Baby steps.

The walk to and from work got old sometimes. The days were starting to feel a bit all the same. And sometimes they would find their minds kind of eating them from the inside while they were folding or ironing or pricing. There was a certain type of stress in being this bored. They would pray and think and try to do each job as best they could to make the day go faster, but some days it was impossible. Really they were used to being their own agents. Doing what they wanted. Like, if they were halfway through something and it got terrible, they were used to just leaving and doing something else. This was one of the good things they were learning, Diane said. This was one of the things that would hold them in good stead for a future. This was life on life's terms – boredom, commitment, smiling. Peggy and Greta would talk about it sometimes. Maybe it would be better if they were earning money. Maybe. Diane said they were earning money – they were both getting the sickness benefit.

When they went to the Workbridge interview, they thought maybe they could stop volunteering at the shop and just do a course. But when they talked to Diane she said, first, how did they know they were even going to get on a course – were they counting their chickens before they hatched? Second, did they owe the shop? Had it given them a chance when no one else had? Maybe they could tell Workbridge they already had jobs and could the course be around the shop? She didn't tell them these things. She just asked questions. They all knew in the end it was up to Greta and Peggy. Diane was just asking questions.

People seemed to get better if they had jobs. But surely not jobs like this, Peggy said. Diane laughed. Peggy and Greta didn't like it at all when Diane laughed at them. Maybe she was laughing with them but they didn't like it at all. Peggy and Greta had a point, they were sure they did. Some people had amazing jobs. Some people saved animals and ran big businesses. But they were being nice to rich kids and not being paid. This was a thought they kept to themselves. They didn't tell Diane because Diane laughed.

Greta and Peggy walked most places. The outdoors was for getting from one indoors to the next. They didn't think they liked it. The picnic had been distracting – getting to the picnic by bus, carrying the quiche, the people at the picnic. Neither of them had noticed the outdoors that day. They had been standing right beside a tall pine which may have been quite old, but they were trying to disappear, so they weren't paying any attention to the tree, or the way the sand shifted so gradually to lawn and soil.

But one day Peggy and Greta were walking home through the Gardens and the light shifted and they looked up and for the first time noticed the way the sky pulled above them. They looked from one horizon to the other. They could almost see the hills. Then, as they looked down from the sky, everything snapped into a very distinct three dimensions. The trees had separate leaves. Blades of grass stood out from each other. The light played through the branches and drew them into negative space. There were kinds of bright things in some of the trees. Of course they were flowers but they hadn't noticed them before now. Not since they'd looked at them in picture books as kids. It would be impossible to explain. Even years later, they would try but it was impossible to explain – even to each other.

'Can you see that?' Peggy asked.

Greta nodded. 'I think so.'

And then they said nothing and both sat down where they were on the grass and looked around at everything.

'Do you think it's drugs?' Greta asked.

'Huh?'

'Like drugs coming out of our muscles?'

'Maybe it's god,' Peggy said.

'Maybe we're going to die.' Greta looked at the back of her hand.

'Brain tumour,' Peggy said. They didn't want to close their eyes. It had been bad before and any kind of shift must be a shift for the best, unless they really were dying. But realistically, at this point, feeling as lost as they did – can't go back, not sure how to go forward – maybe dying would be a relief. They thought about it a lot. They didn't tell anyone, but they thought about it. Mainly they thought about bleeding to death. It sounded like it would be slow and relaxed. They'd tried a couple of times when they were drinking. It didn't work very well, mainly because they were drunk. Some days they were sure it was the last day and they'd see that they needed to drink to end it, and they'd drink and cry for a bit but still be sure they were going to kill themselves, then they would drink a bit more and think, 'Fuck them,' and they'd drink a bit more and think, 'They deserve to die, not me,' and they'd change the plan and start a new plan about how maybe someone else needed to bleed to death. Then they'd drink some more. Towards the end of their drinking, after there were two of them, they'd plan together and talk about the plan, and it would get bigger and bigger and more and more people would be implicated and they would cheer each other on and drink some more and get fed up with how long it was all taking and have a bit of a lie-down and pass out and wake up the next morning with really bad hangovers and Orla knocking on the door, because did they have the breadknife? Roxana and Jimmy had stolen some bread, Orla shouted, but it wasn't sliced. Did they want toast? Generally, they wanted toast. Thought they wanted toast, but then when it was in front of them they couldn't stomach even a slice and they would look at Orla and Roxana and think, 'We should have killed everyone last night when we had the chance.'

'And ourselves,' Greta would breathe under her breath.

'Amen,' Peggy would say. 'A-fucking-men.'

Then Jimmy and Roxana would put on the radio and it was usually the Americana show and they would start saying to each other, how would they get more drink? Talking lots and in a whiny way. And Peggy and Greta would stare at a point on the wall and think about how they could get more drink and not share it with Orla and Roxana, and their head would cut into the thinking and they would remember the half bottle of rum that Jimmy had hidden under his bed that he thought none of them knew about and now all they had to do was wait until Orla and Roxana left.

The three-dimensional vision made them feel a bit like they were living in something made-up. At school they'd been given shoeboxes to make tiny scenes in – green sawdust for grass, a tree, another tree. An adult would cut a hole in one end of the box to look at the tiny scene through. People were moving through it – walking over the millions of blades of grass, under the trees on fire with flowers. Maybe it was make-believe? It was certainly dragging them into the past. It was this part of town as well – but all of the parts of town were like that. Sometimes it felt like it would be good to move away, but people said not to change anything for a couple of years. It made sense. They had a rhythm to their weeks now. They knew which meetings they went to. They knew where all the meetings were. They had the job. The sky sure was big. Peggy looked over at Greta looking at her hands then she turned and looked at Peggy and they both laughed and felt deeply grateful they hadn't drunk for an hour, even a second before this happened because nothing like this ever happened when they drank.

12

When they got home, Heidi was in the kitchen.

'Where's Dell?' Greta asked. Heidi shrugged. It was odd seeing any of them by themselves. It had been weird for the months that Heidi had been away. Heidi shrugged because she didn't care, not because she didn't know.

Peggy started opening doors in the cupboards. 'Will she be home for dinner?'

Heidi shrugged again. They looked at her. 'It's just,' Greta said, 'we were going to make dinner and we just need to know how many to cook for.'

'I know.' Heidi didn't move from where she was standing, and she didn't have anything else to say. They stood looking at each other. No one had anything else to say. It was awkward. Then, just as Greta and Peggy were about to say something, Heidi said, 'You should just cook for her and if she doesn't come then someone can have it for lunch tomorrow.'

It was a weird thought. One dinner sitting by itself. A lunch for one of them. Greta and Peggy nodded, though, because – it made sense. Really. And probably Dell would be home any minute. Usually Dell and Heidi were rostered on together, but Heidi had been away from work for a while and maybe their rosters had got a bit separated. All of the workplaces were still working the second woman out. Working out that the words 'second woman' didn't apply – they were both the same woman. Everyone was trying to work things like this out without talking about it or acknowledging it so it was all a bit chaotic, but even the chaos was pushed down.

Greta started getting pots out from under the sink. 'How was work?'

'I'm not home for dinner,' Heidi said, watching them get all the stuff ready.

'Oh,' Greta said. 'Cool.'

'Is Dell home for dinner?' Peggy asked.

Heidi shrugged. She wasn't saying. Now they were cooking for three, and that was stranger and shook them even more. The lack of symmetry.

'Shall we cook for you too, and you and Dell can have it for lunch if Dell doesn't come home for dinner?' Peggy was starting to rave a bit. There was a dull panic simmering inside them. Their hearts were pounding and a pain was starting to spread over their chest. Greta pulled at the yoke of her jumper and they were both breathing faster.

'Nah,' said Heidi. 'I'll buy lunch.'

'Okay,' Greta said, and she sat down for a bit.

'Where are you off to?' Peggy said, trying to sound casual but not feeling casual at all.

'Out,' Heidi said, but she didn't go anywhere. She just kept standing there staring at them. The scar was settling back into her face. She'd never not look exactly like Dell, but each day she looked more and more like herself, like Dell did. She looked down, then, and picked something off her cardigan. 'Okay,' she said, and looked out the window. 'Gotta go.'

'Okay,' Greta said.

'Righto,' said Peggy. 'Have a nice night.'

They ended up making the quiche again. It was round.

They cut it into quarters and put two quarters in the fridge and sat in silence and ate two of the quarters. Neither of them felt good when they went to bed that night.

'I don't think I like the quiche anymore,' Greta said.

'Yeah,' Peggy said. 'Maybe we've had it too much.'

'We have had it a lot in the last little while.'

'Yeah,' Peggy said, and they rolled over to try and get comfortable, to try and get the whole thing out of their minds.

'Tomorrow's another day,' Greta said, and they both laughed because people said it to them as a positive thing, but it felt terrifying after the day they'd had, after the interaction with Heidi.

'What is eating her?' Greta asked.

Peggy shrugged in the dark.

'She's so angry,' Greta said. 'All the time.'

'If she's not angry, she's mean,' said Peggy. She leaned over, trying to put her hand on something in the dark.

'What are you doing?' Greta said.

'The notebook,' she said. 'For the calls. There was one last night.' The notebook was getting full. Dell had helped them rule columns on each page – date, time. Peggy wrote on the inside cover in the dark. The inside cover was a mess. Usually they put the date there and then copied it into the columns later.

Greta shifted and the pillow sort of scrunched. Then she shifted her head around on it. 'We should get some new pillows,' she said. 'These pillows are shit.'

'Yeah,' Peggy answered. 'They're okay if you put both of them together but they're awful by themselves.'

'Yeah,' Greta said. Still moving her head about.

'Why the fuck did we get such awful pillows?' When they first went to the dole office they'd been given a small amount of money to set up the flat.

'What were we thinking?' Peggy asked.

'They were on special,' Greta said. 'At Briscoes.'

'You get what you pay for,' said Peggy.

'There was a sale on,' Peggy said and they both laughed. It was an in-joke that they'd only got now they were in a flat and making a house and not moving from place to place with just what they had in their bag. Relying on who they could pick up and sometimes sleeping outside or in cars they could break into. Now they were privileged to get all sorts of jokes they'd never got before.

'A sale,' Peggy said, and she was drifting off.

'A sale.' Greta let out one last huffing laugh. 'A sale.'

13

The real problem was that every day was feeling the same. At the start this was the best thing. There was a degree of certainty. They would wake up in the same place they'd gone to sleep. They would wake up together, by themselves, without anyone else. They would wake up and know what was in the fridge – approximately – and what they had to do for the day. They would wake up not worrying about where the next drink would come from. It was a unique experience to start with. It felt good. But now it was getting a little old. Some of their friends were starting all sorts of drama to try and break it up. Their friends would deny it, but from the outside it looked like they were deliberately making things weird so their day would be slightly different. At the meetings most days, someone new was crying. Something big had happened. Usually of the person's own making. They had maybe shouted at someone at work and that was not okay. Maybe they yelled at their flatmates and again, this was not okay. Most things happened as a result of shouting. Shouting was a way to ensure something would change, even if it was for the worse.

Greta and Peggy decided they were more about watching. The morning after the pillow conversation they woke up and the house seemed quiet. They went out to the kitchen. Greta had a shower while Peggy went to the toilet and brushed her teeth. Then Peggy had a shower and Greta did her hair. It all seemed very quiet.

'It's quiet,' Greta said finally.

Peggy had her head under the shower so she didn't hear at first and then, a minute later said, 'It's quiet, eh?'

'Yeah,' Greta said.

Peggy turned the shower off while she stood under it. She stood for a moment, naked, letting the water drip off her and the cold air in the bathroom wipe up her body on the tail draught of warm air rising to the roof.

Heidi was sitting at the table, eating Weet-Bix and looking at the Weet-Bix box. Reading it like it held the answers to everything.

When Greta sat down Heidi turned the box around and pointed to a piece of text. 'Has it always said that?' she asked.

'Huh?'

'This.' She pointed again and this time shook the box a little, moved it further away from Greta. 'Has it always said this. About where the wheat comes from.'

Greta looked at her and Heidi banged the box again and Greta looked at the box. 'I think so.'

'Huh,' Heidi said and sat back. She was looking at Greta now. 'Of course you would.'

'I haven't really paid much attention,' Greta said. 'To the box.' Heidi didn't shift her glare. 'I don't really like Weet-Bix.'

'Maybe you should,' Heidi said.

'What?'

'Pay more attention.'

'I don't really like Weet-Bix.'

'Convenient,' said Heidi.

'Where's Dell?' Greta said. Not exactly changing the subject.

Heidi shrugged. 'You tell me,' she said.

'I don't know where she is,' Greta said.

'Huh,' Heidi said.

'I haven't seen her since yesterday,' Greta said.

'Tuesday,' Peggy said. She'd stopped what she was doing and was just standing and thinking.

'Tuesday,' Greta said.

Heidi shrugged. 'Oh well.' And she took a spoonful of Weet-Bix from her bowl and looked at the box again.

Greta and Peggy looked at each other. Then Dell came in.

Heidi didn't look up. The scar on her face was bigger when she was angrier. All the anger was inside her though, seeping out as sarcasm and irony.

'Morning,' Greta said, and in her agitation she knocked over her mug as she raised her hand to wave.

Dell opened her eyes wide.

'What?' Heidi said.

'Stop fucking with them,' Dell said.

'Fuck you,' Heidi said.

They looked so strange together. Like a thing at war with itself.

'Where have you been?' Heidi said.

'Nowhere.' Dell opened the fridge.

'See?' Heidi was talking to Peggy and Greta now. 'You have to watch her. You can't trust her.' Heidi was looking at them like Dell wasn't there anymore. 'She's up to something.'

Everyone was quiet for a minute.

'Has she asked you to keep track of anything?' Heidi said.

Peggy and Greta shook their head.

'Has she told you not to tell me?' Heidi asked.

Peggy and Greta looked at her. They thought they could hear Dell laughing in the background as she turned on the jug.

'Doesn't that seem dodgy to you?' Heidi asked.

'No,' said Peggy.

'Does nothing about this seem dodgy?' Heidi asked.

'Only you,' Greta said.

'I always thought Ian was a bad idea,' Heidi said. 'Remember that. Butter wouldn't melt in her mouth, but she's crafty as fuck.'

'Do you want a coffee?' Dell asked.

Heidi nodded and her body changed in that moment. She slid in a way that took her body through an odd shape until it came to rest in a position that was the same as Dell's would have been had she been sitting at the table reading the Weet-Bix box. Heidi looked at her watch. She was smiling now. Her scar had settled. 'We might have to go to work soon, eh?' she said to Dell, pleasantly.

'Yeah,' said Dell. Looking at her own watch, and putting some Weet-Bix in a bowl. 'I'll just eat these,' she said.

'Cool,' Heidi said. 'I'll wait while you do.' She sat back and looked at Greta and Peggy. 'What are you up to today?'

'Work,' they said.

'Nice,' Heidi and Dell said. Heidi was like a single fish in the school of fishes that was her and Dell. Swimming out by herself, then slipping seamlessly back into the school so you couldn't distinguish her. It was unnerving. There were no rules, but it wasn't nice to be reminded of what they were. Everyone ignored it – the fact they'd been black-out drunk that night, that they'd been terrible people who had done despicable things. That the only ones who were two now were the worst of the women. There was no real hope of redemption because everyone pretended not to see it but saw it so clearly. No one wanted to see it and everyone was kidding themselves they couldn't. But it was like Heidi was trying to remind everyone again and again. Like she was trying to break Peggy and Greta so they couldn't walk out the door or eat or stay sober or stay alive. It was like Peggy and Greta would be all right if they worked together like one complete unit, but Heidi seemed hell-bent on explaining them back to themselves as two separate people.

'We should go grocery shopping tonight,' Dell said. 'After work.'

'That's a good idea,' Heidi said. 'Shall we meet here at six?'

'We were going to a meeting.' Greta looked at Peggy then back at Heidi.

Heidi stopped for a moment and looked up, making a play of thinking. 'If we go to Big Fresh we can go to the meeting down the road from there – it starts at eight.'

'Okay,' Peggy said, and she turned back to packing their lunches. There weren't any carrots left. She'd chopped up broccoli into tiny little pieces and sprinkled it over some butter then squashed the other half of the bread on top.

'Will that work?' Greta said.

'The meeting?' Peggy asked.

'The broccoli,' Greta said, pointing vaguely in the direction of the sandwiches. Heidi had thrown everyone. They were annoying each other.

'Won't it?' Peggy asked.

'Smells like farts,' Greta said.

'It'll taste like bean sprouts, won't it?' She was looking around now, almost desperately. There was a really old apple in the fruit bowl. That was about it. The half of the quiche was gone.

'It'll be okay,' Greta said.

Peggy was still looking around. There was half a lemon on the bench. Greta and Peggy thought Heidi and Dell had left it there and Heidi and Dell thought Greta and Peggy had left it there. None of them wanted to throw it out in case the others wanted it.

'There's nothing else in the house,' Greta said, then she sighed. 'Lunch is all I look forward to.'

'It's not that bad,' Peggy said.

'It's going yellow,' Greta said about the broccoli. It was soft as well – there was no crunch left in it.

Heidi laughed loudly and abruptly. The other three looked at her. She looked up. 'Trouble in paradise.' She smiled.

'We could buy a carrot on the way,' Peggy said.

'And grate it at work?' Greta said.

Peggy made a face like 'Why not?'

'I'm brushing my teeth again,' Greta said.

'Me too,' Peggy said, racing to put the sandwiches in a plastic bag and that bag in their army surplus bag.

They stood side by side, brushing their teeth.

'Before we got sober,' Greta said, through the brush and the foam of the cheap non-mouthwash toothpaste, 'we always had enough money for food.'

Peggy shook her head.

They both brushed for a bit then Peggy spat. 'You're remembering it wrong,' she said.

'I don't think I am,' Greta said.

'We never ate,' Peggy said, leaning low so she could drink water out of the tap to rinse her mouth.

'But if we wanted to.' Greta had the toothbrush in her mouth and was using her hands to signal. 'We had the money to eat whatever we wanted. Or the means.'

'I don't agree,' Peggy said.

Greta rolled her eyes. It was on the tip of her tongue – those fucking terrible sandwiches. She wanted a new pair of stockings and she wanted to have some fucking fun. Instead, groceries and another fucking meeting.

'Maybe there'll be something at work.' Peggy was applying mascara now. Sometimes one of the bakeries in the area dropped in food that no one had bought the day before. There wasn't much that was vegetarian, but sometimes Peggy and Greta would open up the filled rolls, take out the ham and pretend.

'We did have money,' Greta said.

'Sometimes,' Peggy said. 'At the end. When there were two of us and Orla had kicked us out of the flat it would rain for days and our clothes would be wet from sleeping outside and we would stand outside offices waiting for old men who wanted to have sex so we could be inside for a while and dry off. Sometimes they would bring friends. Sometimes they would take photos, sometimes they would smash us in the face. If things went well, we would steal alcohol from their fridges while they slept.' She was still doing her make-up, and wasn't looking at Greta. 'But if they gave us any money – which was never guaranteed, because once we were in their houses, they were the bosses, and because we looked like shit, they did whatever they wanted – but if they gave us money, we would spend it all on alcohol.' Peggy stepped back and looked at herself. 'So, I guess, technically, you're right – we could have stolen food instead of alcohol. But we didn't – not once.' She washed the make-up off her hands. 'But tonight we don't really have time for all that because tonight we are going to take the money we didn't spend on alcohol and go to the supermarket and buy some food that will be ours and then we are going to a meeting and we are going to thank whatever fucking thing it is that's keeping us sober from the bottom of our fucking terrible hearts that we don't have to be raped or killed tonight and then we are going to come home and sleep under our roof and tomorrow – if we're lucky beyond anything we deserve – we will have a fucking carrot to grate into our fucking sandwiches.'

Greta spat her toothpaste out. Peggy was right. They both knew it, and maybe the bakery would bring in some old food for the volunteers, and their Workbridge appointment was this week and maybe something good would come of that. Right now, though, they needed to put on mascara and finish their make-up because they liked it when they were both made-up the same – it felt safer.

Peggy had the tartan skirt on. Greta had wanted to wear it today, but Peggy had it on – so really it was like Greta was wearing it. All day she could watch it move around the store on the body – the only one on the planet exactly the same as hers. So, in some ways it was even better. Peggy wouldn't be able to see the skirt at all. Just that weird flash of it when she walked or ducked down to pick stuff up off the floor. But Greta could look at it on them all day.

When she came out into the kitchen Peggy had the bag packed. She held it out to Greta. 'Do you want to carry it?'

'Okay.' Greta shrugged. It was embarrassing to step back after that lecture. It was hard to just get there. 'I'm sorry,' she mumbled.

'That's okay,' Peggy said.

'Trouble in paradise?' Heidi said from the sink, doing the dishes.

'Nope,' they said together.

'Glad to hear it.'

Then Dell was in the room with Heidi and Dell's handbag, it was smaller and not a backpack. They didn't need to take much with them to work. Just a wallet and some lipstick. They usually bought lunch at the food court in the mall.

'So, tonight,' Dell said, holding the bag out to Heidi, who maybe was ignoring her. When Heidi didn't take the handbag, Dell put it over her shoulder in a smooth movement. If you didn't live with her, if you weren't used to them being apart, you might not have noticed it. It was like that – they all filled in each other's missing bits. If one of them was tired the other one would keep them going. If one was unsure the other would put forward a good case. If one was thinking maybe alcohol was the answer the other one would remind them.

Peggy and Greta were pleased to be out of the house. Walking down the street, everything made more sense. Walking down the street towards the shop was something they did every day and something people saw them do every day. The cars drove past, surely some of the same cars that drove past yesterday. There was an order, a politeness, and Heidi was trying to disrupt it all.

'What are you looking at?' Greta asked.

'Our bag,' Peggy said.

Greta looked down at the bag and pulled it up so she could see it better. 'Do we need another one?'

Peggy shrugged. 'I feel like this bag is totally adequate. We shouldn't waste money on that.'

'We'd rather have a carrot,' Greta said and hugged Peggy as they walked, smiling a bit. Peggy leaned into her shoulder.

'A carrot seems like a more urgent priority at this juncture.' They both laughed.

'We could try some other bread,' Greta said.

Peggy shrugged. 'I quite like the bread we have.'

'That book at home has a recipe for baking pita bread,' Greta said.

'Does home-baked bread last?' Peggy asked. 'Like a whole week?'

'Probably,' Greta said. The cars were coming past them faster now. They were about to cross a busy street. You had to take the lights across two lanes going one way and then stop at an island in the middle and wait for the lights again and walk over the two lanes going the other way. 'Probably factory bread lasts longer,' Greta said.

'Factory is usually better,' Peggy said. 'For lasting length.'

'Fuck, I'm hungry.' They were passing a bagel shop. In the end they'd forgotten to have breakfast because of Heidi and Dell fighting with each other.

'Hm,' Peggy said.

They both laughed. At treatment, the therapist had asked the group how they were feeling, and Theo had said, 'I don't know. Hungry?' There had been a chart with small yellow faces and each one had an emotion word under it. *Happy* had a smile. *Angry* had eyebrows that went down in the middle like the letter *v. Surprised* also had eyebrows – they were high above the yellow face's eyes – but not many of the others had eyebrows. Not many. One had pink cheeks – that was *Embarrassed*, and they weren't sure how it was helpful until they felt the heat rise in their cheeks and remembered the pink circles. 'Is this embarrassed,' Peggy had whispered to Greta, and Greta had nodded but really, she was only guessing.

Dorrit wasn't at the shop when they got there, so they slid down the door and sat on the concrete. Both of them pulled their knees up, hugging them with their arms.

'Gets a bit old,' Peggy said. Greta nodded. Peggy looked at her and swept a piece of her hair out of Greta's mouth. 'But the day after tomorrow we've got the Workbridge appointment.'

'Yeah,' Greta said.

'But we shouldn't put too much focus on that,' Peggy said. 'Because who knows what will happen.'

'Not us,' Greta said.

'That's right,' said Peggy.

Then they both stared at the other side of the street. It was almost like having your eyes shut. People came into their vision and out again as they walked along the street. It was a bit of a walking town, walking and biking. Not many people they knew had cars, that's why it was so great that people picked them up for meetings. It was a walking and biking town, but it was spread out wide over the plain, so lots of people still had cars.

Dorrit arrived in a fluster. 'Shit,' she kept saying under her breath. She dropped the key and they all went down to pick it up and almost smashed their heads together. 'Sorry,' Dorrit said. 'Sorry,' said Peggy and Greta.

Dorrit fumbled with the key, trying to get it the right way round. If they ate the sandwiches now, they would have nothing for lunch, but they were so hungry. Tonight, they would all go and get food and tomorrow they could have breakfast – a breakfast that would last them until lunchtime, when they'd have a delicious sandwich without broccoli. There was money in their account now – it had gone in at midnight. But they needed to save that money for the supermarket tonight.

Dorrit got the door open, and Greta and Peggy followed her in and started getting the shop ready.

If they bought a sandwich today it would be like five bucks and that could buy a bag of six pita breads – or more, maybe – and that was six sandwiches, or more, maybe. But they were so hungry. There wasn't a supermarket near the shop. One day, Dell said, there would be supermarkets everywhere, but not today. Today they needed to work hard to forget they were hungry.

'We could wash down the changing-room walls,' Greta said to Dorrit after they'd settled down a bit from their bad start.

Dorrit nodded, she was checking the float in the till. Then she looked up and smiled. 'That would be great. Thank you.' And went back to counting the money.

Greta and Peggy went to the kitchen and found a bucket and some sugar soap. They filled the jug so it almost overflowed, and boiled it. It was so full it sputtered and hot water spat all over the bench but eventually it turned off. They poured the boiling water into the bucket over the top of the sugar soap – it bubbled up and looked interesting. Then they filled the jug again with cold water from the tap and poured it over the boiling water. They ducked down beside the bucket and put a hand each in it to check the temperature. It felt fine. Only one of them needed to check, really, but it was nice when you pulled your hand out and it was covered in foam.

The cleaning and the scrubbing helped with the hunger, but they were still hungry. Every time the door opened, they'd look up to see if it was the people from the café, but it never was. They had to wait until lunchtime and then they ate the terrible sandwiches in the sun. It turned out they didn't even have hummus in them.

'I thought they had hummus in them.' Greta was looking in the sandwich. She had pulled the bread apart so she could see inside. It was very obviously just butter and broccoli. There was very little need to ask. She was making a point. There was no point in fighting with yourself, but sometimes they were hungry enough to try. Fear and anger were the things that took people's attention faster than anything else. Heidi was trying to make them frightened and angry so that they'd fight. They both saw that now. Peggy didn't even answer. She just ate her sandwich, closed her eyes and put her face up to the light.

'Should we try and make bread?' Peggy said.

'Maybe.' Greta ate the sandwich now. She was hungry. It was food. Then she opened her eyes and looked at Peggy. Peggy was looking the other way. 'Fuck.' Greta put her sandwich in her mouth and dug deep into their bag. She pulled out a chocolate-covered stick of liquorice. It was slim like their fingers and covered in dark chocolate. She held it out to Peggy, who was still looking away.

'I just want . . .' Peggy started, then she turned round and saw the chocolate liquorice. Her mouth dropped. 'Where did we get that?'

'We've had it for weeks,' Greta said. She put it in both her hands and started to bend it so it would break in two. 'I found it in the bottom of the bag when we were cleaning.'

'How did we not eat it?'

Greta shrugged in amazement. It seemed so unlikely.

'Wait.' Peggy was looking at the half that Greta had handed her. 'Wait. Have you been hiding this from me?'

'What?' Greta said. It wasn't a 'What are you thinking?' what, it was an 'I don't have a clue what you're talking about' what. It was impossible – wasn't it?

'When did you find it?' Peggy asked.

'This morning,' Greta said. She was eating hers now. 'When I went out the back to do my lipstick.'

'Did you smell it?' Peggy asked.

'What? No. Maybe. Just eat the fucking thing.'

They both took a bite. It was old, Greta was right about that, but it was still good. There was so much sugar in alcohol.

Some of the people in the meetings carried sweets in their handbags and briefcases. Greta and Peggy had thought about it for a moment, but buying bread had seemed more important and they didn't have money for everything. Right now, though, the people with the sweets in their handbags and briefcases made a lot of sense.

'Did Diane give us this?' Peggy asked. Her mouth was as full as it could be with the half of the small twist of chocolate-covered liquorice.

Greta shrugged. 'I suppose so.'

They savoured things. One day, Dell said, they would have more of everything than they needed. They could buy a whole box of chocolate-covered liquorice. Today they didn't know where the next bit of food was coming from. Diane said chocolate-covered liquorice got her through early sobriety. That even now the smell of it made her feel better. It settled her down. She had given them this piece – but when? Neither of them could remember, and why had she given them only one? Surely she wasn't that tight. Had one of them not eaten theirs then? Had they saved it? Had they gone halves on one and saved the other for later? Maybe Diane had given them only one as a test? To see what they'd do – to see if they were getting less selfish. Maybe Diane couldn't see both of them anymore? Perhaps they didn't fit in anyone's reality anymore. They couldn't remember. It was all a fog. They could remember things people did to them at primary school. That time they waited in a queue almost all of lunchtime to go on the flying fox, and then someone cut in front of them right when it was their turn. They remembered that they never got what they wanted and someone else always got all the attention. But they had no idea where the liquorice had come from.

'Were you hiding it?' Peggy asked.

'What?' Greta was chewing. They both looked at each other, chewed. 'Is that even possible?'

They didn't know.

'I found it in the bag,' Greta said. 'This morning. And then we were cleaning the changing rooms and I forgot about it and then we were here, and I remembered it again.'

'Heidi makes me crazy,' Peggy said.

Greta nodded. 'Heidi and Dell.'

'They don't agree on anything,' Peggy said.

Greta nodded again.

'What do we need for bread?' Peggy said.

Greta dug into their canvas bag and pulled out the notebook Dell had given them for the phone calls. She opened it up to the back pages which they used for things other than the phone calls.

'It was in the Alison Holst book,' Greta said. 'I copied it out.'

'When?' Peggy asked.

'The same time I was hiding the liquorice,' Greta said. 'We need yeast and flour and that's about it.'

'Water,' Peggy said, looking at the recipe. 'We need water.'

'Yeah,' Greta said and they both laughed.

'Do you know where the yeast is at the Big Fresh?' Peggy asked.

'Do we know where *anything* is at the Big Fresh?' Greta asked.

Peggy laughed. 'Touché,' she said.

Greta closed the notebook up and folded it a bit. It was getting dog-eared.

'Is that notebook weird?' Peggy said.

Greta looked at it.

'Like her giving us that notebook when we already had a

130

notebook and it sort of came out of the blue. Where did that come from?'

'Yeah,' Greta said. 'What is that about?'

'We'll still do it though,' Peggy said. 'Eh?'

Greta opened up to the place they wrote down the phone calls, diligently. 'Oh, yeah.' Greta nodded vigorously. 'Totally.'

Peggy looked at their watch on Greta's wrist. 'We better get going,' she said. Holding Greta's arm for a minute.

The shop was quiet in the afternoon. They did more cleaning and a truck came in with clothes and they sorted through those for a while. The time went faster when they were working through the clothes. Some of the work was boring and some of the work was interesting, and pricing and ironing and putting the clothes on coat hangers was okay. There were lots of winter clothes. That was one of the hard things with shopping in the shop. Some people at the end of each season put that season's clothes away and part of that process was getting rid of things they didn't like anymore or that didn't fit anymore. Dorrit had explained it to them when the winter jumpers started arriving in spring. They put them out, though. Sometimes the weather would change quickly, and people would come rushing in wearing a T-shirt, looking for something warm to pull on. Also, sometimes people thought ahead. Some of the winter clothes were really nice and worth putting away over summer. Also, really, the city they lived in never got that warm. Except a few days a year, when it got unbearable, but for most of the time you could wear a cardigan or a sweatshirt and you wouldn't be too hot. Greta and Peggy liked to wear long sleeves all year round. Sometimes people in the meetings would say, 'That'll change.' But it never would. There was something about their wrists they didn't like. Something about always wanting to cut them open when they looked at them. Imagining cutting them open had become a self-soothing thing, not a self-harm thing. If their wrists were covered, they could indulge in the fantasy but not kill themselves. Sometimes people in the meetings would say, 'That'll change.' Not in reply to anything Greta and Peggy were telling them about their wrists, because they had never told anyone – ever – but because of something the people were saying about themselves. Sometimes it had already changed for them, and then they were saying 'That changed', but it hadn't changed for Greta and Peggy, ever. They always thought about cutting their wrists open and it always made them feel better.

Also, they thought the long sleeves made them look smaller and, really, all they ever wanted was to be smaller. Smaller in the body. Smaller in the world. They wanted to take up less space. Cutting their wrists would make them take up less room. If the shop wasn't busy, or the speaker at the meeting wasn't interesting, they would look off into the distance and imagine shrinking and shrinking and suddenly just not being there anymore. Not being anywhere. Just being gone, but not in any big way that would make people angry, just in a way that made people feel like they had misplaced them. That maybe people might say to each other in a few weeks, 'Do you remember Greta and Peggy?' and the other person would say, 'Hm. Were they the blonde ones?' and the first person would say, 'I don't know.' And the other one would say, 'Oh, you mean Michelle and Marsha, or Debra and Britney. There's no Greta and Peggy,' and the first person would say, 'Oh, right.'

It would be good to have never been in the first place. That's what it all came down to. And seeing as how that wasn't possible, it would be nice just to be forgotten.

14

Everyone was meeting at six at the flat. Greta and Peggy got there first because they finished work earlier than Heidi and Dell because Dorrit closed up the shop. Greta and Peggy were hungry again. There were some Weet-Bix left and Peggy cut them in half and put butter on them.

'Know what would make these good,' Greta said with her mouth full.

'Honey,' Peggy and Greta said at the same time. They added it to the shopping list someone had written and left on the table.

Dell and Heidi got home and got changed. Dell had brought a calculator from work.

'Is that okay?' Peggy asked. Was it stealing if you just borrowed it?

'She asked,' Heidi shouted from the bedroom.

'I asked,' Dell said. It was a revolutionary idea.

'What if they'd said no?' Greta asked, her mouth still claggy after the dry Weet-Bix.

Dell shrugged. 'I guess we would have just had to do it in our head.'

Greta and Peggy nodded slowly.

'Does anyone know how much any of this stuff costs?' Heidi asked, looking at the shopping list.

No one did.

'We have a pamphlet.' Peggy went to the rubbish bin and pulled out a pamphlet from the supermarket.

'Don't worry,' said Heidi. 'How much do we have to spend?'

'Eighty dollars,' Dell said.

They all nodded.

'Okay.' Heidi looked at the list. 'Are there things here we absolutely have to have?' They were all standing around the list now and looking at it.

'Yeah.' Peggy nodded.

'Okay,' said Heidi. 'I recommend we put marks next to the "must-haves" and then we put other marks next to the "nice-to-haves" and we get the "must-haves" first and then we have our calculator and we see what eighty bucks gets us.'

It seemed like a good idea.

'We probably won't get it exactly right the first time,' Greta said. Everyone looked at her. It was emotional genius. They were all scared. They nodded, but none of them were sure it was worth doing if they couldn't get it perfect the first time. More than one of them thought about saying, 'Shall we just not bother?' They looked around at the others to see if it was the right time to say it, but before they could Heidi said, 'Okay, let's go.'

They caught the bus down to the supermarket. They were pretty sure they could catch a bus home but also Dell and Heidi had a taxi chit left over from a late night they did at the shop. While Heidi had been away, their boss had started to tell them to take a taxi home and they'd left a taxi chit in the till. It was there every week, even though now that Heidi was home they were fine to walk. They were all fine to walk anywhere they wanted because there were always two of them. They didn't need a taxi chit for late nights so they could, theoretically, use the taxi chit tonight, although it wasn't exactly what the taxi chit had been given to Heidi and Dell for. There had been a lot of talk about the weekly taxi chit ever since Heidi came home and started going to work with Dell again, but they hadn't broached the subject with their boss, so the taxi chit kept being there. It wasn't necessary, and maybe Dell and Heidi should have pointed that out – like when you get too much change – but, also, they weren't paid very much and also maybe Heidi would go away again. It was Heidi who'd said this. 'They don't know I'm back for good,' she'd said. And they had to agree, this was correct. Heidi and Dell's boss did not know that Heidi was back for good. The other three had looked at Heidi. She knew they were looking at her, but she stayed looking at the taxi chit which at the time had been in the middle of the dining table like it was on trial.

Heidi and Dell brought the taxi chit with them to the supermarket. None of them really knew how taxi chits worked and assumed the boss had already paid for the taxi trip and the chit was a voucher, but Greta was pretty sure they would be charged after the chit was used, in which case they would know it was used for something other than coming home from a late night at the shop. Out of everyone, Greta and Peggy were the greatest advocates for not using the taxi chit. Heidi and Dell got paid and sometimes they would cover things when Greta and Peggy's benefit hadn't come through. All four of them needed Heidi and Dell to keep the job. But mostly Greta and Peggy needed Heidi and Dell to keep their job.

The bus was late, but it was okay, they still had plenty of time to get to the supermarket. They'd get their shopping and then go to the meeting down the road from the supermarket.

They would take all their shopping bags. Maybe there wouldn't be that many bags. Realistically, they couldn't know on their first time. When the bus arrived, it was full and the four of them had to stand. They didn't mind. They talked to each other and looked around the bus. Most people were in suits and coming home from work. No one looked at them. They all concentrated hard on looking at something which wasn't the two sets of women who looked exactly like each other because they'd been caught being sluts and drunk in a moment when none of them and none of their friends had been. No one wanted to see that. It was like this everywhere and it meant Peggy and Greta and all the others were free to look at everyone – intently. All of them had made a study of it. The bus was full of people looking away from them. How many of them were going to get groceries no one knew, but when the bus stopped outside the supermarket a lot of people got out.

'Maybe someone will give us a ride home from the meeting,' Greta said as they got a trolley. It was a good point. People in meetings often said that. If you got your own way there, they would give you a lift home. Maybe even with shopping. It felt wholesome. Being able to go to the meeting with bags of food, saying, 'We just went shopping.'

The supermarket was busy but there was still room. You could fill a bag with buns, and it was cheap. So, they did that. Even though buns weren't on their list. Some of the vegetables they wanted weren't in season and were expensive, so they stood in front of them and negotiated. It was a bit like the blind leading the blind, but they imagined if someone saw them from down the aisle they would look like anyone else. Just flatmates getting their weekly shopping. But no one would look at them for long, because no matter how well they'd trained themselves not to see it, people were freaked out by them.

'What's like courgettes though?' one of them said.

'Carrots?' To Peggy, every problem could be solved with carrots.

'They're the same shape,' Dell said, reaching out and touching a carrot. 'But do they cook the same?'

They all shook their heads. 'Do they taste the same?' Heidi asked.

They shook their heads some more. They didn't think so. Carrots, they decided, were not like courgettes. But maybe pumpkin was. They'd try it. Pumpkins were cheaper but also were scarier. No one quite knew what was inside them. They bought broccoli because broccoli was cheap. It felt like every time they had been to the supermarket up the road – to make the quiche – broccoli had been cheap. 'Should we get two?' Heidi asked.

'Does it last?' Peggy said. After the sandwiches today, she was scared they would end up with broccoli again.

Everyone shrugged and Heidi put one in the trolley and Dell added it to the calculator.

One of them had written down 'Fruit'. They looked. Apples were cheap and so were bananas. All the oranges were from overseas. They all agreed that they probably all liked apples, even though, right now, there was an apple that had been left to go bad in the fruit bowl at home. They promised each other they'd eat them, and put apples in the trolley.

Things were confusing. Especially around the grains. There were different types of flour and the yeast was out in the open and needed to be refrigerated but only once it was opened. Around the aisle where the tea and coffee were, the calculator hit eighty dollars. They looked in the trolley. It looked pretty good. They even had biscuits. It seemed kind of positive. They went to the checkout and each of them got twenty dollars out of their pocket and handed it to Heidi, who handed the notes to the checkout person. They even got some change.

It wasn't too much to carry, not between the four of them, and they had plenty of time to walk to the meeting. They crossed the busy road and walked down the street flanked by factories and other industrial places. The meeting was in the offices of a problem-gambling charity. It used to be in a school, but the school was being done up.

'Incredibly,' Peggy said as they walked, 'we didn't get anything that needs refrigerating.'

'We did really well for our first time,' Greta said, and they all agreed.

They all had their sunglasses on now. The sun was low, and because of the long flat plain the sun shone straight at them. They were walking into it. Maybe they looked like movie stars or gangsters. Grocery-shopping renegades. Quiche-baking outlaws.

When they got to the building there were still a few people outside smoking who smiled and waved at them. People in the meetings tried not to look away from them because, really, it could have been any of them. One guy, Billy, waved with the hand he was holding a cigarette in.

'Been shopping?' he said. They all nodded. 'Did you go down there?' He pointed behind himself so that the smoke from the cigarette drew a line over his shoulder. They all nodded. 'Good on you,' he said. 'It's way cheaper.' He looked happy for them. Like they'd won something.

Billy was three years sober. Greta and Peggy liked him. He seemed kind, not too kind though. He seemed like a 'good sort'. Even Diane said so – Billy was a good guy. He was a mechanic. He'd been a mechanic before he got sober, but now he was a better mechanic. They all walked past Billy and the others who were smoking. They still had their sunglasses on because none of them had any hands free. They were greeted like vanquishing heroes returned from the hunt. 'Look at you,' some of the older women said. 'Supermarket shopping.' People in the meetings were always happy when other people in the meetings got better and, just like they thought it would be, buying food from the supermarket was a sign of getting better.

They sat down and Heidi asked Kadie if, afterwards, she could give them all a ride home and their shopping. Kadie nodded enthusiastically. People in the meetings loved giving people rides home. Yes. For sure. Yes. The boot was empty, they could put the bags in the boot. She just had to do the dishes. Heidi said they could all help with the dishes, and Peggy and Dell and Greta all nodded and said, 'Yeah, totally.'

At the end of the meeting, the dishes didn't take very long. Two of them washed, two of them dried and Kadie checked the room was cleaned up and locked up. Then they all stood at the front door and Kadie turned the lights off and pulled the door so that it locked and then they tried it a couple of times each to check it was locked and it was time to go home.

By the time they got home it was quite late. Kadie didn't want to come in for a cup of tea, so when they got inside they put the food away. Some of the cupboards hadn't been used before and were dusty. They hadn't bought a dishcloth so Greta used a tea towel and water. There was hardly any dishwashing liquid left. They hadn't thought to put it on the list and now they had no more money. But it would be okay. Heidi and Dell said there was dishwashing liquid in the kitchen at work and they could borrow some from there.

'We didn't use the taxi chit,' Heidi pointed out. Which was true.

Around eleven, everything was in the wiped-down cupboards and they were sitting in the lounge each with a cup of instant coffee.

'It seems weird,' Greta said. 'There are some things you shouldn't have to buy.'

The others nodded.

'Like coffee,' Dell said. They nodded again. 'Like, everyone needs coffee. They give away instant coffee at hotels.' They all nodded, but Greta and Peggy had only been to hotels when they were on a job and they didn't really notice the coffee. But it did seem unfair. No one got paid much and you had to pay for everything – it seemed hard out. But all of them felt pretty happy about how tonight had gone.

'We should do this again.' Heidi looked into her coffee, but she knew everyone would be nodding.

'Where does Kadie live?' Greta asked. It had just hit her that maybe she had gone a long way out of her way to drop them home. 'Should we have given her some petrol money?'

Dell shook her head. 'Nah. She's literally down the road.'

'It's totally on her way,' Heidi said.

'Have you been to their place?' Peggy asked.

Dell and Heidi nodded.

'Oh.' Sometimes Peggy and Greta had no idea about Dell and Heidi's life. They'd been to the shop in the mall twice. Once to drop something off, and once because they'd decided to go to the mall.

The four of them were in the lounge, not talking, staring at the wall like they were winding up for the night. Heidi didn't look quite so settled in. There was something about how she was looking at Dell. It felt like since she'd come back, she was always looking at Dell, like Dell owed her something. Then she looked away and said, 'I think we should go to bed.' She sat up in the chair like she was getting ready to leave. 'We have work.'

'I might stay up for a bit,' Dell said.

'Okay.' Heidi slouched back into the couch like she wasn't going anywhere at all.

Peggy and Greta looked at each other. The silence had been fine before, but now it felt weighty. Like someone was making a point. It had been raining on the night they'd split into two. The night they all arrived. They called it a night, but it was early in the morning as far as anyone was able to work out. It might not have even been raining, it's just that the raining seemed right. Like they all came down with it. Or maybe it was the rain that split them in two. They hadn't met Heidi and Dell until months after that night. There might have been a time when Heidi and Dell got on better, but Peggy and Greta hadn't seen it. They aggravated each other completely.

'Oh, well,' Greta said.

'Time for us to go to bed,' Peggy said, and they got up.

Peggy and Greta went into the bathroom and stood in front of the mirror and brushed their teeth. They had two toothbrushes now. Someone had brought a box of them into the shop. They were free samples. 'Not for sale' they said, but that didn't count for the secondhand shop. Dorrit had given them one each while they were pricing them together. There wasn't a lot to say. Being around Heidi and Dell made them aware of themselves. They might never have bought a toothbrush each. The toothbrushes looked strange now. They tried not to look at them.

'We should catch a bus to the estuary,' Greta said. It wasn't a surprise the picnic happened at the beach near the estuary and they'd talked about it the night Heidi came home. One thing led to another. They walked down the same track.

'Yeah,' Peggy said. They both closed their eyes so they couldn't see themself looking back at them. They wanted to feel what it was like to be alone for a minute. Just for experiment's sake, and they were on the estuary and it was years ago, before the rainy night that was actually early in the morning and maybe not rainy at all. For a heartbeat, there was only one of them. One woman standing beside the estuary, watching a flock of birds fly in a murmuration like one breathing thing.

'We could invite someone,' Greta said. They had their eyes open now. 'Like, to come with us.' She was smiling in the mirror but only with her mouth, trying to see her gums. All their gums were getting better.

'Yeah,' Peggy said. 'But we'll probably go by ourselves.' She spat into the sink.

'Yeah,' Greta said, standing back now, looking at their teeth in a usual grin. 'Probably.'

'Thank god for you,' Peggy said.

'Thank god,' Greta said.

15

In the weeks before, it felt like the Workbridge appointment would never come, but finally it was tomorrow. Peggy and Greta couldn't settle and were flighty at work, and at meetings they didn't hear a thing. The appointment would be a game-changer. They would be on their way. They would get on the graphic design course and then they would get a job and they would get some money and they might even move overseas or get a big apartment in town. Their bodies rang out with the possibilities and how great their life would be after the appointment. They got home and were pacing and talking and talking and talking. Heidi said, 'Do you need to call Diane?' They thought yeah, maybe they could tell Diane how great everything was going to be. Maybe Diane could give them some hints about how to get exactly what they wanted.

Diane said maybe they shouldn't think too much about what might happen. Maybe the appointment wouldn't turn up anything. Maybe something else would happen. No matter what happened at the appointment, they were in the right place now, which suggested they'd be in the right place afterwards, no matter how disappointed in the outcome they might feel. No matter how happy they might be. That's how it worked. You were where you were meant to be, because that's where you were.

'What about war?' Peggy asked.

'There's powers much bigger than us,' Diane said. 'Weather, gravity, time. And they land us where they land us. We are where we're meant to be because that's where we are.' It sounded like Diane was eating on the other end of the phone.

Peggy and Greta's heads were touching. They held the handset so they could both hear. The coil cord ran back to the wall between them.

'What about rape?' Greta asked.

'I don't know about war and I don't know about rape,' Diane said. 'And you make a good point. This is what I think – it isn't what you need to think and it isn't what everyone in the meetings thinks, this is just what I think. Life isn't god. Life is life. God is what gives us the power to get through life. Terrible things happen. Not as part of any plan. There's no reason for terrible things to happen, but every now and then there's the tiniest bit of grace that gets us through. No one's more deserving and no one's less deserving, and we can't make ourselves more deserving or less deserving. It's not that kind of thing. All we can do is make ourselves available to that grace. If we get too caught up in ourselves, in what should happen to us, or what we deserve, we might miss it. The grace – it's quiet. And if we miss it, life is much harder to get through.'

Everyone was quiet. Peggy and Greta felt a sense of letting something go but they were still holding the phone. A wave of something ran through them from head to toe. It was like they'd been carrying something for a long time and set it down.

'Chop wood. Carry water,' Diane said. She said it a lot. Peggy and Greta never asked what it meant. They wanted her to think they knew what it meant.

'What does that mean?' Peggy asked.

'Do the work in front of us,' Diane said. 'That's when we're the most useful to the most people. When we're useful, we're not worrying about ourselves and we're less likely to miss it.' Diane yawned. It was late. 'Good luck with the meeting,' she said. 'I have to go.'

They all said goodnight and Greta and Peggy said thank you and Diane hung up.

The excitement and anticipation for the Workbridge appointment had made way for something else. A peacefulness right now. Peggy and Greta brushed their teeth and washed their face and went to bed and slept.

Peggy and Greta didn't have much nice to wear. Nice, like what the world would think was nice. They had clothes they liked but nothing they thought was suitable for the meeting at Workbridge. They had nothing concrete to base this on, just thoughts. They tried to not wear ripped stockings and they put on some make-up but toned it down a bit and then they got all the bits of paper they had to take and put them in the bag and ate breakfast and brushed their teeth and caught a bus to the Workbridge office, which was in a neighbouring suburb. Peggy and Greta worked out they wanted to be there about fifteen minutes before the appointment. That seemed about right. It was how much earlier they would get to work before opening time. The receptionist looked at them and quickly looked at the appointment book, told them they were early, and they said they knew, and she showed them where they could sit and wait. There were no magazines. It wasn't a doctor's surgery but there were posters and pamphlets and a few other people waiting but not many. They were all looking at the floor, or their hands, or the walls, anywhere but at Peggy and Greta, so Peggy and Greta were able to look at them and around the room and out the window. They were on the second floor, so they could see the other side of the road and people coming and going. Then one of the receptionists came over and told them it was time for their appointment.

The woman was at a desk. She stood up when Greta and Peggy came in, and thanked the receptionist. She said they might need another chair and the receptionist brought one in and Peggy and Greta sat down. The woman was looking at the computer now, but she reached out and Greta handed her the documents they'd been asked to bring.

'I'm Zara.' She kept typing for a minute, then stopped, looked at the screen one last time and turned to face Greta and Peggy. She was about thirty. Greta and Peggy weren't great at guessing ages, but she looked about that age. She was wearing a jacket. It was navy blue.

'So, what brings you here?' Zara looked through the papers they'd brought.

'Our friends came and saw you a while back,' Greta said.

'And we wondered if maybe we could talk to you,' Peggy said.

'What did your friends talk to us about?' Zara asked.

'They've started a course,' Greta said.

'Would you like to start a course?' Zara was back at her computer, tapping something in, moving the mouse.

Greta and Peggy shrugged. 'We quite like art,' Greta said.

'What are you doing at the moment?' Zara asked.

'We work at the Salvation Army shop,' Greta said, and Peggy nodded.

'Is it volunteer work?' It looked like Zara was reading the questions from her computer, but they suspected that what was on the screen had nothing to do with them. 'Do you like it?'

They shrugged.

'Yeah,' Peggy said, looking at Greta, but neither of them looked convinced.

'Do you like retail?' Zara asked.

They both nodded. Did they, though? They were unsure. They both hoped Zara wouldn't ask what they had done before they went to treatment. Did she know about that? Had their case manager sent her all the details? Greta and Peggy breathed faster. Maybe this was a bad idea.

'You're not under any obligation to take up anything we offer you,' Zara said. 'But we have some pretty great courses. We have a one-day course that helps you work out what job you want to do and what job you'd be best at. Usually' – she laughed a little – 'there's some crossover.' Then she laughed properly. Greta and Peggy did not laugh. 'Would that be a good place to start?' Zara asked.

Greta and Peggy nodded, but they wanted to shrug again. Was it a good place to start? They had no idea but realised it was probably good to show enthusiasm.

'It's always good to start where you are,' Zara said. 'First things first, that sort of thing. And you know, employment is pretty great.'

They all nodded, then. Agreed. Agreed.

Zara looked at the computer. 'There's a course in about two weeks. It's called "What colour is your parachute?" Have you heard of the book?'

Neither of them had heard of the book.

'It's a good course,' Zara said. 'Shall I book you in?'

'Yeah,' Greta and Peggy said together.

'Do you have a diary?' Zara asked.

Greta and Peggy did not have a diary.

Zara wrote out the time, the date and the place on a business card and handed it to Greta, who put it in their wallet, in the pocket meant for credit cards. Greta and Peggy didn't have any credit cards anymore.

Everyone said thanks and nice to meet you, and Greta and Peggy left, saying thanks to the receptionist, and that was it. It seemed good. It seemed like that was a good outcome and the course sounded good. Soon they would know what they wanted to do and what they would be good at and whether there was any crossover between those two things.

They weren't going in to the store today. They asked if they could give it a miss because they had the appointment and by the time they got there it would be almost time to go home, and Dorrit said that was fine. There were other volunteers who were keen to come in and learn the ropes. There was a roster. Which was fine. Greta and Peggy couldn't expect to work there every day. Other people wanted work experience.

When they got home it was only three o'clock and the house was quiet, and it was kind of nice. They sat in the lounge and just sat for a minute and then Greta said, 'What the fuck did we used to do to fill all this time?'

Peggy said, 'Drink.'

'And think about drink,' said Greta.

'And how to get drink,' Peggy said.

'And try and get money to drink.'

'And recover from drinking too much.'

They both laughed. It wasn't their joke. They heard it all the time in meetings. How boring getting sober was at first, when the rhythms of the old life were still there but there was no drinking. They sat for another minute in silence, then Peggy said, 'Do you want a cup of tea?'

And Greta said, 'Yeah.' Like she had just decided, like Peggy had convinced her.

'We could make dinner,' Peggy shouted from the kitchen.

She was looking in the fridge – she'd gone there to get milk but then she noticed the food they'd got from the supermarket. There was still some broccoli, and potatoes. None of them were sure where the potatoes were supposed to go but there was a large plastic basket at the bottom of the fridge with 'Vegetables' written on it, and potatoes were a vegetable, so they put them there. There was no one to ask. They talked about calling Diane but suspected it was the sort of thing that they should be deciding for themselves – taking responsibility for.

'Yeah,' Greta shouted from the lounge. There was nothing to distract them. When they sat in the lounge feeling anxious or bored, there was nothing left that could take their mind somewhere more exciting. Soon there would always be something to take their minds off things. That's what Dell said. Take their minds away from the things standing in front of them, but for now they spent a lot of time wandering about. Looking at the walls. When Peggy and Greta got the art books out of the library, Dell and Heidi got murder mysteries. Maybe they could read – like really read. Maybe that was something they might like doing. Other people had started hobbies. They weren't the hobby type. They said it when they were alone. They really didn't seem like the sort of people who would have hobbies.

Peggy came in with Greta's cup of tea and sat down again. They really had very little to say these days. They'd sat for hours, days, leaned on each other and talked shit in those last months of drinking after there were suddenly two of them. Talked nothing but shit. Never stopped. Schemed. Worked out how they would take over the world. Worried at each other – at the world. Fought everything. Fought each other. But since they'd got sober, they spent more and more time quiet. Looking at each other but with nothing to say.

They talked about the shop and the meetings. They prayed together, tried to meditate. But there was so little to say. It might have been because of how fragile everything felt. There wasn't really a safe topic. The future seemed so foggy. There was nothing ahead but more drinking. It didn't seem possible that two fuck-ups like them could stay sober. It just seemed ridiculous. So, it was best not to look.

Which left only the past, but what a terrifying corner of the dark that was. Was it a good idea to talk about the things that had happened? It was all so dotted and pitted and black in some areas and too bright in others. They didn't remember much but what they did remember was horrible and it made them thirsty. So, they only had right now, maybe this morning, maybe what they would have for dinner, and it got old.

They were buoying each other up constantly. They wanted to not drink so badly, they pretended a lot to each other. Making out they were happier than they were. It wasn't meant to be like this. They wanted so much for each other to stay sober. They didn't want to do anything to threaten the other, so they acted happy. There was no space for being unhappy or discontented. That was dangerous. Ungrateful people drank again. Someone had told them that for nothing. So, they lied.

Maybe later. When they were more secure, when they didn't feel like it would all fall apart with the slightest push, they could tell the truth to each other, but for now it had to be like this, false smiles – faking it until they made it. And maybe it wasn't such a lie if it was helping to keep them both alive. There were times neither of them wanted to go to a meeting – times when they'd come home from work tired and low, but they did it for each other. Said, 'Time to go, then, I guess,' and the other one would say, 'Yeah. I'll just get our bag.' Neither of them was any good at internal motivation.

Neither of them could do this without the other and maybe that was why they spent more and more time in silence or talking about the weather.

'If we roasted the potatoes and steamed the broccoli,' Peggy said. 'What would we have with that?'

Greta thought about it. 'Do we have any eggs?' she asked.

Peggy thought about it and tried to remember the fridge. 'Yeah,' she said. 'We must have some eggs.'

'We can't have the quiche again though,' Greta said. It was getting a bit beyond a joke.

'But we could try to cook an omelette,' Peggy said. It was Diane's idea really. She'd written it down on a scrap piece of paper she'd found in her handbag at a meeting. She'd asked them how cooking was going, and they said they were still making the quiche and she hadn't laughed. She'd looked at them with a neutral face and said, 'That's great. You could make an omelette one night,' and they looked at her blankly. Was this even something people outside of restaurants could make? They nodded slowly. 'I have a great recipe for an omelette,' she said, and wrote it down. When they looked at it, they suspected it wasn't really a special recipe – it was just a basic omelette, but this was the love she had for them. She wanted them to maintain their dignity, but she also wanted them to stop cooking the quiche every night. At that moment, she wanted more for them than they wanted for themselves. That was how it worked, really. When they started helping other people, they would start to understand this love. She said they would, and she was right. It was a strange kind of care, a powerless care, like whispering into a gale-force wind. Like picking up one piece of rubbish at a time. But it was pure as well, it was special. They'd only ever experienced it for each other before.

'Yeah.' Greta smiled. They were doing okay. They were suiting up and showing up. Heidi and Dell would come home from work and they would have dinner for them – they would have come home early and made them dinner. 'Roast potatoes, steamed broccoli and an omelette. That sounds like a meal. For sure.'

They looked at each other now and all the bullshit fell away for a minute. They looked at each other in faith and with trust, like it would all be all right or at least it was all right, right now.

'Let's do it.' Greta stood up.

When Heidi and Dell walked in the door, Greta and Peggy knew something was wrong. It wasn't anything as spooky or arrogant as 'vibes', it was something in the way they moved around each other in the room. Where they were standing and moving in relation to each other. They kept reaching for the same things and bumping into each other and not apologising, just looking at each other – neither of them willing to give an inch, both trying to take up the same space. Greta and Peggy tried to make calming conversation. It just made Heidi and Dell angrier.

'It wasn't a good day. It was a shit day.'

'It might have been a shit day for you, but that's because you're not paying any attention to me.'

Greta and Peggy retreated to the kitchen and worked on the dinner. It seemed like the safest place. They weren't helping. It felt like nothing was going to help at this point.

The omelette had come out okay, but it had been sitting for a while in the oven, staying warm, drying out. By the time everything went on the plates it looked pretty bad. The broccoli was over-steamed. Greta said she didn't realise you could even over-steam something. Peggy agreed. It seemed like something that was self-monitoring. Like things would just stop when they were steamed enough and not go further. But here they were, in the kitchen – Heidi and Dell bitching and moaning at each other a couple of feet away. Peggy and Greta looked down at the plates and they looked terrible. The potatoes were browned but they were also raw inside. Hard. It was a very bad dinner and it looked like it was sizing up to be a bad night. Greta and Peggy looked at each other. They'd serve it, of course they would, because there was nothing else and they'd bought this with their twenty dollars each and there was no time to start anything else. Peggy wondered if maybe they could boil the potatoes. They were roasted on the outside and she wasn't quite sure what would happen to the crisp outsides if they boiled them now but maybe it was worth them being soggy if they were cooked. They both poked at the plate with a knife.

'Is there dinner or not?' Dell shouted from the dining table.

Faking it seemed like two-fifths of it. If they could convince themselves, maybe they could convince Heidi and Dell.

'Coming,' Greta shouted, and they looked at each other again.

There was chutney in the fridge. One of their friends from the meeting had started making chutney as a hobby, to try and fill the long hours left by not drinking. They put a spoonful on the side of each of the plates and at least it wasn't all earth-toned anymore. The chutney was orange but less autumnal. They both took a deep breath and picked up two plates each and carried them through to the table.

'Fuck,' Dell and Heidi said under their breath. It was the first thing they'd agreed on all night. As expected, they turned from each other to Greta and Peggy, who started to eat with fake gusto. Savouring every bite.

'Fuck.' Dell and Heidi indicated at the plates and the contents to Greta and Peggy.

Greta and Peggy nodded and made 'Mm' noises, like, 'I know, great, eh? Aren't we the lucky ones?'

Dell got up. 'Fuck this.' She left the plate on the table and walked out of the room. Heidi stood up and getting her jacket off the back of the dining chair followed Dell. The front door shut.

Greta and Peggy ate in silence. If you worked around the raw bits of potato, the outside was okay. It was both a blessing and a curse that they'd cut the potatoes so thick. It was why they hadn't cooked, but it also meant there was more surface area for the cooked, crisp bits to be peeled off. The broccoli was fine. Everyone used to eat broccoli this way. It was boiled rather than steamed. It was soft, almost like soup. Did people make broccoli soup? That might be a nice thing to have on a Saturday afternoon – with scones. Did people make scones at home? Greta and Peggy chatted happily. As they were doing the dishes, they realised they had time to walk down to the meeting in town. It was a bit colder out, but it would be okay if they wrapped up tight. It had been a good day, really. They checked that all the electrical things were off in the house and put on a hat each and a jacket. Greta wore the denim one, so Peggy picked up the duffel coat off the floor. It was probably too warm for the night, but it would be okay, they weren't walking far. They walked down the road hand in hand, talking about how good the Workbridge appointment had been. How big the moon was. How nice it was to be walking sober in the evening and knowing they'd be home soon and inside and in bed, and to wake up the next morning and know where they were going and be able to make it there without drama. They wondered if the shop had been busy. If anything new had come in.

16

Dorrit was surprisingly interested in how the appointment had gone at Workbridge. And encouraging. She blocked Peggy and Greta out of the roster on the day of the 'What colour is your parachute?' course and chatted about it every time she saw Peggy or Greta in the shop that morning. Saying how great it was. A new way it would be great, every time she saw them. So, the day sort of flew because it always seemed easier when the people you worked with were in a good mood. At lunchtime some food arrived from the bakery, and Dorrit suggested Greta and Peggy take first lunch and choose what they wanted from the box. It didn't look like there was anything vegetarian, but then at the bottom of the box, under some filled rolls and pastries, there were a couple of egg sandwiches wrapped up. They took these and a cream doughnut on the side. It was old school – with a dollop of raspberry jam in the middle of the cream. They sat in the car park out the back, and Peggy ripped the doughnut carefully in half. It would have been logical to split it lengthwise, but then one of them would get more cream than the other. It was mock cream, which always tasted better than real cream. They ate the doughnut first. It was messy and delicious. Then they ate the egg sandwiches in silence.

'Couldn't we make these?' Peggy was turning what was left

of her sandwich over and looking at it from underneath.

Greta nodded, her mouth full. 'Surely,' she said. 'What is it anyway?'

'Egg,' Peggy said. 'And parsley, maybe.'

'Mayonnaise?' Greta said. She was at it now too, opening the slices of bread away from each other.

Peggy wasn't sure. 'I reckon we could just start with a boiled egg and mush it up.' She made a smashing action with her hand and the sandwich.

Eggs weren't cheap but they weren't completely out of the question.

Nothing came in from outside after they'd had lunch. They were just sitting there. Not looking at anything, unless one of them found a magazine. Generally, they would spend time looking at some point in the distance. Like just sitting in silence and staring out at the street. It was uninterrupted when they were together. And sometimes it was uncomfortable and sometimes it was okay and sometimes it was nice. Greta and Peggy were pretty much never apart. Most of the women who had another woman exactly the same were together all the time. It was early days, everyone was trying to work out how it would work, so it felt best if everyone just stayed where they could see each other. It was easy for Peggy and Greta – a lot of the time they wished they could be even closer together, but it wasn't like that for all of them. Peggy and Greta were the lucky ones. The lucky unlucky ones. It was early days, and surely one day they could all live how they wanted but for now this was best. They looked strange when they were apart – it made people uncomfortable. When they were together, it was easy for everyone to read them as one. When they were apart, they looked like half-people.

'Do you think Heidi will leave again?' Greta asked.

Peggy shrugged. 'Maybe Dell will leave.'

'Maybe she already has.'

They both nodded.

'Maybe that's why Heidi's so angry.'

'Because Dell's getting away with it,' Peggy said.

'Do you want to leave?' Greta asked.

Peggy shook her head.

'Me neither,' Greta said.

'It's fine really,' Peggy said. 'Safer, maybe.'

Greta nodded. 'I guess it's lucky we see things the same way.'

'Yeah.'

'It's probably time to go back.' Greta looked behind them, back into the shop.

'Those jumpers look warm,' Peggy said.

'Why would someone throw out so many good jumpers?'

'Maybe they died,' Peggy said.

They looked at each other for a moment.

'Wow,' Greta said. 'I didn't think of that.'

'Or maybe they just got some new jumpers,' Peggy said, picking up the paper bag and Gladwrap the sandwiches had come in.

'Yeah,' Greta said. 'That's probably it.'

17

Greta and Peggy were close in the dark. Both awake in bed. Listening to Heidi and Dell, who were shouting – but only sometimes. Sometimes they were whispering loudly. They were upset, with each other possibly, but it was hard to tell. Greta's mouth was close to Peggy's forehead. Somehow Peggy had ended up further down the bed. Neither of them moved. They were trying to listen. They were both listening hard, barely breathing – trying to stay completely still so they could hear. Nothing Heidi and Dell said made any sense. At times, Peggy and Greta couldn't even tell which one of them was shouting. Their voices sounded strange, like they both felt completely unwatched. If they weren't as angry as they were, they'd have remembered that Peggy and Greta could hear everything they were saying, but they must have forgotten in the heat of it all. Peggy and Greta had never heard them like this before – speaking in shorthand, finishing each other's sentences in a weird cadence that sounded more like thought than speech. Peggy and Greta never talked to each other like this. It was like Heidi and Dell had been doing it longer, had become practised. It was disconcerting. Then, they fell into audible phrases.

'It's not,' one of them said.

'People would disagree,' said the other.

'You can't keep fucking with their head.'

'Telling the truth is not fucking with people's heads.' A frustrated groaning sound from the one that said this.

Then nothing but the sound of them moving around, waving their arms at each other perhaps. Incoherently saying things. Only the odd phrase or word making sense in all the strange noise. 'Not here,' Peggy and Greta picked out. 'A long way away.' Or were they talking about time? 'Suspicious.' 'Dangerous.' 'Secret.' They kept talking about a game. Were they saying that the other was playing some sort of game? Or was someone else entirely playing a game with them?

'You need to come clean.' They were sure that was Heidi.

And Dell laughed – it could have been to demonstrate how stupid Heidi was being, but it could have been exasperation. The sound of someone who wanted to give up but couldn't.

Mostly, when women like Peggy and Greta and Heidi and Dell fought, they fought about who came first, who had a greater claim to the one life they were sharing. This was a fight that happened when the one life got crowded, when there weren't enough clothes or money or space. It was a ridiculous fight – neither of them had been here first. Being first was a thing that made no sense in relation to any of them. This was not what Heidi and Dell were fighting about, and whenever Ian's name came up it was like he was just an object – like a tennis racket, or a cricket bat. It sounded like, if anything, Heidi was angry that Dell kept going away but Dell had never left.

'You could leave for good.' That was Heidi.

'That would defeat the purpose.' Dell, they were sure it was Dell, but it made no sense.

'You think you're helping but you're not.'

'Not helping?' Dell said. 'Or not helping *you* the way *you* want help and in the exact timeline *you* think help should come?'

'You're playing it all wrong,' Heidi said. Now Peggy and Greta could keep up with the back and forward.

'Ian was a mistake,' Dell said.

'So fucking easy for you to say,' Heidi said.

'We both agreed it looked like the right way to go.'

'Well, it wasn't.'

'Well, we both know that now,' Dell said.

'Fuck,' Heidi again.

'I think if we had just . . .'

'Fuck,' Heidi said. 'I just can't with you anymore.'

'You're fucking pathological.'

'I'm pathological?'

Neither of them said anything for a moment, then Dell said, 'You're the one that keeps fucking with their heads. They're not fucking ready.'

Peggy and Greta looked at each other. Were they talking about them? But then one of them shouted, 'You.'

'But I do.'

'You.'

'That's rich.' And they were off again. Dell saying words like 'important' and Heidi laughing and groaning. Then the two of them fell into making incoherent noises at each other.

'You're like fucking cancer,' one of them finally said.

'We both are, fucktard,' shouted the other one.

'You're like metastatic brain cancer.'

'I wish I was that far away.' Then the walking around again. One of them punched the wall.

Peggy sneezed and everything went quiet outside their bedroom and then it started again, but this time it sounded like a normal fight. Like the sneeze had reminded them that

Greta and Peggy were there and could hear them.

'I'm going to bed,' Heidi said.

'My bed,' Dell said.

'I'll sleep on the fucking couch,' Heidi said, and they heard her throwing things around the bedroom. She was getting a pillow or something but taking the opportunity to throw around some of their clothes. 'Such a fucking shambles,' she shouted. Then she was in the lounge again. 'You're such a pig,' Heidi said. Greta and Peggy knew that Heidi and Dell were both responsible for the way the room looked.

'Well.' Dell was winding up again.

'I'm going to fucking sleep,' Heidi said, and they could hear her settling herself on the couch. 'So I can go to our fucking terrible job tomorrow.'

'Quit,' Dell said.

'You quit,' Heidi said.

'I was here first,' Dell said. This fight was not at all related to the fight they'd been having minutes before. This was a fake fight, and completely for the benefit of Peggy and Greta.

'I was,' Heidi said.

'Fuck you,' Dell said, and slammed the bedroom door and it was quiet, except for Heidi shifting on the couch.

'I need a wee,' Peggy whispered, as quietly as she could.

'You'll have to wait,' Greta said.

'I know.' Peggy squeezed her legs together and started to jiggle.

'How long?' Peggy asked.

'What?'

They were whispering – barely audible.

'Do I have to wait?' Peggy asked.

At first Greta shrugged and then she said, 'Half an hour?'

Peggy scrunched her face up. Greta was probably right.

Half an hour at the least. Unless they started shouting at each other again. Then she could go out sooner. Make like the shouting had woken her up. Rub her eyes as she walked to the toilet like she was fast asleep and hadn't really heard anything, instead of wide awake and hanging on every word and sound. Peggy started to hope they would start shouting again.

Really, Greta and Peggy made it worse. They were a reminder. Heidi and Dell would have been happy if it had never happened, but it had and now it was like this. Peggy and Greta wouldn't tell a soul, not even each other – especially not each other – but they were happy it had happened. Nothing they'd done in their lives as one person had come to anything good. Everything they tried fucked up. They were baffled, but like this, close in the dark, close in the light, it worked. It wasn't a silver bullet, but it was helping. It wasn't like everything happened for a reason. Fuck that. It was like Diane said, they were where they should be because that's where they were. There wasn't another option, but this one was working out okay for them. They tried to feel sorry for Heidi and Dell, but they were tired of the shouting and the challenge. Greta yawned.

'Don't go to sleep,' Peggy said. It had only been ten minutes.

'I'm really tired,' Greta said. 'We're okay if one of us goes to sleep.'

'I'll be alone,' Peggy said.

'We spent almost our whole life awake by ourselves in the dark,' Greta said. She was almost asleep now.

They could have had separate rooms, but they didn't have the money – it was their room. That was how it was.

'Maybe when we do the parachute course we'll come out as different,' Greta said, sleepily. 'Maybe you'll come out as good at plastic surgery and you'll make lots of money and you can buy two houses close to each other and we can have different lives.' She rubbed her nose but didn't open her eyes.

They both laughed. It was ridiculous. Now that they were together, thinking about being apart was like thinking about living without a spleen or a kidney or a colon – you could do it, but it would mean changing everything.

2006

18

Neither of them was reading. They read more than they used to but neither of them was reading right now. Greta and Peggy sat on their bed, staring out the large bay window with books on their laps. It was getting darker. Not as dark as their room from twelve years ago but darker now it was October. There was something about Sundays, no matter what city you lived in. Especially Sundays in spring. Spring was the worst season in the city they lived in now. Everyone said so. Possibly because they got hopeful that the weather was getting better when it wasn't. Possibly because the wind got worse. They'd been staring out the window for a while. Then it was time, so they both closed their books and swung their legs over opposite sides of the bed. They both had sweatshirts beside them, and they put these on. Pulling them over their heads but not in one fluid movement – a bit of pulling, a bit of crawling into and out of. Both of them smoothed the part of the bed they'd been sitting on, and left the room. They were older now and they knew each other very well. Some of the sameness had worn off. But not as much as it could have in twelve years. They still felt like the same things to eat and they sometimes did the same thing at the same time – reached for something and bumped hands, bent down and bumped heads. There was a rhythm inside each of them that was still in sync.

In the bathroom they stood next to each other and brushed their teeth. Every now and then stopping and touching something on their own face. Still exactly the same faces, weakening, wrinkling in time with each other. They had to share everything. Sometimes people said they shouldn't have to. Sometimes people said they should be allowed separate tax numbers and bank accounts, but nobody said it for very long because there were only a few of the women – it had never happened again – and they were getting older and it affected almost no one else. So, anyone who said it quickly forgot about it. Peggy and Greta were fine with the sharing, it made people more comfortable and that made their lives easier. That's the story they told themselves. If it had happened again, if there were newer ones or richer ones then maybe there would have been a movement, but even though they waited (not every day, not desperately) there was only the handful of them, and they were easy to forget about. They were almost invisible. Every now and then people would stare but even that didn't last long. People put it down to a trick of the light, or tiredness. On the whole and most of the time, the two of them read as one – just like all of them did. Generally, they were okay.

Peggy and Greta spat out the toothpaste and rinsed their toothbrushes one after the other. They put on make-up and jackets, one helping the other with an arm that was inside out. Each of them had a handbag now because they each had a phone they carried everywhere. It was the same number, but they'd been able to get two SIM cards. They'd lied about losing one and the shop had given them a replacement. They checked their phones were in their bags, looked around the flat and turned on the light so it would be bright when they got home, and left.

They were twelve years sober today. They'd get tom yum

then go to a meeting. The tom yum in the new city wasn't as good as the tom yum in the city they'd got sober in. It didn't taste quite as good when you didn't have to go through every pocket for enough change. It was okay though. On their way to tom yum, they'd pick up a cake at the supermarket to share with everyone at the meeting, to say thanks. A lot had changed, and a lot had stayed the same.

They got a text as they walked to the supermarket. Both their phones vibrated at the same time and they got them out and read the text. It was from Heidi. *See you at tom yum. Happy Birthday XX.*

The air was cold and the sky high over them but not as big as the sky in the city they'd left – the hills here held it in. They felt grateful and free. They still wanted to be sober more than anything else they wanted, and today they were sober. They still went to meetings, they'd never not gone to meetings, they helped out more than they used to. Sometimes it felt like it was much easier to be sober and some days it felt harder than ever, but it still came down to doing the next indicated thing. It was a long game, but it could still only be played one moment at a time. And they still had each other. Heidi had moved to the new city a few months after they had. Dell was supposed to come too but Heidi had knocked on their door by herself. There had been a disagreement – a difference of opinion about the best way forward. Heidi wouldn't talk about it and they weren't sure who had won but Heidi had come to the new city and Dell had stayed put. Peggy and Greta still looked behind Heidi sometimes, and beside her, and they thought they could hear Dell in another room. It had been six years and the habit died hard. It was nice to have Heidi, but they still hoped Dell would turn up one day.

The supermarket was bright and there were a lot of people

shopping. Peggy had a beanie on and she kept it on as they walked through the automatic doors. The bakery was on the other side of the supermarket, but they could walk straight there once they were through the fruit and vegetable section. They stood in front of the cakes and buns and took turns picking up plastic packages and holding them so they could both read the ingredients.

'Peggy?' someone said behind them, and they both turned round. 'Greta?' It was Dorrit. They both hugged her.

'What are you doing here?' Peggy asked.

'Up for work.' Dorrit sort of pointed with her hand, like work was a fixed thing that stayed in one place in time. 'I'm holed up in a hotel and wanted some chips.' She held the chips up and they all laughed. 'I haven't seen either of you in ages. Since we were in the shop.'

Peggy and Greta nodded. 'It's been ages,' Peggy said.

'I haven't seen you since you left the Salvation Army shop,' Dorrit said, and they all nodded. She wasn't wrong. 'But what have you been up to?' she said.

They knew how to answer the question. It had worn off over the years – the oddness of them. There had been no more of them, and people had had over a decade to get used to the small number of them who were still around. The general population had perfected its blindness to the women who had divided. No one would say anything – not out loud – but Peggy and Greta and all the others knew this was a privilege rather than a right. It was contingent on them behaving in certain ways. All of them were acute studies in how to not be disturbing.

So, without ever speaking to anyone about it, not even each other, Peggy and Greta knew that Dorrit, along with anyone else who asked the question, wanted to know what they had been 'up to' within strict limits. Generally, people wanted to know: what they did for work, where they lived and whether they had a partner or any children. It was okay, perhaps, to tell someone about specific hobbies – if those hobbies filled a particular space in their lives and were light or whimsical. The question was, of course, completely performative in the end because Dorrit, like everyone else, knew they were trying to keep two people alive on one person's wages, which meant they rented a cheap, run-down flat and that on the whole the only people they had sex with were each other. But no one talked about it. Peggy and Greta were pretty sure that deep down inside Dorrit knew they knew she understood these things, but the question was asked like a step in a process of politeness that was part of the way everyone was able to not see it. Like how someone seeing double might close one eye in order to see one of something rather than two.

'Same old, same old,' said Peggy.

'How about you?' Greta said.

'Oh.' Dorrit looked up, trying to look like someone trying to work out what to say. 'I got married.' She held out her hand which had a wedding ring on. 'I've got three kids.'

'Cool,' Greta said.

'Wow,' Peggy said.

'And I work for this insurance company now. That's why I'm up here.'

'Awesome,' Greta said.

'Yeah,' Dorrit said.

Then they stood in silence until Greta, to stop it getting awkward, said, 'Three kids. Awesome.' And they all smiled and shook their heads slowly.

'So good to see you,' Dorrit said.

'So good,' said Peggy, and they said goodbye and see you

around sometime and got on with their shopping.

Peggy and Greta chose a chocolate coffee roll filled with mock cream. It was in a hard plastic container so they could carry it to dinner and then the meeting.

'Do they have candles?' Greta said when they were in the checkout line. 'At the meeting?'

'Yeah,' Peggy said. 'Surely.'

'It's no big deal,' Greta said. She meant the candles, because the fact that a hopeless drunk like them had stayed sober and made a better life for themselves was a huge deal.

The tom yum was good at the place they could walk to. Not as good as the place out by where they worked, but pretty good for not having to get on a train. It was hot and sour with thin rice noodles, if that was what you wanted. The broccoli might have been the best thing about it, but the tofu was also pretty great. They usually went to the place they could walk to. It was downstairs. The door was on the street that all the public servants walked along. It wasn't a flash place. It was one of the few places on the street that was open at night. It was dark and because they went there quite often the owners said hello as they came in. There were plastic cloths on the tables and a cup with chopsticks and open-mouthed spoons poking out of it. It was often not that full but tonight there were a few people sitting at tables. Peggy and Greta talked to each other so the other diners wouldn't be uncomfortable. It made people nervous if they were too quiet.

'I'm not sure what I'll get,' Peggy said.

'Hm,' said Greta. 'It all looks so good.'

Then Heidi arrived and they all hugged, and she sat at the table. Although no one she'd met in this city knew that Heidi had been Heidi to a Dell, it was more comfortable for people if she sat against a wall and didn't draw too much attention to the space beside her. Because people had learned to read Heidi and Dell as one when they were together, they imagined that by themselves they looked more like a half. It was more disconcerting, it appeared, when one of them lived a long way away from the other. There was an imbalance to it that no one could put their finger on – it was just a bad feeling about the woman by herself, something like animosity or frustration. While they went all sorts of places by themselves now, people could tell if they hadn't seen each other for a while, hadn't been in each other's company, in physical contact. Heidi had experimented and, she told Peggy and Greta, it seemed it was not being close to Dell that made her more disconcerting to others. There was nothing she could do about that though. Dell wouldn't come and Heidi had no desire to travel back to the city where they'd all lived in the flat when they first got sober. It was an impasse – like they were in a battle of wills with each other. So Heidi patched it over with politeness and consideration. Heidi talked to Peggy and Greta about these things, which made them uneasy, but all they could do was listen and nod. They were all patching something over with politeness and consideration. They couldn't afford to be rude.

'You two look nice,' she said.

For a few years, towards the end of their twenties, they'd tried to look different. When they'd first moved to the new city, Greta had a short blonde crop and Peggy had long, dark hair with a blunt fringe. She swung it up in pigtails sometimes, then wound and wound it so she had two buns. Then they turned thirty-three and Heidi, more and more, would joke that maybe they needed to tone it down a bit. Heidi was a real-estate agent. Greta once told her she looked about fifty when she was in her work clothes. It was jealousy, really. Heidi's life had opened up since she'd got away from Dell. As Heidi had settled herself into being alone and learnt how to make people feel less and less awkward or angry around her, opportunities had opened up. But she was never fully free. Since Peggy and Greta first met them, Heidi and Dell had been at war with each other. For years it had confused and infuriated Peggy and Greta, but now that Heidi was here and Dell was there it was slowly becoming easier to see that from the beginning Heidi had wanted to be alone and Dell had wanted to be with Heidi. Peggy and Greta watched it and talked about it. 'Why doesn't she just stop calling her?' 'Why doesn't she just move up here?' But when they had mentioned it – 'Why don't you just stop calling her?' – Heidi had reacted badly, and they saw it was even more impossible because they were each other, so underneath the thrust of their opposing objectives a part of Heidi wanted to be with Dell and a part of Dell wanted to be alone. Neither of them could win. They were never at rest. They could never let the other rest. But maybe this was better. Maybe if one of them just dropped out, they could find some common ground, and maybe it could be Heidi because she was so much more together than Dell seemed to be. When Peggy and Greta suggested this to Heidi she reacted with even more venom and Peggy and Greta would never be sure if this was because they had been wrong or because they were right. Dell was working cash jobs and most of the time she kept the money at her house but every now and then someone would pay Dell's money into their account and Heidi would call her – ostensibly to tell her to leave her alone but subconsciously to hear her voice. Heidi saw her own neediness walking around in Dell and Dell, they were sure, could see her underlying selfishness writ large in Heidi.

'We still have to stay in touch so much,' Heidi told them with an exhausted sigh as the spring rolls arrived. To keep their stories straight. It was extremely tricky when Dell got in trouble with the police. They could lose their real-estate licence, Heidi said, dipping the spring roll in the chilli sauce and looking at it. Heidi herself was floating quite close to the wind. She drove illegally. She'd bought a car by doing something dodgy with the ownership papers. Then she'd somehow got a credit card – Peggy and Greta didn't want to ask. For her work she mostly took taxis but occasionally she wanted to drive.

'Like a fucking grown-up,' she said.

Greta and Peggy nodded and smiled, and Heidi said, 'Am I right?'

'Yeah,' Peggy and Greta said for the benefit of the people at the table next to them.

Greta and Peggy thought people might feel more comfortable if they looked different but, really, it didn't work. They were still identical and sometimes the fact they looked different ornamentally made the way they were similar even more disconcerting. They would never fully fit in. That's what they told each other sometime late in 2003, a few months after their thirty-third birthday, as they both shaved all their hair off. A fresh start. The older they got the less people really paid attention. Maybe one day it would work, but for now they just wanted to have the same haircut. They'd always shared a wardrobe and the whole different haircut thing had started to look so hard won, like they were trying so hard and it wasn't working, and having the same haircut was so much easier. 'Fuck,' Heidi had said when she saw them. 'That was a mistake.' And she laughed and laughed. Peggy and Greta rubbed their heads and looked concerned. Heidi tried to stop laughing, and put a hand on each of their arms. 'It'll grow back,' she said. 'It'll totally grow back.' She called them Seven of Nine and said, 'Let's go get a fucking coffee.' And Greta and Peggy tried not to look at themselves in the glass along the street or at each other.

Their hair was mid-length now, not dyed. It fell into their faces as they looked down at the soup. They both tucked it behind their right ear at the same time.

'Oop,' Heidi said, smirking to herself as she twisted some noodles around her fork. 'Your weird is showing.' And then she laughed outright.

Peggy and Greta laughed too and then Heidi looked at her phone. 'What time's the meeting?'

'Seven-thirty,' Greta said.

'Cool,' Heidi said and put the forkful of noodles in her mouth.

The waiter came over and asked if everything was okay.

'Great,' they all said together.

It hadn't gone the way they thought it would go. They'd thought people would want to investigate. That's what TV told them, and movies, that there would be an angry mob or a new religion, but the undoing was on a slow subconscious level. Greta and Peggy often laughed about how decidedly *unlike* being in a movie or a film or a book it was. They were there and everyone thought they understood what that meant, and no one wanted a fuss, and everyone just got on with things. But, while everyone else ignored it, Peggy and Greta had to live it. So, they had very little interest in any other intimate relationships. They preferred each other's company and hanging out with Heidi. Occasionally they'd go out with people they worked with in order to read as less disconcerting when they were at work. Although they had sex with other people when they wanted, it was always quite a pragmatic thing and generally they woke up or rolled over wishing they were at home with the other one. They still had sex with each other but, from the outside, their home life didn't look overly intimate. They talked but they didn't share much with each other – there was very little need to talk when they were by themselves. They were no more interested in the other's day – past a level of politeness they could imitate if other people were around – than they might be interested in hearing about the day of their liver or the hypodermis of their skin. Nor did they have the ability to talk about their separate days. If they tried to explain, it was hard for the other to grasp. It was almost impossible to separate their own day from the one they were being told. It was hard to imagine it. And on imagining it there was a strange wiping of their own day. A lot of their time at home was spent engaged in their own activities. One moving past the other, like basketballers sharing a court with a game of tennis.

It was as if they were coming to the way they should have always been. Like they were levelling up into what they really were. Like the friendship and intimacy they'd had in those first years was some hangover from other relationships, like they'd thought they should act that way. That was the way they acted with other people who slept in their beds and brushed their teeth with them, but as they went on they realised there was very little need for it. Little by little, when they were alone, they experimented with less and less conversation and less and less politeness and it felt much better, much more comfortable. They still slept in the same bed. They still stood next to each other and brushed their teeth together and went to the same meetings and talked to Diane and shared one wardrobe. But it was so different from how it had been at the start.

They still had the knack, though. When they were in

public they would chatter away and touch each other and be polite and what they observed to be 'caring' with each other. But if they went out, which they did no more and no less than anyone else, they were always happy to get home and be alone together and silent.

'How's work been?' Peggy asked Heidi. They had almost finished their soup.

'Yeah,' Heidi said. 'Good. You?'

19

They woke up each morning at the same time. Maybe they could afford two beds now, but it never came up. The flat they lived in was split in two by a glass ranchslider – which was strange but worked. They lived mainly in the back part of the house. There was a large room with a kitchenette, next to the refrigerator a washing machine and dryer, and next to the washing machine and dryer a door that led to the bedroom they slept in. It was odd to walk through a door directly from a bedroom into a kitchen, but this was the bedroom they slept in. There was another bedroom on the other side of the ranch-slider but this one was full of computer parts and computers. There was a lounge beside the computer-parts bedroom with a couch and a coffee table that Heidi had brought round for them because, she said, it was weird to have no furniture in your lounge. They'd never asked Heidi where she got the couch and table. She sometimes staged the houses she was selling, and they assumed this was an extension of that. Occasionally, they brought women home to have sex with and the couch was useful for this because, almost exclusively, the bedroom in the back of the house was for sleeping in and having sex with each other. Probably they slept in the same bed because it had never occurred to them to sleep in separate beds.

When they woke up, they knew who was going out to work

and who was staying home. There wasn't a lot of rhythm to it, but it was apparent as soon as they woke up, and without talking to each other. They both got up at the same time. It was sunny the morning after their birthday meeting and there were bagels for breakfast which they'd bought when they got the cake. Peggy had a shower and Greta split a bagel and put it in the toaster – it took a bit of squashing and wriggling because the bagel was bigger than the slot. The griller on the oven didn't work.

They had a job in a call centre now. The 'What colour is your parachute?' course started it all. They both seemed good at analytical work. Which had seemed odd. At least, it had seemed odd to the facilitator of the 'What colour is your parachute?' course. Usually 'girls who dressed like they dressed' were more artistically inclined. They offered to take the quiz again, but he said no, it was all right, things had changed. At first, Peggy and Greta thought he meant that there were women who had divided into two – that had changed. That had changed overnight and quite recently. But probably what he was talking about was that maybe women were able to do analytical work now – that had changed.

They were INTJ. Both of them. He said it was interesting. He had been doing a few of them. He used the word 'them'. It was strange because Greta and Peggy didn't feel like they were part of any group – none of them felt any great affinity with the others. Greta and Peggy got on with Heidi and Dell, but they imagined they would have even if it hadn't happened. From the outside it looked like a whole new person had been added, in some huge, creative disruption, but actually it was a small, quiet splitting. Like, all the things they'd held inside themselves were now outside themselves. It was hard to explain. Most people didn't want to hear about it – not when

180

it had first happened and not now.

Any disappointment about not being artists had faded when Peggy and Greta started doing School Certificate calculus and physics by correspondence. They realised that all the places art hit them, maths and science hit them too. There was creativity and beauty in the derivatives and integers, and the physics explained the world back to them like a painting. The correspondence school packages would arrive, and they'd sit side by side at the dining table in the old flat in the old city, completing the worksheets, leaning against each other, trance-like. Two hands working like one. It made them incredibly happy and they were good at it.

They had a computer sciences degree now – between them. People needed a birth certificate to go to university and they only had one so they couldn't both go. In the campus office they asked politely if, perhaps, there wasn't a way around the one birth certificate rule, given their particular circumstances? Wasn't there some way they could both go to university? But it got awkward quickly, so they said, maybe they could do the degree together? The university advisor pretended not to hear what they'd said in a way that made them think that perhaps if they didn't say it again, they might get away with it. Then the university advisor broke the silence by saying, 'There's some forms to sign,' and leaned back to get the forms that needed to be filled out. 'One set of forms,' he said. 'One degree. You can fill them out over there.'

The computer sciences degree turned out to be good training in technical skills but also in sharing work. It laid the foundation for a good working relationship. They left each other good notes so one could pick up seamlessly from the other. They worked well together and got excellent grades. For a moment, it looked like they might get a good job. But the better jobs were a lot more nervous about the two of them. There were more background checks and they always wanted both of them to come in for the interview and it was uncomfortable. Sometimes there were people in the room who had never seen two women like them, but the biggest problem was that everyone knew what it meant if there were two of you. They'd been drunk when it happened – very drunk. Only the worst women had split into two. So the better jobs were harder to get despite their grades and letters of recommendation.

They tried lying a few times – applying as one person and then doing the job as two – but it always bit them. Someone would make an offhand in-joke, referring to something that had happened the day before, and then it was weird and people got uncomfortable and immediately looked at Peggy or Greta as the source of the discomfort. 'Does she look, like, out of kilter?' 'Yeah, there's something up with her.' The city they moved to was more progressive and there were more government jobs, but it felt smaller and someone was always bound to see them doing shopping, going for lunch in the weekend, walking beside the beach. So, lying wasn't going to work either.

They went back to sex work for a while – it was a cash business, but after a few years and a couple of calls from the tax department they'd started to pay tax as contractors who worked in the entertainment industry, just like they'd watched people do years before because it was still illegal. It meant they could work indoors more. Businesses made exceptions for them, but they always wanted something in return. Sometimes they'd both work – together. Men liked that. Not all men. But they only got paid for one. All men understood that – that they only really needed to pay for one.

Especially when they knew they were paying tax. One birth certificate, one IRD number – only paying for one girl. When anyone asked what they'd been 'up to', this was the sort of thing Peggy and Greta knew not to say.

Through all of it, they went to meetings and didn't drink and called Diane and complained and Diane told them to 'hold on'. Be honest, pay the tax, pay the bills and hold on. They'd say thanks and goodbye, look at each other, curl their lips, roll their eyes and hold on for one more day, or one more hour, or just for now. The only time they got any relief was when they were helping other people. There was something about thinking about someone else that eased it all just enough.

The sex money was barely enough to survive on, but luckily they had computers. They bought parts wholesale and built CPUs for people. They'd also fix computers that were broken. Not publicly but as favours for people they knew. People they knew would pay them for the computers and the fixes and the cheat codes for software and the pirated software, but it was a favour. The money the people gave them wasn't taxable, they told each other and Diane. They overheard Diane talking to someone after a meeting one night. 'Look,' she said, 'if everyone's going to make it this hard for them then, fuck it, surely they can bend the rules a bit.' Diane realised it was hard for them to make a proper living. That's the story Peggy and Greta told each other, citing comments she'd made in exasperation when they told her about another job they didn't get and another piece of bureaucracy unwavering in the face of logic.

'There are two of us,' Peggy shouted once at a WINZ case manager. 'You are sitting here looking at both of us.' A security guard came over and tried to grab her arm. She pulled it away.

'We're fucking leaving,' Greta said, and they left without the emergency grant they'd been hoping to buy food with. That's what they'd been 'up to'.

It fucked Peggy and Greta off. All of it. They would rant about it at meetings and to Diane. And then they ranted about how no one in the meetings understood. There were hardly any of them left in the meetings, and how would anyone else feel being treated like this? If the boot was on the other foot? No one spoke back in meetings, so they never found out.

Being this angry made them crazy – it hurt their head. And one night they found themselves with a bottle of wine on the bench of their flat and both of them looking at it like it held all the answers, and luckily ('Was it luck?' Diane said) it hit them like a truck – everything that came after a drink, all the ways drink was not the solution at all. All the pain and the hardship came smashing back at them like it was in the room with them, playing out all around them like virtual reality, and they took the wine bottle out onto the street and put it on the pavement outside their house and came back inside and realised they needed to do something very quickly to make them not angry anymore. And, eventually, like months later, after a lot of hard work, Peggy said to Greta, 'It's gone.' And Greta stopped what she was doing and felt around in her body and it was gone. They were still angry, it was still fucking unfair – it just wasn't crippling them anymore. They hadn't noticed the fight leaving, just that it was gone now.

About six months later they saw the ad for the call centre. They wouldn't have applied if they'd still been angry. If they were still fighting how unfair it was, they would have seen the ad as another example of how fucked everything was and how now they had to apply for this job that was so far beneath their skills.

The useful thing about the job at the call centre was that the call centre wanted you to be more like a machine than a person. 'It's like having a spare,' their boss, Duncan, joked at the interview. They both laughed, because he seemed happy with that. He couldn't pay for both of them, though. There was the one tax number thing, but also some people wouldn't like it if they both came to work together day after day. That would take a lot of effort for some of the people at the call centre. People didn't like to offend people, and no one knew how not to offend people like Peggy and Greta – they'd have to work at it, and that took effort. Some people were better at it than others and Duncan had to be fair to the ones who found it harder to read them as one. It was asking too much. People would get uncomfortable. People could do it on the street or in the supermarket – in passing – but this was people's workplace. You couldn't ask them to do that.

Peggy and Greta said it was fine. They could handle that, no sweat. They had in the past and they could again. They didn't say it out loud, but a small amount of regular money was easier than not being sure. They'd get commission on top of the awfully low base rate. They asked, respectfully, if they could do double shifts. Duncan said it was a very good question, but he thought probably not. He'd have to file the tax returns and there were labour laws and they only had one tax number and it would be hard to explain. Greta and Peggy said that, really, it wasn't that hard to explain. They would be happy to explain it. But Duncan said no, it didn't seem fair. Nobody talked much about any of it, but most people were pretty sure Peggy and Greta shouldn't get an advantage from it. Most people were sure that just because one day there were suddenly two of you that shouldn't entitle you to anything that people who were still only one couldn't get. That's what

Duncan said he thought most people would think. 'But we'll never know,' Duncan said, and he was right, because no one talked about it. It had been weird of them to ask, but Duncan seemed immune to awkwardness. Duncan needed call centre staff and he was just trying to make it turn out in a way that worked for him.

'That's what I'm offering,' he said.

Peggy and Greta nodded, and Peggy said, 'We'll take it,' and they all laughed.

The call centre was a train ride out of town. None of them could get a driver's licence – legitimately. It made the transport authorities nervous, what with the alcoholism and the giving one licence to two people on account of the one birth certificate. In the end, though, the train was okay. It was comfortable. They were going against the traffic, so there was always a seat, and the one of them going to work could read if they wanted or look out the window or just listen to music. It was fine – and the job was, too. They would sit in a room full of other people with headsets on, answering calls and answering questions about computers and phones but most often the internet. Everything about the internet was a bit confusing to everyone except the people who worked in the call centre. Most of the people who worked in the call centre had watched the internet coming. They'd built modems and written JavaScript and downloaded files from all over the world. They'd found their way into places they shouldn't be – just for the fun of it. The call centre was filled with people who understood more than perhaps anyone else in the country how big the internet was going to be. The rules were being redrawn. No one at the call centre asked what Peggy or Greta had been 'up to'. They asked what they were playing and what they were building and whether they wanted an AutoCAD crack keygen, 'cause they had one, if Peggy or Greta were in the market for one, just between Peggy or Greta and them but also, if anyone wanted to know if they knew anyone capable of writing an AutoCAD keygen – let them know too. All the call centre people were doing dark, great things. It felt like a place Peggy and Greta could make work. It would take some effort on their part, but it had the potential to work out well. Everyone was doing something secret.

When people rang the call centre, everyone had to stick to the script. They all wanted to explain too much. That's what Duncan told them. 'No one wants to hear all that,' he said when they tried to explain something fundamental to him. 'Stick to the script. People just want their internet to work. Get in, get out.' Each day there was a number of calls they needed to complete. At the front of the big office they worked in there was a whiteboard with all their names on it. Every couple of hours Duncan would come down and rub out the number of total calls and change it to a bigger number. Twice a day he'd rearrange the names so that the person with the most calls was at the top of the whiteboard. The secret, Donna told one of them at afternoon tea, one day when they were standing in the car park getting some sun, was that how many calls you did in a day had very little to do with skill. 'Some calls are just easier,' Donna said. Donna had been one of the first people at the call centre to talk to them. Donna and Peggy or Greta both had their faces to the sun, like they were some kind of reptile. They weren't looking at each other. 'Some calls just take less time.' Sometimes people hadn't rebooted the computer after they attached the router. Sometimes one of the phones in the house was off the hook and the person ringing didn't realise it. Sometimes a cord was plugged into the wrong place. But sometimes there was a real problem.

On all their desks was a large folder with dividers. The further you got down the script, the more trouble you were in. You started at the start of the script and, after welcoming people, you asked how you could help. Then they would say something and even though they thought their question was new and difficult, some keywords they said would tell you which divider to turn to and at the top of the first page was a question and you asked that question and the answer to that question would tell you what page number to go to in the section. It was a bit like a choose-your-own-adventure book. Often, it was very tempting to second-guess the manual. To jump ahead or just give the person the answer. But almost all of Duncan's job was to listen to their calls and make sure they weren't doing that. It was fine. It was a perfectly reasonable way to spend the day and there was lunch and twice a day Peggy or Greta's system would stop for fifteen minutes and so would four other people's in the office and they'd all go into the staffroom and grab an instant coffee and sometimes there was a cake or biscuits.

At first, Peggy and Greta were a little unsure what the one of them who wasn't working at the call centre would do all day. But there was cleaning and cooking and the life admin things that made it possible for the other one to go to work. If one of them did this, it would save them some money – they wouldn't eat out so much, and because their things were looked after they didn't need new things as often. They still had the computer work, but it was thinning out a bit and if they wanted to make a proper go of it they'd have to advertise wider than their group of friends, and then they couldn't pretend it was favours and god only knew the clusterfuck that it would cause at the tax department.

A couple of weeks into the call centre job, someone posted

on one of the message boards that someone was looking for comment moderators for a sports website. The website was in America, but the moderator could be anywhere. They didn't want to advertise or use agencies because they were disrupting the space and also, they wanted to pay everyone under the table. Moderation wasn't completely in Peggy and Greta's wheelhouse, but the website was going to pay on a per-comment basis and Peggy and Greta thought they might be able to build a script that parsed the comments for certain words and released them automatically. If they didn't need to read every comment, they could get through hundreds, maybe thousands a day. Peggy and Greta knew nothing about American sport, but they looked up some of the sports on Wikipedia and then at some of the comments that were already on the sports website and agreed they could handle it. They emailed the website and were sent an online exercise which was really just reading some rules for the comments and then flagging the comments that didn't meet the rules. The rules for the comments meant the script would be even easier to write. They didn't talk to anyone from the website directly, just sent their bank account number to another email address. Then they were sent a URL to download a small piece of software which alerted them each time a new comment was assigned to them. So, the one of them who wasn't going to the call centre sat at home and watched the software, moderated the comments and worked on the script that would free them up to fix computers, write cracks and play games.

Sometimes they wondered if one of them should always stick to the call centre and the other should always work at home, but it was probably good for them both to get out and be with people, so one of them didn't start acting shut in, and it really did take both of them to do the job properly. Besides,

Duncan had hired both of them and it seemed like the honest thing to do was to give the call centre both of them.

One Sunday they looked at each other and realised things were pretty great. Within a couple of months, it had all turned around. They were doing okay at the call centre and were paid an amount that would easily support one of them. The comment moderation was going well and paid almost enough to cover the shortfall from the call centre job. The script was coming along, and they decided that as soon as it was working, they'd take on some more moderation work. There was more and more of it around. They had nights free to go to meetings and help out a bit, and on the nights they didn't go to meetings they had a growing network of people to talk to and play games with online and every now and then Duncan would organise things for the call centre staff – bowling, movies. There was a social club.

Being apart during the day was okay, because they each had a phone now and they could be in touch, but in a lot of ways that was for the benefit of others. The two of them knew what the other was up to because they both did both jobs and they were both the same.

At the call centre, Duncan wanted them to wear name tags or let him put just one of their names on the whiteboard, so people knew who was working. 'It's not fair on the others,' he'd said.

'You could,' the one of them working said. 'But how will you know you've got it right?'

'Because you'd tell me,' Duncan said. They were in his office.

'Truth is' – and she sat closer to him, like it was a secret – 'sometimes even we can't tell.' And then the one of them who was in the office with him sat back and let the silence get

190

awkward, so even though he'd think it and sometimes mutter things about it under his breath, he never mentioned it again out loud.

Niall worked at the desk next to them and was often there before they were.

'Greta?' Niall asked, hesitantly.

'Sure.'

'Cool,' Niall said. 'Cool, cool. Can we talk about a customer I think we both talked to yesterday?'

'Sure.' Everyone was friendly and, realistically, people used names less often than they thought they'd have to. All the call centre staff used fake names on calls. One side of the room was the 'Anne and John' side and the other was the 'Jane and Dave' side. The names had been user-tested. People didn't feel threatened by Anne and John and Jane and Dave. Peggy or Greta were Anne, and Niall was John along with ten other people.

When they were at home, working as a moderator, they often wouldn't change out of their pyjamas. They would mooch around the house, making cups of red bush tea with soy milk, watching the comments roll in and their script working in real time. Sometimes people said awful things. Sometimes people said okay things but in awful ways. Peggy or Greta were able to have conversations with other people on the message boards at the same time as they watched the comments and their script, but every now and then things would go crazy and they were flat out. The at-home job was like that – slow periods of fractured concentration punctuated by frantic, focused activity. In the slow periods they watched the script, refining and sometimes letting it run on the software. In the busy times they had to ignore the script and just do the job like they were the script. Someone from the website would message them through the interface. 'Have you got a fucking eye on this?' 'What the fuck are you doing?' but they were thousands of miles away and there was no time to answer them, anyway. They had to show they had their eye on it. Around lunchtime, or usually a bit after if there had been a clusterfuck, they logged off the interface and made some toast and ate it in front of the computer and went back over the last shambles and looked at how the script had handled it. They were always refining, and it was getting better and better.

Eventually it was time to finish at the call centre. Another set of people, who had been working there longer and got paid more, arrived for the night shift. Peggy or Greta walked to the train station. Sometimes they walked with people from work, but most of the call centre people lived in the suburb close to the office. Peggy and Greta wondered if maybe they should live out closer to work, but they hadn't moved yet. They would catch the train home and there would always be a seat like there was in the morning, and the city would come into view and they were happy they lived in town.

Around five o'clock the one of them working at home started making dinner. They worked until the other one got home, but they could work and make dinner at the same time. They set something going and ducked into the kitchen to cut things up and put rice on. The interface binged every time a new message came in and they could hear it over the cutting and the boiling.

Three nights a week they went to a meeting – there were a couple in walking distance. And the other four nights they stayed at home and watched TV shows they'd stolen from the internet or got from the video store down the road. There were always laptops around the house in various states of repair, and they watched TV on these. They could have watched separately, but generally – like, they couldn't remember the last time it wasn't like this – they wanted to watch the same thing, and would. Sometimes sitting up in bed eating dinner, sometimes on the couch. Their flat was small and damp and sometimes they only wanted to heat one room. The door between the kitchen and the bedroom meant the heat from cooking would warm both rooms. Dinner was always good. They went to the library on weekends to borrow cookbooks so they could try new recipes out. They had a library card between them and it was one of the best things they had.

20

Duncan sent an email inviting everyone to a party for Guy Fawkes. They were both invited. Peggy and Greta only had one work email, but he made it clear they were both invited. 'Both come,' he wrote. The party would be at the call centre. There was a barbecue they set up in the car park sometimes and Duncan shouted some beers and people would bring more. Greta and Peggy would bring salads and bread, and sometimes vegetarian sausages but that was always tricky. 'If you don't want to eat meat,' Niall would say, 'why eat vegetarian sausages?' So they didn't bring sausages often. Just salads and bread.

Greta arrived about five-thirty with a couple of plastic bags full of bowls that clinked together. She walked over to Peggy who was standing beside the trestle table they'd set up in the shade next to the barbecue. They put the salads on the table and undid the Gladwrap. Greta took her backpack off and took out the bread they'd made, which was wrapped in a tea towel. Peggy had mixed and kneaded it lightly the night before, leaving Greta to turn it out, prove it and bake it. Peggy dug into the backpack Greta had brought and pulled out a chopping board and a knife. Duncan had some sliced white bread to wrap the sausages in and Peggy and Greta looked at each other as they realised maybe the bread was too much.

Greta said to Duncan, 'Sorry, maybe the bread is a bit much.'

'Nah,' he said. 'You can never have too much bread,' and everyone nodded and made agreeing noises.

Peggy grabbed a Pump bottle out of the bottom of the backpack and drank long from it.

'There's Coke,' Niall said, pointing towards the drinks table with the hand holding his beer.

'All good, thanks.' Peggy pushed the pop-up top of the bottle down with the palm of her hand. 'How was today?' she asked no one in particular.

Niall shrugged.

'It was okay.' Billy took a drink from the bottle of beer he was holding.

'The system's playing up,' Greta said, grabbing a glass from the table as she talked. 'I think it's slower than it should be.' She wasn't really talking to Peggy and she put her hand out for the Pump bottle and Peggy pulled the top up and passed the bottle to her without looking. Neither of them looked. The others looked, though. Not noticeably but Duncan noticed it. It sent the tiniest ripple through the group. Greta and Peggy didn't pick it up or they picked it up and thought it wasn't about them. They were okay together, like this, with the people from work. Everyone could assimilate it, like when someone gets a new haircut, or they push their hair behind their ear, and you remember they have a helix piercing.

'When's the new system coming?' Greta poured water from the bottle into her glass and handed the bottle back to Peggy again without looking or acknowledging the movement.

'No shop talk,' Duncan shouted, looking at the barbecue, turning over sausages. Everyone laughed.

'They've put the roll-out back again,' Donna said.

'Have they started beta?' Niall asked. No one knew but

they suspected not. It was quite likely they would start testing at their office. It was one of the biggest.

'It'll be a nightmare,' Duncan said. He was that kind of boss.

'It couldn't be worse than the elderly horse we're riding home,' Billy said. The others nodded.

There was a strange line everyone navigated. They could say some things to Duncan but not all things. It was a boundary they skirted and didn't always get right. There were things it was a good idea not to complain about. Complaining about the system was risky. It was verging on saying they couldn't do their jobs and if they couldn't do their jobs, they weren't doing their jobs and that was probably not something they wanted to advertise. Realistically, the system was fine. It was slow and buggy, but it did everything they needed it to do. No one would complain about it if the new system hadn't been announced. The complaining was their way of saying goodbye and thank you.

'Yeah.' Duncan stopped cooking and was looking out over the car park and taking a sip of his beer. 'I guess so. The roll-out will be hard. Don't be deluded about that, but maybe you're right, maybe it will be easier because we're aiming for something better. Like in the long run.'

'Great speech, boss.' Peggy patted him on the shoulder, and they all laughed. Duncan was the first to laugh. He didn't really want to be a boss, but what else was there? He couldn't be a call centre operator all his life. His girlfriend wanted to have a baby. Management was more transferable.

The writing was pretty much on the wall. They all knew that in the back of their minds. The biggest telecommunications company in the country had just relocated its whole call centre to the Philippines – everyone would eventually. The call centre workers were the ghosts in the machine. The chess master inside the automaton. People thought a lot more was automatic than it was. 'Automagical,' Donna called it. If they wanted to win, the big companies had to go to places where ghosts were the cheapest, and the big companies still thought business was a game of winners and losers, that they knew all the players and everyone had agreed on the rules and objectives, but they were mistaken, and while they were mistaken there were new players entering who knew the rules were changeable and that the only objective was to perpetuate the game. The old businesses were playing to win, and the new players were playing to survive, and this instability made it look like anyone could play. Most people at the call centre were building something in their spare time. Something they hoped to sell to one of the new companies in Silicon Valley. Peggy and Greta hadn't set out to do that, but as their moderating script got better and better, they wondered if it might end up like that. Lots of people were trying to write the perfect script for moderating, but there was something about the way Peggy and Greta had to make such a close study of how people talked to each other – so they didn't offend – that made them wonder if maybe theirs was working better than other people's.

Some people at work spoke like it was inevitable – getting rich. It was easy to believe it. There were people who had made more money than most of them would make if they worked their whole lives in the call centre. But everyone wanted more. Especially the companies who thought they could win. The company that ran the call centre had made seven billion dollars in the last year. But they hadn't won, and there was only so much you could do with the product – so everyone was cutting costs and people were the biggest cost.

'It's a good sign,' Donna said. 'The system. Even if it's not good. It's a good sign. The investment.'

'Yeah,' Billy said.

'They test everything down here,' June said. She'd had quite a lot to drink and was slurring her words a bit. 'Like because of ACC.'

No one was quite sure what she was talking about, so there was silence in response to what she said.

'Like EFTPOS,' she said. She was trying to explain. She saw the need for explanation. 'EFTPOS,' she said again, raising her wine glass this time to emphasise it. ''Cause they can't get sued.'

'Isn't that just for personal injury?' Greta said.

'And suing,' June said. She was nodding her head now, agreeing with herself because maybe no one else was.

'Oh.' Greta left it there. She looked at Peggy, neither of them fully understood.

Niall tried to break the uncomfortable silence. 'You gotta watch those EFTPOS machines.' A few people laughed, more in relief than anything else.

'Kill you,' June said and looked down like she was finished.

Duncan cut one of the sausages on the barbecue and spread it apart to see if it was cooked. He started putting some of the sausages on a plate he'd balanced on the wooden trolley the gas barbecue sat in. When eight or so of them were on the plate he lifted them up and Niall went over to get the plate off him.

'Do you want one?' Niall asked Duncan.

'Not just yet, thanks,' Duncan said, and he took another sip from his beer bottle.

Niall carried the plate of sausages over to the trestle table. People picked up slices of bread and buttered them in their hands.

'There's some onions.' Duncan started picking up the

sliced onions off the barbecue with tongs and putting them on another plate. Donna leaned over and got the plate of onions and put it on the table.

'Do you want one?' she asked.

'Not just yet,' Duncan said. Then, 'Oh. Go on then.'

Donna buttered him a piece of bread. 'Onions?' she asked over her shoulder.

'Yeah. Thanks,' Duncan said.

Everyone else was talking, so no one really took much notice except Greta and Peggy. They were in a conversation that only required nodding, so they watched Donna butter the bread and take it to Duncan. When Duncan had it, she went back for the sauce container. This is how people helped each other out, Peggy and Greta thought, these small dances of politeness and care. They talked about it sometimes. How it must be lonely, and how people weren't meant to be alone – like, just one of them – and even though everyone thought they were weird, it was being by yourself that didn't entirely make sense. Like the whole of society was trying to correct that one fault.

'That's why people get married,' Greta had said one Saturday when they were lying in bed talking about it.

Peggy nodded her head. 'And the sex.'

Greta agreed but also said, 'But not just for the sex. You can get sex anywhere.'

Peggy had to agree that maybe the sex was secondary. Maybe the care was the primary reason. Humans were born with spares – two arms, two lungs, four chambers in the heart. They had to manufacture the rest. Everyone needed to care for someone, and everyone needed to be cared for by someone.

'Babies,' Peggy said.

Greta nodded.

Although they didn't talk much now, they still tried

to explain themselves to each other through these long conversations. Writing their own mythology, trying to find their place. Making it as dull as possible, so they could move around undercover. It was no big deal – they were exactly like how people had two kidneys. Nothing to see here. These conversations helped them when they had to be out amongst it – they were like coaching sessions. Sometimes one of them would panic and the other could say, 'Two kidneys,' and they could keep walking down the street, or get on the bus. They were happier in the blind spot. 'Where's the milk?' Domestic blindness. They imagined all of them did it. Heidi was doing it. Working out the rules, looking for clues. She talked to them about it sometimes, but it felt more like she was laying bait – seeing if they'd say something useful. No one had shared anything useful except with themselves – there was no website with useful tips and tricks. It was almost like they were competing with one another. All of them trying to solve the puzzle first.

'What are you up to for the weekend?' asked Donna.

They both shrugged. 'Not sure,' said Greta.

'You?' asked Peggy.

'Um.' Donna looked up at the sky a bit like she was acting at remembering. 'Going out,' she said, and scrunched her nose up.

'Cool,' said Peggy.

'We might go out,' Greta said almost at the same time.

'Movies,' Donna said, and they all nodded. The movies was a good idea.

'How was work?' Greta asked.

'Okay,' Donna said. 'People were angry.' She shrugged, to punctuate.

'People are angry.' Peggy was still holding the Pump bottle, but it was empty now so she was throwing it up and down. Spinning it a bit in the air then catching it.

'They certainly don't like the internets,' Donna said, and they all laughed.

'I'm not sure most of them know what to do with it,' Peggy said, and they all nodded and shook their heads.

'But they've got to have it,' Greta said.

'Now,' Donna said.

'Do you want salad?' Duncan shouted from the barbecue. 'You should get some now before they eat it all.'

Greta and Peggy nodded and went over to the table, turning to look at Donna and Donna nodded and walked over too. Duncan had brought out some plates from the staffroom and they filled them with salad. A few of them had brought out the wheelie chairs from their desks. Duncan told them to be careful with them, like he did whenever they had a barbecue, so everyone was making sure all the wheels were on the ground at the same time and they weren't being scratched by the asphalt in the car park. No one wanted Duncan to get in trouble. Greta, Peggy and Donna sat on one of the kerbs in the car park under a short tree that was giving a bit of shade. Niall, Billy and Mary wandered over, balancing their food and drink.

People found places to sit or stood around in groups eating and talking. Who was playing what, who was watching what – usually illegally. 'Where are you watching that?' 'Um, it fell off the back of a truck.' Who was listening to what. There wasn't much crossover, but every now and then people would say, 'Oh yeah. I love that.' People listened even if they didn't love it. There was politeness and care everywhere. People drank and ate a bit more and talked and then someone turned their car stereo on, and people moved back and forth in time with the music as they talked. Some people brought out fireworks and as the sun went down people's faces lit up orange and red and blue and people stopped talking to watch the lights spin and jump and sparkle. Around nine-thirty, everyone helped Duncan clean up.

Most people were catching the train back into town. They were going out to dance and drink more. Niall and Michelle volunteered to keep an eye on June, promised to get her home safe. The train into town was bright compared with the darkness they'd been in, but they stood around and kept talking. When they got to the train station in town Donna asked, 'Are you two coming out?'

Greta and Peggy looked around like they were mulling it over. 'Nah,' Greta said and they both lifted the bags full of the bowls and everyone agreed the bowls would make it hard.

'And you don't drink,' June said. Then, quietly, 'Sorry.'

Greta and Peggy said, 'All good. All good. Have fun. Goodnight.' They left before anyone said, 'I didn't know you didn't drink,' or 'Why don't you drink?' or 'Surely you could have just one drink?'

When they got home the fireworks were in full swing around the neighbourhood. They both fell into the couch and sat the bowls beside them on the floor and just looked out the window for a while at the black sky light up with sudden explosions of colour. They could sleep in tomorrow, but they probably wouldn't. They woke up at the same time every day.

'That was nice.' Greta was still in small-talk mode.

'Yeah,' Peggy said. Then they just sat in silence and their phones vibrated and it was a message from Donna wanting to know if they wanted to come to lunch with her and her girlfriend.

Sure, Peggy typed, and they both stood up to brush their teeth.

21

During the night, it rained. It woke them up and they got up for a cup of tea and then went back to bed and fell asleep for a few more hours. It was the weekend, so they could have slept in. But they woke up at the same time each day whether they set an alarm or not. They lived near the motorway now and sometimes they thought it was because it always got busy at the same time each day, but that seemed unlikely. There was something internal. Even when daylight saving came on. Like time was part of them or someone was waking them up from inside.

They yawned and stretched. They hardly looked at each other now. To begin with it had been a bit of a novelty but now there didn't seem to be much need. They knew each other like they knew themselves. Greta had the first shower this morning and Peggy put on the coffee. They had a stovetop, so it took a while. It was good to take things slowly. Everyone said so. Especially on the weekend. The weekdays could be a bit of a rush, so it was nice to move around the house slowly. To just move from one room to the next with no real purpose. There was no need for efficiency on the weekend. It was all on a whim. They didn't have to log in to their work email. They could look at the news and check the message boards they liked. There was no need to look at work messages. Other people moderated websites over the weekend.

Peggy found an avocado in the fruit bowl. They'd put it in a paper bag with a kiwifruit to ripen it. It was so hard when they got it. Each week a box of fruit and vegetables was delivered. Fruit and vegetables that were on special or hadn't sold during the week. But sometimes there were nice things in it, like the avocado. Even though it was hard the avocado was a nice, unexpected thing. Peggy took it out of the paper bag, and it was softer now. She put some toast in the toaster and ran a sharp knife around the stone of the avocado. It didn't look too bad inside. It had some brown patches, but it wasn't too bad. The toaster popped and she spread half the avocado on the two pieces then cut up a tomato and put the slices on top and ground some salt over it all. Greta, out of the shower, picked up the plate and Peggy went to have a shower. When she came out Greta had made her a new plate of avocado and tomato toast that was almost identical to the first.

Greta was sitting in a chair in the spare room, one foot up on the chair, reading, pushing the arrow on the keyboard down, down as she read. It was a news site they liked, an independent news site. Peggy pulled up a chair beside her. The chairs touched and Greta shuffled over so Peggy could sit partially on the same seat. They took turns scrolling through articles. Not talking, just reading. Peggy was finished eating and Greta closed the site and they checked one of the message boards. There were a couple of newsletters and they read those and then Peggy stretched and swallowed and looked around the flat. They stood up and Peggy filled the sink and washed her plate and then Greta washed her plate and they put everything away and made the bed.

They went for a walk. There was a garden close to where they lived so they went there. Part of the garden was sectioned off into a scented garden – for the blind, it said. That was where Peggy and Greta liked to go most. They ran their hands through the bushes and the smells rose up to them. Some of the plants smelled sharp and some of them were round and sweet. It was good to be out of the house, and not at the call centre. In the fresh air. They sat for an hour or so watching the other people in the park. There weren't many but the ones who were there were all different. There were short ones and tall ones, ones with dark hair and ones with light hair and some had children with them, and some were running, and some were on bikes. They wore yellow and black and red and pink. Some talked and others listened. Sometimes people would walk in pairs and not say a word. It was a menagerie. Greta and Peggy could spend hours watching them. The people looked off balance, out of symmetry walking around by themselves, alone. Sometimes it gave Peggy and Greta vertigo, but they always looked at them. They liked to see them.

Greta's phone vibrated in the pocket of her jacket. It was way too hot for the jacket, but they didn't want to bring a bag. It was Donna. Were they still up for lunch? Peggy read over Greta's shoulder as Greta typed back, *Yeah. Thanks. Wherewhen?* And they stood up and walked home to get a bag each and the other cellphone.

22

Donna was sitting at a table near the window of the café. It was busy but she'd managed to get a table for four. Her girlfriend, Mira, was sitting next to her. Mira worked for a large multinational food corporation. It paid well. She had the same degree as Greta and Peggy. She was their age and Donna was younger. Much younger than the three of them.

'Hi,' Greta said, and touched Mira on the shoulder as she sat down.

'Hi.' Mira reached the hand that wasn't holding a coffee over to touch Greta's. 'Peggy,' she said, and Peggy nodded back, smiling broadly and waving a comical wave at Donna and Mira. Everyone waved back. Peggy and Greta worked their way into their seats opposite Mira and Donna.

'How have you been?' Greta asked.

'Good. Good,' Mira said. And Donna nodded too.

'Sounds like it was a howler last night,' Mira said.

Greta and Peggy laughed. 'You know us,' Peggy said, and everyone laughed because they did.

'Did you stay out long?' Greta asked.

Donna looked a bit worse for wear. She nodded sheepishly. Mira pulled Donna's head towards her and kissed her hair, then ruffled it a bit which made Donna groan theatrically. Everyone laughed again.

Peggy opened the menu. 'Are you having lunch?' she asked, not looking up from the big glossy sheet.

'We're only up to breakfast,' Donna laughed.

'They'll do lunch though,' Mira said.

'Cool.' Greta was looking at the menu now. 'I'm starving.'

'Are you?' Peggy said. 'I'm not very hungry at all.'

'Well,' Greta said. 'You had that huge breakfast and I only had coffee.' It was better to differentiate themselves when they were in company. Peggy and Greta knew the thought of them sitting side by side at the computer eating the exact same breakfast and taking turns scrolling down the page was creepy.

'I didn't think you'd ever stop eating,' Greta said.

Mira and Donna laughed, and Peggy said, 'I'm a growing girl.' And everyone laughed again. Donna and Mira liked hanging out with Peggy and Greta. Peggy and Greta were funny and easy. They were thoughtful. They were a good ear when Donna and Mira needed one and they always said the right things. Donna had gone to them when Mira was talking about going overseas for a job. Mira sometimes called them to ask about technical problems at work, saying they were so underutilised at the call centre.

'What did you do when you got home?' Donna took a sip of coffee. Greta and Peggy could smell it, strong and bitter.

'Not much.' Greta looked at the menu, then pointed her thumb at Peggy. 'She was up playing RollerCoaster Tycoon.' In reality, they'd brushed their teeth in unison, put on white T-shirts, and lain next to each other looking at the ceiling with the same arm bent up and over their heads.

Peggy nodded, and they laughed again. 'I fucking love those rollercoasters,' she said, and they laughed some more.

'So dumb,' Greta said.

Mira and Donna played first-person shooters and *Morrowind*. It was a strange mix of real life and complete fantasy.

'Doesn't it do your head in?' Peggy said. 'The switch.'

Mira and Donna shook their heads.

'It's all fantasy, really,' Donna said.

'But.' Greta looked from one to the other, like they were holding out.

'What?' Mira said.

'One has a lot more tits and swords,' said Greta and they all laughed again.

'There are no tits in RollerCoaster Tycoon,' Peggy said.

'There aren't that many in *Morrowind*,' Donna said. 'It's not *Conan*.'

'Less in RollerCoaster Tycoon though,' Peggy said.

'Less in RollerCoaster Tycoon,' Donna conceded.

The waitress came over and Greta ordered a vegan open sandwich and a juice. Peggy asked for a cup of coffee – black.

'When do you go away?' Greta asked.

'Four months,' Donna said.

'And counting,' Mira said.

'Do you fly straight there?' Peggy asked. The waitress brought her coffee and she said thanks.

'No,' Donna said. 'You can't really. Like, you could but we're not going to.'

'You couldn't,' Greta said. 'Surely? That's, like, twenty thousand kilometres.'

'No,' Donna admitted. 'You probably couldn't fly direct.'

'We stop in Singapore,' Mira said.

'Singapore's a nice airport.' Greta put a forkful of her sandwich in her mouth. Greta had never been to Singapore Airport. They'd never been out of the country. They never would – one birth certificate, one passport, two bodies. They'd read about the new Singapore Airport in an article about SARS. 'It has an outside,' she said, chewing as she said it.

'Yeah,' Donna said. 'We're there about three hours. There are showers and stuff.'

'Nice,' Peggy said. 'A shower will be nice.'

'Yeah,' Mira laughed. 'After ten hours in the air a shower will be nice.'

'And a prayer room,' Greta said. It had been in the article. She was eating and looking at her food.

Mira looked at her. Peggy saw but didn't fully understand what Greta had said wrong. Greta felt it and, making light of it, said, 'If you need that sort of thing.' And everyone laughed again.

They sat talking for a while after they'd finished eating, empty plates and glasses and cups in front of them. Greta and Mira worked themselves into a deep conversation about a finite state machine Mira was developing for a vending machine, and Donna and Peggy went up to pay. Peggy dug around in their wallet.

'You two,' Donna said.

'What?' Peggy asked, counting out the change.

'You always have the right amount of cash.'

'Do we?' Peggy asked, and it stopped her a bit – did they? 'We don't have one of those,' Peggy said, pointing to Donna's EFTPOS card.

'Don't you?' Donna said, possibly shocked, possibly surprised, and Peggy realised what she'd done.

'On us,' Peggy said, trying to cover it up, and she laughed and Donna punched in her PIN.

Mira and Donna were going for a walk around by the water. Greta and Peggy decided to walk down with them and then walk home that way. There were lots of people by the museum and kids on skateboards and bikes and people with dogs walked back and forth. 'Like Sims,' Greta said, and they laughed. It was like The Sims. A small girl riding on a three-wheeled plastic bike passed them then stopped and looked back at Greta and Peggy. Peggy waved, smiled, and the girl turned and scooted away fast to where her mother and father were. It was easy to brush it off. Greta and Peggy knew what the girl was looking at. Everyone did, but it was easy to pass it off as the type of thing a child does with any adult they don't know. That part of their development where they're just coming to terms with the fact that they're autonomous, that people can see them. No one had to walk around it, it was so small you could just step over it, not having to change your path or even mention it. Greta and Peggy knew how to handle it. This was one of the reasons it was important for them to stay sober. Drunk, or angry, they would've blown it up. 'What?' 'What are you looking at, kid?' They needed to stay calm and let it pass. It would settle if they just left it alone. People would realise there was nothing to see. Nothing that concerned them. It had sunk into the manners of society. It was part of the oil that kept the cogs going.

But they knew they still stuck out. Now and then they would see others on the street and sometimes they would smile and sometimes they wouldn't. It was a small group of women at a moment in time. A literal moment. One moment they had been one way, and the next they weren't. They'd turned to their left and their right and they were this way, and everything had to carry on. By the time they were sober, it was already normal. At first the other one of them was like an article of clothing on a chair. Then they were putting the article of clothing on, then the article of clothing was melting into them, then it was like a limb, and then it was like nothing.

Greta and Peggy said goodbye to Mira and Donna and walked home in silence.

They still had it. They liked to go out like this now and then to put money in the bank. To be in the world. To chat. To be with Mira and Donna. To walk around. It made it so much easier to blend in when they wanted to walk in silence, like they were now, if people could see them like that – easy and talking and laughing and with individuals. Another small girl riding on a three-wheeled plastic bike passed them and didn't look back. They lived in a small town. Everyone did.

23

They played RollerCoaster Tycoon that night. They both loved it, neither of them thought it was dumb. One of them would control the game with the mouse and keyboard while the other watched, leaning on her, so as much of the side of her body would be in contact as possible. Sometimes they would lean the sides of their faces together so their ears would be close, cutting off the sound, and they would hear like one person – out of their two uncovered ears. The one controlling would take her hand off the keyboard and they would play like one person with two hands – a left hand on the keyboard, a right hand on the mouse. They would play for hours like this. Because they loved the game and because they loved making rollercoasters. 'I love these fucking rollercoasters,' Greta said.

The tiny people would come in and in and in the park, and they would pay the entry fee. They would go on the paths Greta and Peggy had built and ride the Ferris wheels and merry-go-rounds (always build the slow games first). And while they were riding, Greta and Peggy would build a go-kart track and start theming the areas, adding shops where the people could buy food and balloons. They always built an information centre and gave away the maps – it was best if people knew where they were going. Then, when the people were taken care of – busy – and there were employees to sweep and a mechanic to maintain the Ferris wheel and the merry-go-round and the go-karts and they were pretty sure no one would die on any of the rides, they would build a path and a gate but close it and start on a new rollercoaster.

This was on the new parks. They had more than one game on the go. They would check in with random people that walked around their existing parks – seeing what they wanted. If they wanted anything, Peggy and Greta would try and keep them happy. They would sometimes close a rollercoaster and add a water feature to it. Playing for hours. The people kept coming and paying their entry fee but they also bought pizza and balloons and sometimes Peggy and Greta would charge a small amount for the maps and it would allow them to employ one more man in a panda suit who could show visitors around if they got lost.

Outside, the sun moved across the sky. The light moved away from Peggy and Greta as it sank behind the hill until there was no sun, and eventually they got hungry and had to stop. They closed the park for the night. Some parks they left open and just shut down the computer. They watched the screen go black then they sat for a moment and sighed and looked at their flat and for a moment the small scurrying people would walk back and forth on the walls and any light space they looked at. The people moved by themselves, but deep inside them was a destiny made up of code, and this was what Greta and Peggy loved the best. The way the people looked like they could go anywhere. Like they could be anything they wanted to be but, really, they were just lines of assembly under a thin layer of C. The people had different names, but they all looked the same.

Greta and Peggy stretched, stood up and went to the kitchen to make dinner. They put some bread in the toaster and Greta got peanut butter out of the cupboard and margarine out of the fridge.

'Do we always have the right amount of cash?' Greta said.

'When?' Peggy said.

'Like, when we pay for things,' Greta said. 'Do we always have the right amount of cash?'

'We always have cash,' Peggy said.

Greta nodded. 'Yeah. That's what I thought.'

'That would be weird,' Peggy said. 'If we always had the right amount.'

'Yeah,' Greta said.

'Did Donna say that?' Peggy asked.

'Yeah.'

'People just think that because everyone has a card now,' Peggy said.

'That's what I said.'

There was hardly any margarine left. There had been a discussion in the staffroom at work that peanut butter didn't need butter. 'It's got it in its name,' Niall had said. 'It's like eating butter on top of butter.' Peggy had kept quiet during the conversation, because Niall was master-cleansing, but it was the first thing she'd asked Greta when she got home. 'Is peanut butter butter?' They'd tried it, but without margarine they missed the extra fat and salt.

All the vegans they knew were freegan now. The chatroom where people used to post recipes for scrambled tofu and soaking times for beans was only for sharing what time Starbucks threw out the sandwiches they didn't sell and how to get weevils out of rice. Peggy and Greta hid it well – still being vegan. No one ever really knew. It was bourgeois to be fussy about what you ate when people were starving. The freegans ate anything they found. The prime minister of

Britain had called Africa's poverty 'the fundamental moral challenge of our generation'. Vegans were part of the problem, one of the people on the 'Making Poverty History' Reddit said. Peggy and Greta agreed. They felt bad but this was the way it was. They couldn't bring themselves to eat meat or milk or cheese or eggs or honey. They understood completely why that was bad, but it was just the way they were, so they tried to eat things that came from close by, and toast. The peanuts had been grown in Australia.

They were watching a TV show about the office of a paper company. There was an American version, but they also watched the older British version. They bit-torrented episodes. They weren't very good seeds, but they downloaded a lot. They'd found an old computer in a skip on one of their walks. It was a heavy laptop that didn't work when they plugged it in. They fixed it, but it was so big they only used it for file-sharing now and watching the things they downloaded. It was set up in the computer bedroom, but they'd bring it into the lounge if they were going to watch a lot.

They sat on the couch, reclining with their legs tangled, and ate toast and watched the episodes without laughing. They liked the show well enough and it gave them something to talk to everyone at work about, but they didn't laugh a lot. Lots of people didn't, it was that kind of show. That's what people talked about at work – that maybe it was a bit too close to the bone. That you only laughed to get some relief from the tension of it being like working. A bit too much like working at the call centre.

'A bit much exactly like working at the call centre,' Donna had said, and everyone laughed. Greta and Peggy laughed, too. Being separated during the day was probably the worst thing about their pretty good life. They were hoping that, if they got good enough, or if the script worked out, they could start some kind of small business and just work from home. There were more and more jobs they could do online. Moderating was just the start. That's what they thought. It was completely anonymous. The companies didn't want to know who they were or how many of them were working under one username. They just wanted to make sure the job was done. They were being paid straight into a PayPal account. They could use PayPal on eBay and get most of the things they needed shipped to an address in America that would ship them to their doorstep. Everyone used Trade Me, but they couldn't use PayPal on Trade Me. It was complicated, but the point was no one needed to know about the money they earned online. They were writing code as well. That paid much better but was harder to come by and when you came across it you couldn't ask too many questions. There were white-hat hacking jobs. Niall talked about it a lot. So, Greta and Peggy were teaching themselves how to break in to things, too. Nothing large, because that was the quickest way to get caught, just small things, popping in, having a look, putting things back the way they found them. The problem – and Niall said this was the problem too – was that as they got better and better the idea of doing computer security seemed less and less appealing. It seemed like inserting a middleman between them and the wide-open door into the place where the money was.

They didn't want to work for anyone else. That was what they hoped for. They wanted to work together and not have to be apart. Being apart was like an irritation.

Greta moved her hand so that it was on Peggy's thigh and moved it between her legs. Peggy didn't take her eyes off the screen but shifted into Greta's hand and moved her own hand up Greta's skirt and inside her underwear. At first, always, it felt like it could happen or not – like they could take it or leave it. Sometimes they'd stop but mostly, if they got this far, they were probably not going to stop. Their faces were closer now because of the position of their hands, they'd moved their whole bodies and their faces were closer. They breathed open-mouthed on each other's faces and as they slipped their hands inside each other they found ears, lips, tongues with their mouths. They shifted again, kneeling now, hands working, Peggy fighting to get her jeans off one-handed, while her other hand pushed Greta's underwear off clumsily, never wanting to go too far from her vagina, which was warm and wet and calling her deeper and deeper inside. Two fingers in. Her thumb massaging everything else. Dizzy with the feeling of Greta and the feeling of Greta inside her – mirror-imaged in the swim of it. Wet mouth, wet everywhere. Exactly the same breasts under two different shirts, soft and sucked. They were lying beside each other before they knew it – both wanting so badly to taste the other and be tasted. And still they hadn't seen each other – eyes closed, touch overwhelming sight. Beside each other. Both nestled in between the other's legs. Boundaries completely gone. Slowing to make it last longer, then unable to keep it slow anymore. Hands inside, tongues inside, close and coming. And in that moment noticing each other – in a way that they didn't at any other time – as two separate entities. And then it was gone, and they rolled onto their backs on the lounge floor as a bad joke was going on in the background, and looked at the ceiling. The other one was gone again. They had been separated just for that exact moment. Now they were one again, looking at the same ceiling and not saying another word to each other. Some nights they fell asleep when they came. When they woke up the next morning, wherever they were, they could smell themselves on their hands and they looked at the ceiling to get their bearings and one of them got up and had a shower and the other put two pieces of toast in the toaster because there weren't any bagels.

24

'But won't you help her?' Greta and Peggy were looking at Heidi.

'No,' Heidi replied, and laughed.

'But really,' Greta said, not laughing. 'You have to help her, don't you?'

None of them said anything for a moment while they thought about whether she did. Dell was in the other city in the other island an hour's flight from where they were. She'd stolen a car and crashed the car and run away.

'But she's in trouble,' Peggy said.

'She could come and stay here.' Greta looked at her coffee. They were in a busy café. Heidi had been on the phone when Peggy and Greta arrived. Peggy and Greta had ordered coffee. Greta had got cake – it was her turn to eat in public.

Heidi shook her head and screwed up her face a bit. Dell was always involved in something, but they'd never had to have this particular conversation in public. None of them knew exactly how to do it around so many nice people having brunch, and it seemed that now it was underway there was no stopping it.

'Maybe you can do something?' Peggy asked.

'Can I, though?' Heidi laughed.

'You can't just leave her,' Greta said. None of them had

any idea for whose benefit she was saying that – not even Greta. Maybe she thought the people at the next table could hear them. Maybe she thought this was the way to have this conversation.

'No,' Peggy said, taking Greta's lead, but they all knew she was talking theoretically. From what they'd seen, you couldn't leave someone when they were in trouble.

'Was that the police?' Peggy asked.

'No.' Heidi looked at them as if maybe this was going on a bit long and they didn't need to put on a full melodrama. 'She ran away.'

Peggy and Greta looked around but the other people in the café didn't seem to give a fuck. Maybe the whole show was unnecessary. Maybe they could all just sit there quietly.

'So, who was on the phone?' Peggy said. 'How did you find out?'

Heidi looked bored with the whole thing. 'I found that.' She pointed to a palm-sized game console with an LCD screen that was lying beside her coffee cup and saucer.

'Is that a Game & Watch?' Peggy said, picking it up.

Greta looked around. 'Has that been there the whole time?' She was pointing at where the console had been, next to the coffee cup and saucer.

'It's *Lion*,' Peggy said. She was playing the game now, and the high-pitched vibrato that came out of it cut through the sound of the café.

'It's from when I was a kid,' Heidi said, 'and it made me think about Dell and I called her, and she just wanted to check that I'd used the credit card in the last hour.'

'Why?' Greta said.

'Alibi,' Peggy said, not looking up from the game.

'Where was it?' Greta said, wanting more than anything to

look around again.

'It was in my bag,' Heidi said.

'Did you put it there?' Peggy said. Now Peggy wanted to look around.

'No,' Heidi said. 'I didn't know it was there until I put my card back after I'd paid for the coffee.'

The Game & Watch was still beeping, but Peggy wasn't playing it anymore, and she lost and lost and lost and the console made the noise of the game being over.

'Did *you* put it in your bag?' Greta asked.

'No,' Heidi said.

They sat in silence for a moment.

'Dell must have,' Heidi said.

'Was she here?' Peggy said, starting the question loud then pulling it back under her breath.

'I came home last week,' Heidi said, 'and a few things had been moved around and some money was missing and now I've found this, so I figure it must have been her.'

'But you didn't see her?' Greta asked.

Heidi shook her head.

'She's like the invisible man,' Greta said through a mouthful of cake. 'Disappearing into thin air. Poof,' she added, making an exploding motion with her hand. Peggy and Greta hadn't talked to Dell since Heidi had come to the new city.

'Maybe we should talk to her?' Peggy said.

'Nah.' Heidi sipped from her coffee which looked like it was still too hot to drink. 'It's all fucking games.'

'And you're not playing?' Peggy said.

'No,' Heidi said.

'But shouldn't you?' Greta said, still eating cake.

'She needs your help,' Peggy said. The conversation was derailing. Peggy and Greta were doing their best, but this wasn't the conversation they'd prepped for. They'd thought it was going to be a casual coffee. They knew how to do a casual coffee in public. They hadn't seen many conversations like this, and they were overthinking things.

Since she'd been by herself, Heidi had become natural and almost seamless in public. 'Yeah,' she said. 'Well, I'm not playing the way she wants me to.'

What made it harder was that Peggy and Greta knew they couldn't say anything about how maybe, deep down, Heidi cared about Dell and wanted to be back with her or maybe Dell just wanted to be left alone and that's why she had snuck in and out and left the game. To Heidi, the situation read simply because she was invested in the roles they'd been assigned: needy Dell had left her the Game & Play to stop Heidi from living her best independent life, and now Dell was in trouble and Heidi was implicated.

'But. What would you do if she got arrested?' Peggy said.

'Yeah.' Heidi stared at them. 'That's kind of my fucking point.'

'Yeah,' Greta and Peggy said together.

'So, you should help her,' Peggy said. 'Like for yourself.'

'I've got my own strategy,' Heidi said.

'But you could team up,' Greta said.

Heidi shrugged. 'She's not my friend, or my family, or a workmate, or anything. Realistically, she's just a malfunction. No offence,' she added.

'None taken,' Greta and Peggy said together.

'But. What would you do if she got arrested?' Peggy asked. She was repeating herself now – like she'd rounded back on a dialogue tree. She was shaking her head. Greta was as well, opening her mouth, miming what Peggy was saying.

'That's what I'm saying,' Heidi said. 'Dell and I fundamentally disagree about the best way to do this.' And she waved her hand between Peggy and Greta, which made them both look around to make sure no one saw it. No one had seen it.

'But,' Greta said.

'She wants to run around trying to fight everything.' Heidi was getting angry. 'Look at this – like today. Like, if I just carry on living my life – I'm fine. Doing what's expected, playing by the rules. We're fine. She's fucking stealing cars like it's fucking Grand Theft Auto and I'm out having a nice cup of coffee like a normal person and through having a nice cup of coffee I save both our arses.'

'So, you're kind of a team anyway,' Peggy said.

'Dell brings nothing to the table,' Heidi said. 'Look, I'm sorry I even mentioned it. It's not a big deal. She's on her way out of the city to lay low for a few days now.'

'You'd miss her.' It was more a question than a statement. But what was left of the statement, Greta was making for all of them. They weren't monsters. 'Like, if she did leave. Like properly.'

'I guess I'd find out,' Heidi said. 'I haven't seen her in years. If she wanted to go away properly, she would.'

Equivalency was often mistaken for intimacy. Proximity was important – Peggy put her hand on Greta's leg – but Dell and Heidi had never been close, not like Peggy and Greta were. They'd never settled into being two. They hated each other in a way that was only possible because they were the same person.

'But you've known she's there. Like, while you're up here. Like a shadow,' Peggy said. 'That must mean something.'

'She's not helpful,' Heidi said. 'Do you know what she is? She's a fucking status effect – and not a good one. Dell is a fucking nausea potion.'

'Or cancer,' Greta said, and everyone looked at her for a moment because she'd said too much.

'I feel like you both want the same thing,' Peggy said, and the moment she said it she and Greta realised they'd been wrong about everything. It wasn't about being together or being apart. It was about how to live. Heidi and Dell were locked in a deep, elemental disagreement about whether to fight or whether to surrender and it would never be settled. They'd be at war for ever. Greta had been right to bring up the fight in the flat all those years ago – somehow this irreparable fissure had its roots in Ian. Greta and Peggy saw, now, that Dell and Heidi had been in cahoots and Heidi had almost lost everything and it had broken something in them finally.

'Maybe Dell's trying to make it up to you,' Greta said.

And Heidi looked at her with so much hate it would never be mentioned again. In that one look, Peggy and Greta realised they would never understand.

'We love you.' No one was sure who Peggy was saying this to. Heidi looked behind her, half expecting to see someone close by – a waiter, maybe, or maybe someone they knew from work or someone who could overhear. But it was just as possible she really was saying it to Heidi. Peggy's face was giving nothing away, possibly because even Peggy didn't know what she was saying. It happens. People say things all the time they don't really understand. One thing leads to another. There was a pattern to a conversation. They all knew it – they'd made a study of it. They weren't monsters. Any of the people in the café would do the same. It was just a set of questions and answers – like the manual at the call centre.

No one was originally moral. No one was particularly ethical, it had gone too far for that. Tribes, villages, towns, cities, global communities. There were pathways and they all moved around in them. So maybe they were talking in earnest, out of love and concern for each other, in an attempt to understand the difficulty Heidi was experiencing, but also maybe it was just the next thing that needed to be said in the conversation theatre so they could maintain their cover. If they'd been in an empty café, none of them would be talking. Heidi would have told them the news, possibly – it was information, and information wants to be free – but there would have been no discussion. They all knew. Greta and Peggy would have nodded and that would have been the end, just like it had been every other time.

'Do you want another coffee?' Heidi said. Greta and Peggy nodded. Heidi put the Game & Play in her bag and got up to order more coffee. Greta and Peggy talked about the weather and dug at the bottom of their empty cups with their spoons until Heidi came back.

'Did you watch *The Office*?' Peggy asked her.

Heidi shook her head. She didn't even like *The Office*. But they were all just closing things down now. Making sure it was shut away.

They said goodbye to Heidi and walked home. A lot of people were out shopping. Not for any particular reason – just because they'd woken up and thought to themselves all at once, 'I'm going to go shopping today.' Everyone wanted something. The sun was quite warm. Greta and Peggy looked weirder in sunglasses, but they needed them because it was very bright. Sometimes young guys would call out of the windows of passing cars. 'Agent Smith,' they'd yell. And it would be excruciating, and everyone would look and sometimes Peggy or Greta would knee-jerk take their sunglasses off so that when people turned round, they wouldn't be able to find what the boys were shouting at. But today they wanted to wear their sunglasses. They wore their sunglasses and they didn't need to explain it.

25

Three of the people from the meetings were having a party. They were all turning thirty. One of them handed Peggy and Greta an invitation at coffee after a mid-week meeting.

'Will you come?' she said. Peggy and Greta were looking at the invitation.

'Yeah,' Peggy said, and they both smiled and nodded. 'Can we bring anything?'

'Maybe a plate of food?' she said. 'Maybe something to drink? It's BYO. Some people might be "drinking" drinking but there'll be lots of sober people there.'

'Cool,' Peggy said. 'Cool.' It was always nice to know what to expect. They were often surprised, even now, the events that people didn't drink at. They'd gone to Niall's kid's third birthday fully expecting to spend at least some of the time saying 'No, thanks' to offers of wine. 'They'll probably have champagne,' Peggy had said as they were doing their make-up in the mirror before they left, and Greta agreed. It didn't matter overly, but it was nice to be emotionally prepared. But no one drank at the third birthday party. Everyone was watching the kids and looking after the kids and standing around in groups talking about the kids with glasses of soft drink and cups of coffee. These days, no one asked much after 'No, thanks'. People didn't drink for all sorts of reasons. Peggy and Greta weren't sure when it had changed, but it had. They often talked with Heidi about it. Ten years ago, you almost had to present a certificate. People took offence if you said you weren't drinking. Heidi suspected it was amplified by the fact they were hanging around with different people now, but even she agreed it seemed to have changed.

The thirtieth birthday party was on a Saturday night. Peggy and Greta spent the day making a platter of roast capsicums and tiny pastry packages filled with spiced potato and peas. They roasted aubergine and made baba ganoush and cooked the chickpeas they'd soaked overnight for hummus. By about six they were finished, and Peggy put on some music and they danced around the house trying on outfits and doing their hair and putting on make-up. The party started at eight and they aimed to be there about quarter past. It was hard hosting during that very start bit when no one was turning up and you wondered if anyone would. They probably wouldn't stay long, so they were fine with being part of the first shift.

'You look nice,' Peggy said. They were doing final touches in front of the big mirror on the dresser in their bedroom.

'Aw, cheers,' Greta said and hugged her. 'You too. I like that T-shirt with that skirt.'

'Thanks,' Peggy said. 'You invented it.'

'Huh?' Greta was putting in some earrings so wasn't totally listening.

'You wore them together a couple of months ago.' Peggy used the knuckle of her pointer finger to pull a tiny smudge of lipstick back into the boundary of her lips.

'Oh,' Greta said. She was applying more mascara now, her mouth open. She stood back. 'I remember now. Well, it looks good on you.' They both laughed.

They were chatting because it wasn't a normal night. They were excited and also they were getting ready for being around people – there were so many things that could go wrong in such an unusual setting. They needed to be prepared.

The taxi arrived and they carried the platter and pastries down the path. There weren't many people in the hall when they got there. The big empty room was decorated with crêpe-paper streamers and some fairy lights. There was a rented sound system and some lights that spun around the room and every now and then hit the disco ball hung from the centre of the ceiling. The decorations and the lights made the space seem even bigger and emptier. The music was loud and bouncing off the walls with no bodies to soften it. The three people having the party were standing in a huddle near one of the speakers talking to each other when Peggy and Greta walked in. The woman who had invited them turned round, smiled broadly and walked over to hug them.

'It's so good to see you.' She looked at the platter and the baskets of pastries and said, 'Thank you. Wow. Did you buy these?'

Peggy and Greta shook their heads.

'Wow,' she said. 'I didn't even know people could make these. I thought there was a factory.' They all laughed. 'Oh,' she said. 'We have a table for food.' She walked them over to a couple of trestle tables that had been set up and covered with white butcher's paper.

Peggy and Greta put down the platter and the pastries and picked up a paper cup and filled it with the sparkling water they'd brought in Peggy's handbag. Then they stood to the side and watched.

By quarter to nine, the hall was at least half full and people had started dancing. Heidi arrived carrying a couple of pizzas.

She leaned in and air-kissed the hosts on both cheeks, then walked over to Peggy and Greta, who hadn't moved far from the food tables.

'Hi,' said Heidi. It might have been the unfamiliar setting or maybe it was the uneasy conversation they'd had in the café, but it occurred to Peggy and Greta that it could be Dell. That it was all an elaborate hoax. That despite all of Heidi's remonstrations, she and Dell were working together – in some kind of co-op play. They hadn't seen or talked to Dell in years. They looked at Heidi's scars – counting them off. The scars had settled over time and there was better make-up now. She always wore her hair over the ear there was only half of. Maybe Dell and Heidi were alternating in the role of Heidi. It was a mindfuck, and for a minute Peggy and Greta couldn't do anything but stare. They'd all been so close. Slept under the same roof for years. When Heidi had come home after being with Ian, they'd helped her get back on her feet. They'd shared the weirdest experience and now Peggy and Greta realised they were as much in the dark as everyone else. They had no way of telling them apart or proving that what Heidi had been telling them about Dell or about the accident or herself was true. Everything Heidi and Dell wanted could be solved if they could be one again. Had they found a way to do it?

'How's Dell?' Peggy said it. It came out unmeasured and sounded wrong.

'Hello to you, too,' Heidi said, and put the pizzas down. People noticed Heidi when she talked to them. Heidi had almost perfected looking like there was only one of her, but when Heidi talked to Peggy and Greta in a crowded room like this, she seemed slightly different from anyone else who talked to Peggy and Greta. People looked at her and sometimes they scowled. Once, a guy yelled at her from across a room. Called her a slut. No matter what Heidi did – no matter how good she got – when she was talking to Peggy and Greta people got interested and sometimes, if the room was loud enough and crowded enough, they got angry. Peggy and Greta were frightened that one day Heidi would worry about this and that her standing as a single person would mean more to her than Peggy and Greta's friendship and they wouldn't hear from her again.

Heidi hugged them both in turn, and as she pulled each of them in they smelled her, hard. Would her smell give her away? What had Dell smelled like?

'Great party,' Heidi said.

'Yeah,' said Peggy.

'How's Dell,' Greta said, taking a sip from the paper cup she was holding. She'd seen other people do it. To make a comment look offhand, not important, just niceties, but in the fluster of it all she'd forgotten that Peggy had already asked, and Peggy elbowed her very subtly, not to stop her but just because she couldn't control herself.

'Um . . .' Heidi was filling a paper cup of her own. Lifting the bottles of soft drink and juice that had filled the table to a tilt to see what they were. 'I don't really know.' She took the lid off some orange juice that was mixed with sparkling water.

'It'd be nice to see her sometime,' Greta said.

'You just have to look at me,' Heidi said, and laughed.

'To spend time with her,' Peggy said. 'To spend time with both of you.'

'Yeah,' Heidi said. 'I don't think you'd like that so much.'

'Why not?' They said it together. They were completely thrown – the lights, the thump of the bass from the speakers. That was all.

'Dell's not how you remember her,' Heidi said, and then put her index finger to the side of her head and rolled her head back and forward, making a mad face. She was sipping from the cup now. 'Do you want to dance?' she said, turning fully round to Peggy and Greta. 'Remember this song? We loved this song.' Without waiting for a reply, she walked onto the dancefloor and started dancing with a guy they knew from the meetings.

Peggy and Greta were left standing by themselves. 'Fuck,' Peggy said, and shook her head.

'What is wrong with us?' Greta said. 'We're going fucking crazy.'

'Persecution complex much?' said Peggy.

'We have to apologise to her,' Greta said. 'Fuck.'

Peggy nodded. Heidi was dancing and every now and then turning and waving them over. They put their cups down and walked onto the dancefloor. The lights illuminated everything and then passed into darkness. A spray of white ran over all of them like stars. The music was loud. It was a great night.

Peggy and Greta leaned close to Heidi and shouted, 'Sorry,' and Heidi said, 'What?' and they shouted it again, louder.

'Oh,' Heidi said. 'Oh. No.' She stepped back from them, they were all still dancing, and shook her head and waved her hand and mouthed, 'It's no big deal,' and smiled the widest smile as she swung her head from side to side, letting her long hair whip across her face. Hiding it, then revealing it, so it looked like she was there then gone, then there again.

Later in the night, much later, Heidi found them. She was holding her phone out to them and waving for them to follow her. The three of them stood on the street and Heidi put her phone to speaker.

'Dell,' she said.

'Yeah,' Dell said. It was Dell, they could tell by the way Heidi looked when Dell spoke – like they used to, like it was twelve years ago, and they were in the flat and Dell was speaking to them from another room.

'Dell,' said Heidi. 'Peggy and Greta are here.'

'Oh,' Dell said. 'Hi.'

'Hi,' said Peggy and Greta. They were overjoyed. They had been dancing for hours and that made them happy and now, here they were, all together again on the street under a bright moon.

'How are you?' Peggy asked.

'Good,' Dell said. 'Good.'

Heidi saw someone she knew, handed the phone to Peggy and Greta, and walked away.

'How are you?' Dell asked.

'Good,' said Peggy. 'We're really good. It's so good to hear you.'

There was silence for a moment, just Peggy and Greta laughing – overjoyed.

'Cool,' Dell said.

'Cool,' they said.

'Is Heidi gone?' Dell asked.

Peggy and Greta looked. Heidi was well out of earshot, talking animatedly with a group of women. 'Yeah,' they said. 'She's talking to someone else.'

'Oh, cool,' Dell said. 'Cool. Quite a party, eh?'

'Yeah,' Greta and Peggy said together.

'Yeah,' said Dell. 'So, um, yeah, I don't know if Heidi's told you but I'm kind of doing something quite important.'

'Oh?' they said.

'Yeah. I know, right. So, I was thinking – it's so great to hear from you – did I say that? So great. So, yeah, I was wondering, like, you guys might be able to help out. I just need you to look after something. Heidi doesn't need to know. It's nothing big – it's kind of like that notebook. You still have that notebook, eh? That was no big deal, eh? It's not big, this other thing. I could post it to you. I have a pen, you could give me your address.'

'Oh,' Peggy said. 'Like the Game & Play?'

'What?' said Dell.

'I'm really sorry,' said Greta. 'I mean . . .'

'It's not big,' Dell said.

'Yeah, but.'

'Have you been good?' Greta said.

'Fuck you,' Dell said. 'It's not even just for me,' and she hung up.

They looked at the phone and then Heidi came over and they handed her the phone. 'Want to dance some more?' Heidi said. Peggy and Greta looked down the street.

'Come on,' Heidi said, grabbing Peggy by the arm, and they all went back into the hall.

26

The next day, Peggy and Greta decided to go to the supermarket on the other side of town. They had plenty of food. It was Sunday, though, and they felt like something special for lunch and someone had told them at the party that the supermarket by the waterfront was stocking vegan sausage rolls from England. The woman they'd talked to was also vegan. They often saw each other at meetings and talked about what they were eating or what they were wearing on their feet. She always had good shoes on.

She came over to tell them she'd imported a culture for making tempeh and she'd made a box with a lightbulb in it to keep the tempeh warm while it fermented. 'Indonesian warm,' she said. They all laughed. She was pretty sure she'd bought the city out of bulk dried soybeans. 'Do you want some?' Peggy and Greta nodded. They would love some of her homemade tempeh.

'Cool,' she said. 'Cool.' Then, as she was walking away, she remembered the English vegan sausage rolls at the super-market across town and turned back to tell them. They'd been in the freezer when she was at the supermarket a couple of days ago. She'd eaten them while she was in England a few years back. They had all sorts of vegan food in England.

'Thank god for mad cow disease,' she said. And they all

looked around a bit to make sure no one had heard them, then laughed conspiratorially.

Peggy and Greta woke up thinking about the vegan sausage rolls. How nice it would be to have vegan sausage rolls for lunch. For breakfast, even. They'd stepped out of their clothes. They'd got home later than they had thought they would and both of them still had their make-up on. They looked pretty bad, but it only took a shower and a cup of coffee to get them ready to go. Peggy grabbed a backpack – they would probably get more than just sausage rolls. They headed off, walking past the parliament buildings and straight down to the waterfront. It was still early when they got there and there were people running and cycling and even some on rollerblades and skateboards. It was overcast, so the water was dark and choppy. There was energy in the air, maybe it was the wind, but it was also the people. Most of them swept past Peggy and Greta without a second glance. Peggy had her hair up and only Greta had sunglasses on, but it was also that people were in their own early Sunday morning worlds. Everyone had work tomorrow. Peggy and Greta had work tomorrow but that felt like it was a long time away as they walked around the waterfront surrounded by the motion of the other early morning people.

The supermarket was busy too. People walked through the aisles carrying newspapers, looking for fresh bread and eggs. Peggy and Greta looked through the glass doors of the large stand-up refrigerators. There were lots of readymade meat meals and then there were frozen meats done in special ways – crumbed, rolled. When they got to the ice cream, they figured they'd gone too far. So, they went back to where they'd started and walked slowly again, looking up and down the shelves as they walked. Then Peggy spotted them. They were right next to the meat sausage rolls. The door opened with a suck and they both read the label and it was true. They were vegan sausage rolls and Peggy and Greta had a packet of them.

The walk home would take about forty-five minutes. The sausage rolls were frozen, so they wrapped them in Peggy's sweatshirt. They walked through town because it was interesting, and the wind had picked up even though the sun was out now and warm. The end of town up by the parliament buildings was deserted. It was crowded during the week but dead on the weekend. When Peggy and Greta got home, they were hungry. One of them turned the oven on and the other went to the bedroom to put their coats and backpack away. She found half a lettuce in the refrigerator and some chickpeas they hadn't used for the hummus, which might be nice. 'I'll make a salad as well,' she said towards the bedroom door, which always shut by itself. 'Cool,' she replied from the bedroom. 'Thanks.' She stood at the sink and washed her hands. There were some tomatoes somewhere, but she wasn't sure where. Tomatoes with chickpeas would be good with the sausage rolls. A car's reflection slid across the bedroom wall as she heard it accelerate. The street was a cul-de-sac but every now and then a car went past, and you could always hear it from the bedroom. She looked behind herself and there was a lemon in the fruit bowl, and they had some olive oil. The jackets were warm with the walking and the sun, and she held them up against her face before hanging them up. She couldn't find the tomatoes anywhere.

She stopped what she was doing and looked at the door, from the kitchen, from the bedroom – she walked over to it and she opened it and there was only one of her.

27

She sat for a long time on the floor in the frame of the open door, staring at the hinges, keeping it open with her feet. She couldn't look into either the kitchen or the bedroom. She was keeping the whole house balanced with her stillness. Like the slightest glance would collapse everything into a decided state, and it would be settled. It felt like maybe it wasn't quite decided yet – like if she did the right thing, she would be two again and this would be a funny story to look back on – just a hiccup. Then she stood up, not shifting her eyes, breathing deeply, gasping perhaps for something. The door swung towards her and she reached out her hand to stop it. She was dizzy. She hadn't eaten, and she was hungry and stiff from sitting on the floor. It was starting to get dark outside and the oven was still on. The close smell of warmth pushed at her face.

Finally, she looked around, not knowing which room to step into but knowing she couldn't stay in between them any longer.

She walked the house, opening other doors, but she knew. She'd known from the second it had happened. A chill ran over her, like someone had skinned her. Like her muscle and viscera were out in the air. She could feel every hair on her head and when she blinked she felt her eyelids slide over her eyes. Her teeth felt too big for her single mouth. She opened it and moved her jaw side to side. The house was unfamiliar to her. But it was hers. The clothes were hers. The computers. The job. There were two phones on the table. She moved tentatively towards the bathroom. There were still two toothbrushes on the bench, and she reached out for them but couldn't quite reach from the door and didn't want to go in, in case the bathroom door shut.

There were messages on the phones, but none were to do with this. She needed to talk to Heidi, and Heidi was the last person she should talk to. She needed to get herself straight before she talked to Heidi.

It got darker, and colder. And she sat in the frame of the door again and looked at the hinges. She got up occasionally, walked around the house, and then came back to the door and the hinges. She'd find herself there, like it was a surprise. She'd think, 'This is ridiculous, I should get up.' And then half an hour later she would find herself still there, her mind having been somewhere else. Then she got up and found herself on the floor again, in the doorway in between the bedroom and kitchen. Then it was two in the morning and one of them had to be at work in seven hours and one of them had to be in front of the computer to moderate the comments and write the code that was due by lunchtime. She needed to work out which one was easier to call in sick for. Was she sick? They were not sick. Did she need to tell Duncan? Was it that sort of situation? Theoretically there was only one of them, on paper, in pay, in tax, but did Duncan need to know that now there really was just one of them? Would she keep her job if there was only one of her? Would people miss the other one? Which one would she be? She tried out both names but had no idea. The names were no use. Names were for everyone else. There had only been a Greta so there could be a not-Peggy and vice versa. It was just a convenience. The names had just come. They'd talked about it in whispers in the dark, inches away from each other so no one would overhear and think they were crazy. 'Some people call me Peggy.' 'That one guy used to call me Greta.'

She couldn't remember which room she'd been in and the names were no help at all. Had she been in the bedroom? Someone had turned on the oven – the oven was on, it had been on for a long time when she'd first found herself sitting in the door frame, alone. But was she the one who turned the oven on? There was only one of her now. When they'd first talked about it, they'd thought it was a doubling thing. An extra one, hiccuped in from a parallel universe. But the question 'Which one of us was here first?' was ridiculous and impossible to answer except with a simple 'Me'. It wasn't a doubling, it was a division. They had been divided over two bodies. She had been divided and now they were in one body – perfectly overlapped, so you couldn't see there were two of them.

Now, in the cold and the dark, the question seemed to be, which one of them was here last? Which one of them was left? And the answer was still 'Me'.

She lay down on the floor and curled into a shape that was tight, but she could still see the hinges of the door. A pain, a moaning gape, grew deep inside her. It pulled every part of her into it so every part of her just felt loss, reverberated with a low, loud shriek of no. She cried and the crying accelerated into a body shake and her throat was raw. She had trouble breathing, she almost drowned in her tears and snot and still the pain centred just under her ribs drew everything into its emptiness. She hit her face with her fists and then hit the floor with her head. There was none of the relief of denial. There was no phantom limb. She was gone. There was no way of hiding from it in any kind of hope. They hadn't been that stupid.

From force of habit, when the sun came up, she rang Diane and talked about work and didn't mention that there was only one of them now. She was under no illusion it was temporary. She wasn't avoiding it or anything like that. If she told people they wouldn't want to know, just like they hadn't wanted to know when it first happened, and she couldn't handle that. Not right now. But after she'd hung up, she rang Diane back.

'Hello?' Diane sounded confused.

'Also,' she said. 'She's gone.'

'Who?' Diane asked.

She thought about it. 'I'm by myself,' she said.

'Where,' Diane said.

'I don't know. Maybe inside me?'

There was silence on the phone for what seemed like a long time.

'So.' She said it like she was asking a question.

'Maybe one of you popped out,' Diane said. 'For bread.'

'We have bread,' she said.

'Does this happen?' She'd never heard Diane sound uncomfortable, not once in the twelve years they'd known her. She sounded like she would rather cut off her arm than have this conversation.

'Not that I know of,' she said.

'Yeah.' There was a noise in the background like standing up. 'We can't talk about this,' Diane said. 'You need to talk to someone else about this. I can't help you with this.'

'Oh,' she said. 'Sure. Okay. I understand. Thanks.'

'Have a good day,' Diane said, and the phone clicked before

241

she could say goodbye.

She looked at the phone. It wasn't Diane's fault. Diane wasn't perfect. If anyone looked at the situation for too long, it ruined their lives – no one wanted that. Not even the handful of women who couldn't ignore it. She needed to call Heidi, but she didn't. Maybe she needed to call Dell. Maybe Kitty and Erin were in the phonebook. She looked at the phone. She needed to either go to work or stay at home and work. She couldn't afford the flat if she didn't do both jobs. She looked around the flat. But maybe she didn't need such a big flat now. Maybe she could flat with someone else. Her spine ran cold. So, she tried again, just to feel the discomfort, like she was picking a scab – maybe she needed to move in with someone else.

The phones started to ring. It was Heidi.

'Hello?' She sounded like she was asking a question.

'Greta?' Heidi said.

'Is it?' she said.

'Hey, do you still have that pizza stone?'

'Yep.' She had to sit down.

'I'm thinking of making pizza, can I borrow it?'

'How's Dell?'

'Can I pick it up today? I wanted to use it tonight,' Heidi said.

'I'm not sure anyone will be here,' she said.

'Is the key in the same place?'

'How's Dell?' she said.

'Oh. Um. Scheming? Dishonest? A thief?' said Heidi. Another phone was ringing. 'Gotta go. I'll pop round about one. Thanks.'

She needed a shower. She walked to the bedroom and found some clothes and put some toast in the toaster and turned the shower on. If she didn't log in to the moderation job, that was the same as calling in sick. That was how she figured it worked. She didn't have a manager as such. She could mop it all up tonight when she got home from the call centre. Or they would realise sooner that she wasn't there and put someone else on her work. Surely that was how it worked. It would be easier to phone in sick for the call centre job, but she needed to get out of the house. She was running late. She'd been up all night and now she was running late.

She ran to the train station and decided to stand up all the way to work. She checked the phones. She had both phones. Just in case someone called. She only needed one of the phones, because they were both connected to the same number, but she wanted both of them. The train was busy, she had to stand. As she stared down the carriage, she saw two women sitting next to each other. An earbud each in their ears. They were identical. She hadn't seen them before, which seemed unlikely. She thought she knew all of them. But she hadn't seen these ones before. They weren't twins, she could tell by the way they moved around each other. They were like her – like she had been.

She caught their eyes and smiled, then waved, and they looked away. Out the window, in unison, like a dance to whatever they were listening to. In profile one of them had a flatter nose and she realised they were twins. She ran her waving hand down her clothes, to cover it up. She looked down at her feet and the shoes she'd put on. They were flat pumps but, in the rush to get dressed, one was black and one was navy. She looked around to see if anyone else could see or was looking, but no one else was looking.

In reality it didn't matter. It hit her as she looked at the shoes again. Either of the names would work. It wasn't going to change anything – even if she went back to the old name. Someone in the train was laughing – they must have been listening to something. But she couldn't. She tried the old name on for size, the one on their birth certificate, but it upset her so much – like it had the power to kill her from inside. People changed their names all the time. She practised it in her head. 'We're changing our names. We're just going to have one name from now on. To make it easier for everyone.' It sounded strange but okay. Could she pull it off? She wasn't ready to come clean. She was worrying about the name, because she wanted two things at once: to deceive everyone and at the same time be honest with them. She thought if she got the name right, she wouldn't have to tell them that there was only one of her now. But that was ridiculous. What was a name, anyway? It was more about the people at work than about Greta and Peggy. People felt better if they thought they could tell the difference. They liked to think there were fundamental differences. It was less creepy. She thought that if she could make the name transition first, revert both of them back to their old name, then maybe people would see the differences disappear and then she could break it to them that there was actually only one of them now. It was so complicated – a lie was always more complicated than the truth. The truth was easier to remember. They'd spent years making everyone feel okay about them and this would destroy everything.

She felt the air all around her and the weight of both the phones in her pockets – one of the phones should be at home. 'Should I make potatoes or rice?' 'Is it rubbish night tonight?' The name was a distraction. The name was a symbol of the terrible thing that had happened and her complete inability to work out how to deal with it. The train would stop soon, and she'd take her one body into the call centre and start her new life of making people feel comfortable with the fact that she had been one person and then she was two people and now she was one person again. The man laughed again in the train. Comedy was tragedy plus time. She didn't know how she could go on and it was ridiculous.

28

She was late to work and flustered by the time she got there. She passed the whiteboard and *Peggy/Greta* was halfway down the leaderboard. No one had made any calls yet; the number of calls column was wiped clean. All the names were where everyone had ended up on Friday. She walked to her desk and went to put her bag on the desk and some things fell out on the floor. A packet of cashew nuts, a tampon and their wallet. She leaned over to pick everything up and the zip on her wallet wasn't shut and change and cards fell all over the floor from the height she'd lifted them to. She bent to pick them up and then Donna's feet were beside her.

'Hi,' Donna was holding two cups of coffee.

She nodded at Donna.

'Tough morning?' Donna held out one of the coffees.

'Oh.' She looked around the office like she was trying to remember, so she looked like she was answering honestly. 'Oh. No. All good.' She took the cup from Donna and drank it.

'Cool.' Donna looked over at her desk. Duncan was standing beside it. 'Oh. Gotta go.' Donna was gone, and it seemed like it was going to be that easy. She worked all morning, not looking up. She had morning tea with Niall and June, and they talked about things and it looked like very little was different except her, and that didn't seem to have made a ripple on anything. She had lunch at her desk. It was busy, easy, and then before she knew it it was five o'clock and she could go home. And it was going to be this easy.

At home she went straight to the bedroom door. She stood and swung it open and shut, watching as it went, trying to look behind it as she swung it. Then she remembered the computer and realised she still had a day's work to do. She sat in front of it and logged in and it was fine, there were no messages, just a whole bunch of comments to read and release. The login would work anywhere and she wondered if maybe she could log in at the call centre. She started reading the comments. The script was there but it wasn't working – she shut it down and started it up again and it still didn't work. 'Fuck,' she said, and started reading the comments – skim-reading them for keywords then reading them more deeply after that. She settled into the work and after an hour or so she got up and made some noodles.

Maybe it was going to be all right. Maybe it would even be better. She was tired but lots of people worked hard. She might be able to keep the flat. She went to lean into someone who wasn't there and the groaning hole deep inside her opened up again and she had to read the comments through tears.

29

She walked around a lot in the days following – like she was looking for something. It was a mindfuck and in her clear-headed moments she knew there was nothing to find. She wasn't either of them, she was both of them and if someone used one of the names it meant nothing. It didn't matter at all. She was the same. In every single way. Nothing had changed about her – except instead of being split over two bodies she was back in one. Like she had been for all the terrible years before that night twelve years ago. She had never looked after herself until there were two of her, and now everything had collapsed again and she was by herself, so it made sense to go back to the old name, the name she was called when she did all the terrible things.

She was one again. She had been two, and now she was one again. Heidi had called Peggy and Greta slippery sometimes – like they were clumsy, like she hadn't been careful enough, and maybe Heidi was right. She needed to go back to the old name – it was the honest thing to do. But this going back and forward about it in her head was a coping mechanism, delaying the hurt. She berated herself for not being able to just do it. She talked to herself a lot more than they had talked to each other. It was incessant. Then she wondered if maybe she was someone completely new. If she was going to change her name, why not change it to something completely new? But the old name would still be on all the records. She could be two people, she had been – but not like that. But did she need to? Why not just let people call her what they wanted?

'Peggy,' Donna said to her the next day at work, and she said, 'Yes.'

'I'm having a fucking rough time,' Donna said, and then a look of disgust went over her face for an instant. 'Wait,' she said. 'Are you Greta?'

'Well,' she started.

'Fuck you,' Donna said. 'Both of you. That's fucked up.' And Donna didn't speak to her for the rest of the day and the next day she only talked to her about work and then only over email. That was just the start. She upset everyone in the call centre. She was always in the wrong place at the wrong time and just the sight of her annoyed people, she could read it in their faces. Everything that had worked before didn't work anymore, and it got worse each day.

She put off calling Heidi for almost a week. When she'd got home on the first day, the pizza stone was gone and there was a block of chocolate waiting on the bench with a handwritten note pulled from a diary that just said *Thanks – Heidi*. Heidi had called a few times, but they didn't always reply straight away. It wouldn't have seemed odd from Heidi's end. Then finally, after a week, she called Heidi.

'Oh, hi,' Heidi said. She could hear her repositioning herself on a couch or a bed. Sitting up. 'How are you two?'

'Good,' she said.

'Cool.' Heidi was looking at something now, she could hear her rustling paper around on a table.

'Are you free for dinner tonight?'

'Oh.' Heidi was probably looking at her watch or at the

time on the clock beside her bed. 'Yeah. Seven?'

'Yeah.'

'Tom yum?'

'Yeah. Cool. See you there.'

They hung up and she looked around the flat. Now she had to go. There wasn't another way to do it. Unless – she looked at her phone – unless she called again and said they'd forgotten about something and couldn't go.

The tom yum place was busy, but Heidi had a table for three. Heidi's face changed a little when she saw her come in. It was only for a second, but it changed, like she was seeing the whole thing all at once. Like what had happened was written all over her body and the way she held herself. She walked over and sat down opposite Heidi.

'Oh,' said Heidi.

'Yeah,' she said.

'Hm.'

They sat in silence for a minute.

'What happened?'

She shrugged. Then she made an exploding action with one hand and mouthed, 'Poof.'

'You're kidding?' Heidi said.

She shook her head.

'Oh.' Heidi looked down now. 'Peggy.' For a moment her heart rose but then Heidi looked at her and said, 'Peggy?' and she shrugged again. They looked at their menus. 'Fuck,' Heidi said suddenly. 'You're neither of them, eh?' Then, 'Wait. Is it correcting itself?' Heidi lowered her menu and looked at her. 'Is everything going back to the way it was?'

They ordered tom yum but didn't say much else. Then Heidi said, 'Does it matter?'

She shrugged.

'The name,' Heidi said.

'It seems to,' she said.

'Oh,' Heidi said.

She looked around. 'I'm going to the loo.'

Meeting Heidi had been a mistake, but she was here now. She looked at herself in the mirror above the basin. She thought about the layout of the restaurant and whether she could leave without Heidi seeing her.

A woman paying her bill watched her as she walked back to the table. When she got there the food had arrived.

'I'm almost positive you could carry "Peggy",' Heidi said.

'It was your gut feeling,' she said. 'When you first saw me.'

Heidi nodded. 'I'm pretty sure I only corrected myself to be polite. You know. We hate that.'

'We hate that.' Something settled a little bit. 'Do it again,' she said.

'Peggy,' Heidi said, but they both knew it wasn't right. 'That's not going to work.'

'No. It's like the first time,' she said. 'It's like I'm back how I was before the first time happened. But different. Missing something. Or with too much of something.'

The soup was hot. They blew on it. It was hard to tell when it was cool because there was so much spice in it. Even when it was cold, it bit. There were mushrooms and noodles in it and hunks of tofu, slippery between their chopsticks.

'I don't suppose ...' she said, but Heidi shook her head before she could finish.

'Dell's still here. I checked while you were in the bathroom.'

'Yeah,' she said. 'It's not really like that.'

'No,' Heidi said.

'I don't really know anyone else.'

'Kitty and Erin?' Heidi said.

'Yeah, but I wouldn't know how to get hold of them.'

'Carola and Lotte?'

She frowned with her whole face. 'Oh god,' she said. 'Carola and Lotte? I'd rather never know. I hate them.'

'Yeah,' Heidi said. 'You're right. I only really bump into them anyway. I don't have a number or know where they work or anything.'

'We've spent years trying to not be in the same place as them,' she said, and then she groaned like she just couldn't bring herself to think about Carola and Lotte.

'Is there anyone else?' Heidi asked.

There wasn't. It had been such a limited thing in the tiny part of the town where they lived – between the four avenues – and only a split second. It was amazing there were as many of them as there were. People knew about them, but they were such a small moment in time.

'Have you thought about Facebook?'

They both laughed. It felt good to laugh.

'It really doesn't matter,' she said. She had tilted the bowl towards her and was using the ceramic spoon now. 'Like, not really. It's not like there's anything to be done.'

'You'll be fine,' Heidi said. 'Like, it will take you close to death. But you'll be fine.'

'Is that what it was like for you?' she said. 'When you left Dell?'

'Yeah,' Heidi said through a mouthful of noodles. 'No. Look, Dell is just a thorn in my fucking side. I don't miss her at all. If you've got to be alone, it's much easier if it happens like this – the same way you got not-alone.'

She nodded. There was a clear space on every side of her. She kept turning to watch herself, but she wasn't there. She hadn't had to carry on a whole conversation for a long time.

Not for twelve years. It was all wrong. She was working with every ounce of her strength to keep herself sitting at the table and eating the noodles. They were hot. The soup burned her mouth numb. First her tongue, then, with the next mouthful, the roof of her mouth and in between her teeth. Soon her whole mouth was bigger, swollen with the scald. Heidi wasn't talking much anymore. She was blowing on her soup and looking at her phone beside her on the table.

'Margaret,' Heidi said, and shook her head.

'I know,' she said.

'Who the fuck calls their kid Margaret?' asked Heidi.

'My drunk mum,' said Margaret, through her numb mouth.

'It's terrible.'

'Mmm.'

'Patron saint of expectant mothers,' Heidi said, and they both started laughing. 'Your mother was a narcissist.'

'She told me it meant pearl,' Margaret said.

'She would,' Heidi said.

'Heathen,' Margaret said, and then, 'Fuck.'

'You could just take one of the other ones. People shorten their names all the time.'

'It doesn't seem right,' she said. 'People get upset. They think I'm trying to fuck with them.'

'It's a terrible name.'

'Yeah,' she said. 'It's my name.'

'People change their names all the time,' Heidi said.

'If I change it, I have to do things – bureaucratically. If I don't change it, I have to do nothing – less than nothing.'

'What will you do about work?' Heidi said. There was something in her tone and in her eyes. She could see opportunities opening up. 'You can't do both jobs.'

Margaret shrugged. 'I kind of have been,' she said finally.
Heidi looked over her spoon.

'I can't sleep,' she said.

'Is that sustainable?' Heidi put down her spoon and wiped her mouth with the serviette.

'I can't actually see any other way through,' said Margaret. Heidi didn't say anything.

'I need both jobs to pay for the flat and everything.'

'There's only one of you eating now,' Heidi said.

'I'm not sure it will make a huge difference,' she said. 'The real cost is the rent.'

'You could get a credit card now,' Heidi said. 'Like, a proper one and a proper job. Now there's just one of you.'

'I'll need proof,' she said.

Heidi nodded and looked at her soup again. 'Do you, though?' she said, and she sort of waved her hand. 'Really it's just going back to normal. The way they've been pretending it is this whole time.'

'Do you think?'

'I think this has definitely happened before,' Heidi said.

'Like this, though?'

'Probably,' said Heidi. 'It was like this the first time.'

Margaret didn't say anything.

'You're not that special,' Heidi said.

'No,' she laughed. 'Probably not.' They both laughed.

'It must have.' And then Heidi stopped eating for a moment. 'Really,' she said, 'you're living the dream.'

Margaret laughed like she was an actor in a play.

'Like, it'll be bad for a while.' Heidi leaned forward slightly, like she was confiding in her, or supporting her. 'But, eventually, it won't be tough, and you'll get over it and then . . .' she wiped her hand in between them both like she was wiping away something on glass, clearing a space, clearing it all away.

Margaret let her spoon sit in the soup and looked behind Heidi. She wanted her to think she was thinking about it. But she didn't need to. Probably nothing would be right ever again. 'You're probably right,' she said, and knew she could never talk to Heidi about it again. Heidi had no idea.

'Maybe it won't be perfect,' Heidi said. 'But there are a lot of advantages.' Heidi meant administratively. She was talking about money and sex. Dell hadn't been around for a long time and she was only present in Heidi's life through barriers and problems.

Margaret, the name, sat strangely on her. She panicked that maybe she'd been too fast to take it on again. That maybe the other two would be back. That if she was Margaret the other two wouldn't be able to find her because there'd be no room. Others must have disappeared – died, been killed, moved as far away as they could, which was never very far. Some must have gone mad and been incarcerated. Twelve years later, more of them must be living in ones than living in twos. That was also the nature of human beings. To split up, to live independently of anyone else.

'Yeah,' Margaret said. 'You're probably right.'

'You just need to leave work. Fuck, most people at meetings don't even notice. Everyone's worried about themselves.'

'Diane doesn't want to know.'

'Diane can't get her head around it. People have spent over a decade trying to ignore it. We never talk to anyone about it except each other and yeah, you can't spook the horses, but they'll forget. They've been trying to forget for twelve years. They don't want to know. No one wants to know and that's why this will be a seamless transition to better living.'

A chill ran down Margaret's spine. Heidi was thinking about what it meant to her, and it made Margaret see what it meant to her. If it had happened to Margaret, the possibility of it was in the world – it would have to be assimilated into the world, which meant Heidi could allege that it had happened to her. In the way she walked, in the way she held herself. It was like how a crossword was always easier to do the day after it was published. Margaret could feel Heidi watching her with a new attentiveness.

'Yeah,' Margaret said, and tilted her bowl further, so the soup swam to one corner and was deep enough again for her spoon to collect it. 'You'd tell me though, eh?' Margaret said. 'Like if you knew anything?'

'Probably not,' Heidi said. 'Not yet.'

They sat in silence for a moment, but it wasn't uncomfortable. All of Heidi's cards were on the table.

'Realistically,' said Heidi. 'If this shows you anything, it's that it wasn't supposed to happen. None of it was. This' – she pointed at Margaret with her spoon – 'is everything being put right, returning us all back to normal. We've passed the test, killed the dragon. Levelled up. It'll happen to all of us before the year's out.' She hadn't looked this happy in years. 'I guarantee it. It's just a fuck-up, and your fuck-up has been unfucked.'

30

Once Margaret started looking, there were lots of women who looked like her. There was very little outstanding about them. They were of average height. They weren't unusually skinny. They weren't exactly average but there were a lot of women that looked like Peggy and Greta.

She went out a lot. She would work for five hours when she got home, or sometimes go to a meeting and then go out to the bars and nightclubs around the city. She would sit and drink Coke or lime and soda and watch all the women who looked like them. Often, she would talk to them and for a while they would stand at her shoulder and she felt the hum come off them the way it used to when she was two. No one needed to know much about her and often they would come home with her. There weren't many hours in the day. Not for working and fucking. But she fitted it all in. No matter what time she went to bed she woke up at the same time. She would ask if they wanted to stay but no one wanted that much. Not after they'd just met.

The first woman she slept with came home with her effortlessly after only a couple of hours in the bar. She said her name was Rachel. Rachel had a bob like they had worn in the early nineties. Margaret ran her hands through Rachel's hair as they kissed. It was straight and shiny. There was slightly more of it, but she seemed to be able to forget that. She held Rachel's face in both her hands and felt the angle of her cheekbones and the way Rachel's jaw felt as her mouth worked. Rachel's neck was millimetres shorter and Margaret hit the clavicle faster than she'd thought she would, but Rachel's breasts were perfect and for a second Margaret was able to explain herself back to herself as a separate, complete thing, not waiting or looking for anything or anyone, not wrong. They were in the spare bedroom, with all the computers. Every part of the house reminded her except for this room. Greta and Peggy had sex in this room but not as often, and the hum of the computers was enough to change the temperature. It was early in the morning. Sex early in the morning tended to be in Peggy and Greta's bed in the other room. They would roll into each other and hardly wake. Kissing softly, penetrating slowly – eyes never opened. In rhythm, lacklustre stroke for stroke so that it felt like masturbating. Leaning more than anything, then coming and falling back to sleep as the calm and pleasure rolled through them.

Her hand was in Rachel now. Knuckle-deep in her, thumb on her clitoris – gently rolling it in the wet and warmth that leaked from her. Her chin was on Rachel's shoulder, so she could look at the wall, not be confused by the face or the ears or the hair. Everything was dampness and grip in the high march towards the jumping off place. Rachel fumbled for her half-heartedly, settled for her thigh, grabbed, held. Rachel's voice humid in her ear. The low moans backgrounded by the urgency of someone drunk on what they wanted. Rachel didn't know her from Adam – Margaret hadn't told her her name. But she was here now. Could Rachel trust her to take her all the way? She inserted another finger, her pinkie slipping back towards Rachel's anus which throbbed and sucked as she moved towards and away from her. Towards and away. Close, close, then as far away as she dared. Finally, Rachel came and for a second Margaret was held there, pulled further in and the woman was panting in her ear and then reaching for her and then kissing her breasts, looking up at her. Then her stomach, and her thigh, still sharp from Rachel's grip – fingernails almost breaking skin. Then Rachel eased Margaret's legs open and her mouth sat differently but it was okay. With nothing to do she ran her hands through Rachel's hair while her tongue mapped out the boundary of Margaret's clitoris, breathing on it as she did. She moved slightly with Rachel and then Rachel had two fingers in her, deep, she felt herself widen and then it was everything all at once and in perfect time. Tongue quickly over her clitoris, hand deep in her cunt. The boundary between them became clearer and she arched her back and her head fell back and she called out fuck and for a split second she was two again. And then in the aftermath the air came in between them, and she could feel all of Rachel and it was all wrong. The space she took up. The way she moved. The strange way she couldn't synchronise their breathing. But it had been close. For a second in time. For the first time since it happened, Margaret felt right.

Rachel didn't stay. She got up and started pulling on her clothes and Margaret realised she wanted Rachel to stay.

'You don't have to go,' she said.

'Nah,' said Rachel. 'I do.'

'But it's really early.' She was squinting at her phone.

'Nah.' Rachel was pulling her boots on now. 'Thank you' – and she kissed her – 'but I need to go.'

'Can I have your phone number?' Margaret was sitting up now.

'No,' Rachel said.

'I might see you at the bar,' Margaret said.

Rachel shrugged. 'You never know.' But she wasn't looking at her. They probably wouldn't see each other again.

'That was good though?' Margaret realised how she sounded. Rachel was drunk and she was sober, and she sounded whiny.

'It was great.' Rachel kissed her on the top of her head and left.

Margaret kept going back to the bar. Not drinking, just looking, and sometimes she found what she was looking for and sometimes she didn't. But when she woke up, always at the same time that they woke up, she was alone. No one wanted to be leaned on that much, she realised. They could tell that there was something different about her. Something needy. They circled her. Kept her at a distance, even when they were knuckle-deep in each other. So, she stopped saying 'You could stay' and instead just said 'Thanks', and joined the march towards what she wanted. That moment. She never got used to coming alone. She learnt to masturbate but that was even stranger.

She videoed herself, close up, so all she could see were her hands and her cunt and she watched it while she made herself come. Using the exact same strokes. A copy of a copy. It was the closest she could get, and it was better than having anyone else there. She would stop going to the bar so often, maybe. She knew she wouldn't stop going to the bar, but for now the video worked fine, if she let it rest as close to her face as she could. She missed the smell and the taste, but it was as close as she was going to get. She was back at the bar the following night.

She had lunch with Heidi on Saturdays. They'd stopped going for tom yum. 'There's a new Korean place,' she'd said to

Heidi about a month after it happened. She'd looked up all the new places in the area. Had said it a few times in the mirror before she left home to meet Heidi. 'There's a new Korean place,' she said to herself in the mirror. Looking for any flinch. The first time she said it, she cried a bit. They needed to say goodbye to the tom yum place, and she wouldn't go there again with Heidi. Maybe she would go by herself. Later. When she was feeling better.

31

Margaret went to meetings three times a week. It was the place where things were most the same. The place she could let her guard down, where she was least likely to make a mistake. She threw herself in. At first some people called her Greta and asked where Peggy was. Others called her Peggy and asked where Greta was and then, gradually, she started introducing herself as Margaret and the people in the meetings took her word for it and it was relatively seamless. New people were coming all the time, and the ones who had known them for a long time believed her and moved on.

It was Wednesday. For the last six months, on Wednesdays, Peggy and Greta had set up each week for the meeting. So, it was ready when everyone else got there. Margaret did it by herself now. She arrived forty-five minutes early, opened the door and put on the kettle. She'd bought a small carton of milk from the dairy on the way, and there was a plastic container of instant coffee, another of generic-looking tea bags, and a large one with white sugar in it. She opened the top of the sugar container and, seeing it, went to the drawer next to the sink and got a teaspoon. She fished out the clots that were made when people put wet teaspoons back into the container to get more sugar. People did that. The people that came to the meeting. Some of the meetings were using single-use cups and sugar wrapped individually in packets even though the venue provided some coffee mugs and a dishwasher. Still, she'd always brought her own cup from home when there were two of her, and she continued to bring one now.

Peggy and Greta had tried to help out where they could. It was annoying sometimes but it had made them happy. She needed to be setting up the room and fishing the clots out of the sugar to stay close. So much had changed and so much would change, and there were the bars. She looked out the window. The next-door neighbours' backyard was close. She could see their washing on the line. It was a big house. There were lots of men living in it. She hadn't talked to Diane about the bars. If there had been two of them going to the bars, eventually one of them would have said, 'The worst ideas are the ones we don't want to share with her.' And they would have been right. They would have been able to provide evidence. Be able to say, 'Remember when we went back to sex work? And we didn't tell her about the money we were keeping in the closet and not paying tax on and how we decided to have a client over at our place so we would get all the money, and he stole *all* the money in our closet, and we had nothing? Remember? For all that work? Nothing.' They would have been right.

Being sober in this way was a continuing journey into places and events that seemed completely different but were probably the same.

She got her phone out and rang Diane. People started arriving for the meeting. It was all set up. She walked outside to talk on the phone and waved at them, smiling and indicating the phone. People smiled back. Some gave her sideways hugs, some rubbed her arm, some just smiled. It was that same feeling of being home that Peggy and Greta had found in the other city. Some strange kinship. She hadn't noticed it for a while, but it was like this. It used to come over them when they weren't fully expecting it. It felt like what they'd thought god must feel like.

Diane picked up. Margaret had walked a long way from the meeting room so no one would hear. The first bit of a conversation like this was the worst. The saying hello and asking how Diane was and answering when Diane asked her. She wanted to blurt it out. Always, she just wanted to shout it. For years they'd rehearsed everything, worked out how to make the thing they'd done sound the best it could. But in the last few years, since the angry bottle of wine that had turned up at their flat, they'd just wanted to blurt things out using whatever language they could summon.

'I've been going to bars a lot,' she said when Diane asked how she was. 'By myself.'

'What for?' Diane said.

'Sex,' she said. 'Mainly.'

'How do you feel about that?'

'The sex?'

'Yeah, if you want,' said Diane.

'I like the sex,' she said.

'We all like the sex.' They both laughed.

'I'm just not sure about the bars.'

'Hm,' Diane said.

'Or the way I'm getting the sex.' There was a certain kind of power in being a sober person at a bar full of drunk people, which Margaret was increasingly uncomfortable with. 'That's probably what's eating me up the most,' she said. 'If I'm honest.'

'Being around all that booze must be tricky too,' Diane said.

'Yeah,' Margaret said. She felt more and more like she was in the wrong place.

'Sometimes I tell myself I'm going somewhere for one reason and actually there's another reason I can't quite see,' Diane said.

'Yeah,' said Margaret. 'There could be a bit of that.'

'Sometimes I get a bit of a hit off just being around the stuff,' said Diane.

'Yeah,' Margaret said.

They only talked for five minutes and Diane didn't tell her what to do, but Margaret felt better than she had in weeks when she hung up. Diane didn't have an opinion. It really was up to Margaret. Diane talked about her experience – how it was hard to know where to get sex when you didn't drink. Talking about it shone some light on it and in the light Margaret could see it for what it was – there were corners she hadn't seen into before. Sometimes she went to the old solutions for new problems. Sometimes, when you'd used a hammer for a long time, even if it was a long time ago, every problem still looked like a nail.

32

Margaret looked at the clock at the bottom of the screen. It was 3:30am.

It had been a busy night on the sports website. She was barely getting away with just working at night. Every couple of days there would be a message from the head moderator saying something like 'Did you see this?' and 'I think this needs faster attention'. She'd reply. Buy herself more time. Sometimes she logged in to the moderation board at work, at lunchtimes. She wasn't supposed to, had to do it in secret, minimising the screen to the point it was useless anyway. Really all she was doing was logging in, so it looked like she was working. She wasn't able to work. They monitored everything at the call centre. Duncan called her in and showed her the log and the first few times she said she must have done it by mistake. It was a lame excuse, but she just needed a bit more time.

'Greta,' he said. 'You can't do this.'

She nodded. The next time he called her into the office he gave them both a verbal warning. She was going to say 'It was an accident' again, but they both knew she'd signed in and visited a couple of pages and that was not what people did when they were accidentally somewhere.

She continued to be weird at work. The tiredness was

adding to it. She couldn't carry on even the most mundane conversations. Donna and Mira had stopped asking if they wanted to go out for lunch in the weekend. She sat by herself in the staffroom at the short breaks, or went for a walk outside. She gave everyone a bad feeling.

Eventually no one stopped by Peggy and Greta's desk anymore and Margaret started eating lunch at it every day, so she never saw anyone in the staffroom and she always made sure to walk to the train station by herself. Sometimes she'd get on the train early and one of their workmates would come on the train, see her and pretend they hadn't so they could sit somewhere else.

Earlier tonight she was walking home from the station and realised she was going to leave the call centre job. There were always messages and emails about other work she could do at home. Some of the work was way more lucrative. A site where people uploaded pictures of their pets needed people to check that none of the photos included sexually explicit content. The script was working better and better on the words and she was pretty sure she'd be able to train it to analyse images. There was this other thing, a friend-type thing, which needed people to check for hate speech and advertising. Both needed maximum discretion because the sites had told shareholders they could do all the moderation through an algorithm and the pet site had lots of very young users.

Now it was 4:00am. The script was humming away behind the email window happily. 'Automagical,' she said to herself, and she smiled at the script – she never knew if she was ahead of anyone, but she was in the ballpark, and she didn't need it to be a crazy success. She just needed it to work well enough for her to check a lot of items quickly so she could make as much money as possible.

33

On her last day, they brought out the barbecue and she brought in some beers and steaks and made salad. In the end it was a kind sort of farewell. People asked where Greta was and others asked where Peggy was, and she said, 'Oh, I think she's here.' And people would look around a bit and say, 'Oh. Okay. Cool.'

People were politely interested in where she was going and when she told them she was going to freelance from home some of them said, 'Living the dream.' She smiled and nodded. 'You'll put on weight,' Duncan said. She must have looked confused for a moment and he said, 'All that food, just sitting there waiting for you to eat it.' She laughed. 'And your kitchen will get clean,' June shouted from across the group. She laughed at that too. There was a lot of housework to do when there was just one of her, but she was keeping up. She had to keep telling herself that. That everyone else did it. That really she'd been spoilt for twelve years. That really this was what grown-ups did. This was growing up. And then while doing the housework she would find herself sitting in the doorway between the kitchen and the bedroom again, looking at the hinges and looking at her watch, and she'd been sitting there for an hour. There wasn't time for that kind of self-indulgence. It was such a bind: the grieving took so much time and the loss meant there was much less time for grieving.

Finally, everyone said, 'Speech. Speech.' She stood up and lifted her bottle of water in front of her and said, 'We just want to say – thank you. We've been really looked after here. You have all been great and we've enjoyed working here. Thank you and cheers.' And everyone applauded, lifted their glasses and cans and bottles and said 'Hear, hear' and 'Cheers' and things like that because there wasn't really a word for what you said after a toast and if there was, this group of people did not know it.

She helped Duncan tidy up after everyone left. They filled large black bags with cans and paper plates and the leftover food which wouldn't last until Monday. They talked mainly about the clearing up. As they were facing away from each other he said, 'When did she go?' And she didn't stop picking up what she was picking up and just made a small, non-committal 'Mm' noise.

'The other one,' Duncan said.

'Oh,' she said, like she hadn't really thought about it.

'I reckon you've been by yourself for about two months,' Duncan said. Maybe to help her out.

'Yeah,' she said, making a noise of agreement. 'About that.'

'Did she leave?' he asked.

'Yeah,' she said, wiping down a bench.

'Like, on her feet, or in a car?' he said.

'Something like that,' she said.

'Did you have a fight?'

She thought about it for a moment. 'No.' But it was more like a question.

'My sister.' He was continuing to pack up. 'She just disappeared.' He waited a moment to see if Margaret would say something else. 'Like . . .' He tipped a bowl of chips into the black bag and it made a rustling noise. 'She was one, when we were growing up, and then she was two – like you two – and then one day she was one again. Like, just like that.'

'Oh,' she said. And neither of them said anything, and for what seemed like a long time there was just the noise of cleaning up and then she said, 'It was like that.'

'My sister,' Duncan said. Stopping now, looking out the window. 'Well, you know what happened there.'

She nodded. Duncan's sister, the only one he mentioned, so that Margaret had always thought she'd always been just one, had killed herself. 'Yeah, well. Just saying.' Then he mumbled, 'Keep going to meetings. Don't pick up a drink.' He went to another room and when he came back he said, 'Don't forget. I can write you a reference. It will be a really good one. You two have been really good workers.'

They walked to the station together and as his train arrived they shook hands and he said, 'All the best. We'll miss you both.' And she said, 'Thank you for everything.' And he was gone, and she had promised to go back and visit and maybe she would. One day.

34

The next morning it was Saturday and for a long time Margaret couldn't get out of bed. She woke up and couldn't get out of bed. The sun came into the room and it got hotter and stuffier and she lay on her back and looked at the ceiling and then rolled over and looked at the wall and the space that was empty next to her and she shut her eyes and rested with them shut and listened to the noise of her own breathing and her pulse in her ears and behind her eyes and in her temples. An hour went by, then two and then it was one o'clock in the afternoon. She checked her phone, but no one had called, and no one had messaged, and she realised no one missed her. She was hungry. Dizzy. Probably more from thirst than hunger, but she was hungry, and she just couldn't get up and there was no one to get her any food and she was between a rock and a hard place. Hungry and wanting to stay in bed. She couldn't have it all. That was life – compromise.

When they were drinking, when they were maybe not even eighteen, a guy had told them that was their problem – they were never willing to compromise. And then he'd stormed out and they'd laughed. Both of them had the memory, but there had only been one of them when it happened.

'Do you remember that, too?' one of them would whisper.

'Of course,' the other one would say.

They talked about it, late at night, inches from each other, in whispers. But now there was no one for Margaret to turn to. No one to talk to about any of it. Heidi didn't want to know, and Margaret didn't know any of the others well enough anymore to even know how to contact them and was she even one of them now?

On the night it happened, Peggy and Greta found themselves next to each other. Everything except the handful of them was in the right place when it happened. Everyone else was sober and together – in themselves. Margaret had been blacked out. She was walking around and moving around but not all of her was in the margins of her body, so her guard was down – she had no defence.

Peggy and Greta asked the others. It had to be quick because it was rude, and you had to catch them off guard. You got one shot. Someone had asked them – that was how they'd started to understand it, and that's why they started asking the others.

'Blackouts, eh?' they'd say.

'Yeah.'

'Were you blacked out the night this happened?' Pointing at each other, not pointing at the other two.

'Yeah. What?'

'Nothing.'

Now, it seemed, they'd been wrong. They'd been sober this time and maybe there was no real connection between the blackouts and the drinking, maybe they were random and would continue to happen. So, what was the use of not drinking? And wouldn't a drink make it all feel better?

She opened her eyes, looked at the ceiling and then shut her eyes tight again and tried to make it happen, but it wasn't going to. It was the dizziness and the hunger that did it. Gave her the impression that if she just tried enough, she could make it happen again, so there'd be two of them again.

A negative version of the sunlight in the windows projected onto her eyelids and for a moment she could feel them both in the bed. The bed gave a little with the weight of them both and she could feel warmth in the top of her arm, and she opened her eyes in surprise, in hope, but there was only space.

She remembered there was bread in the fridge that she'd brought home from her going-away barbecue last night. Soft and white – not like they normally ate. Also tomatoes, and she could either eat the bread fresh and soft or toast it. Or she could do both and have a selection.

She rolled out of bed and onto her knees, like they did in the old days, and prayed. Words she'd been taught, and then, quietly, 'Take me,' then, 'Or fix this.' She cried and lay on the floor on her side with her eyes open, looking under the bed, and then she saw something. She reached out. It was a long way from her, and she had to stretch. Once she had it in her hand, she looked at it. It was a phone she'd never seen before. She pushed the power button and some black pixels played on the small grey screen and were gone. She pushed the power button again and nothing happened. She was sitting up now. She looked behind her, like there was someone there. Like someone was watching her, or at least with her in the room. She looked at the phone again – she was sure it was a phone.

It looked old and like a toy. A small white rectangular box, thicker than the flip-phone Margaret used now, with a stubby blue aerial that looked like the cap of a felt-tip pen. Three-quarters of it fitted in the palm of her hand. If she put her index finger out it balanced comfortably. The screen was small. Most of the phone was buttons made of hard plastic that clicked when she pushed them. When she lifted it up and looked over the top of it, she could see through the parts of the buttons that protruded from the body of the phone, and under the clear plastic bubbles were blue labels with white numbers and yellow Kanji and English characters. Just like on her phone, 2 was ABC, 3 was DEF, and so on. The grey screen was surrounded by a watery border of light blue. Swimming in the border were small cartoons in fine black outlines. Each picture had zip ribbons around it to show sound and movement – a vehicle raced while the front of it rotated, the antennae on an egg beeped, a square-looking duck quacked. At the bottom of the screen in bubble letters filled in yellow, bordered in blue it said TAMAGOTCHI. The small egg-like digipets had been huge and then disappeared, superseded by new games. They looked like a joke next to The Sims and Animal Crossing. She held it out. Maybe it wasn't a phone – maybe it was a Tamagotchi in the shape of a phone? But it had three diagonal lines at the top and three dots at the bottom. One set of holes for listening, one for talking, and the numbers and the letters. It was a relic of a crossroads – phones for kids, games for phones. History would only go one way and because the phone was both it felt older than it really was. The idea of it was ancient. From here it looked like it was hedging the wrong bets.

Margaret reached for her phone on the bedside table and the weight difference was noticeable even though they were both small objects that did the same thing. Her phone was light and slim and smooth. She flipped it open and looked at the buttons, which were moulded from a single sheet of plastic – soft and easy to depress. She could flip her phone open and work it from one hand. The phone from under the bed was hard and stiff – there wasn't a soft piece of plastic on it. She'd seen phones like it, and she'd seen Tamagotchi, but not something like this. She pushed the power button, but it was still dead.

Neither of the chargers for the phones Peggy and Greta

used fitted the Tamagotchi phone. She crawled under the bed again but there was nothing there. She slid herself over towards the bottom drawer beside the bed. She knew it was a shambles. She shook it and pulled it open. It was full of cords and plugs and compact discs used to load software. There were even a couple of floppy disks, an old portable CD player and a Walkman which was the same size as a cassette tape. She pulled things out one by one. The cords pulled still more cords out. She untangled them as they came. Then she was really hungry and walked, with a few cords in her hands and the Tamagotchi phone nestled under her arm, to the fridge and took out some hummus and carried it back to the bedroom in her mouth while she untangled cords.

In the end everything was laid out on the floor. All the cords were in order of appliance. There were eight chargers. She stood up eating a sandwich now and looked at all the cords and plugs and discs lined up on their bedroom floor like it was a garage sale. She looked at the chargers especially. She was scared to look at the chargers because she knew none of them would fit. She looked at her watch. There was an electronics shop that would be open for a few hours yet – a backstop, she liked that. The charger would cost a lot. A lot more than she should be spending on a whim. She needed all the money she had now that she didn't have a regular job. She looked out the window, chewing loudly and open-mouthed, rolling the new phone over and over in her hand. Then she snapped back to the chargers. Three of them were for bigger appliances. There was a 4.5×3.0, which was probably for a laptop they'd picked up from someone and repaired and sold. Why would they still have that? Maybe they'd bought a better charger. Maybe it didn't work? There was a Toshiba 6.3x3.0 and some other plug-looking plug. Then there were several with the flatter pins, which were more likely to be for a phone. Several people had brought them phones that weren't working. One had stopped working because it got wet. Not very wet, their friend had explained to them. It had been in a bag and it rained and maybe two drops had got on it and then it hadn't worked again. But then the phones got better and cheaper and people brought them phones less often and then there were phones in the secondhand shops, and they intrigued Peggy and Greta. They kept thinking about that conversation with Dell all those years ago about the device that you could take everywhere that they would always be looking at. Whenever they went anywhere, they carried an iPod and their phone. They had to attach their iPod to their laptop, then download the music and podcasts they wanted to listen to. They had a big brickish iPod. There were smaller ones, but they liked the big one – it felt like it would last longer, and they'd had it for years and they didn't have enough money to replace it. They bought better phones. They couldn't afford it, but the call centre job had given them an employee discount because the internet company had shares in a phone company. At least two of the chargers were from phones they had owned and discarded. She looked at the Tamagotchi phone again. Maybe they'd had three old phones, but she knew they'd never had a phone like this.

She bent down and picked up the possible chargers and sat on the bed cross-legged trying each one in the Tamagotchi phone. She hadn't let go of it all afternoon. None of the chargers fitted. She could see just from looking at the charging port that none of them would fit. She thought about forcing a couple of them, thinking it would be worth it, but then realised there was a chance she could break the whole thing. She liked the phone. She had no idea where it had come from. There had been several people in the house but none of them had come into this bedroom. It was possible it belonged to one of the women she'd brought home, but it seemed very unlikely that it had found its way into the bedroom from the computer room or the kitchen floor or the lounge.

Things were always turning up.

The thought came into her head like it wasn't hers. It stopped her and she tested it. There was a notebook in the bottom drawer. It was the one they'd used to write down the phone calls years ago after they'd punched Tyra. She opened the notebook to an empty page and with a stubby, blunt pencil started a list: the cheese grater, the liquorice, the right amount of cash. Where had Heidi got the sofa and the coffee table? Why did Dell have a spare notebook? The taxi chit, the tea and coffee – Dell and Heidi said they came from work, but they'd never pushed them. The Game & Play. She looked around again. 'Dell?' she asked the room – but there was no reply because it was ridiculous.

She kept making the list. It was starting to look like a list of things to be grateful for, things that had turned up at just the right time, reasons to believe they were being looked after by something, that maybe they didn't need to drink – not right now, not for the next five minutes. The laptop, waking up at the same time every day, the Tamagotchi phone – but not a charger. She shut the notebook and looked down. None of them would work. She looked at her watch and thought about the electronics shop and it seemed like even before she had decided she was going she was putting on her coat and pulling on a pair of jeans and ripping off another hunk of bread and putting it in her mouth as she picked up her keys and wallet and a bag to carry everything in. Doing it all with the Tamagotchi phone in her hand or under her arm or balanced on her thigh when she sat down to tie up her laces. She put it carefully in the side pocket of her jacket and zipped it up.

35

There were only men working in the electronics shop, which she never liked. But they were a lot like the guys she'd worked with at the call centre, which gave her a bit of confidence. All the men were wearing lanyards with swipe cards and security keys. She stood at a distance at one of the counters while two men finished a jokey conversation. One of them looked up and she came forward with the Tamagotchi phone already in her hand.

'I think I've lost my charger,' she said, and put the phone on the counter.

'Okay.' The guy wasn't looking at her. He was still looking at the computer on the desk for a moment and then he did look, and he picked up the phone and turned it over in his hand and laughed. 'Where'd you get this?'

She shrugged. 'You know?' she said and laughed. An exhale standing in for a laugh, just to get him on her side.

'This is really old.' He turned it over in his hand again. 'Like, maybe ten years old.'

'Oh,' she said.

'Yeah, I don't know if we can get a charger for this,' he said, typing on the computer. 'I don't think they even came out here.' He typed some more. 'Yeah, see.' He turned the screen round. 'Yeah.' He shook his head. 'It's like a PHS or a PAS. It's just meant for in a small area. It's like a walkie talkie. It's from Japan, they've never been here. It won't work here. I don't even think the game will work here – the pet. It would never have worked here. It's like a . . .' He searched for the words. 'Like a schoolgirl phone. Like – anime,' he finally said. 'Do you know anime?'

She nodded and read the screen.

'It was only in Japan,' he said, 'and only for like a few years. And for, like, kids.'

She nodded again and looked at him now. 'Can I get a charger?' she asked.

He looked at the phone again, turned it over and looked at the recharging port at the bottom. 'Theoretically,' he said. 'It won't work though.'

'I probably don't need it to work,' she said. 'I just need to turn it on.'

He nodded. 'Yeah.' He looked at it. 'Hang on.' He went out the back with the phone and she was left standing by the counter looking around the store. It wasn't very busy. It was Saturday afternoon. She noticed a woman at the back of the store, restacking shelves, and knew immediately there was another one of her at home, exactly the same, and then the door opened to the storeroom and there she was. One out the back, one in the store – it was probably working pretty well. So many of them were in technology. It was probably because you could work without being around people. Also, all the technology jobs needed ghosts in machines. They needed double the workforce. All the machines looked like they were labour-saving, but they weren't. Not really. They were all Mechanical Turks. Working away behind the screen to make it look seamless from the outside. That would all change, she thought, watching the woman hand the woman who looked exactly the same a box full of compact discs. Realistically, soon there would be no use for them at all.

The guy was back with a charger, but it didn't fit. He'd brought it over to show her, he'd already tried it out the back. 'Yeah,' he said. 'Sorry. That was sort of my last idea.'

'Could I get a new battery for it?' she asked.

He looked at the back of the phone. 'Nah. I don't think so. You could try like eBay or something. Craigslist?' He handed it back to her. 'Sorry.'

'All good,' she said.

'Yeah,' he said. 'I've never seen one of these Tamagotchi phones. It's crazy.'

She nodded and walked out of the store.

36

When she got home, she turned the house upside down. It made sense that if the phone was in the house the charger would be as well. Which also made no sense at all. If someone had left it in the house by accident it was unlikely they would have brought the charger with them. People used old phones all the time. People loved a gimmick. She took a photo of the phone and put it in one of the chatrooms.

'Holy shit,' someone replied almost immediately. 'Where the fuck did you find that?'

'PHS only?' she wrote.

'Yup,' someone else replied, and went on, 'It only works on Japan's personal handyphone system and I don't think that even exists anymore. It was a low-priced wireless service,' they explained. 'Big with teenage girls.' She knew all about the PHS and the reply looked like it had been copied and pasted from Wikipedia but that was the risk of asking this room, someone always wanted to explain things rather than just answer the question. Especially to her.

'I always wanted one,' someone else said. 'You can blast your monster to another Tamagotchi phone. So, someone else can look after it if you're away from it. Instead of having to watch it die while you're in class or a meeting. I think it's called a Tamapichi – the phone. But, yeah, what he said – it

281

only works on PHS.'

It was less use than a pager. The network was dead – it had never worked outside Japan, ever. It made no sense that anyone she'd invited round would have had a phone like this. Or at least had a phone like this they carried around. She'd cleaned under the bed countless times. She stopped, the cutlery drawer open in her hand. She looked around the house. Since she'd been alone, she hadn't cleaned much. There was so much to do. She was having trouble just keeping on top of the dishes and laundry. She went to the bedroom and looked under the bed. It was dusty and there were a couple of plastic bags under there from food she'd brought to bed. She hadn't cleaned under there since she'd been alone.

She looked further and further under the bed. She was getting covered in dust as she slithered further and further under. There was nothing. No charger, anyway. One of them would have noticed the phone, because they were always cleaning the flat and that included under the bed. There was time for that when there were two of them. She lay for a moment face down under the bed in the filth and the dust. The phone must have arrived since she'd been alone. She had to stop. She had to go and get some work done, or eat, or turn on music, or do something that normal people did. She needed to stop looking for the charger. There was a knock at the door. She pulled herself out from under the bed. It was Heidi.

'Fuck,' Heidi said. 'Filthy much?'

Margaret brushed one hand through her hair and the other down the front of her shirt. A dusty strand of hair came off in her hands. She was still holding the new phone. 'Cleaning,' she said.

'You didn't get the pizza stone out of the letterbox.' Heidi held up a plastic bag the shape of the pizza stone. 'I put it there weeks ago.' She walked into the kitchen and looked around at the mess. Drawers pulled out. Contents all over the place.

'Cleaning,' Margaret said again.

Heidi put the pizza-stone-filled plastic bag on the table.

She walked over to the kettle and turned it on. 'Do you want a cuppa?'

Margaret nodded. 'Yeah.'

'Have you eaten?'

Margaret shook her head. 'Some bread,' she said. 'A tomato.'

'Cool.' Heidi set down a paper bag on the bench and pulled two sandwiches out of it. She looked through the cupboards to find a plate.

'Cool,' Margaret said. She remembered the notebook and pencil were in the back pocket of her jeans. *Sandwiches*, she scrawled quickly, before Heidi could see her.

'You could go have a shower,' Heidi said. 'While I sort this.'

'Oh.' She looked at the bathroom. 'Yeah. Cool. Thanks.'

The bathroom misted up quickly. There was no real ventilation. The shower was tall. The whole flat had high ceilings and the shower was very tall. It had a fabric shower curtain. She brushed her hand over the misted mirror to clear enough space to look at her face. She hadn't cleaned under the bed since she'd been alone. She was sure now that the phone had arrived after it had happened, so she had even less idea who could have put it there. Sometimes things turned up because there were two of them. 'Did you buy this kiwifruit?' But there was only one of them now, unless she was sleep-walking. She looked at her face and wet hair. Was she sleep-walking?

'Has Dell been back?' she asked as she walked into the kitchen. Heidi was looking at the Tamagotchi phone.

'Thanks,' Margaret said, and grabbed it off her. With her

free hand she picked up the plate Heidi had put her sandwich on. She sat at the table and used her free hand to alternate between picking up the sandwich and drying her hair. The bag with the pizza stone was on the table. Once her hair was dry, she absentmindedly pulled the bag off, still gripping the phone. The pizza stone fell out with a clunk, but the bag wasn't empty. She held it higher and a small white dock attached to a plug fell out of it. It was a charger. She looked at it. Waiting to see if it was really there. It had pink Kanji printed on it and a picture of three small monsters.

'Did you bring this?' she asked.

'What?' Heidi's mouth was full.

Margaret held up the charger like it was a serpent. Like it was alive.

Heidi looked at it. 'It was in the letterbox,' she said, and took another bite of her sandwich. 'With the pizza stone.'

'But you didn't bring it?'

'I did not bring it,' she said. She was reading something as she ate. It was a free circular that came, even though Peggy and Greta had put a No Junk Mail sign on their letterbox.

Margaret put the charger down and laid the phone on the table next to it. She hardly needed to check. The phone sat in the dock perfectly and the charging port clicked into place. Margaret rested the notebook on her knee under the table. *Charger* she wrote without looking. She put the last of the sandwich in her mouth and stood up. She held the phone in the dock with the power cord leading out of it like a tail. She looked around her. There was a powerboard under the table, and she plugged it into one of the travel adapters that was plugged into the socket.

'What's that?' Heidi asked.

Margaret shrugged.

Heidi looked around. 'You need to get out more.'

Margaret nodded, then she remembered. 'I was out this afternoon,' she said.

'Where'd you go?' Heidi asked.

'Out,' she said. The phone was too low to turn on yet. She left it sitting on the floor beside the powerboard. She'd have to leave it for a while.

'You need to clean up as well,' Heidi said.

Margaret looked around. 'It's hard.'

'I know,' Heidi said. 'We all know. Everyone. But you just need a system. Maybe you need a smaller place, now.'

'I'm working from here now,' Margaret said.

'Oh?' Heidi looked up.

'I quit the call centre.' She was wiping crumbs off the table with her finger. 'I'm going to work at home.'

Heidi frowned in a way designed to show she was thinking, and she nodded. 'Sounds like a good idea.'

Margaret nodded.

'Things are going to be so much fucking easier for you now,' Heidi said. 'You can claim back the office, the internet, computers and clothes. You only have to look after yourself. You can get a driver's licence and a passport. You can travel.'

Margaret nodded. She was digging a trough between the sprinkled crumbs on the table.

'It's just, Greta . . .' Heidi said.

'Margaret,' she said.

Heidi made a face like it was all sinking in. Like she was planning her next move, in the light of some new move that Margaret didn't realise she'd made.

'I told you,' Margaret said. 'When we had tom yum.'

'You didn't seem convinced.' Heidi was turning a page in the circular over then back.

'I'm convinced now.'

'Really?'

Margaret looked around the kitchen. 'For now,' she said.

'Makes sense,' Heidi said and looked through the junk mail some more. Then she looked up. 'We could go for a walk?'

'I have to work,' Margaret said. The phone's small red light was flashing less and less. It was charging up.

Heidi only stayed another ten minutes. She had little patience for this kind of thing. She couldn't stay too long in proximity to it. Heidi was busy. A deep kind of busy. She was busy in her soul, and this sort of thing, an untidy kitchen with a person newly alone, agitated her. Heidi left, making an excuse – another thing to do, a thing she'd forgotten about that she needed to do – and the phone charged some more, and Margaret was alone with it at last. Alone with it charged enough to be turned on, and she crawled under the table on all fours and then down on her elbows so she could hold it in both hands. She turned it on, and it hummed a little with the effort of coming to life and in the bottom of the tiny screen was a small envelope with a 1 on top of it. She used the hard, clicky arrow keys on the face of the phone to navigate to the envelope and opened it and there was a message. There were a couple of read messages and no unread messages – like it was a brand-new phone. She clumsily navigated to the message and there it was, black pixels carving out letters on the grey pixels. *Are u awake? Is there snow there?*

37

Margaret carried the phone everywhere. She sat it on the bathroom bench and looked at it as she brushed her teeth. She looked at it a lot. First just to make sure it wouldn't go away and then to make sure she didn't miss it when it chimed. She didn't want to starve the tiny pixelated monster who needed food and medicine and fun but more importantly she didn't want to miss any of the messages. The envelope in the corner of the screen would change and sometimes it vibrated. Buzzed across tables. The phone wasn't small enough to fit in her pocket so she had to carry it in her hand. She would stuff it under the belt of her pants. She wore it around the house this way. She slept with it beside her and sometimes it would squeal in the night and she'd wake up to feed the monster or read a message. Sometimes another monster would be there, and she would look after that as well.

There would be a rise in her body when the messages arrived. *K.*, then maybe a couple of hours later *Eh.. is it? What time ur sis timing?* Then:

Hee.. reached. I wait on top k.

K.

Kk .. :) dm got say anything?

Ok.:-).

K.

k.

k.

Sometimes there were days' worth of *k*'s and *No*'s and *Ya*'s. She wrote all the messages in the notebook next to the times and dates they arrived. She carried the notebook everywhere too – not just for the messages but for recording anything she hadn't noticed before.

She replied to the messages. She would try sometimes. *Wru?* or, *What u want?* The messages that followed any question were elusive. One night, as she was leaving to go to a meeting, she sent *U Peggy?* and then, straight after, *U Greta?* The next message was a *K* and she wondered if she hadn't asked the question properly. *Dell with u?* she sent. Then there was a run of messages in quick succession:

Ask.

K fyn.

K.

K d.

A few days later it hummed, and the message read *Sorry d v seriously forgot.* She lost a day's work trying to figure out what it meant. Around six at night she realised it meant nothing. She started another list – all the things that had just disappeared and two hours later, she looked up from the notebook and there was no order or balance – no way of making sense of it. She was being played with. Another message arrived, she wrote it down and it meant nothing.

Over the next couple of weeks, she picked up several new jobs. She wrote a small piece of code which sent an alert when a decent job came through the messageboard. She created a file of letters of interest using a Mad Libs system so she didn't have to always be writing emails for jobs that would take a day and not pay enough to cover administration. She was working as a moderator on several new sites and also doing sales. Chatting with people who wanted to buy phones and subscriptions to porn. She was the 'Want to talk to a salesperson?' bubble that most people thought was a robot.

Early one morning a new job came up. Not through the normal channels. They had a chatroom for everyone working online and by themselves. It was like a water-cooler. They were a small part of 4chan. They shared hacks and codes and keysets. The Tamagotchi phone had woken her up at 3am and she'd left the notebook by her desktop. She'd turned on the screen for some light just as the message about the job arrived in the chatroom. Someone had written that there was a video-sharing platform which needed moderators – lots of moderators. Someone else replied to say that they were working there, and people needed to know there was some terrible stuff. They wrote it in a way that said they wanted people to know they were working with the terrible stuff and were cool with it. They wanted people to know they were tough and progressive and dead enough inside that they could watch anything. Like most of the things people wrote in the chatrooms, it was an act of swagger. That, or the person was trying to protect the work they had with the video-sharing platform. While the company didn't mind how many people they had moderating – more got done – sometimes the work got crowded and there was less for the individual moderators to do. Either way, he – and Margaret was sure it was a man – was an idiot. Any hint of explicit or disturbing content meant more money. Much more money. There was an email address for the video-sharing platform.

Margaret stopped for a second and thought about the most terrible thing she could imagine being videoed and shared, and then she imagined a more terrible thing. Over the last couple of weeks, she'd realised what she wanted was more money. Things came and went without any reason or meaning – she had no control over her world. No matter what she did, things would come, and things would go. But money meant something tangible and quantitative. Things had a value and so did her time. Money was a way to convert her time into things. More money meant more things. Then she could control what turned up and what disappeared. The only way to get more money was to increase her hourly rate, because the hours in the day were fixed. This job could be it. But, also, this was the sort of thing that ruined people's lives.

She'd seen the other parts of 4chan – the places that held the worst. This was the sort of thing that desensitised you to a point you couldn't operate in the world. They'd said the same thing about video games. And probably rock 'n' roll.

The Tamagotchi phone vibrated. She pulled it over to where she could see it. *K.* it said. Then another message straight away, *HF*, and then another, *I vil tell u after eat u start.* The moderating algorithm she'd built was working pretty well. It was learning. She was sure she could teach it to see. She thought about the cheese grater not being there and then suddenly being there. She thought of all the things she'd lost – where did they go? Nothing was solid, there was no way of keeping hold of anything. The rules kept changing. It wasn't the blackout and it wasn't an accident. Things turned up and things went away – nothing was stable or had any objective value. Nothing was real. And if this was true for the things in the world she lived in, then it was true for her and everyone else. Their lives meant nothing, and they could disappear in a heartbeat. She touched the wall beside her and remembered the day in the park when everything had switched into three dimensions. That had felt real, and so did the wall, but what if the idea of real had been programmed into her with the same set of instructions that had made the wall? Nothing meant anything, because the meaning of everything lay outside this place – the place where all the things and all the people and she existed. Their morals were some element in an equation – her happiness, her love, her fear. She understood, and that was her superpower. Nothing could frighten her or upset her again, because she'd lost everything in the flick of a switch, in the tap of a hand. She'd been left all by herself and her grief was just the outcome of a series of inputs. Her grief didn't belong to her. Nothing did, none of it was real and none of it mattered.

She sent an email and carried on with what she was doing. She got a reply within minutes. The email had a set of attachments and a link to a form for her payment details. One of the attachments was a zip file with a piece of software she needed to download to her computer, so they could tell when she was working for them, so they could pay her properly. Not for anything creepy, the email joked.

She opened the zip file and looked at what was inside. There were pieces missing, but it looked like all it could do was turn itself on when she was working for them. Everyone else used timesheets. She downloaded it.

The next day, she was transcribing into an XML editor and tagging anything that needed tagging when a second email arrived. She clicked away from the editing window and read it. There was a link and it took her to a post on the video-sharing platform and she realised that the moderation was taking place after the videos had already been shared. People would report the offensive material and send a link, then the links were sent to moderators. There was a login on the page, and she logged in using the username and password from the email. Under the video was a box where she had to check 'Yes' or 'No'. If she ticked no, there was a checklist where she had to give a reason the video needed to be taken off the site. The video began to play – it showed a small dog and a man with his fist in its anus. She tried to click 'No' but it wasn't going to work until she watched the whole video. The dog's back broke and then it died. 'No,' she clicked. 'Violence,' she clicked, then she thought about it and clicked 'Sex' as well. Nausea overcame her and she felt cold and sweaty and knew she would vomit and that this was how she was going to make money from now on.

2018

38

Margaret stood at the kitchen sink and looked out the window at the backyard. It had been raining – for days. The deck was wet and the trees that flanked the deck were wet and the concrete steps that led down to the back door from the deck were wet. It was like being under the ground. She wasn't sure how they'd managed it. The deck and a small concrete courtyard were above the kitchen. When she looked out the window, the concrete courtyard was at eye level and the deck was above her. She had to walk up steps to get there. When it was sunny, they had dinner up there, under a large pōhutukawa tree that was almost falling out of the side of the hill. It leaned further and further down. The deck was under the hill. And the kitchen was under the deck, and then it stopped. That was as far as it went. Except the front door was at the top of more steps, so actually it did get lower – the street was under the kitchen. You walked down the street to town. You didn't notice it on the downhill but when you came home there was a slight puff if you were going fast. She was often going fast.

Heidi was talking. She'd been talking for a while. On and on about something. It was important, but Margaret was looking out the window. There'd been rats under the deck and in the walls of the house. Margaret had put poison out and now she hadn't seen a rat for a few weeks, not since she'd seen a really sick-looking rat struggling across the deck. Everyone knew how rat poison worked. The rats got thirsty after eating it so they went back to the nest where they died of thirst and then the others would eat them, and the others would get poisoned and die of thirst and new rats would eat them.

Margaret took a long sip from the lukewarm cup of peppermint tea she was drinking. Heidi was angry about the government. She was right to be. They were all doing as much as they could. Protesting and writing letters, and they'd stopped buying as much, but it wasn't enough. That was the tough part of being forty-eight. At twenty-four or even thirty-six, you could fool yourself that it might make a difference. That if you tried this one last thing it might make a difference. But now Margaret and Heidi and all the people they knew had tried everything and time was running out – now more than ever before. With every day it seemed like there was less and less they could do on the small scale of their homes and selves. Heidi realised this. It was just that at the moment she was wound up, energised by the anger that nothing they did could change anything properly – it might have, but it hadn't. It was time for big change and no one who could make big change would.

'I said we'd go,' Heidi said. That was how it worked – the keeping living. None of them were ever broken on the same day – not completely. Margaret and Heidi were like a couple of hikers stuck up in the mountains freezing to death. One of them would say, 'I'm tired. I'm going to take off my clothes now and go to sleep,' and the other would say, 'No. Wait. Half a k more.'

Margaret nodded. 'Okay. Yeah, that sounds good. Let me know if I can do anything.'

'We're making signs on Sunday,' Heidi said.

'Right,' Margaret said. She didn't say what she was thinking. That making signs seemed like activity for activity's sake, that signs were not going to save anyone. She just said 'Right' because that's how the keeping going worked. Heidi did not need to know what Margaret thought about the signs because Heidi knew the signs were a waste of time.

'It's not about the signs,' said Heidi.

'No,' said Margaret. 'It's about the hanging out together and making the signs.'

'Yeah.' They were reminding themselves. 'People are scared of protesting but hanging out and doing crafts is doable.'

'I'll be there.'

'Yeah.' Heidi was unpacking the vegetables. They were both members of a co-op. The fruit and vegetables would arrive at the community hall and one of them would go and pick them up and drop them off at the other's house on their way home. Heidi lived in the house behind Margaret's with her wife Bisi and their kid Ash. Heidi was smelling a fennel bulb, sniffing in between everything she was saying. She was saying a lot.

Margaret and Heidi had aged well for a while, but the last few years had been hard on them. Margaret had wanted her hair to go grey – she'd thought it would be easier than the slow gradual dimming. But then as she got more grey hairs, she'd thought a lot about dyeing it again. When she brushed her teeth, she looked in the mirror and she looked haggard. It was the only word you could use. She was fat as well. She hadn't changed a thing about her life, but she was fat and getting fatter and everything tasted bad. Really bad. She'd be dead in thirty years – if she was lucky, and she'd been luckier than plenty of people they knew. She was still sober, and she still went to meetings and called Diane and did what she could to help other people. She'd been able to carry on. Even though she was alone. 'What am I? Chopped liver?' Heidi would say. Margaret had been able to minimise the harm she'd done other people and she knew where she was, and she was safe most of the time. She had a job and a place to stay and that was more than most people had now. Heidi was still close, too.

Which was a lot more than most of them had. Most of the women who had split into two had been separated now. You hardly ever saw any of them walking down the street together anymore. But Margaret could still spot them – could tell they were one half of something. Nobody noticed it now except for the women who had experienced it. The women didn't usually stay in touch with each other. Sometimes one of them would send a Facebook request and it wouldn't be replied to. Sometimes one of them would see another at a mall and say hello, as a reflex, and the other one would say, 'Do I know you?' and it would be embarrassing. Some of them were dead. All over the country there were ones where there used to be twos. Sometimes neither of them was left. At first, everyone else had worked hard to not see them, then it had become second nature, and now the women weren't there to be seen.

Heidi had been left alone early. She'd arrived in the new town without Dell. No one knew in this town. She liked it that way. She'd worked hard even though she couldn't get a good job, or a legitimate driver's licence. Then Margaret had become one. Maybe it was the length and the circumstances of their singleness that allowed them to stay friends, when everyone else was trying to isolate themselves from each other. Heidi lived in hope that what had happened to Peggy and Greta would happen to her and Dell, and maybe that's why she kept Margaret close. But Dell kept calling and getting in trouble and needing money and fighting, fighting, fighting.

All the things Heidi and Dell had done for each other and all the things that Peggy and Greta had done for each other, Heidi and Margaret did for each other in those years. Everything two people who were genetically, emotionally and spatially distinct from each other could do. Heidi met Bisi and lied about Dell – said she was her sister, and then they had Ash, who was nearly nine now. Even though Heidi had Bisi and Ash, she and Margaret still helped each other. Heidi picked up the vegetables from the co-op. Margaret made sure the jug was boiled and that she had picked some peppermint from the garden.

Six years ago, Dell had died. In the end it was quick and nothing to do with Dell at all – a sudden tear forced deep parts of her heart apart. It was quick and vicious. She'd been standing at a bus stop and simply fallen to the ground. Their mother was devastated. Heidi had gone to see the body and then had a fight with their mother and left before the funeral, which she'd paid for. Margaret thought about the day they'd been grocery shopping, over a decade ago. The walk to the meeting, her arm warm against her other arm. Time had passed. They didn't issue a death certificate, which meant for all intents and purposes that Heidi was the only one now. She'd flourished. It was a jumping-off place, and she got a good job – an important job that she loved.

'I don't know what this is,' Heidi said. 'What is this?'

Margaret looked over. It looked like a squash, but it was green. 'It looks like a muppet,' she said and they both laughed. 'Or that pot plant out of *Little Shop of Horrors*.'

Heidi held it up and made it say 'Feed me Seymour' and they both laughed again. Then she put it down and looked at her phone for the email from the co-op with the list of things in the box.

Heidi had probably saved Margaret's life. After she was alone, Margaret saw what was going on and it made her dangerous. She said things and did things and hurt people and she only stayed sober so that she didn't miss anything. 'Was that always there?' she'd say to Heidi, because Heidi was the last one who would hang out with her. 'What?' Heidi would say, tired. 'That box of matches,' Margaret would say, and she'd write it in her notebook, not even hiding it from Heidi now. There was nothing Heidi could say, but she stayed. She made Margaret go for walks, and Margaret would say things like, 'Does that tree look the same as that other tree? Are they running out of tree designs? Is that what happened to us?'

In the end it was only Margaret running out of will that brought her back. She realised no one would ever understand – it hadn't happened to anyone else they knew, and to the rest of the women who looked exactly like each other, what had happened to Peggy and Greta seemed like a blessing. *Poof* and she was one again. One day, looking at Heidi's face, she realised that all her shouting and explaining wasn't changing anything and that if she kept it up her life would be worse – so she shut up. It wasn't about winning, it was about surviving. They were living in a sandbox. Like the small people in the rollercoaster park, if there was any point it had nothing to do with them. There was no meaning to wrestle from anything. Nothing she could do would change anything. Dell was dead, and maybe there was some peace in death, but nothing was what it seemed and maybe the end she dreamed of didn't exist and it was just more pain, so Margaret gave up, even on that. How she lived now was under the weight of a deep despair, by herself, with the knowledge of what they were dealing with.

'Is it fennel?' Heidi asked. 'Oh, no, that's the fennel bulb.'

She pointed at the two bulbs sitting next to each other. 'It's not a potato.'

Margaret shook her head.

'Wait.' Heidi picked up the vegetable again. 'Is that kohlrabi?'

Margaret googled 'kohlrabi' and held up the screen to Heidi. Everything was in their phones now. Their whole lives and the whole world in slim black screens that could do anything.

'Maybe?' Heidi said.

'Ash would know,' Margaret said.

'They certainly would,' Heidi said.

Margaret and Heidi stood in silence and looked at the vegetable, but it wasn't giving anything away.

'Do you want to stay for dinner?' said Margaret.

'Do you have work?' Heidi was looking at her phone now. Double-tapping pictures on Instagram, flicking back and forth to Twitter.

Margaret looked at her phone. 'Yeah. But you could, like, watch something? Or just hang out until dinner.'

Heidi frowned like it sounded pretty good. 'Yeah,' she said. 'Okay. What are you making?'

The vegetables were lined up on Margaret's bench in a small Noah's ark parade. Heidi's fennel bulb, Margaret's fennel bulb. She never forgot what it was like not to be alone. She was always lonely. Even when Heidi was standing this close to her and they were looking at the vegetables together. She never talked to Heidi about it, because she knew Heidi loved her independence. Dell was dead and Heidi was sad, but they'd been apart for a long time before Dell died. Heidi had always wanted to be free of Dell. But what had Peggy and Greta wanted? They'd been happy, they'd worked well together, they were grateful every day for each other – all they wanted was to be close. Some of the people in meetings talked about how everything that happens is for the best. Had Heidi and Margaret both ended up with what they wanted? Heidi had been left alone, and Peggy and Greta were as close as they could be in Margaret. But Heidi was happy and Margaret never would be. Like someone who'd messed up the syntax of a wish – she went over and over it every day of her life. What had Peggy and Greta done? But it wasn't cause and effect, and this is what made Margaret angriest of all. The simulation was flawless, but the narrative was full of causal fallacies and cliché. Life was long and boring. The day-to-day was a shambles and the big picture was a cliché. The world was ending – what would they do?

'You could go away and come back with the family for dinner?' Margaret said. She hadn't seen any of them for a day or so. She liked Ash. They were kind and smart and interested in interesting things.

'Yeah.' Heidi looked out the window. 'Yeah. How about I do that?'

'If you let Bisi know now, she won't start dinner. Is Ash out tonight?'

Heidi laughed. 'I think you overestimate the social life of a nine-year-old. I'll head home and let you know if we can't make it.'

'Sounds good,' said Margaret. 'I can get that work done.'

'No rest for the wicked,' Heidi said.

Margaret still worked from home. She had never fully re-assimilated into the workforce. But it was different now, it would be easy for her to get a good job. It had been twenty-four years and no one remembered. People still found her annoying, but the heat had gone out of it. 'I just don't like her,' she sometimes overheard them saying. It hadn't changed a thing for anyone except for the women directly involved – to everyone else, it was as minor as a change in theme song. That was what was cunning about it. No one cared about them, because they had been at rock bottom when it happened. Most of them had no family or friends or work, and that was that.

Margaret thought about it a lot. She was sure Heidi did too, but they never talked about it. No one talked about it. It was a massive part of her life that she never talked about. When she talked at meetings about the time in her life when she was two, she was able to say 'I' and 'me' and, sometimes, she even remembered it that way. For a while Margaret had tried to talk to Heidi about it and one night, when she tried again, she explained how she was having trouble remembering what it had been like when she'd been Peggy and Greta. Heidi said that was the best way to do it. It was the best way to be – it was what she tried to do herself. Forget there even was a Dell. Which was harder for Heidi because, at the time they were having the conversation, Dell was still living in the city where they'd all met, only a few kilometres from their old flat, and she could turn up at any time. But Heidi recommended acting as if there had only ever been one of her. Bisi would say, perhaps from another room, 'Heidi, would your sister like that coat I'm throwing out?' And Margaret would shake her head and look at Heidi with her eyebrows raised and Heidi would say, 'Shut up' and 'Like you're so perfect, Margretapeggy.'

Margaret was not so perfect. No one knew about Margaret. She operated largely as a voice over the phone and if she had to come into meetings with clients, she was quiet and polite and nodded. 'You know why you're so successful?' someone said to her once. She shook her head and they said, 'You're like a man.' She'd nodded slowly. The string of women who still came through Margaret's bedroom didn't know, Diane had forgotten, no one at the meetings remembered, and she didn't talk to anyone else who she wasn't being paid by. And still, every two or three or five days or a couple of times an hour, the Tamagotchi phone would beep and there would be another message that made no sense to her and she would write it in the spreadsheet she'd started after the notebook had got too full. And every now and then she would get the notebook out and flip back to the first message that came on the day she found the phone. *Are u awake? Is there snow there?*

Heidi didn't know she still had the Tamagotchi phone – she hadn't seen it since the day it had arrived. But Bisi didn't know about Dell. 'We're all doing what we can,' said Heidi, and Margaret knew that was her way of saying they weren't going to talk about it anymore, and they didn't. When Heidi came back after the fight with her mother before Dell's funeral, Margaret had held back tears and asked her how she was and when Heidi said, 'Fine,' she said, 'Cool.'

Heidi's phone lit up.

'Ash says they're pretty sure it's not kohlrabi.'

'Mystery,' Margaret said.

Heidi picked it up again. 'I've never seen anything like it before.'

'New tool of play,' Margaret said. 'Came in on the update.'

Heidi laughed but in a warning way that said she wasn't having any of that today.

39

Heidi went home and a few hours later messaged that they would bring bread. Bisi had been making bread. They all had, but Bisi had made a new loaf with caraway and linseed and had been working from home all day so had had time to let it rise and proof, and it was looking good. Heidi explained it all in the message. Margaret suspected she'd dictated it. Heidi was a bit in love with the way her phone spoke back to her. Margaret and Bisi called it her friend. Heidi was committed, and she persisted even though it didn't work as easily as it would one day, for sure.

'Alexa,' they'd hear her say in another room, and they'd look at each other, stifling laughs. 'Alexa, make an appointment.'

'Alexa, calendar appointment.'

'Alexa, make a reminder.'

'Alexa, create a reminder.'

They would laugh outright, and Heidi would hear them and laugh too. 'I'm teaching her,' she'd say. 'She's getting way better.' Which was probably true. 'Ten years from now, when you're using a seamless natural language interface, you'll have me to thank,' she'd shout. Then they'd hear Alexa say, 'Here are the Google results I have for that.'

And everyone would laugh again, including Ash. Nine years old seemed like a nice age, Margaret would think as she watched them laughing with Bisi. But Ash had always been a pretty great kid. Heidi and Bisi were amazing parents in a very light-touch way. 'It's only having one,' Bisi said once. 'It's easy when there's only one. And Ash is a fucking great person. We can't take credit for most of that.'

Ash was lying on a chair in Margaret's lounge now, legs flung over the arms on one side, looking at their phone. Everyone was looking at their phones. The bread was in the oven smothered in garlic and oil. Margaret had roasted the fennel bulb and was cooking some potatoes to mash with it. She'd made a large pot of spinach dhal. Everything would be ready soon. Margaret's house was an extension of Heidi and Bisi's house and vice versa. Generally, everyone just lay around. Sometimes they would all sit for hours just doing their own thing, but they liked to be in the same room doing it. Ash liked to draw as much as look at their phone. Right now, they were on TikTok. They had earbuds in and every now and then they would act into their phone, lip-syncing something. Bisi was usually looking at Instagram or Twitter or an article Twitter had sent her to. She was interested in injustice. She liked to get angry. All the social media platforms were anger machines. They all admitted it. They talked a lot about algorithms and about how rage gets attention and everything online was geared towards that. But it didn't stop them going back and scrolling through the platforms for ages. They all talked about doing something different. Heidi had switched her phone's display to monochrome, but she still found it hard not to spend hours, head bowed, sucked into it, scrolling down and then back to the top – they all did.

Margaret was working, quietly, for at least three of the biggest social media companies through a third-party contractor. She'd been one of the first moderators. The human moderators were hired as a stop-gap. For years, the companies had said that soon they would be able to do the moderation automatically, with algorithms, but they still couldn't. Margaret had spent years looking at terrible videos, longer than most people lasted. She'd got faster and better and it was noticed by one of the people she reported to, and one day there was an email and they wanted to track her for an algorithm and then that project didn't work but in tracking her they noticed something. Like everyone else, Margaret had abandoned the idea that she could teach the programme to identify content that breached the vague and ever-changing content guidelines, so instead she'd built a page and integrated it into the right-hand side of her screen. The page included a menu of options to help her filter content into silos. She could change the menus as the guidelines changed. The manuals were only occasionally updated, and most of the changes in policy were done on the fly by subject-matter experts and emailed to the moderators.

When she showed her page at the Skype meeting a couple of years ago, it became clear to her that her small piece of programming was the most up-to-date and complete representation of all the current policies. A blush went through her as she realised this might be her big thing. Her excitement was followed almost immediately by the terror of realising she was showing it to them and that she had never asserted any rights over what she'd made, because it had always been just for her so she could look at more videos and images and comments so that she could earn more each hour and win the mathematical game she'd set herself. The approach was new to them. The execution looked sound, they said. Would she like a job?

'I'd be willing to sell it to you,' she said. Not sure where the

307

confidence had come from.

'We don't want to buy it,' a man in Toronto said. 'We could whip this up in no time.'

'Now that you've seen it,' she said.

'It's very similar to what we've been working on,' he said.

She took the job. It was an international team and they built the single review tool in less than six months. About halfway through beta-testing at a presentation, Margaret made an offhand comment about the amount of data they were collecting about the moderators through the tool and wouldn't that make an interesting management device. They jumped on it. She'd said it to show off. Part of her was angry at herself for not being more savvy about the way she'd handed over her work. She'd always said she didn't really want to have anything to do with the features that made it possible to track every worker and everything they did, but then she went to the meeting and some guy was getting applause for his ugly code and she couldn't hold herself back.

After the tool was built and the tracking software completed, the company wasn't quite sure what to do with her, so they gave her the supervising role. These days she kept the menus up to date and supervised a small team of moderators in the Philippines. They paid her a small retainer which was acting exactly as that, the NDA still stood, and they didn't have to buy anything off her because her tool was still the product of an employee. There was a supervisor on the ground, so her role was more technical. The moderators went to her when things weren't working or if they wanted to query the results the tool returned on their productivity. There were moderation centres all over the world – Hungary, Spain, China, Canada, Brazil, Argentina and Mexico. In India alone there were centres in Bangalore, Coimbatore, Gurgaon,

Noida, Hyderabad, Kochi, Kolkata, Mangalore, Mumbai and Pune. There was a centre in Arizona and one in Florida. She worked with Manila, because the directors thought the time difference between her and the Philippines was more compatible, which it wasn't. So she still worked strange hours. Her role got smaller and smaller as the years went by – they largely forgot about her, which meant she was paid for fewer and fewer hours, which meant she needed to find more work.

She built a tool for Mechanical Turk, an algorithm that searched for certain words and certain rates of pay. Some weeks, she slept near her computer and set the alert so it woke her up when a job came through that looked like it would fit one of the small programmes she'd written for other jobs. She'd written a programme that could sort images based on colour planes and a programme that could find words and take actions based on those words. She'd even built one that could listen to audiobooks and use voice recognition to create documents that were automatically grammar-checked. There were better jobs, but she kept doing it. Everything about Mechanical Turk was unfair, and she liked the idea that her cheats fucked with it a bit. She shared them all online and more and more people were using them to try and scrape out some kind of existence from the app.

There was quite a bit of computer security work available and it paid much more than putting images into folders or data de-duplicating. It was a word-of-mouth thing, and because it was commercially sensitive she never got any real credit for her work. She was generally called in when there was a problem – and then only quietly. Someone would call someone, and they would message her, and she would try to fix it from home. But every now and then they'd want to meet her face to face. A few times she'd asked Heidi to go. Heidi was managing online sales for a medical device company, so she was often out of the office legitimately at meetings. No one asked when she put Margaret's meetings in her diary. Margaret had to brief her quite carefully, but Heidi was a lot happier around people. She would say she was Margaret, or whatever Margaret had said her name was on that occasion, and she'd take the meeting and sometimes, because she felt that Margaret should really be able to handle all this by herself, she'd agree to things that were very difficult for Margaret. Nothing so far had been impossible. Margaret was always smarter than anyone realised. 'Smarter than you give yourself credit for,' Heidi would say. She was in the shadows and never able to shine. 'Which might be the smartest thing I do,' Margaret would say.

They heard Heidi talking to Alexa in the kitchen as she checked on the bread in the oven.

'Alexa, set timer.'

'All right. For how long?'

'Five minutes.'

'Sorry. I don't know how to help with that yet.'

'Alexa.'

'I'm still learning.'

'Fuck.'

Heidi came back into the lounge looking at her phone. They all looked up from their phones, even Ash, and laughed together.

'Seamless,' Heidi said. They laughed some more – Heidi and her family.

Margaret looked to her right and then her left but she was alone. It had been hard to get here. Every day. There was never a moment when she could remember, with anything like comfort, the time before she wasn't alone. She tried, thinking that it would help her adjust to the new aloneness. But she still did this. Went into rooms talking to someone when there was no one in the house. Looking to her right to share a laugh and then the startle of no one being there and then the look to the left before she realised she was alone. Like, really alone.

40

Dinner went well. Afterwards, they sat around for a few hours talking about the news. Heidi talked again about the need to do something. It was hot and the oceans were getting hotter, and they all nodded and none of them wanted to say that anything they could do seemed pointless in the face of it. But if they had, Heidi would say that's what everyone had thought about nuclear weapons and the ozone layer, and she'd be right. Then Ash cut up some plums that had come off a friend's tree and put them on a plate like boats in a harbour. People's eyes started to droop, and Heidi reminded everyone it was a school night. She and Bisi and Ash went home, walking up the driveway carrying the reusable bags they'd brought the plums and the salad and the bread in. Margaret stood in the cool night and watched them walk away for as long as she could see them and looked up at the sky and watched the trees moving in the breeze and went inside and she was alone again.

She cleared away dishes and glasses from the lounge, then stopped and felt in the pocket of her oversized sweatshirt for the Tamagotchi phone. She made sure no one saw it, but she carried it everywhere. Her monster was pixel-gliding across the screen – the black squares grouping and regrouping to make it bounce slightly and then fly. She used the arrow button to navigate through the food, lightbulb, game, medicine and duck icons to the chart. It wasn't hungry but it wasn't happy either. She'd have to play with it. The game was infuriating. A song would play, then the monster would turn from one side to the other. She had to guess which way it would stop by pressing either the left or right button. There was no skill involved, it was all luck. The monster would flick right, left, right, left, and she'd push a button and it would stop – not always where it had been heading. When she got it wrong the monster got angry. She had to get it right at least three times out of five to make it happy. She'd lost count of how many had died – sometimes it was carelessness, but sometimes she would swear off it, angry that none of the messages made sense, that her messages were never answered – but this monster was doing okay. It would go to sleep soon, and she would turn off its light and put the phone in the charger beside her bed. The phone needed charging twice a day now. She could never discipline any of the monsters. Ever. They just wouldn't take it.

K, came a message.

Ash looks well, she replied to the number – the only number that ever sent messages.

Then she sent, *Yeah. They're a great kid.* It was a new thing, a theory. She thought she could teach the number by sending both sides of the conversation.

Are you ever sad you didn't have kids? she sent.

Then, straight away, *No.*

Then, again, *No. Some people are just not the parenting type.*

She laughed. Surrounded by the sound of being the only one laughing at a joke they'd made themselves. The replies she sent went nowhere. *U collect it*, the number sent. She looked back at the last few messages.

I am on d way.

K k thanx.

May b lol.

Then, *I love u:-)*, which it would occasionally send over and over again.

She brushed her teeth and went to bed.

She was up the next morning before her Tamagotchi monster – the tiny screen of the phone was black with a *Z* rising stiltedly in grey. Her proper phone, the one she used for real, was lighting up. There'd been a data breach. Not at any of the companies she worked with directly – no one actually worked for any of the companies directly – but at one of the big social media companies which she might be working for in some of her covert jobs but was definitely working for in the moderation job. It sat in the background humming away most days. An all-staff email came from the senior management team of the contractors she supervised the moderation for. It was a firebreak. *You may have read,* it said. *We can assure you.*

She read the email with one eye shut. She went to the news site that had broken the story and read the article. Then there were messages from the moderators she supposedly supervised, asking what the email meant. There was one from the supervisor on the ground too. Everyone thought she would know something.

She put her phone down, got out of bed, kneeled beside it and prayed. It seemed to keep her away from a drink. She knew something was watching now – something was playing with all of them. It was vengeful, probably – human, maybe, or post-human. She didn't know exactly how it worked, but she didn't want to set any alarm bells off or draw attention to herself. She was biding her time, watching, trying to be unwatched. So, she kept doing what she'd done on the first day she was sober, and the second – she kept going. She picked up the battered notebook from her bedside table and turned to sit on the floor, her back resting on the bed. She had to write in small printing and some pages were written over and over, illegible, but it felt best to keep it this way – analogue. She was using a spreadsheet for the messages, but the messages weren't anything anyone couldn't find by looking at the phone. She was the one noticing the things that turned up and disappeared and she wasn't ready to put that information anywhere it could be found. She started every day writing in the notebook. It got her head right. Some days she wrote *Nothing*, but these days were fewer and further apart. She was already worried about how much work she had to do today. Worried that somehow she would be implicated in the data breach. She had a rule that she never took on a job that she didn't honestly think was 'right'. There was a sliding scale of what was right. Depending on how close rent was. She was reading the article now but still thinking about the day ahead. *Data breach*, she wrote in her tiniest writing in the notebook.

The political consulting firm had come to her. In a roundabout way. Not directly, they never did anything directly, but she was pretty sure she knew who they were. Someone had developed a profiling system using general online information – social media 'likes' and smartphone data. Margaret was told none of this outright, but she'd found it out by asking around. She was told they wanted an app that could collect people's data. This was not an unusual request – it was pretty much using the social media platform as it was set up to be used – for advertising. She'd done it a million times before. What did not sit well with her was a sentence, nested in the message, that said the consultancy were pretty sure there was a way to harvest not only the data of the person who used the app but also of their online networks. The sentence was cleverly constructed. It said a lot more than the words it was made up of, but only a few people would understand this second, coded meaning. It was asking for a decision – are you with us or against us? If Margaret was against them, if she said anything about it, they would be able to quote the text back as it was written, and it would mean what the words said, and she would look like she was overreacting and a bit paranoid. But what they were asking for didn't seem right. No one read the terms and conditions and that was their fault, but she couldn't quite justify it. The contractor had wanted to talk to her on the phone. She said she didn't want to, but they'd insisted, and she had an uncomfortable conversation where it felt like she just said no, over and over, for an hour. Until she said she didn't have time and there was only one of her. She couldn't get it done for them on time.

The contractor followed up the phone call with a message saying that by agreeing to the phone call she'd implicitly signed a disclosure sanction. She wrote back and said she understood, and they knew she did. 'What you see is what you get with Margaret,' a guy had said at a meeting once, and everyone nodded, and she realised none of them had any idea. What they saw was what they wanted to get.

Another contractor working for the political consulting firm wrote a week later pitching her the same job in different words. She didn't have much going on – she had a lot going on but it was all boring her. It had got her attention the first time and now, with the contractor's new way of explaining the job, she felt like she could justify it – to other people probably, and to herself absolutely – because the rent was due and she had been thinking about it for a week and she'd almost worked out an elegant and canny way of executing it.

She stayed on the floor and read a couple more articles. It was definitely the programme she'd written. The silly game with the spiders that ran all over you and your friends, grabbing copies of everything and bringing them home, leaving you with a definitive answer to the question, which Hogwarts house do I belong to? Or, which cocktail am I? Or, what is the date of my death? The whistle-blower was a guy she'd heard of. None of them had met one another – they all worked on their separate parts, separately, all of them contracted by different companies. He had positioned himself. Had some photos taken to go with the article. She spread her fingers to zoom in – he'd had his hair done. She could understand it, how he was trying to emphasise the sacrifice he was making, but no one ever did anything unless it benefited them. Her included.

The job was wrong. She shouldn't have taken the job. She knew it the minute she read the first message. She knew it even more surely when she read the second message. She hadn't needed money to pay the rent – she already had money. What she wanted was the challenge of it, was what she told herself, but she realised as soon as she accepted it that what she liked was the destructive capability of it. That it had the potential to corrupt everything in a way that might undermine the game. That it might contaminate the experiment she felt like she was living in. It was like the people in the rollercoaster park, but it was real people who could be made to line up and ride. It was a way of taking control of the players. The world was on fire with this sort of thing, and she'd been in its path for years. She'd said no for years without any fanfare and as a way of not drawing attention to herself, then she'd said yes to this, and by saying it she was shouting at the fire, from inside the fire, making more fire: 'Here I am.' And she rested the notebook on her thigh and wrote, as the media storm raged and the messages kept arriving, *I'm seen*, and immediately wished she was invisible again.

She checked her messages and found the correspondence between her and the contractor who was acting on behalf of the consultancy. She'd given them nothing. He, stupidly, had repeated back to her something he'd heard someone else say that she said, but it was completely deniable. She checked the next message and she'd neither confirmed nor denied it. She was clever like that. Crafty. It came from ducking and diving. You can't con a con, Diane had said once. She'd heard it before, but as she looked through the messages, she saw herself quite clearly for a moment. Everything was calculated. She had justified it to herself, but here she was, message after message, trying to do the job without leaving a trace that she'd done it. None of it read like she was proud of what she was doing.

Probably, she'd get away with it – in the world. The bigger problem was the conflict of interest. She'd been protecting the users in her moderation role while fucking them by helping build the app. If she'd said no, any number of other people would have done what she did. It wasn't the biggest part of the job and she wasn't any smarter than hundreds of other people. She'd never sought any kind of praise or attention. No one would know it was her. But she wasn't sure, reading over it all now, if she could act like this and stay sober. She had to live with herself and if she couldn't live with herself, she'd have to drink, and, realistically, if she drank again, she might as well fire a gun at her face. If she was lucky, she'd die fast, but she'd had friends who drank for years and got sicker and sicker. Angrier and angrier. But just couldn't die. When Greta and Peggy were twenty-five and still living in the other city and still studying and living in cold flats, a friend shot herself in the face and survived. She had two teeth left and no palate, but the bullet had missed everything important. She was blind and was hard to understand and she came back to meetings and was still sober now as far as Margaret knew. 'How are you?' Greta had asked, at the time, just after she got out of hospital. 'I can't lie,' she'd said. 'Things are pretty fucked.' Greta and Peggy nodded. 'But there are small moments when it's bearable,' she said. 'I'm pretty sure anyone would say the same thing.' And they laughed with her, because she was right. 'Women don't shoot themselves in the head,' someone had said to Margaret years later, when she'd told the story, trying to use it as an example of how suffering was relative.

Margaret looked away from her phone. She would probably be fine. At least, she had to carry on as if she'd be fine, if there was any chance of her being fine in the end. She looked back and there was a new message from the company that contracted her for a company that contracted them for the social media platform. The message gave very clear instructions about what to tell the moderators. She got off the floor and went to her desk. She had a nice office now. It was at the front of the house, so she could watch the street go by and the sun came in for most of the morning. She sat at her computer. She should probably get something to drink or eat – a cup of tea or an apple, then she saw her flask beside the computer still half full of ginger water. She took a swig. It was exactly what she needed.

The computer woke up and she drafted a message to the moderators, copying and pasting from the contractor's one. Before she could send it, there were more messages from the moderators. Some of them had been asked to pass on information – by customers, by the contracting company, by people who said they were from the social media platform. In a perfect world, the message she was writing would be sent by a people manager, but there was a gap – as soon as anyone imagines a job being done by non-humans then the people doing that job stop acting like people. So, there was no manager. She was the one they contacted most often, so she was the one they contacted now. That's why the contractor had sent her the 'What to say' email, because they knew there was no one else and she was the one the moderators would contact. She had no real authority or experience to be writing the message. What they did was up to them, she typed at the end, after the corporate-speak she'd copied and pasted, but there was no need to do anything they didn't want to, or they felt was wrong. They couldn't be compelled to give over any information. She sent the message, knowing it would stop some messages but start a whole new group of them from people who hadn't quite put two and two together. Someone high up would read it, too, so there was a chance she'd have to explain her ad-lib. She was playing both sides – part of the problem and part of the solution. It was unethical but also necessary. Everything was hidden under layers of deceit. She just needed to navigate it all for a couple of days, and no one would pay her any attention and she'd be fine.

She worked until six, when it looked like it was settling down for a bit, then she got up, had a shower and made some toast. She needed to make some more bread, but it would have to wait a while. She should probably get back to the computer. There was a whole bunch of other work for other contractors that she needed to do. She put the jug on the gas-top and the Tamagotchi phone beeped. She'd taken it out of the charger that morning and without noticing had tucked it into the band of the trackpants she slept in. It was in the pocket of her sweatshirt now. There was a message. She scrolled through it. Numbers and then some words that meant nothing to her. Were they names, she wondered for the thousandth time since the phone had appeared. There was no pattern. She worked out patterns all the time. She understood rules, she understood calculations, she understood codes, but there was no pattern here. She got her phone out, opened the spreadsheet, and copied the message into a cell. And then she sent a message back. She sent the same message she'd been sent, but she changed one number. The message wouldn't arrive anyway because it never did. She did it out of habit. Habit that looked like hope.

The toast was crisp and nutty. She stood at the bench eating it and scrolling through Instagram and then had a look at TikTok. It was terrible but it interested her because Ash loved it so much. Then she looked at Tinder, and there was nothing. No one. Everything would be fine. The panic had slowed down. She'd heard nothing from the consultancy she'd made the app for, and the story had disappeared from almost every news site and social media feed. It was almost over and there was nothing to see here and it looked as if she'd gotten away with it.

41

She woke up with a vague sense she could have a day off. She never had to set her alarm. Although she'd moved flats several times, she always woke up at the same time. The first move dispelled the idea that it was the motorway that woke her up. There had been very little traffic until a bypass onto a motorway was built and the road outside her house became a thoroughfare for the suburbs above them. She lived in a valley now. Her bedroom got slightly more light but she didn't think the waking up had anything to do with nature. When daylight saving came on or went off, she still woke up at the same time – according to the clock, not the sunrise or the birdsong.

She leaned over, picked up her phone and looked at her calendar. There was a list of things she needed to do, and she had ticked these off one by one until she couldn't tick off any more. There was one job left and, really, she needed to do it but maybe not until the afternoon. She could pop out for a coffee maybe. She messaged Heidi but Heidi was busy. She got up and had a cup of tea and then a shower and had some breakfast. The Tamagotchi phone didn't make a sound. She fed the monster and played with it. To begin with, she hadn't cared about the monster-pets. She was interested in the messages. Sometimes, new pets turned up out of nowhere for her to look after, but she let those die, too. The other monsters were coming from the same number as the messages, though, and after one of the visiting monsters died there wasn't a message for nearly a week. So, she started looking after the monsters. It was tedious. They would call her at inopportune times, needing to be fed, wanting to play and sometimes not needing anything, which meant they needed discipline. She turned off the alert sometimes and found that by leaving the clock in 'set' mode she could have a break from them. She was getting good at looking after them while she was doing other things. This morning when she checked the monster's hunger and happiness it was fine, and no messages came. Everything in the house was quiet.

She put on some jeans and an old band T-shirt. Her hair was still wet when she logged in. This was habit. Work was the path of least resistance. There was always more to do and while she was sitting there she felt safe. She could have gone for a walk into town, but by herself it felt weird. She was much more comfortable here in front of the desktop computer, getting stuff done. She thought about watching a movie or TV show, but it felt like such an indulgence. She'd tried it a few times, but she ended up feeling agitated sitting in one spot, knowing there was more work to get done. That having the morning off was more trouble than working. So, today, she worked, getting up occasionally to drink tea or eat, and then it was night and she looked at her watch and walked to a meeting.

She said hi to everyone as she walked in and hugged a few people she was happy to see and sat halfway from the front and listened and felt better and afterwards they were going out for coffee so she went too.

The café was crowded after the meeting, but they got seats for everyone over a few tables. There were plenty of them who were animated and filled any quiet bits. Mostly Margaret just sat and watched it all, not talking more than anyone else, but not talking any less. She was sitting at a table with Carola and Lotte. There were other people at the table, but Margaret's eyes always came to rest on them. Carola and Lotte were still identical and still together. Margaret had known them tangentially in the other city. Their parents had moved them here soon after it happened – to look after them. Their parents were rich, and they'd had everything they needed and most of what they wanted. Carola and Lotte were still together in a particularly successful way. They were friends and they had a house and they always seemed very, very happy, like Peggy and Greta would have been, she couldn't help thinking. When she went up to order a coffee, another, older woman came with her. 'They're great, eh?' she said.

'Yeah,' Margaret said.

'Didn't you used to be . . .' the woman said, but she ran out of steam. 'It's just someone mentioned it,' she tried.

'Yeah,' said Margaret, because there were people in the queue who knew, and if she tried to be cagey they'd catch her out. Margaret had always found it hard to look at Carola and Lotte, and she'd tried not to think about them unless they were right in front of her. When they'd first arrived, Heidi, Peggy and Greta had figured out which meetings Carola and Lotte went to and worked hard at never seeing them. On the whole, it worked – but not tonight.

She stayed at the café for an hour or so. It got late enough that she could say goodbye without it looking weird, and she walked towards home. The park near her house was dark because someone had knocked one of the streetlights out. There were shadows and some men sitting on the park seats. She had her earbuds in but wasn't listening to anything, she just wanted to make sure no one thought she wanted to be talked to. She walked, head down but not overly fast, not like she was running or anything. It was a tenuous balance. She got through the park and then the road was relatively well-lit, but people had died here too. Women. One man. When she got home, the house was dark because she hadn't left the lights on, because it had been light when she'd left. She cursed herself as she tried to get the key in the door in the dark. She'd taken her keys out when she'd left the café. Held her keys all the way home between her fingers. It looked weak to look behind yourself, so she didn't, but she'd wanted to. She finally made the key fit the lock and when she was inside she was still alone. The house was quiet. There was no one there. But she said, 'Hi. I'm home.' Just in case anyone was watching her from the street, or anyone was waiting for her in the house.

42

There had been a run of messages on the Tamagotchi phone since the data breach. Sometimes when she looked back at the notebook she wondered if perhaps she'd not copied something down years ago. That maybe it was missing the most important message of all – the Rosetta Stone. But she'd never know. She didn't tell anyone about any of it. It was okay to have one secret – two if you counted the data breach and the app. But no one said that. Not in the meetings. In the meetings, she heard, 'Your secrets will keep you sick.' In the meetings, she heard, 'The truth will set you free.' But she justified it. In the meetings, she heard, 'Anything you're justifying is probably not true.' She knew that what she heard in meetings was probably what she needed to hear. She agreed with all of it, felt in her gut that it was probably right. Whenever she met with Heidi, the phone, the notebook and the spreadsheet stood between them like a mountain. When she went to meetings, she sometimes felt different. Different was probably the most dangerous thing she could feel. Her ego would kill her. Her ego wanted her to be apart – better or worse than everyone else, but always apart. It was her ego that had got her into this. She didn't want anyone telling her how stupid it was to keep the Tamagotchi phone and the spreadsheet recording its messages. So she didn't tell anyone, and the secret kept a large back door to drinking open – swinging wildly in a gale.

She'd got away with the data breach and then the Tamagotchi phone had got busy. She felt like all she had were things she was keeping to herself. It made her think about the coffee the other night and Carola and Lotte. Since the coffee the other night, everything made her think about Carola and Lotte. Everything that had gone wrong, everything stopping her from coming clean, felt like their fault. Everything missing felt like it was missing because Carola and Lotte had taken it from her. She played the coffee night over and over, and she was sure they'd been looking at her. Seeing straight through her. Judging her for keeping a secret. Sure, she was keeping a secret, but they were responsible for the circumstances that led to her having to keep secrets. She tried to not think about them. That's how Diane suggested she deal with it. If she was honest with herself, Margaret knew she was resentful. Blowing it out of all proportion in her head. Thinking they were doing things to her when they were just doing things.

Diane said to her, 'What does it affect in you?'

'It affects my security,' Margaret said. 'And my self-esteem. And my relationship with them and with other people.'

'What part do you play in it?'

Margaret was quiet for a moment. 'I guess . . .' She made some noises with her mouth, but she knew almost straight away, almost before Diane had finished asking the question. 'I'm lonely,' she said. She was so close to telling her about the Tamagotchi phone. 'I'm jealous. I guess I'm kind of slavering after what they have instead of looking at what I've got.'

'And what do you have?' Margaret was pretty sure Diane was making dinner. She could hear a tap being turned on and off. It occurred to her how lucky she was. That this woman would pick up the phone in the middle of making dinner and talk to her in a non-judgemental, non-emotional way in order to save both their lives. Margaret did it for other people. This was how it worked. You passed it on. Suddenly the equation came into focus.

'You,' Margaret said.

'Yeah.' She imagined Diane, phone between shoulder and ear – chopping.

'Heidi and Bisi.'

'Yeah.'

'I'm sober.'

'There you go.'

Margaret didn't say anything.

'Does anything you know about yourself or me suggest we can stay sober by ourselves?'

'No,' said Margaret. She could feel her body filling with a lightness.

'Did we do anything to deserve to be sober that maybe someone else like us didn't do?'

'No,' Margaret said. 'I was an arsehole.'

'I was a drunk arsehole one minute' – Diane was eating something now, her mouth was full – 'and the next minute I was sober.'

'Yeah.'

'I was a terrible person,' Diane said. 'I hurt everyone who came in contact with me.'

'I smashed and burned everything that came near,' Margaret said.

'Grace,' Diane said.

'A gift unearned,' Margaret said. The sun came out behind her. The room filled with a soft light, but inside Margaret it was blinding.

'I'm sorry you're so lonely,' Diane said. 'I imagine it's really tough.'

'Yeah,' Margaret said.

'I don't know if you being alone is a bad thing or a good thing for you, I can't judge that.'

'Me neither.'

'I just know there are lots of people left to help and if we can stay sober that would be great, because then we can help them.' The tap was on again. 'And for that grace to keep me sober, I can't afford resentment. Some people can. I can't.'

Margaret nodded. 'Thanks.'

'Thank you,' said Diane.

Margaret was so close to telling her. About the Tamagotchi phone, the messages, the spreadsheet – maybe even about the data breach and the app. But she didn't. When things were in the open, there was always light on them and for some reason, she wanted to keep this in the dark – for herself. She realised she wasn't being smart, but that was the way it was today. She'd mentioned it to Diane years ago. In passing, not properly. It was a clever kind of lie. 'Oh, yeah, I've got two phones.' Saying it without saying it. She fell back on that for years. I've told Diane, she'd think to herself, knowing full well she hadn't. She was smart. She still sometimes thought it was enough, and that she'd done it. Diane had never had another one of her, so Margaret told herself she didn't need to mention the Tamagotchi phone again, and that Diane wouldn't understand anyway. But she knew she hadn't told Diane, and that Diane probably understood enough that it was important she told her.

Whenever there was a run of messages on the Tamagotchi phone, she would find herself sitting and watching it. She'd be eating and would catch herself looking at nothing but the tiny grey screen set into the hard white plastic rectangular cube. Sometimes she didn't sleep. Sometimes it was three in the morning before she realised she was still looking at it. Then she'd look away and the messages would slow down, and she'd feel an incredible loss. Sometimes she'd try to fill it with sex, or food, or daydreaming about cutting her arms open.

This time it was midday when she realised she'd been looking at the phone for a while. She was sitting at her desk and had no idea how long she'd been looking at it. She looked at the last line of code she'd written. Then at her messages on her desktop, and she'd sent one at about ten o'clock. She looked out the window and decided to tell Heidi everything. Heidi would understand. She picked up the Tamagotchi phone. *Telling Heidi*, she typed, and sent the message.

43

Heidi said she was busy right now because someone had just arrived, but she'd come round in half an hour or so. Margaret looked at her watch. It was just after two.

She paced back and forth, waiting. Regretting that she'd called. Going over and over in her head how she might tell the story of the Tamagotchi phone in a way that would get her exactly what she wanted. She was a little unsure what it was she wanted. But she'd spent a lot of time trying to work it out in her head. She would say this and then Heidi would say that, and she would reply with this. Heidi would probably be sarcastic. Maybe that was why she'd decided to tell her and not anyone else. There were lots of people she could tell. She walked back and forth. She walked all around the house.

She went into the bedroom and was startled by a loud noise outside. She looked out the window and saw Greta and Peggy. They were walking past on the street outside. They were shouting at each other. It looked like they could be fighting or laughing. It had been so long. She ran into the office and thumped on the window as they passed. They didn't hear her. Or they pretended not to hear her. She ran out the front door and out the gate and she was in front of them and they didn't acknowledge her. Maybe they were angry at her? She didn't want to speak, because she was unsure of what she was seeing. Then they walked past her. She fitted into the space between them. It was hardly enough space, but they passed her without touching her. Maybe they turned slightly, at the exact moment they passed her, and that made enough room for her. Margaret turned, heart thumping, breath racing. She watched them walk away from her for as long as she could and then they turned a corner and were gone.

'Hey.' It was Heidi. She was standing in front of Margaret like she'd come out of nowhere.

Margaret changed her focus to see her. Heidi had been walking towards her as Greta and Peggy walked away, and now she couldn't get past her to follow them.

'Whoa. Have you eaten?' Heidi said, not in a caring way. She had an odd look on her face, like she'd a gutsful of today, like someone had fucked her off and she wasn't going to take another ounce of anyone's shit.

Margaret looked behind Heidi now. They were definitely gone. 'Did you see them?' she said.

Heidi looked over her shoulder, then back at Margaret, then over her shoulder again. 'Who?'

Margaret didn't want to say it until Heidi said it, and Heidi wasn't going to say it. She could see that now.

'I passed a couple of women,' Heidi said, 'and a guy walking a dog.' She was looking back now, talking to Margaret but looking back to where she'd come from.

'Yeah,' Margaret said, and it all started in her head, so many voices with an opinion about who it was she had seen and whether it was what she thought she had seen. Had they smiled at her? Now when she thought back, they had both looked at her and smiled, then looked away and passed her in that way that meant she didn't touch either of them. One voice in her head spoke above the others, calmly and clearly.

She couldn't be sure now what she'd seen, but she was certain of how she'd felt. When she first saw them as they walked towards her, as they passed her so close and she watched them walk away, she was made right in a way she hadn't known was possible again. It was different from all the ways she'd been trying to manufacture that feeling by herself since the night in the doorway all those years ago. It was so different. She'd tried to accept this life for twelve years, but when the feeling passed on either side of her, so close, and left her standing alone as it walked away, she realised this had never been acceptable to her, only bearable. She'd thought she was living a life – she'd tried to tell herself that – but really it was nothing. She'd spent twelve years by herself feeling nothing and kidding herself that she was okay. For that split second, as they passed by on either side, she realised how terrible being alone had been.

She reorganised herself. She stepped back into this body and the role she played in this body. She shifted and laughed. 'Cute dog?' she said to Heidi. 'I love a cute dog.' And then the Tamagotchi phone beeped.

'What the fuck is that?' Heidi said. She moved towards Margaret, reaching out like she was going to touch the Tamagotchi phone tucked into the top of her trackpants.

Margaret snatched it out and laughed. 'Paranoid client,' she said, and looked at the screen. *U dn't hve to tell H :).* And there was no need for the message, because there was no way she was telling Heidi now. Not a chance.

Heidi looked at it. 'Is that the kid's phone you found that day?' she said. 'In the kitchen? The day I brought back the pizza stone.'

'Huh?' Margaret raised her eyebrows. Acting like she didn't know what she was talking about.

With both of them, lying was more than pretending or

acting. All of the alcoholics lied in a deeper way, because every lie to someone else was birthed in a lie to themselves. Margaret needed Heidi to think it was not the same phone she'd seen twelve years ago – that Margaret had not held on to the phone for twelve years. So, in her mind and in her soul, she made it not the same phone. This was a new phone, given to her a few days ago by a paranoid client who wanted to communicate with her this way because the client was eccentric as well as paranoid. Margaret had not held on to the phone for years – this was a new phone. It was the truth now. It had never been different. She looked at the phone and it was at once genuine and for effect. She looked at it to cement the lie and then she looked at Heidi like she was really considering what she was about to say. She pursed her lips and shook her head. 'No.' She smiled. 'No. The client just gave it to me last week.' The best way to lie was not to tell too much. There was a temptation, when it was quiet, to fill in the gaps, but if she could wait it out it would be more effective. It was the truth, so she just looked Heidi in the eye and smiled and let the quietness sit.

'Oh,' Heidi said finally. 'My mistake.'

'Do you want a tea?' Margaret said.

Everything was possible. It made perfect sense that Greta and Peggy would be here, and that Heidi would finally see the phone. The atmosphere was full of carbon and the sea was full of plastic. Everything was where it shouldn't be. Whales had stomachs full of rice sacks and snack bags and tangles of nylon rope. There were orca in the harbour. When they tried to swim in the sea it was salp-thick. Everything was possible – it was infinitely replayable. She'd been stuck in it her whole life, maybe more than once, so surely there were broken-edged cases. It made perfect sense that Peggy and Greta would be gone and then here again and then gone. There were ghosts walking right beside her – showing her the way she'd come. Stakes were being driven up as she progressed further through the skill-tree. The world was ending. It was hotter than it should be. Margaret could almost feel it all as she watched the jug boil. It was unseen and yet it was all coming into sharp focus.

It made perfect sense that Greta and Peggy would be here today. It was a sign she was doing well, getting closer, uncovering more and more emergent gameplay – forcing stranger and stranger content out of the procedural generation system. Everything lost was somewhere. Because that's how it worked – every lost opportunity could be played out at another time. Everyone else was probably an NPC, except for Margaret. She had everything she needed to succeed. She was collecting everything she needed to succeed, and seeing Peggy and Greta today was part of what she needed to succeed. 'A cute dog,' Margaret had said, but it was all she was capable of saying. It was all so clear to Margaret and then, as if with a snap of the fingers, it sounded crazy.

Margaret looked out at the deck. She didn't know who the women were. She had no idea. Probably she was out of her mind with grief. Maybe none of it had happened – maybe she'd made it all up in her head to save herself, because she couldn't save just one of her. Maybe she'd conjured a scenario in which she could look after herself, literally. Maybe she'd drunk so much that night that her brain had finally stopped in its tracks, and she'd been living in her wet, wet brain ever since. Maybe her body, her real body, had been sitting in a chair drooling in a hospital for twenty-four years. No one would talk about it. The two women on the street hadn't even looked like her. Of course they hadn't stopped. She was old and desperate-looking, running out of her house and onto the street, shouting at them. Of course two women who probably didn't even look that much like each other had walked past her without saying anything. It hadn't been Peggy and Greta at all. It was a trick of the light. She could feel it trying to settle in. She was becoming convinced of it now, and completely unconvinced at the same time. This was what was left from being divided. She was always in two minds. That's what was left. At least two things being true at any one time. Never being able to come down on one side. Holding all possibilities in the air so they didn't drop – weighing them up to try and get at what was real among the branches and branches of the game tree.

She kept it a secret – this residual ability, this hangover of being divided. She could hold all of it in her head, and anything that tried to settle never did. While everyone else settled into any new order, she saw everything all at once. She had been one, then divided, then one again, but no one mentioned it – Diane didn't mention it, wouldn't talk about it. Shame conveniently covered it up and moved everyone on.

Above all of this racket, there were three possibilities in her mind: the fraction of human-level civilisations that reach a post-human stage (that is, one capable of running high-fidelity ancestor simulations) is very close to zero. The fraction of post-human civilisations that are interested in running simulations of their evolutionary history, or variations thereof, is very close to zero. And, the fraction of all people who have had these kinds of experiences and who are living in a simulation is very close to one.

At least one of these three things was almost certainly true.

44

When Margaret came back with the tea, Heidi had the Tamagotchi phone in her hand. She had no idea how Heidi had got it. Margaret never left it anywhere where it could just be seen. She almost dropped the mugs. Panic ran through her like electricity. There were wireless signals everywhere, and for an instant she felt all of them running through her. There was a part of her already reaching over the coffee table and pulling the phone from Heidi's hand. But most of her stood there, holding the mugs, rearranging her face, while Heidi got round to looking up from the phone.

'I didn't know you had this.' Heidi held the phone up slightly towards her, like she was holding bait for a falcon, or something more dangerous.

'Huh?' It was always her first response. It bought time. Confusion was a currency.

'Have you had it all this time?'

The lying kicked in faster than the truth. It never changed. She didn't even think which would be better – she just lied. 'Paranoid client,' she said, putting down a mug next to Heidi. Heidi didn't let go of the Tamagotchi phone.

'Oh.' She turned it over. 'I thought it was my one.'

'Yours?' Margaret held a mug in both hands and blew on the tea.

'From that day.'

There was a silence. It was so tempting to fill the silence, but she wouldn't make an amateur mistake. It was a game of chicken, really, especially with Heidi. The game was performed in this space between them. Both of them knew the other was lying, but they'd been taught to deal with just what they were told. That trying to work out what was behind the language was crazy-making. It wasn't worth the effort.

'You know.' Heidi started pushing buttons on the phone and the electricity ran through Margaret again.

Margaret screwed her face up like she really didn't know. Like she was trying to remember but couldn't. Inside, her mind raced, her pulse raced, she could almost see what Heidi was about to do. She was terrified Heidi would really do it, and it was coming at her like a large truck.

'With the pizza stone?' Heidi said. 'I left a phone just like this at your house that day.'

Margaret wound herself into the deep, soft chair opposite the couch. She sat on her feet and looked into her tea. 'Did you?'

'Yeah,' Heidi said. 'You were being weird, and I left my Tamagotchi phone there.'

Margaret nodded. 'I don't think so.'

'Do you remember?'

'I remember it differently,' she said. 'I remember a Tamagotchi phone that day, but I found it under my bed before you came with the pizza stone.'

'I left the pizza stone in the letterbox,' said Heidi. 'And you were sulking and sad, and not out of bed . . .'

'I'd been out trying to buy a charger,' Margaret said. She should have kept quiet, but she blurted it out.

'Well, you looked bad. And I came round because I was

worried about you and the pizza stone was still in the letterbox and I brought it in, and I had my Tamagotchi phone and I put it on the table and then I never saw it again.'

'This isn't that Tamagotchi phone,' Margaret said.

'Oh,' Heidi said, and looked at her. Really looked at her.

'This is a new Tamagotchi phone that a client gave me last week because he thought it was funny and then he realised he could message me on it – like a pager.'

'It looks like my phone,' Heidi said, mock-questioning herself. 'It seems weird there'd be two of them. It looks like the phone from that day.'

'It's not that phone,' Margaret said.

'It's got unread messages on it,' Heidi said. She would be in it in a second. Scrolling through the messages.

'Well, the client is annoying.'

Heidi nodded. 'What is this?' she said, reading one of the messages which was just numbers, from last week. 'C++?' She was one message away from the message with her name in it.

'Python.' Margaret held out her hand.

Heidi looked at Margaret, then at the Tamagotchi phone. Finally she handed it over. It was like they were twenty-four years younger – in the kitchen, talking about the wording on a Weet-Bix box. The good lives they'd had seemed to fall from them like scales. Like everything was a fight, and Heidi was just home from Ian's, acting like no one could be trusted. Heidi didn't seem like that anymore, but she was. She pushed her hair behind her severed ear – Margaret hadn't seen her do it in years. Neither of them trusted the other because they didn't trust themselves or the situation. Their lives had been so strange, and the strangeness made them feel vulnerable. They had an idea that the rules didn't fully apply to them. It was the most dangerous place their minds went. The idea that they were special, somehow singled out – that idea could kill them. They'd seen it. They'd seen it with Dell.

'What are you thinking about?' Heidi asked.

'Dell.' She was tired. Sometimes her body would fool her into just telling the truth.

Heidi nodded, and they sat in silence for a moment, both thinking about Dell. 'What did you want?' Heidi asked. She was sipping her tea now.

'Huh?'

'You messaged me.'

'Oh. Just to say I hate those girls,' said Margaret.

'Carola and Lotte?'

'I hate them.'

'Like *hate* hate?'

'Like, "they're taking up space in my head" hate them.'

'Like, "drinking poison and expecting them to die" hate,' said Heidi and they both laughed a bit. 'They're all right.'

'I know that,' Margaret said. 'But I'm not.' And they laughed again. 'I'm jealous.'

'Yeah,' Heidi said. 'That's usually what it's about for me. Ungrateful.'

'Ungrateful,' Margaret said. 'It was driving me nuts. I couldn't work. Then you came over and I haven't thought about it for, like' – she looked at her watch – 'half an hour.'

'Lucky I wasn't busy.'

'Blessed,' said Margaret, and they laughed again.

'I'm sure that's the phone from that day,' Heidi said.

Margaret looked at her like she'd forgotten about it. 'Huh?' Heidi didn't flinch.

'It's not yours,' Margaret said. 'You didn't bring it round.'

'I know I didn't bring it round.'

'It was in the letterbox already,' Margaret said.

340

'I know it was in the letterbox already.'

'It wasn't in the letterbox,' Margaret said.

'I know it wasn't in the letterbox,' said Heidi. 'I was testing you.'

'Anyway, it's not that phone.'

'I know it's not that phone,' Heidi said.

'It's not yours.'

'I know it's not mine,' Heidi said. 'But it's that phone, isn't it?'

Margaret arranged her face, hoping she looked like she was thinking, like it really wasn't that important.

'Have you had that phone all this time?' Heidi said. 'Is it sending you messages?'

'Is that what you think is happening?' Margaret said.

Heidi sipped her tea and looked away. 'I don't know,' she said. 'I don't really care. It's not my business.'

'I wonder what happened to your Tamagotchi phone,' Margaret said.

'I never had a Tamagotchi phone,' Heidi said.

It was a game. Margaret had known from the start it was a game. The nature of the game was confusing. Was it chicken, or was it a fishing game? Did Heidi know everything? Or did she know nothing? If she knew everything, she was trying to fool Margaret into showing her what she was up against. If she knew nothing, it was like when you say, 'What about that accident?' and the other person says, 'Oh, yeah,' as a way to find out if there's been an accident. Margaret used it sometimes when she was working. 'What about that problem on the second page?' And they would say, 'Yeah,' and she could tell from that 'Yeah' where they were at. She looked at Heidi, and Heidi looked at her. Margaret wasn't being straight with Heidi, and it made her assume Heidi wasn't being straight with her. They were closer to each other than anyone else in the world. If they weren't being straight with each other, then they weren't being straight with anyone else.

'Do you want to come round for dinner?' Heidi asked now. It was a simple question, but so much hinged on it.

'Yes,' Margaret said, like she was answering a million-dollar question on a game show. 'I have some work to finish, but I'd love to. What can I bring?'

'Dessert,' said Heidi, without missing a beat.

'Cool. I'll make a cake.'

'Nice.' Heidi took one final gulp of tea and made to stand up and leave. She took one last look at the Tamagotchi phone on the coffee table. Margaret was pretty sure she did it in a way that she could be sure Margaret saw her.

'Why don't we just take that phone and drive a fucking truck over it?' Heidi said.

Margaret shrugged.

'The phone is not making your life any better,' Heidi said.

Margaret looked down at her shirt and wiped something invisible off it, then she looked up and said, 'Oh, nah. I'm good.'

They looked at each other for a moment. Inside, Margaret was screaming. All she wanted to do was tell Heidi the truth. She was so close. She was inches away. One noise, a nod, and the secret would be gone. But she couldn't.

'Seven?' Heidi asked.

'Seven.'

They hugged each other and Heidi poked her finger gently into Margaret's forehead. 'Don't let them live rent-free in your head.'

Margaret smiled and nodded. 'Yeah,' she said.

Heidi turned round and picked up her stuff. 'Be fucking

grateful. We've dodged death for another day.'

'So far,' Margaret said and they both laughed. Properly laughed, like they were vulnerable and open, and they let themselves laugh as if it was safe and they could trust each other with their lives, which they did. Just not with the truth.

45

Margaret made the cake while she was working. She made herself some miso and noodles for lunch. There was some cucumber left and she cut that up into the bowl once the rice noodles had softened. The cake was in the oven and she ate the noodles at her desk while she read through code. Back and back and back. Something wasn't working somewhere. She hadn't run it for ages. Why had she not done that? The mistake was somewhere. She'd run it through a parser, but it wasn't picking anything up so she had to go back through the whole thing. It was like getting chewing gum out of hair or finding a needle in a haystack. Margaret had never seen a haystack.

The oven timer went off and she went into the kitchen. She pulled the cake half out of the oven and drove a sharp knife into it which came out clean. She pulled the cake all the way out and set it on the bench to cool.

The Tamagotchi phone beeped. *Wen ru coming*, it said. She wrote it in the spreadsheet.

She couldn't find the mistake. She should have worked all night, cancelled dinner at Heidi's and kept working, but she didn't. Instead, she wrote a message saying it was more complicated than she'd anticipated, and she'd have it by tomorrow. She wasn't sure she'd have it by tomorrow, but she knew she wouldn't have it by tonight, because she didn't stay up all night anymore. It wasn't for her, it was for everyone else. She was modelling healthy work behaviour. That's what they'd talked about years ago. She wrapped the cake, tin and all, in a clean tea towel and put on a jacket. No one needed to work all night. Working all night was reinforcing the power imbalance and it needed no help from her. She put the Tamagotchi phone in her bag, under her wallet so it couldn't be seen. She couldn't leave the monster alone around dinner time – it got hungry. She'd take it into the bathroom with her after she'd been at Heidi's for a while and feed it then – she'd done it plenty of times before.

When she got to Heidi's house, it was only a couple of minutes after seven. Bisi opened the door and Margaret walked in and popped the cake on the bench in their big open kitchen. Ash was playing Overwatch in the lounge. Margaret watched for a while. Ash changed avatar because they needed healers. Then someone else became a tank. The players did it all without talking to each other. People said the games were isolating, but in this one the players were acting like one mind. Everyone was thinking about the goal, not the individual kill, and happily playing one game in multiple bodies.

'Do you talk to each other before you start?' she asked Ash.

'Not always,' Ash said, without stopping.

'How do you know when to change?'

'Oh,' Ash said. 'We need healers. I can play a healer.'

'Does everyone do that?'

Ash shrugged. 'Mostly.'

'What if you don't want to?' said Margaret.

Ash shrugged. 'I guess we lose.'

'Oh,' Margaret said. 'Cool.'

*

Dinner was nice. Heidi and Margaret were back to normal. Everyone laughed and ate and talked about things. Bisi and Heidi had made a lentil loaf. 'Like it's 1972,' Heidi said, and they all laughed. Ash had made a salad. They'd eaten all of it and now were using pieces of bread to soak up the dressing at the bottom of the bowl. Heidi was looking at her phone.

'Did you bring dessert?' she asked.

'Oh,' Margaret said. 'Yes.'

Heidi looked at her phone again. She seemed a bit on edge, like she was waiting for something. 'Well, go on then.'

'Oh,' Margaret said. 'Yeah. I'll go and get it.'

She went to the kitchen to get the cake. She took her time, put some of the plates in the dishwasher. The conversation in the dining room became quieter, like they didn't want her to hear something. She disregarded it. It was probably just Ash talking. They talked more quietly than Bisi and Heidi. She wiped down the bench and put a pot in the sink and filled it with warm water and detergent so it would soak. As she walked into the dining room, someone dropped something on the table.

'What are you doing?' she said, both of her.

'I just don't think you two need this anymore,' Heidi said. Peggy and Greta's handbag was on the table and their wallet was beside it, and Heidi was holding the Tamagotchi phone. 'Like, we could just get rid of it.'

They were in the dining room now – Peggy and Greta, fully through the doorway, all of them in the dining room. No part of them left in the kitchen. Standing right arm to identical left arm, like the seams hadn't fully come clean yet.

'Oh,' they said.

Bisi and Ash were looking at them now, laughing. Laughing about the Tamagotchi phone and how ridiculous it was that

Peggy and Greta had it. But Heidi wasn't laughing. Her eyes held something of a plea in them. 'Like, we could just throw it away,' she said.

Greta looked at Peggy, and Peggy looked at Greta. They both looked behind themselves, trying to see back into where they'd come from. It was the kitchen. Just the kitchen. Greta and Peggy were looking into the kitchen. The rules were, there were no rules that anyone involved had access to. It was an open world, but not their open world. Whether they were Margaret or Peggy and Greta, and no matter how hard they tried, they had never been able to wrest any control out of it. New decision points and victory conditions were generated through a combination of human-generated assets and algorithms coupled with computer-generated randomness and processing power – somewhere. Somewhere outside of the place where they were doing all this, somewhere far in the future, something was playing. *If two, then. If one, then. If two repeats, then.*

'We forgot the cake,' Peggy said to Greta. Both of them were empty-handed.

'Don't try to change the subject.' Heidi looked at her phone. 'There's not a lot of time.'

'We brought cake,' Greta blurted out, looking at Peggy, who shrugged.

'Don't change the subject,' Heidi said again.

Peggy and Greta looked at Ash and Bisi, who seemed unfazed. Margaret becoming two again had been quickly assimilated into the joke of it. It was like all that had happened was someone had sneezed. A function had run over the top, making it all normal again – settling it all into place. New task: now she is two.

'How long have you had this?' Bisi reached out so that

Heidi would give the phone to her.

Greta answered, 'Like. Twelve years. We found it under our bed – in that old flat. We thought it was funny. It doesn't work.'

'Do you carry it around all the time?' Ash said.

'Why didn't you tell us?' Bisi said. 'Why would you lie about a thing like that?'

'Such liars,' Ash said.

'Who are these messages from?' Bisi asked.

'We don't know. That's why we kept it.'

'That and the monster,' Ash said.

'Yeah,' Peggy said. 'And the monster.'

Ash and Bisi laughed. Ash laughed the most and reached out so that Bisi would hand them the Tamagotchi phone. It looked strange in Ash's hands, odd out in the open. Peggy and Greta felt ill, like they were watching a TV show for too long and it was getting late and they were tired and should have gone to sleep hours ago. Maybe they were watching all this unfold from their bed late at night. Maybe this was game feel. Maybe it was a TV show, and they were lying down in a way that blocked some nerve that was vital to send blood all the way around their bodies. Ash took a photo of the Tamagotchi phone using their smartphone. Then they made a small video, moving the phone back and forth in front of the camera.

'It's like a relic,' Ash said, and started playing with the monster, who was hungry.

'Those messages are probably just some weird glitchy echo,' Bisi said. 'They're probably stored somewhere in the phone and they're just, like, clearing out.'

Peggy and Greta nodded even though it made no sense. It was like Bisi was telling a story, programming it into truth. Ash nodded too, even though Peggy and Greta knew it made no sense. Heidi watched the phone go from person to person.

Greta and Peggy turned and walked back into the kitchen, flinching as they went through the doorway. No one noticed they were gone. Bisi had made her point – Peggy and Greta would lie even when there was no gain in it. They were untrustworthy. If one of them said right now, 'I think we're all living in a simulation,' it would be a lie. Bisi was watching Ash play with the monster. If Peggy and Greta said, 'There was only one of us five minutes ago,' Bisi would say, 'Oh,' and scrunch up her face, and Ash would say, 'Maybe. All good,' and Heidi wouldn't do anything but look worried and unhappy.

They stood at the bench. It felt like they needed the bench to hold themselves up. They looked at each other's hands. Then they looked at the sink and the way the burnt-on food was soaking off the pot they'd put in the sink – five minutes ago. In a movie, they would have vomited into the sink. The first time it had happened she'd been drunk, and by the time they sobered up it was almost already assimilated – cemented into the fabric of everything, including them. The second time it happened they'd been awake, but she'd made no real memory of it. It had settled in everyone but never fully in her. This time she was blindingly awake. They felt more than awake. They were aware of everything. They could feel the air on the exposed parts of their skin. They could feel their hair growing. There was a version of the next five minutes which was them freaking out. They ran it over in their heads. Exactly what that would accomplish. They looked out the window. They would need to go back into the dining room soon. They worked the cake out of the tin and onto a dinner plate. It was the same cake. Everything was the same. The phone had triggered something, but only a very limited change in task. It wasn't a test of her resilience, or her courage, just of her as an object. Maybe Margaret was the NPC? What was she like as two? What was she like as one after being two? What was she like as two again?

They breathed, feeling every inch of their throat and lungs, almost feeling the oxygen exchange in their blood. They found a knife and rested it on top of the cake and one of them carried the plate into the dining room and placed it on the table.

'Thanks,' Heidi said.

'Cheers,' said Greta. There was a sound, and the front door opened. Peggy and Greta could hear someone taking off their shoes and putting them into the rack. There was the rustle of a jacket, and Dell walked through the door. And Bisi and Ash said hello.

'Fuck,' Heidi said. She looked at Peggy and Greta for help, but they had no idea what she wanted. 'See?' she seemed to be indicating. 'We had a chance and we missed it.'

'We're having cake,' Bisi said. 'But there's some dinner-dinner if you want that.'

'Oh,' said Dell, and she pulled up a chair. 'I'll have cake.' And Bisi and Ash laughed.

Dell sat next to Heidi. It was unmistakably Dell – exactly the same as Heidi, but without the scars. Her hair was cropped short to show off both her complete ears.

Greta cut the cake, trying not to look at Peggy, while Peggy tried not to look at her. Dell was not dead, that was clear. But had she ever been? Was this a trick Heidi and Bisi and Ash had been playing on them? Surely not Ash? All the news about Dell had come through Heidi. There had been times when they'd asked about Dell, and Heidi had said, 'Huh?' and they'd asked again and Heidi had said, 'Fine – she's fine.' Had Heidi just not changed her name? Had she been manufacturing the news about Dell for those years when she was away but not yet dead? Was Heidi the game master? Had Heidi and Dell become Adelaide at some stage, like Peggy and Greta had become Margaret?

But no, no. Peggy and Greta decided. Heidi and Dell would have done anything to be Adelaide again. If it had happened, they would have shouted it from the rooftops. Dell had died – maybe in a lie, maybe for real – and she was here now. Dell was dead and alive. Both things were true, but Peggy and Greta were the only ones who could see it. They looked at Heidi, her disquieted face – and they saw that Heidi could see it too. Heidi and Dell had seen it right from the start and they'd never told them.

Greta looked at Peggy, and Peggy at Greta. People were missing. Everywhere. People were missing and coming back and coming back different. Who knew what had been settled into Peggy and Greta's minds as they interacted with the broader level? Who knew what they'd forgotten? What they were able to ignore? Across the table from them, Dell looked sober but sad. Ash had stopped playing with the Tamagotchi phone and was eating the cake they had made.

Bisi slid the Tamagotchi phone towards Dell. 'We've just been laughing at this,' she said.

'Oh,' Dell said.

'They've had it for years,' Bisi said.

'They take it everywhere,' said Ash.

'And they've been hiding it,' Bisi laughed. 'They found it under their bed in that old flat. Remember the old flat?'

'I wasn't there,' Dell said, her mouth full of cake, like she was starving.

'But there's no interesting story at all,' Ash laughed again.

'Nothing to see here,' said Greta.

'Then why did you lie?' Dell asked.

Peggy shrugged her shoulders. 'I have no idea.' And they all laughed again.

'We never do,' Greta said.

Then Bisi touched Greta and Peggy on the arm at the same time. 'Cheer up. We're only joking.'

Dell was still eating cake, not saying anything at all. Not even her body was in the conversation. She was eating with one hand and scrolling through her phone with the other. Like she was trying to catch up on everything she'd missed.

The night carried on and they talked about things while Dell ate and looked at her phone, and Greta and Peggy leaned into each other like they used to.

'I'm off to bed,' Dell said. No one really stopped what they were doing, but they all said goodnight.

As Dell stood up, Heidi held out her hand, which stopped Dell. Under her breath she said, 'Fuck.' She dug into her sweatshirt pocket and handed the Tamagotchi phone back to Peggy and Greta, who put it deep in their bag. Dell picked up some plates and went into the kitchen. Peggy and Greta followed her, picking up some of the other plates. In the kitchen, Dell was still looking at her phone.

'Nice night,' Peggy said.

'Mm,' Dell replied.

'How have you been?' Greta asked.

'Fine.' But Dell never lifted her face from her phone.

'How long have you lived here?' It sounded good in their head, but now that Greta had said it out loud it sounded so obvious. Dell looked up, because it sounded like a shriek to her too. 'Like, in the house,' Greta said. 'We were just trying to remember.'

Dell shrugged. 'Not long,' she said.

'Where were you before that, again?' Peggy was rinsing plates, watching the chocolate dissolve off them. She'd made the cake that afternoon. In her kitchen by herself – they both had.

Dell put her phone down. She still held it close but she let her hand fall beside her body. 'Why?' she said. 'Did Heidi say something?'

'No,' they both said at once.

'We were just wondering,' Greta said. 'Like, how did you end up back here?'

'On a bus,' Dell said. 'You all know that.'

'Well. Yeah. I haven't spoken to Heidi about it,' Greta said. 'You've all spoken about it.'

'Not tonight,' Greta said, smiling, trying to make it light.

Dell returned to her phone. 'Well,' she said. 'If you hear anyone say anything different, you should tell me.'

'Yeah,' Peggy said.

'You don't need to tell Heidi,' she said. 'You'd just need to tell me.'

'Yeah,' Peggy said. 'Yeah.'

'Just saying,' Dell said. 'And there's no need to go back and tell Heidi I asked you to tell me, because I'll deny it.'

'Yip,' Peggy said.

'And they all think you're liars.'

'Yip.'

'They talk about it all the time. What huge liars you both are.'

Peggy turned slightly from the sink, her hands still under the tap. 'Are we?'

'I don't know,' said Dell. 'It's just what I hear. But you know that.'

'Totally,' Greta said. 'Totally.'

'So, I'm just saying – and remember it was you who came to me with the whole "where were you before now" business – that if you hear anyone talking about me and where I've been or how I got here, you can tell me and there is no need to talk to Heidi about this conversation because, a, I'll deny it and, b, lying is kind of what you're both famous for at this stage.'

'Totally,' Greta said. 'But where were you before you got here?'

Dell looked at her and said, 'Where were you two?' Then she walked out of the kitchen.

46

Peggy and Greta walked in the dark down the drive. Greta was carrying the tin the cake had been in, and the tea towel. Peggy was carrying their bag. They were alone for the first time in twelve years, but there was nothing to say. The change was only cosmetic. Peggy bumped into Greta and Greta bumped her back. There was nothing they needed to say.

Greta washed her face while Peggy brushed her teeth. The dairy was shut, so they'd have to use the same toothbrush tonight – like they had been for twelve years. Really, they'd never been apart. They'd just been living in a smaller space. They both laughed, and Peggy put her free arm around Greta while Greta massaged moisturiser into her face.

They put on pyjamas and went to bed. After a few moments, Greta rolled over and dropped her arm over Peggy's shoulder, and everything slipped even further into place. Everything that had been wrong before was right and anything odd or uncomfortable was gone. They should have waited. They hadn't needed to speak to Dell. They should have trusted that everything would come clear. What happened to anyone else was none of their business. They had what they had, and they needed to protect it now it was back. The Tamagotchi phone beeped. Greta leaned over and picked it out of its charging dock. It was scuffed badly now, the white washing into grey.

There was a message from the number that had been calling for years. Peggy leaned over and held the phone, so they were both holding it – one hand each. The message said, *U here ANYTHING. Lt me no.* The phone beeped again. *U dn't hve to tell H.* The room swam a bit and they looked at the small grey screen for a long time and then the monster went to sleep, and they needed to turn off the light of the screen so it could sleep in the dark.

They doubted they'd sleep, so they got up. Crept quietly out of the room. They sat in the lounge on the couch. They could have made camomile tea but instead they just sat in the lounge and looked at the wall. They thought about sleeping on the couch. Watching a movie in the dark. But eventually they got up and walked back into the bedroom and got back into bed, where they would be awake for a while yet. Lying on their backs, one arm bent above them, their heads resting on their forearms, the Tamagotchi phone on the pillow now between them.

'Dell,' said Peggy.

'Yeah.' Greta shifted a bit. 'Once upon a time,' she said, 'it was always Dell.'

Peggy rolled so she was holding Greta across the waist. 'And Dell was a superhero,' she said.

'Who was trying to help us,' Greta said.

'From the future,' Peggy said.

'Sending us messages from the future.'

'Dell knows how to navigate time. Dell knows how to navigate everything and she's going to save us when she works out how to save us.'

'And that's where she was,' Greta said.

'Heidi and Dell have never been Adelaide again.'

'No.'

'And there were times when Heidi had no idea where Dell was.'

Greta rolled so she was facing Peggy and pulled herself up on her elbow. 'Heidi was the bad guy all along.'

'Heidi said she was dead.'

'But Dell was trying to save us.'

'And we all live happily ever after,' Peggy said.

'Because Dell is the unsuspected hero,' Greta said.

'Like Thomas Anderson,' Peggy said. 'Dell is like Neo.'

Greta kissed Peggy and they were almost asleep, but as they drifted off, they both said, 'Or the Terminator.'

47

They woke at the same time. Peggy showered while Greta made a smoothie. Peggy drank the smoothie while Greta had a shower. It was great, but as the sun started coming into the house it felt precarious. They didn't want it to break again – they were anxious. They avoided each other, walked around each other, not talking, hoping they could trick it into thinking they didn't want it to be just like this – like they really didn't mind either way. Eventually, about an hour after waking up, they found themselves sitting at the kitchen table together drinking tea. They both looked up, almost surprised to see the other. Like babies finding their hands for the first time. They just looked at each other. Nothing was odder than being in the company of yourself. The first time had been different. They'd been in such a state of flux. Still drunk for a while after it happened, blacked out most of the time. Rediscovering each other as they woke up or came to somewhere. Never really sure if the other one was really there. Never really sure if it was real or some kind of chemical reaction. Then, freshly sober, finding out who they were – surprising each other. Now, stone cold sober, it seemed that this was how they would find each other. Sitting, drinking tea.

'We should try and fix that code,' Greta said.

'Yeah,' Peggy said. There wasn't any need for the

conversation, but they were just sounding it out, in the new house, in the new life. Hearing what it sounded like to confirm your thoughts with yourself.

'I could do the dishes while you start,' Greta said. 'If you wanted.' It was a bit disconcerting, like talking to yourself. Then their smartphone lit up. Peggy put her finger on the print reader at the back. It was a message from a number they didn't recognise. The data breach had flared up again. There might be a government inquiry. Someone had given out their contact details. Then the phone lit up again, and again. Suddenly there were messages from all over – lawyers, moderators, the company they did the moderating for, the social media company, the political consultancy. Everyone wanted something. Some of the messages were threatening.

Peggy looked at Greta and Greta looked at Peggy. It seemed like it was going to be near to impossible for them to keep the job at the moderation contractors – and, if they were fired, the company would keep all the work they'd done. It was highly unethical, the messages said, and they needed an explanation as soon as possible. The explanation was for a paper trail. Really, the situation was gold to the contracting company, because they could scapegoat Peggy and Greta, get rid of them and keep everything they'd made. There were several messages from government officials and at least one from a law enforcement agency. Really, it didn't matter – nothing mattered. It was all a game, but also it mattered more than anything in the world. Everything was fake, but it was all they had. If there was no food, they would starve. They'd lived on the streets in this world, been beaten within an inch of their lives. There was no peace in knowing it was manufactured.

The app had been the start of it. Their one act of rebellion in twenty-four years had set off a reaction that had seen her divide again and might mean that both of them would lose everything. There was no way to win the game. Whether it was a punishment or a reward, it made no difference. All they had was what was in front of them.

Still reading the phone, they both went to the office. There was only one desktop computer, but there was a laptop that they used to watch TV on.

'Can we both log on at once?' Greta said. She plugged the laptop into the multiplug and sat on the armchair opposite the desk.

'Not sure,' Peggy said. 'Probably not. But the messages are coming from everywhere.' They'd turned off the notifications. Peggy on the desktop, Greta on the laptop.

They'd never worked together – not on the same job at the same time. They looked at each other again and saw for the first time that morning that they were both dressed almost the same. A pair of tight jeans with a floral dress over the top.

'Invoices?' Peggy asked, but Greta was already there, in the files. She was sitting on the armchair with her legs crossed.

Peggy went to the messages.

They both realised at the same time. The invoices were there, shouting, itemised very clearly. There was no real way of denying the mess of accusations and questions stampeding into their inboxes.

'We're pretty hard to find in this,' Greta said, hopefully, but she knew that if they had been, they weren't anymore. They were both in the messages now, working through them together, flagging some of the more urgent requests, the ones they couldn't ignore, like the official ones requesting they turn over stuff to the authorities. The ones from the social media company asking for what they had and how well it was secured and who exactly they were being asked to turn stuff over to, and then one from a lawyer for the social media company telling them not to turn anything over until he'd talked to them. There was a very limited amount they had to turn over, he'd written, as contractors.

'What about as citizens?' Greta said.

'Do we need a lawyer?' Peggy asked.

'It would be nice to avoid it,' Greta said. 'Given the whole . . .' and she waved her hand between the two of them.

'Argh,' Peggy said. Pronouncing all the letters so that it sounded like the word in a comic book bubble.

'Hm,' Greta said.

They were only as good as each other. Neither of them would come up with anything outside the box of the other one. There was an advantage to having each other – they could talk about it. But it was like talking to a voice in your head. It was like a pond of anxiety already full to the brim. There was no fresh water, it was stagnant. So in the end there was no advantage, because neither of them had developed differently. They couldn't get out of each other's grip.

They both looked at the messages for a while, working their way back through the shitstorm. As they read each message it all came back to them. Settled into their body and cemented into their understanding. It was exactly like they'd thought it would be when they'd been Margaret. Yesterday they'd been congratulating themselves for getting away with it – was it yesterday? It was yesterday, when, for a moment, there'd been three of them. It was like chewing gum in hair. They were implicated, and they were being asked for documents by some scary people with official-sounding titles and they were being told not to pass the documents on by the lawyers working for the social media company. No matter how tricky it was, they would need a lawyer. That was a good thought.

361

They were happy they'd thought of that. If they were sitting here thinking they could do it themselves, they would have trouble.

'One of us should take this so the other one can fix that code,' Greta said. It felt like an epiphany – surprising and inevitable at the same time. You can't know what you don't know, until you know it.

'Yeah,' said Peggy.

'Which one of us should take this?' Greta asked.

Peggy made the 'hm?' noise, then they both read for a while longer, then Peggy leaned back and breathed out in one long, heavy sigh. 'I really don't think it matters,' she said.

'Yeah,' Greta said.

'Neither of us wants to, though,' said Peggy.

'No,' Greta said.

'I'll flip you for it,' said Peggy finally, and she got a coin out of the small bowl that sat beside the computer.

Peggy flipped the coin. It turned over and over in the air – heads, tails, heads, tails – until it landed.

'Heads,' they said together, and Greta said, 'Okay. Okay. That seems fair.'

'If you do this,' Peggy waved her hand in a circle in front of the screen. 'Then you can fix that coding for that other contract.'

Greta nodded. They were out of practice. So they kept checking in with each other like this. They'd hated it last time, when they were in their thirties – the chatter had agitated them – but it was quite nice now. Having someone to actively sound things out with. They were both getting older, fuzzier. Margaret had started talking to herself. Making ridiculously complex lists and checking them off, like a meditation. A few times in the last year she'd forgotten about big things and people had reminded her and she'd been able to cover it up, but they were not as sharp as they had been, and it was not a good way to be – especially not with the work they did. People already assumed they were out of date. They never were, but people just assumed it when they walked into a room, which was why they tried to walk into a room as little as possible. They were checking in with each other occasionally and it was nice. They were bouncing things off each other, and the office had a nice feel to it.

About midday, they were hungry and decided to break for lunch. They made sandwiches out of the tofu spread and salad in the fridge. They'd been making buckwheat bread for the last few months and it was in the fridge when they looked. There was enough of everything for both of them. They'd never got used to providing for just one of them.

They sat at the table again and looked at their food. Then they found themselves looking at each other. It was shocking, to see what they really looked like. There were mirrors that were flattering and there were mirrors that were not. On the whole, for the years they were just Margaret, they'd become more and more confused about what they looked like. Margaret would see photos and not recognise herself. Admittedly, no one looked like their photo anymore. There were filters and face-tuning tools. Margaret had felt ugly a lot of the time, but in a special way. It was as if she looked like no other human being. She walked into things, too. She had no idea where her body ended and the world started. But now, but now, they were looking at themselves across the table and it was a new way of understanding their body. They were more in their body than they had been when there was only one body. They felt like they understood it more than they had in years. This is where my arm ends and my hand begins, they thought as they looked at each other. This is where my hair parts.

Greta looked at her plate and smiled. 'It's good to be back,' she said.

'Yeah.'

'She was always bumping into things,' Greta said, and she held her left hand up, fingernails facing Peggy, and there was a chunk out of her index finger. Peggy held up hers and they were the same, of course.

'Watermelon,' they said together. They hadn't been paying attention, or maybe they had, and the knife was new and serrated. But maybe Margaret had been paying attention perfectly. It was just that thing where she didn't understand where her hand ended. She'd been looking after Ash at the time. Ash was maybe four. There was a lot of blood and she felt faint and the pain shot up her arm and into her heart. They dropped into a chair and held a tea towel round their finger tightly. Ash came over and patted Margaret's arm and said, 'Ouch.' Margaret was crying hard. It had healed, but their finger was never the same shape. It was a defining moment. An understanding that they would die with their hand this shape. That there was no do-over. Which led to a deeper understanding that they were not coming this way again. Turning forty-one had been the worst thing. They were forty-eight now, but forty-one had been tough. That's what they told people, and people agreed. There was a build-up to forty and then you were forty and you thought, 'Thank god that's over,' and then time went on and you turned forty-one and you thought, 'Didn't we do this?' and you realised you would keep getting older. That's what it felt like. Like time was going forward but – they looked at their hands, the bit missing from their finger – anything was possible.

'If you're lucky,' Greta said.

'If you're lucky you'll keep getting older,' Peggy said, and they were right.

There was a beeping noise from the other room, and they looked at each other. It was the Tamagotchi phone. They'd forgotten about it. The beep went right through them now. They looked at each other. Greta picked up her phone and rang Heidi's number. It rang and rang, then someone picked up but didn't say anything.

'Dell?' Greta said. 'Just ring us. Or come over. We're having lunch. We've got like forty-five minutes.' And there was a knock at the door.

Peggy got up, walked down the hall, opened the door and there was Dell, her phone still to her ear. 'Hi, Dell,' Peggy said.

'Margaret,' said Dell.

'It's Peggy,' Peggy said.

Dell rolled her eyes and sighed. Peggy could hear Greta in Dell's phone, telling her to just hang up already.

Dell took the phone from her ear. She was holding something in her other hand. 'I brought chips,' she said, and held the bag out. 'For lunch.' The bag was open and half empty. There were crumbs down the front of her sweatshirt.

Greta was in the hallway too, now. 'Do you want a sandwich?' she asked, and Dell nodded.

They all went to the kitchen. Peggy went via the bedroom. She put the Tamagotchi phone on the table in front of Dell and sat down. 'We probably don't need this anymore.'

'Don't we?' Dell said.

'Yeah. I don't think so,' Greta said. 'But – thank you.'

'Yeah,' Peggy said. 'Thank you. But you could have been way more helpful.'

Dell shrugged. 'Could I?'

'What have you been doing?' Greta said. She was spreading

Dijon mustard on the bread.

'Nothing much,' Dell said.

'You weren't dead, though,' Peggy said.

'No.'

'Where were you?' Greta said.

'Well, I wasn't dead for very long, at least,' Dell said. 'It was the shortest amount of time – like, for the time it takes to walk through a door, I was dead. Then I was here.'

'When did you get here?' Greta asked.

'Just before two o'clock,' Dell said.

Dell was eating the sandwich now and shaking her head.

'Yesterday?'

'Yesterday.' That was right when there had been three of them.

'Where did you arrive?'

'Next to Heidi,' Dell said.

'Like this?' Greta said, pointing between herself and Peggy.

'No,' Dell said. She'd finished the sandwich now and was eating the chips.

'Do you want another sandwich?' Peggy asked.

'Yeah,' Dell said.

'Did you do this?' Peggy was waving her hand at Greta and back at herself.

'I don't think so,' Dell said. 'Maybe.'

'How did you get the Tamagotchi phone to us?' Greta asked.

'I didn't.' Dell's mouth was full, and she pulled out an identical Tamagotchi phone and put it on the table. 'When I got here, I was holding a bag and that was in it – along with this phone.' She picked up the smartphone to indicate that this was the phone she meant, and then checked it for messages.

Peggy and Greta looked at the Tamagotchi phones. Dell

put down the smartphone. 'I thought it was like a loot box,' she said.

'But what about the Game & Watch?' Greta said. She had the notebook and was flipping through the pages.

'Oh,' Dell said. 'Yeah. I totally put that in Heidi's bag. A friend was coming up and I got a lift with them and I broke into her house and I left it there. I thought she'd see it and call me.'

'And the cheese grater?' Peggy said.

'Stole it from work,' Dell said.

'And the right change?'

'Huh?' She looked up at them now from her sandwich.

'We always have the right change.'

'Wow,' Dell said. 'Yeah, I had nothing to do with that.' Her mouth was full.

'Did you really come on a bus?' Peggy said, but Dell was looking at her smartphone now and sending a message. 'Who are you talking to?' Peggy asked.

'No one,' Dell said.

'You don't know,' Peggy said.

'Don't I?' Dell said. Then she put the phone down and looked at them with all her attention. 'So,' she said. 'Are you having a good day?'

They looked at her, and Greta said, 'It's all right. Bit of a clusterfuck to sort out.'

'Is that the thing you were talking about last night?' Dell said, eating the sandwich again.

'Were we talking about it?' Greta asked, and Dell nodded. 'Yeah. Well, it is slowly untangling itself.'

'Lucky there's two of you,' Dell said.

'Or is it only happening because there's two of us?' Peggy asked.

'Deep,' Dell said, then she looked straight at them. 'Don't be too quick to "untangle" things, that's all. You've been such cowards. You should maybe take this moment and, like, finish what you started.' Then she went back to her phone. 'Sorry,' she said. 'Work.'

'What are you working on?' Greta asked.

'Sales. Selling things.'

'Really?' Peggy said, and Dell nodded.

'What about the notebook,' said Greta, holding it up. 'Why'd you give us the notebook?'

'To write down the phone calls.'

'So, you don't want the notebook back?' Greta said.

Dell took a moment then shook her head.

'It's not some kind of navigational tool?'

'Or a cheat code?' Peggy said.

'I don't think it works like that.' Dell was picking crumbs off the plate.

'Why did you even come over here?' Greta said.

'I was hungry,' Dell said. 'And a bit lonely. Ash is at school, Bisi's gone out. Heidi's at work. Heidi said you work from home.' She looked around the room, at the Tamagotchi phones and the notebook on the table. She picked up the notebook and flicked through it.

'Do you want a glass of water?' Greta said.

Dell nodded. 'Yes, please.'

'What about that message last night? How did you know that was us?'

'I'd seen the phone by then,' she said.

Peggy and Greta were getting confused now.

Dell put down the notebook and drank from the glass of water. 'It's not rocket science.'

'So you haven't been messaging us all this time?' Peggy said.

'No,' Dell said.

'And you don't know who has?'

'No,' Dell said.

'And you haven't come to save us?'

'What from?' Dell said. While they'd been talking, she'd slid all the phones except her smartphone into her bag. Like a shoplifter. The notebook was still on the table.

They sat in silence again, and Greta and Peggy ate their sandwiches.

'It's hot,' Greta said.

'Yeah,' the others chorused.

'I'm so glad we've got the heat pump,' Greta said.

'Yeah,' said Dell. 'Actually. I think I probably do need the notebook.'

Peggy and Greta watched as she put it in the bag with the phones.

Dell finished her sandwich and drank from the glass of water Greta had brought her. 'Well,' she said. 'I better get back to work.' And she laughed, but Greta and Peggy didn't.

They saw her to the door and at the open door they all hugged and said goodbye.

It was a beautiful day. Peggy and Greta hadn't noticed it because they'd been inside for it all. As Dell walked home up the driveway they stood with their back to the sun, and it warmed them. Their clothes felt light without the phone and the notebook, but they had each other now. Maybe they didn't need the phone.

'Are you awake?' Peggy said.

'Is there snow there?' said Greta.

48

Greta cleaned up the lunch dishes and put away the food. Peggy was reading through the messages that had come through in response to the messages Greta had sent about the data breach – which wasn't a breach, but the app working exactly as it was supposed to. Was it their fault that people didn't read the terms and conditions? Yes, they said to each other as Greta sat down beside Peggy to work, yes, it was completely their fault. They had made the app knowing that no one would read the terms and conditions.

An email alert came up at the bottom of both their screens. It was short, so they could read all of it, and it said, *It looks like the app collects data from the user's friends. If that's true, that's terrible.* And Peggy stopped working and looked at Greta and Greta looked at her. The person who'd sent the email knew exactly what the app was doing, because their boss had asked Peggy and Greta to make it work that way. Someone was watching the emails. The email wasn't for Peggy and Greta's benefit, the email was for someone else to see. They were trying to pass the blame on to Greta and Peggy. Peggy and Greta knew how they were supposed to react, but they weren't willing to take the blame. Greta replied with nothing in the body of the email and attached the requirements document. It was a million miles from the act of aggression Dell was advocating, but it was also a long distance from lying down and being walked all over.

It was ridiculous that this was playing out from their small house in a valley in a town on an island that had nothing between it and the end of the world. The email had come from Tel Aviv, where an office full of Americans had been transplanted. They lived in apartments and didn't go out much. Peggy and Greta had seen pictures. It was a sad state of affairs, but all the Americans told themselves and everyone else that they wouldn't be there for long – it was just a stepping stone. The guy emailing was acutely aware that his stepping stone was crumbling. He didn't know Peggy and Greta. They'd spoken on the phone and had meetings, but he didn't care. It was everyone for themselves. Peggy and Greta were further down the food chain than he was. As the afternoon went on it became clear that nothing would really stick to them, but they needed to show they were willing to help. How they acted during this would get around quicker than a fire. How they handled this would determine the work that came in for the next six months. If they wanted to stay, they needed to be interested. No one wanted to play a boring game. It was annoying. But they were handling it. Maybe taking on the app job had been an okay decision. They were making it work. Greta on the phone and messages, and Peggy doing the work in progress that was coming in. It was scary, but they were handling it. They could get it done. It would be fine, and the money was coming in. Peggy was able to deliver the coding before lunch just like she'd said the night before. And then it was three o'clock, and then five o'clock and time to finish up. Everything was sitting in a way that was okay. The guy in Tel Aviv was working through the night, but around two in the afternoon other people started arriving at work and put a fire blanket over his attempt to implicate Peggy and Greta more than they were.

Greta stretched and then so did Peggy and they logged off and stood up and walked into the lounge.

'Do we have plans?' asked Greta.

'I don't think so.' Peggy was looking at their phone and the calendar and there was nothing there. 'Who knows, though?' she said. 'Like, really.'

Greta agreed. 'We could go out?'

Peggy nodded. 'Yeah. We could walk into town?'

Greta got up to find a cardigan.

'We're dressed the same,' Peggy said.

'I'll change,' Greta said. 'I'm ready for a change.' And she walked into the bedroom and Peggy could hear her rustling around. The coat-hangers made a scraping noise in the wardrobe. It was high-pitched and strangely reassuring. Greta could hear Peggy in the lounge pulling the curtains. The house had been quiet before. They realised that now. It had been lonely and quiet and full of secrets they'd been keeping from everyone around them. Although Margaret had been fine in it, dealing with it all, it had been a sad place. But it wasn't like that now. Two bodies instead of one was so much less lonely. Bodies made a difference. They decided that. For them, bodies made a difference.

Greta came out dressed in the geometric skirt a friend had given them. 'You ready?' she asked.

'Yeah,' Peggy said. 'Yeah. Totally.'

49

It felt like months since they'd been out in anything except short sleeves. The heat was coming from another country. But everything was warm. The beaches were full of jellyfish and things were igniting. A fire in the other island had been burning for seven days. Margaret had been at the beach last week. She and Ash were walking over the dunes to the car park. The sea had been cold, like a lake, but the sand was hot and the wind was blowing warm. Margaret said to Ash, 'Can you smell smoke?' and Ash had stopped and smelled the air – like a small rodent coming up from underground – and shook their head. They looked towards the other island, where the fire was. 'The wind's coming the wrong way anyway,' Ash said. Margaret nodded, 'Yeah.'

It had been smoke, though, from another fire closer to the beach. Another piece of bush was on fire. But they didn't find out until they were home, still salty and sticky, and they'd looked at their phones. Dell had been dead, and Margaret had been Margaret, but when they got home from the beach that day – the lakey, icy beach – Dell had said this was how it was all going to end. Everything on fire.

As Greta and Peggy walked down the street tonight, they were looking out for dust. The wind had picked up the dust from a desert on another continent and carried it all the way to where they were. They were both excited, hoping the dust would come. The heat felt too slow, like the end would come too slow. The dust seemed like something to breathe in one final time.

There were people riding bikes and cars driving up their road. Now and then, someone walking a dog passed them and they would both completely concentrate on the dog. Loving it with all their hearts.

The city was as busy as a small capital city at the edge of the earth during the end of the world would be. They were together, and they walked together. For the first time in twelve years they felt safe and unexposed walking at each other's side.

They walked through the park. People were drinking at the picnic table. Some people had strung up a volleyball net and were playing. Peggy and Greta stopped to watch. Then they realised Heidi was playing.

'Wasn't it Dell who played volleyball?' Peggy said. They looked closer, but it was Heidi. She saw them and waved and walked over.

'We saw Dell,' Greta said to her.

'She came round for lunch,' said Peggy.

'Oh,' Heidi said. She was still watching the game, continuing on without her now.

'I thought it was Dell who played volleyball?' Peggy said.

Heidi looked away from the game. 'We both do,' she said, and Peggy and Greta nodded their heads. Of course.

'Did you give us the phone?' Greta said.

Heidi looked at the ground now. 'No.' And she looked back at the volleyball game.

'Well,' Peggy said. 'We gave it to Dell anyway.'

'I wish you hadn't,' Heidi said.

'I bet you do,' Greta said.

'Why do you wish we hadn't?' Peggy said.

'That sort of thing gets her riled up,' Heidi said. 'She always thinks she can figure out the unfathomable things.'

'So the phone doesn't mean anything?' said Peggy.

'Well – you know how it is,' said Heidi.

'No,' said Greta. 'Do you?'

'You know,' Heidi said. Everyone in the volleyball game clapped after a long rally.

'We think we're all living in a simulation,' Greta said.

Heidi shrugged. 'Sounds about right.'

'Do you know what the rules are?' asked Peggy.

'I don't know if it works like that.'

'There are no rules,' Greta said.

'There might be.' Heidi was shifting on her feet, not looking at either of them. 'If there are rules, then they keep changing, so there might as well not be any rules.'

'So nothing means anything?' said Peggy, and Heidi shrugged. 'And nothing matters?'

'Those are two different things,' Heidi said.

Peggy and Greta didn't say anything.

'Those two things only look like the same thing if you think you can win,' Heidi said. 'And you can't.'

'What matters, then?' Greta said.

'The keeping going,' Heidi said.

Peggy pointed to the people playing volleyball and the people watching them and the people just sitting in the park. 'Is that what they're doing?' she said.

'I think so,' Heidi said.

'Is it just wandering about?' Greta said.

'I think so,' Heidi said. 'But what would I know? What did Dell say?'

'Not much,' Greta said.

'She's a fighter,' Heidi said.

'What about you?' Peggy asked.

'Me?' Heidi said. 'I don't think it's as simple as who's fighting and who's surrendering.'

'Dell's fighting,' Peggy blurted out. 'She's going to win.'

Heidi squinted a bit into the sun. 'We're all fighting. We all think we can win. Like, you and me. But Dell's fighting different things.'

'What different things?'

Heidi thought for a minute. 'We're making signs,' she said. 'Dell's trying to stop this sort of thing happening.' And she waved her hand between Peggy and Greta.

'Dell's deluded,' Peggy said.

'I didn't say that,' said Heidi. 'She might be right. I just can't do what Dell does. Not anymore.'

'Did you always know it was fake?' Greta asked.

'Is it fake?' Heidi said.

'It's fake,' Peggy said.

'I mean, yeah, I know it's *fake*, but it's all we've got,' Heidi said. 'So it doesn't really matter what it is, or whose it is. That's what I'm talking about. Dell's trying to fight the things that are out of our hands.'

'Things are getting weirder,' Peggy said. 'Things are getting weirder, eh?'

'Yeah,' Heidi said. 'I guess it's getting old.'

'Did you bring Dell back?' Greta said.

'That's exactly the sort of fighting I'm not doing. It was Dell who came back – no one brought her back,' Heidi said. 'At least, no one we know. Anyway, I don't think it works like that.'

'How does it work, then?'

'I don't know,' Heidi said. 'At least, I don't know how it

works for you, but it seems like stuff happens and we react and that makes more stuff happen. I think that's why it's getting weirder.'

'Edge cases,' Peggy said.

Heidi nodded.

'That's what we thought,' Greta said. 'It's falling apart.'

Heidi nodded. 'We all are.'

They all watched the volleyball game now. The players kept the ball in the air until finally they didn't.

'We thought Dell had magicked the phone to us, somehow. That she was trying to send us messages, or maybe it was a way for her to travel, like, through time or something. We thought she was winning,' Greta said.

'Dell's gone,' Heidi said.

'What?' Peggy and Greta looked at her.

'I think she must have left from your place.'

'Where?'

Heidi shook her head. Her face looked slightly hot from the exercise and her scars showed a bit more. She had her hair pulled up, which she hadn't done for years, and now she'd done it twice in two days. But probably just because it was getting warmer, and Dell had come back from the dead and she couldn't see any reason to be bothered anymore. 'She's off to fight some new impossible thing,' Heidi finally said.

Peggy and Greta could see her ear, and a shudder went through them as they thought about the pain of it. Peggy and Greta had underestimated the unrest in Heidi and Dell for all this time. They'd been far too concerned with themselves, with their own dilemma. With Heidi and Dell, it was something much deeper. It was fundamental. Much earlier than Peggy and Greta had realised, Heidi and Dell had seen what was up. They'd been looking for a way out, even before they'd all moved into the flat together. They had thought Ian was something they could win, that he offered some sort of solution, and they'd decided that Heidi would play him. It had ruined her, and because it was her it had ruined, she saw it more clearly – that there were some things that couldn't be fought. From that point on they could never agree on what was worth fighting and what wasn't. Maybe Dell had kept playing so hard, moving always towards conflict and pain, to make it up to Heidi. Maybe if Dell could prove them right, that things would falter from a headlong assault, then everything – the abuse, the shame, the scars – would be worth it, and Dell could forgive herself – but everything she did had made things a lot worse.

'How are Bisi and Ash?' Peggy said.

'Good,' Heidi nodded.

'That's going to take some explaining,' Peggy said. 'About Dell. You told them that she was your sister.'

Heidi shrugged.

'And that she was dead,' Greta said.

'Wait,' Peggy said. 'Was she not dead?'

Heidi laughed, 'She was dead when I saw her.'

Dell had been dead, and then she hadn't. For them, it had been years of loss. For Dell, it had been a heartbeat. Like walking through a door from death to yesterday.

'We always think we're special because of what happened,' Heidi said. 'Like we have a special grief, special pain, but everyone is dealing with something. This place isn't any kinder on people like Bisi and Ash. They get on, though. We're fucking show ponies.'

Someone from the volleyball game called over to Heidi. 'I need to go and play,' Heidi said, and she looked at them. 'No hard feelings.' They'd been through a lot.

They shook their heads and gave her a hug.

Heidi turned when she was a few feet away from them. 'I always wanted to tell you,' she said. 'Like, I know it means nothing now, but I always wanted to tell you. Dell said it would ruin you.' She looked to her left and then to her right. 'Don't let it ruin you.'

They watched her run back to the game and take her place again and someone served the ball and Heidi hit it back. Peggy and Greta had never fought, in all the time they'd known each other. They'd niggled at each other, little remarks here and there, but never a painful disagreement. Never anything like Dell and Heidi. At the beginning, everyone had tried to lump them together. It was just the normal kind of bigotry. People tried to make people who were different from them all the same. But none of the pairs were the same.

'Do you feel like noodles?' asked Peggy.

Greta thought for a moment. 'Yeah,' she said, surprising herself.

'Malaysian noodles?' Peggy said.

'Tom yum?' Greta said, and Peggy nodded, and they walked down past the arts centre and then past the place where the record store used to be.

'I like it better like this,' Greta said, and Peggy nodded. 'Like, I can deal with it the other way. I'll live. I did live. I even thrived, maybe. But I like it better like this.'

'It's not the natural way of being,' Peggy said. 'But I agree.'

'It's the natural way for us,' Greta said, and Peggy nodded. 'Like, once there were two of us, I realised why it hadn't been working.' She was looking out over the street. 'Like life.'

'Yeah,' Greta said.

'We're lucky,' Peggy said.

'Blessed,' Greta said, and they both mock-shuddered and

laughed. They looked up in time to see a woman walking towards them.

'Carola?' Peggy said. The woman looked up, and didn't respond at first. Then, 'Peggy?' she said. 'Greta.' And she hugged them both.

'Where's Lotte?' Greta asked. The woman looked strange, alone, somehow naked or under-dressed, or in the wrong place.

'Who?' she said. And someone going past on a bike stopped and said, 'Charlotte?' And the woman turned, because Charlotte was her name.

'Hi, Joan,' Charlotte said. 'These are my friends – Greta and Peggy.' And they all said hello and had a short conversation about where everyone was going: Charlotte – home, Joan – to a meeting. And they talked a bit about things – work, mainly. Then they all said goodbye and went their separate ways.

The noodle shop was full, but there were two seats at the end of a long table. Greta and Peggy sat down, and no one even looked. Except the people already sitting at the table, and then just to say hello. The forgetting, the ignoring – in one sense it was a kindness. It gave them space to work things out. There was a hubbub in the restaurant. The hard walls echoed it. Greta and Peggy looked over the menu even though they knew what they were going to order, because there was still a chance that something else would take their fancy, but they wanted tom yum even while they were looking at the menu.

The waitress arrived and they looked up and ordered tom yum noodles and then they looked over the table at each other and there they were.

Acknowledgements

Throughout my life I've been granted many second chances. Through the patience, love and compassion of countless people I feel like I've had the strange and wonderful opportunity to live two lives in one body. There are many people without whom this book would not have been possible. In an attempt to name all of them, I am bound to miss some of them. Please know I am grateful to you all.

Thanks first and always to Sue, Joan, Vaunda, Kay, Sheila and Anna.

Thanks also to Therese, Shona, Becca, Sydney, Noeline, Emma Hislop, Aidan Rasmussen, Rebecca Rasmussen, Selva and Oriol, Cherie Connor, John Brooks, Mirabelle and Iris, Murray Hewitt, Lenni, Anna Sanderson, Anne Kennedy, Chris McIntyre, Sinead Overbye, Anahera Gildea, Annaleese Jochems, Eamonn Marra, Jackson Nieuwland, Carolyn DeCarlo, Alisha Tyson, Helen Heath, Helen Lehndorf, Maria McMillan, Carl Shuker, Anna Smaill, Cassandra Barnett, Sarah Graham, Chris Hilliard, Rose and Tess, Victor Rodger, Simon Sweetman, Elizabeth Knox, Freya Daly Sadgrove, Dominic Hoey, Laurence Fearnley, Sora Kim-Russell, Laura Vincent, Hera Lindsay Bird, Kylie Boxall, Kerry Donovan Brown, Tia Narvaez, Nicky Taylor, Paula Kimble, Gregory Kan, Rose Lu, Emily Writes, Sarah-Jane Parton, Lukasz Buda, Rachel O'Neill, Giovanni Tiso, Justine Fletcher, Lucia, Ambrose and Joseph, Brannavan Gnanalingam, Murdoch Stephens, Jo Randerson, Tracey Monestra, Clare McIntosh, Nina Powles, Chris Tse, Mia Farlane, Chloe Lane, Ebony Lamb, Catherine Robertson, Tayi Tibble, Gem Wilder, Sarah Bainbridge, Claire Mabey, Kirsten Le Harivel, Hannah Mettner, Sam Searle, Nikki-Lee Birdsey,

William Brandt, Gigi Fenster, James Brown, Ken Duncum, Maree Brown, Caitlin Smith, Raewyn Glynn, Tokerau Wilson, Mary-Jane Duffy, Cassandra Rivers, Ingrid Horrocks, Brandy Scott, Elliot Elam, Sharon Lam, Jacqui Moyes, Emily Perkins, Damien Wilkins, Chris Price, Louisa Buchanan, Whiti Hereaka, James George, Megan Dunn, Mark Amery, Frances Cooke, Helen Rickerby, Catherine Woulfe, Jesse Mulligan, Sam Duckor-Jones, Avi Duckor-Jones, Mary Chapman, Andrew Larking, past and present CREW254 and 354 workshops, and all the people I work with at IIML, Whitireia, AUT, Arohata Prison, City Gallery Wellington, Radio New Zealand and everywhere else.

I really appreciated Rebecca Hawkes agreeing to read an early draft of this work and am extremely grateful for her insightful feedback which helped make this book so much better.

In 2018, I was quite shocked that my book *The New Animals* was awarded the Acorn Foundation Fiction Prize. In a lot of ways, this prize gave me the courage to write this book. I am very grateful to the organisers, the judges Anna Smaill, Philip Matthews, Jenna Todd, Alan Taylor, and Jann Medlicott whose generosity makes this award possible.

I am also very grateful for the financial support of Creative New Zealand, which made this book possible.

Thanks to Brent, Bo and Coco. What an incredible gift to live with three such wonderful earthlings.

Thanks to Mum, Dad, Tim, Thea, Rufus, Rocco, Ari, Royce, Tania, James, Terzann, Clete, Athol, Loma, Laura, Hannah, Shane, Anna, Pat, Trevor, Teresa, Aletia, Sammy and Robin.

I'm very grateful for the cover of this book. Thank you Russell Kleyn for the photograph and Franca for allowing us to use your likeness. Thanks to Fergus, Ashleigh and Kirsten who worked on the design of the cover and thanks also to Ebony Lamb for the author photo.

Thanks finally to the team at Victoria University Press who not only made this a book but made it a better book than I could have managed by myself. Fergus Barrowman, Ashleigh Young, Therese Lloyd, Craig Gamble, Kyleigh Hodgson, thanks for the fun and the work. Thanks also to Rachel Barrowman and Jasmine.